WITHIN AND WITHOUT TIME

SECOND EDITION

D. I. HENNESSEY

www.arkharbor.press

WITHIN & WITHOUT TIME © 2021, previously published as WITHOUT TIME ~ WITHIN TIME © 2017, 2019, by Daniel Ignatius, aka D.I.Hennessey. You have been granted the nonexclusive, nontransferable right to access and read the text of this book. Unless otherwise stated, biblical quotations are based on the American Standard Version of the Bible, 1885 by the English Revision Companies. At least one Scripture reference is taken from THE MESSAGE. ©1993, 1994, 1995, 1996, 2000, 2001, 2002. Used by permission of Nav-Press Publishing Group.

Second Edition 2021

ISBN 978-0-9991221-2-9 (Paperback Edition)

ISBN 978-0-9991221-6-7 (Hardcover Edition)

Version 007302023

Cover design by Russ Scalzo, Out of the Stack Publishing,

https://www.outofthestack.com

DEDICATION

In memory of my mother, Gloria, who at age 95, still provided inspiration and encouragement. I'm grateful to her for showing me what unconditional love looks like, and for teaching me that kindness and humility are the greatest powers on earth.

CONTENTS

"In the last days, God says,
I will pour out my Spirit
on every kind of people:
Your sons will prophesy,
also your daughters;
Your young men will see visions,
your old men will dream dreams."

— ACTS 2:17

ON EARTH... AS IT IS IN HEAVEN

Heaven and earth in midnight stillness heard the groans and sighs of the
mysterious Being in whom both worlds were blended.
~ C.H. Spurgeon

Darkness surrounded me suddenly, freezing me with fear. I struggled to make sense of the unfamiliar scene as a cold blast of wind stole my breath away. The place was strange and unfamiliar — feeling ominous and unsettling.

A shrill thundering drew my attention. I turned quickly to see an enormous jet approaching, so close that it looked as if I could reach up and touch it, as fifty thousand pounds of thrust blasted past me just overhead. Its roar was deafening.

That's when I noticed him — an indomitable figure, larger than any man. He was an otherworldly-looking stranger.

He stood watching the huge planes as they moved like enormous behemoths, growing as they approached, from pinpricks of light into brazen beams that flooded the sky. The huge jets pressed the air beneath them as they hung above us in their solemn descent. A color-less night surrounded us; its darkness was thick as coal dust, masking the wider scene's blush.

Gazing downward, I saw a wide highway below us, filled with an endless flood of heavy traffic. It seemed to flow like a stream of light in an odd and chaotic concert. The river of light passed swiftly beneath us, then moved away like a swarm of embers, hot red, in a disordered mix of scattered red and amber flashes. It glowed within rust-colored borders, and huge signs, like eerie-looking green tetragons, flashed their messages as they were illuminated by the brilliant onslaught.

I looked again at the stranger, watching him anxiously. From his enormous broad shoulders, a thick cape undulated in the stiff wind. His resolute face revealed an inexpressible mix of emotion. His hair and bristling beard were stately white, and his bronze-colored skin radiated light.

His eyes seemed to pierce into the darkness before him; they held a look of deep knowledge — more than understanding, they reflected the experience of long history. His bearing seemed to emanate kindness — righteousness even — but his brow was somber, lined with hard-earned wisdom and discernment.

Turning, he spoke to an unnoticed companion who had suddenly materialized, no less dramatic in appearance — the words that he spoke sounded thunderous:

"I weary of this incessant battle," he bemoaned.

His stalwart companion approached and grasped his shoulder;

"Ye are strong of heart Ardent," he consoled, "a lesser one would have fallen long ages ago in so fierce a conflict."

"Speak not such invention," the one called Ardent protested, "were it not for the strength of the Almighty, this ombudsman would have verily fallen at the first contest.

Aye... His strength," he repeated gratefully.

"Then His strength shall continue to sustain us... and to make us prevail," the unflinching companion asserted.

"I must surely take hold of thy words," Ardent avowed, "they are eternal truth. I wish only for the casualties to be less severe -- less lamentable."

"That, my brother, as thou knowest full well, is the purpose of our struggle."

"How is it?" Ardent reasoned aloud, "How has creation's hope -- these children of most glorious design -- become the agony of all the universe? This beautiful creature has become the terror of immortal dreams. All of our heavens cry for the calamity that is Earth!"

"'Tis true..." his partner conceded, "the beguiler of these human hearts has taken a grievous toll. Still, our pursuit is not yet attained. We have labors still to work -- remember the esteemed ones."

A look of mixed hope and solace emboldened Ardent's face.

"Aye," he said determinedly, "the esteemed ones shall prevail... by His unfailing grace!"

Suddenly the two of them turned as if called by an inaudible command.

"Be swift!" — Ardent called to his compatriot – "I will direct our brothers in their assault... Thy duty is to Sterling."

A MASSIVE SWELL erupted beneath Ardent's huge cape, effortlessly forcing the thick fabric into the air behind him. It revealed the concealed enormity of brilliant white cherub wings as they spread upward. Then, with a single blast of his wings, he was catapulted skyward.

Overhead the dark air had filled with a legion of their gallant companions.

"To the fray with Godspeed!" Ardent called to the others; his voice thundered so that it seemed as if the sound of it could be heard to echo from Earth's moon.

Moving with terrific speed, the glittering lights of dock cranes and massive metallic vessels blurred below them. With its smell of thickened oil and foul decay, the harbor swelled in undulating black rolls as they traveled rapidly overhead, converging on the city's unseemly streets.

Ardent dove toward the chosen battleground, his drawn sword flashing with the fire of holy fury. The rush of a thousand sets of wings adjusting for descent crushed the air behind him. "Away ye devils!" His thunderous shout shook against the waiting enemy... "or feel the bite of holy fire!"

"THESE BE OUR'S..." came the frightening reply from below. It shrieked in a cruel foment like the cry of a hundred prehistoric predators in a profane unison... "Yer battle is lost already!" they protested.

"Ye hold vainly to thy lies — Then ye have chosen fire!" Ardent cried, his sword in full flame spelling the signal for the charge. The air overhead had filled with the clash of an immense struggle.

Below them, the huddled forms of four young mortals could be vaguely seen among the shadows, their eyes blind to the fierceness erupting around them. Their struggle was against the cold night -- and the unsettling words of an unassuming messenger before them.

A boy, appearing aged beyond his years, pinched a fresh smoke between his lips and struck a match. The tiny flame lit his face momentarily in the darkened doorway, revealing eyes bloodshot and heavy with the night's imbibing. He stared ruthlessly at the audacious evangelist who was speaking to him. The discarded match sank to the ground like a dying star, illuminating a dozen spent cigarette butts strewn around his feet.

The lone preacher gestured emphatically, obviously making an impassioned point to the three boys. They leered at him with a mixture of contempt and fear. His words seemed to bother them immensely -- and not them alone. The beasts that were invisible to them clamored around the shivering boys, reacting angrily to the preacher's words.

He seemed to be quoting something... words that felt familiar. All those around him appeared to understand perfectly, yet the words were oddly masked. Their utterance carried great force; they struck against the hellish throng with a perceptible burst of thuds, like arrows hitting a thousand targets.

In an unworldly response unheard by the deafened human ears, a wounded shriek rent the night as these words cut through the surrounding devilish hoard.

Breathing murderous cursing, they leaped toward the source of their agony -- rushing toward the defenseless envoy.

Ardent's enormous wings formed a shield around the frail human figure. Then, just as the group of hideous devils attacked in a furious swarm, his mighty wings flung open, brushing them aside.

With a mighty slice of his sword, Ardent drove the legion backward with fiery wounds. They hissed and railed against him, drawing the attention of unnumbered devilish kinsman battling in the air above.

Sensing a pulse of spiritual strength, perhaps from Ardent's invisible touch, the emboldened messenger's eyes flashed brightly as he continued, his words growing in intensity and impact. Impassioned gestures articulated his unbridled conviction. There was an emphatic expression on his face, conveying the supernatural power of his message. Again, a sustained battery of spiritual artillery emanated from his lips toward the gathering hoards above him as he spoke. This time it appeared like a fiery rain of bright pulses, flashing in waves of brilliant light. They pierced the ugly beasts and sent them tumbling backward.

Reeling from the power of this assault, the smitten beasts clamored back to their prey. The grasp of their hellish talons dug deeply into the listening gang members; each quote striking in the angry beasts a greater fury.

Finally, the gang's leader bent lower as if feeling the darkness that crushed his soul -- "shut up!" he shouted. The other boys lurched forward as well, suddenly animated with a dark passion all too familiar. The half-smoked cigarette flung toward the unwelcome evangelist, striking him in the chest. "Shut up, or I'll kill ya!"

The preacher continued; an unnatural boldness filled his words, which flowed with far more than intellectual argument; they seemed to pour from his soul with an inescapable ring of truth.

The leader grabbed the preacher's shirt and pulled hard. His own body was shaking violently with an overwhelming mix of fear and seething anger. It was a fear of the piercing guilt that seemed to stab at his long-dead conscience; anger welled at this inexplicable fear gripping his entire being.

Another quote from the evangelist ripped through the hellish scene with the greatest intensity yet seen. The beasts were flung backward as if stricken with the blow of an enormous concussion, sent tumbling through the air. The boys were physically bent under the strain of their own pricked consciences, their faces contorted with angry rage.

Their closed human ears could not hear the hideous shriek that filled the air around them as a thousand of hell's hosts twisted in torment at the preacher's spirit-filled assault. Their wounded cries sounded like the roar of an ancient monster of unworldly proportions.

The gang leader pressed his fists to his ears, his face filled with hatred. He shouted obscenities, cursing God and the unwelcome protagonist.

Suddenly, the whole host of battling fiends in the surrounding air seized upon the animus growing below and descended in an enraged press, bringing unrestrained their impulsive blood lust. The gang leader drew his blade while the other boys flung themselves onto their tormentor, knocking him to the ground. The long blade flashed in the dim light of a streetlamp before sinking in cruel hate into its overpowered victim.

ARDENT STOOD LOOKING UPWARD toward the silent and invisible commander who instructed him, forbidden until now to intervene. Now with a guiding wave of Ardent's hand, the hoard of hellish creatures was quickly swept away by his angelic troops -- a police siren instantly erupted nearby. The boys jumped to their feet and ran for cover. Ardent looked down at the gasping human figure below him -- "you'll be staying, brave lad; the Master has not done with thee here."

Two patrolmen knelt beside him.

SUDDENLY, the hair at the back of my neck stood on end as I realized that Ardent had turned to look directly at me. I felt my mouth drop open in stunned silence as he bowed his head in a sort of deference. All at once, I became aware of arms releasing me from a strong but gentle grasp that had been bearing me up. As my feet stood on the cold ground, I turned quickly to see who had carried me.

"I am called Chozeq,[1]" said the enormous angelic being bowing low beside me. I recognized him as the powerful personage who had been with Ardent on the airport's tower earlier.

Looking around in shocked amazement, I struggled to make sense of the scene. It was entirely too real to be only a dream – the street was cold under my feet, a stiff winter wind made me shiver and robbed me of breath as I tried to speak. Yet the policemen just steps away seemed oblivious to our presence. The extraordinary pageant I'd just witnessed could not have been real, at least not in any worldly sense of reality I'd ever known.

I heard the first officer speaking into his radio – "victim's name is Rodriguez -- Reverend Juan Rodriguez. Looks like a single stab wound to the chest; tell EMS to step on it."

WHILE HE WAS STILL SPEAKING, an intense flash of light instantly shattered the dark night, sending my already shocked senses reeling as it struck me.

I raised my arms to shield my eyes and felt myself staggering backward. The light was now a steady flood; its heat warmed my chilled body, but the complete change it brought to my surroundings alarmed and frightened me.

My eyes were momentarily blinded, but I could hear an entirely new sea of sounds closing in around me, of alarming voices... voices that I recognized. I struggled to remember!

⌘

2

SCHOOL

"Jimmy? Are you all right?" Kelly's voice cracked in alarm, I could feel her hand on my arm. "What's wrong? What's happening?"

Still staggering backward, something caught my feet, tripping me... I knew immediately from the loud clang as my head hit that I'd fallen into a hall locker, slamming its door. I sat against it rubbing my head. The hall began to come into focus as my eyes adjusted to the bright sun coming through the school's expanse of windows.

"Jimmy, oh my gosh - are you alright?! What happened?" Kelly was kneeling beside me; a group was gathering around.

I stared at her trying to find any words to answer, not really wanting to, unsure if I knew.

"I-I'm okay."

"It's like you blacked out or something. You gasped like a truck was hitting you. Are you sure you're all right?"

Mrs. Blackburn broke through the crowd and leaned over us. "What's going on here?"

"It's okay, Mrs..." I began...

"He just blacked out..." Kelly interrupted.

Mrs. Blackburn studied my face and then noticed the impression my head had made in the locker door. "We'd better get you down to the nurse's office. Do you think you can stand?"

"I'm really fine, I protested." As I stood, a throbbing pain reminded me of the growing lump on the back of my head; I instinctively reached my hand to rub it.

"Let me see that," Mrs. B insisted. "You've got quite a bump on the head; you'd better get some ice on that." The mention of ice caused a chill to return to my chest and shoulders. I shuddered slightly.

The chill had only just begun to fade when we reached the Nurse's office. Mrs. Blackburn led me to a chair in the corner and went to speak privately with Nurse Snyder. From the smug look on her face and the overheard mention of a "drug test," I could tell she had assumed the worst. I tried to appear grateful as she brushed past us to leave; she frowned indignantly down at Kelly and me, not saying a word.

"You're Jim Moretti, right?" Nurse Snyder asked as she offered me an ice bag and wrote on her clipboard, "Sounds like you've had quite a fall." She was a decent person as far as school staff went; all the kids called her by her first name, Betty. Sometimes she tried a little too hard to be friends and fit in, but she meant well and seemed genuine. "What'd ya do, trip, or did someone push you?"

"Neither... at least I don't think... I guess I just lost my balance, that's all."

"Hmm..." she intoned, tapping her finger on her lips as if investigating a mystery. "Let me see that bump of yours." I felt another shiver run through me as she lifted the ice bag and probed the growing knot on the back of my head; she noticed my slight shudder. "Feeling cold? Your skin actually feels a little cool... maybe you'd better lie down for a few minutes. I want to take your temperature." She stopped at the thermostat on the wall and gave it a nudge... "Let's turn up the temp a little bit."

Kelly sat next to me with a worried look on her face; she and I have been friends for as long as we could both remember; her mom and mine were best friends before we were born. We grew up next-door neighbors and did everything together as kids.

She's a great friend, the greatest. The kind you can share anything with... but not this. This was too weird to even talk to her about.

She leaned closer and looked me in the eye... "Are you going to be all right? I really have to get going to Chemistry class... there's a graded lab project today." She squeezed my hand and then looked down, slightly surprised... "Wow, your hand really is cold."

"I've been holding the ice bag..." I reminded her.

"Oh... yeah... guess that's it." She smiled warmly and let go, waving goodbye.

"Bye..." I said, smiling back. Watching her go made me think about how much I was going to miss having her around when her family moves in a few weeks. As she turned and quickly made for the door, I looked down at the hand she was holding and flexed the fingers, touching them against my neck to gauge their coolness. I knew that the ice bag had actually been in my other hand the whole time.

After Betty gave me an all-clear and two Aspirin, I spent the next two periods deep in thought, oblivious to the teachers' questions. My distraction earned me a few extra homework assignments for the evening. I struggled to make sense of the afternoon's events; could I be losing my mind – or maybe worse yet, what if it were true and I really had seen a Vision of some kind? But what could it mean?

By the time I reached home, I was exhausted from thinking about it. All I knew for sure was that it had been the most realistic daydream I'd ever had. Every part of it was still so clear! Usually, I can never remember dreams, but this seemed just as if I was really there! I even remembered the names, Ardent and 'Kozek,' ...I guessed at the spelling ...maybe their names could be a clue.

My mind was jumping through the events as if watching it on TV and someone else had the remote. The police had said that the victim's name was Reverend Rodriguez. I did an online search for the name – plenty of Rodriguez, but no mention of any of them being Reverends.

I finally gave up and headed for bed. The minute I closed my eyes, the images came rushing back. This time they were definitely just dreams and memories, but they were still jarring in their clarity. In my mind's replay, the hideous monsters seemed to be looking straight at me. They gave me chills. As tired as I was, it was impossible to sleep. After tossing and turning for an hour, I finally dropped out of bed to my knees and did what I should have done in the first place... I prayed... hard.

But the harder I prayed, the more chaotic my thoughts became. It was like my prayers were being batted away in a whirlwind of menacing distractions.

I'd known times in the past when it seemed like the heavens were made of brass, but this was like nothing I could remember. In desperation, I finally threw myself to the floor and cried out... "Lord! Help me!"

The sudden change was so dramatic that it startled me, it was like a switch had been thrown, and the cacophony was instantly quieted. In place of the swirling chaos was an intense calm... and a laser-sharp focus that seemed to cut through the heavens. My thoughts were suddenly filled with a rapid pattern of words that I somehow recognized in their essence. Still, they remained indecipherable by my conscious mind, like a forgotten language that remained understood by the deepest part of my soul. I struggled to recognize them, but they remained just beyond the grasp of remembrance, like long past childhood memories veiled in whispers. Yet they were stacked in an orderly sequence, like a grand edifice of truth being built around me block by block, surrounding me like a fortress.

Deep in my hurting soul, they seemed to draw an elaborate picture of eternity. It revealed God's omniscient preparations transcending time. His infallible planning; about a legacy that He is building... a great mystery... an effort into which He has poured His entire being. My mind couldn't comprehend or hope to contain the entire stream of this exquisitely woven tome as if the very heart of God was being poured out. It told of an indescribable and unfathomable love for a broken humanity. Expressing God's intense determination to leave a single legacy as the purpose of all creation. The words echoed and swirled around me before finally receding into a silence so intense that it gripped my very soul and focused my mind in stunned anticipation.

The words had been at once terrifying and soothing, like none I'd ever known – they made my body shake in fear while at the same time bringing the most fantastic thrill to my spirit. As it ended, a sense of awe engulfed me; the image that had been drawn of God's intent in creation was right in front of me. Yet, it was so vast that it was beyond my ability to comprehend it. I began struggling for words to say but was quickly stopped by words that pierced the silence. They paralyzed my spirit.

"James Matthew..."

When I heard my name, the breath left my body. I was frozen in place. ..Who? I struggled to ask the question for which I already knew the answer...

"I am the Word."

WITH A HUGE GASP OF BREATH, I was suddenly aware of my surroundings, lying face down on my bedroom floor. I felt overwhelmed with the implications of the message, which my soul seemed to grasp despite my mind's inability to comprehend it. I began to sob until eventually falling off to sleep.

⌘

3

FUTURE SHOCK

Who of us does not desire to lift the veil that hides the future?

S tepping out of the car into a driving rain, I landed ankle-deep in one of the city's famous potholes. "Bye, Jimmy, I'll pick you up at 10," Mom said as the door closed. She sped off, preoccupied with a list of errands and the usual time crush.

"Can't wait till I get my license," I said under my breath as I shook the water from my drenched sneakers. I pulled my jacket over my head and rushed to the door of Farro's Subs, my Uncle Mike's Sub Shop.

Uncle Mike glanced at the clock as I entered; "Nice 'a you to finally show up," he said with his usual dripping sarcasm.

"Sorry, Uncle Mike," I apologized. "Mom had a few stops to make. I'll work extra hard to make it up."

"Sure, kid, could'a used the extra help 30 minutes ago when the dinner rush was in full swing." Just then, the door burst open with what looked like a dozen college kids soaked from the rain. They started ringing out their jackets and shaking their arms as if they'd just emerged from a swim. "Grab a uniform," uncle Mike commanded. I made my way behind the counter and donned one of the red bib aprons hanging on the wall – 'the uniform,' as Mike called it.

Two weeks had gone by since my 'vision-or-whatever,' I hadn't figured out what to call it, but I still hadn't been able to get it out of my mind. I'd spent every afternoon searching the web for anything I could find on angels, and especially the names Ardent and 'Kozek,' but so far had come up empty. One thing was sure, there was no Reverend Rodriguez listed in town. The more that time had passed, the easier it became to explain it away as just a bizarre daydream.

"You plannin' ta eventually get t' work tonight?"

Mike's verbal jab woke me from my thoughts. "Here, handle the counter while I get the phone," he said, shaking his head in obvious annoyance.

Friday nights were by far the busiest of the week, and tonight we were shorthanded since Jenny had bailed for a new job at the movie theater. Jeremy was already backed up with a half dozen delivery orders. He stood waiting impatiently for the last of them to be filled so he could make his next set of rounds. He stood in a puddle on the kitchen floor from his own drenched clothes.

Mike hung up the phone and started in halving another dozen rolls, laying them out with mechanized precision in an orderly assembly line. I was busy writing order tickets from a new crowd of customers and working the register. Nothing like a rainy night to keep folks inside – the tables were already full. Jeremy, the delivery driver, grabbed the last package from Mike and made for the door; "make sure you get yourself back here pronto," Mike shouted after him.

I took advantage of a lull in new orders to give him a hand with the subs. Another jingle of the door's bell signaled a new entrant; I turned instinctively to greet them. **The face of the man who had just entered stopped me in my tracks.** Although I'd never met him before, I recognized him immediately with a sudden realization that hit me like a swift kick in the stomach.

Before I knew it, the tray I was carrying had tipped, dumping the two large 'Number 1's' onto my feet and sending their contents sliding across the floor.

Several kids about my age followed the man inside. "Pastor Juan!" one of them called out, "your wife said to tell you...."

I couldn't hear the rest of the sentence; the room seemed to swim around me in slow motion – "Pastor Juan..." the name echoed in my head over and over. I could tell that Uncle Mike was yelling beside me and waving his arms. For what seemed like a long instant, I stood frozen, unable to move my eyes or any other muscle for that matter.

<hr />

A LOUD NOISE behind me drew my attention. As I turned, the room suddenly changed around me. I was surrounded by a flurry of activity, with people running everywhere. I recognized that some were wearing what looked like medical garb. The room had completely changed – I was standing in an emergency room!

The scene brought memories flooding back of the night Dad and I were in our accident. The knot in my stomach tightened as I thought of our last moments together. It had been two years already... man, did I ever miss him!

Before I had much time to dwell on that thought, however, lobby doors blew open, and a team of paramedics and policemen burst inside, wheeling a stretcher. They ran straight toward me, nearly knocking me over – I thought I recognized one of the officers... but couldn't place where I'd seen him before. As the stretcher passed in front of me, I looked down at the man it was carrying – I caught my breath in shock, realizing instantly that it was him – it was Rev. Rodriguez! Glancing quickly back to the officers, I recognized them now as the patrolmen who had responded that night...this night ...I struggled to make sense of it.

JUAN WAS TRYING TO SPEAK... "BAIBI..," he gasped, "tell Baibina..."

. . .

"DON'T TRY TO SPEAK," his attendant said, "save your strength."

"We found your address in your wallet," one of the officers said, leaning over him, "a patrolman went to get your wife; she should be here soon."

The stretcher was moved briskly through a set of double doors into a nearby operating room; Juan was lifted onto the operating table, wincing in pain as they laid him down.

A lump was growing in my throat as I watched them work on his gasping body.

The scene was moving fast. The emergency room surgeon was rapidly giving orders to a large cast of attendants who continued to flow into the room. They quickly plugged him with intravenous lines and hooked him up to monitors; the room was a jumble of urgent voices, beeps, and buzzes. They covered his mouth with a mask connected to plastic tubes and turned up the oxygen flow. White sheets quickly covered everything.

I couldn't see what they were doing from where I was standing, but they were apparently preparing to operate. The pace was frenetic. The monitors were beeping erratically – reporting a mix of jumbled heartbeats and unnatural-seeming pauses. The doctor in charge was barking instructions about CCs of this and milligrams of that.

Pastor Juan was growing calmer, the heaving of his chest slowing as he drifted into an anesthetized sleep.

I saw a blood-covered scalpel; someone was mopping sweat from the surgeon's brow with a towel. A pile of reddened gauze was building higher in the attendants' stainless steel tray as they continued to fight the flow coming from Juan's chest. Two pint-sized bags of the crimson fluid hung attached to his intravenous lines, traveling in an urgent torrent to his lifeless-looking arms. The reddened tubes stood out dramatically against the intense whiteness of the room.

It briefly crossed my mind that I usually passed out at the sight of blood but didn't feel the slightest tinge now... weird, to say the least. But then, what wasn't weird about this!

It was about to get much, much weirder!

I heard the EKG monitor sound a loud monotonic alarm and could see that his heartbeat had flat-lined. The attendants were scrambling over him frantically, pushing and prodding and injecting something. The doctor yelled "CLEAR!" and the room was suddenly filled with the concussion of a loud crackling shot from the Defibrillator. Juan's body jerked up off the table and fell back again... the monitor continued its steady wailing. Another "CLEAR!" ...again, Juan was tossed violently... but still no response from his silent heart.

As I watched the scene in a mix of horror and despair, a strange glow began to appear on his arms and face. It grew brighter and brighter until the surface of his skin seemed to lose focus, like a TV image when the colors get out of sync.

The brightness seemed to be rising – emanating from him; it grew thicker and more distinct, taking on a recognizable form – his form. Instead, it rose quickly, floating into the air like a mist that was suddenly free of its confinement, except this mist did not dissipate. It rose in concise unison – a perfect likeness formed of transparent light. I could easily see that it bore a recognizable resemblance to Juan. Yet, it didn't look anything like his physical body.

The glowing likeness seemed to be sleeping at first as it floated higher, then he slowly opened his eyes (if they could be called eyes). He held an expression of utter wonder, not in the least burdened with confusion or fear, but rather with an unmistakable sense of awe. He was intently gazing upward and seemed to be beholding something immensely wonderful to him. However, the ceiling above us looked unchanged to me.

SUDDENLY I HEARD a familiar voice speak to him. It boomed in the small room, causing the hair on my neck and arms to stand straight. I recognized it instantly as Ardent's voice. Turning quickly, I saw him standing behind me near the door. His countenance burned with compassion as he spoke. It was not out of sympathy for Juan's apparent death but rather because he was saddened with the news he had been sent to deliver to him.

"I have been sent to you, noble servant, with a difficult message.

Thy heart cries earnestly for the reward that awaits above. Indeed, I can see that it aches most desperately for thy Master's meeting... still ye have work yet to complete here below.

There is much that ye still must do in the fields of His harvest."

Ardent's words thumped against my chest like raging waters as he spoke in a deep and powerful tone. Juan's image drew its attention from gazing above and looked at Ardent. He was drawn to the ground and appeared to be standing, then bent and bowed low at Ardent's feet.

"Nay! Arise thou heir of the Most High God! Bow not before a servant such as I, but stand and listen, for the word I have for thee is most urgent."

Juan didn't try to speak; he seemed awestruck by Ardent's imposing figure.

"Ye have done well, faithful one. The field of harvest in which ye have labored is hard indeed, but rest assured that our Master's word will not return unto Him void. Even now is the seed of thy message gaining hold in the very enemies that have smitten thee.

"Ye have been faithful in small things; God will reward thee in large. Lo, He has chosen to anoint thee with a portion of faith that has been seldom known to the earth. Ye shall be a powerful witness to this land in the closing days of your mortal time. Use thy gift well, for it is the final hope of countless souls. The hosts of darkness will fear thee and be powerless against thee, but be ever vigilant! Mindful be that no creature framed of the dust of this earth has yet resisted sin, save one. He the darkness faced alone to annihilate death, and all death's minions render impotent. Yet ye know that mankind in its weakness, though thus freed, continues to wear sin's enslavement by flesh's unfettered will. Be strong, therefore! Watch carefully! For ye shall not taste death again before thy Lord's return!"

With that, Ardent stretched forward his hand with palm facing upward and an index finger extended. On its tip could be seen a tiny seed, which shown in a glorious brightness as intense as the sun. It gave such light to the room that it obscured everything else. Yet, despite its intensity, my eyes were not blinded by it but instead were able to look at it entirely unharmed; it was beautiful. Ardent touched the tiny fleck to Juan's forehead, where it quickly filled his entire being with its light as it consumed his form from head to toe. It came bursting forth from his fingertips in spectacular beams. He held his hands up, staring at them in amazement; his face filled with a look of extraordinary peace and wonder.

Then, more suddenly than he had emerged – instantly – the room dimmed to its natural brightness as Juan was returned to the motionless body that lay behind him.

His human form glowed momentarily with the outline of the glorious likeness that had the same instant stood before us. Then his body quickly began to change from its cold white appearance to a warm, lifelike hue. He jolted as he gasped a huge gulp of air, and the monitors jumped back to life with the echo of his reinstated heartbeat.

The attendees who had already begun recording his time and cause of death turned in stunned disbelief at the miraculous recovery. A nurse raced to his side to feel the warmth of his newly ruddy skin and the pulse of his beating heart. The emergency room intern, who had already removed his gloves, quickly grabbed a new pair and returned to work on the untreated chest wound. I heard him muttering in disbelief as he discovered healed scar tissue on Juan's heart muscle. Nothing was left for him to do but close the surgical opening in his chest.

JUAN DREW a long breath and let out a sigh that seemed at once filled with joy and longing. Then, to the utter amazement of everyone in the room, he began to sing in a quiet, nearly breathless voice. His eyes remained closed; by all indications, he was still unconscious. But the words were clearly heard. Everyone stood frozen in rapt attention as they drifted from his lips. They stared at his face, then at one another, as some wiped tears from the corners of their eyes. The aura in the recently hectic emergency room was suddenly tranquil and otherworldly.

His words flowed in a slow, quiet whisper, trailing off after each line then beginning again; they danced along my spine, making me shiver. It was a song I'd never heard before:

To me remains nor place, nor time...
    My country now in every clime...
    I now am calm and free from care...
    On any shore, since You are there...

While place I seek, or place I shun...
    My soul finds happiness in none....
    With You my God to guide my way...
    'Tis equal joy to go or stay.[1]

I turned again to look behind me at Ardent, but to my dismay, he was gone. As I spun my head back around to where Juan was lying, the room began to dissolve once again. In its place was a chaotic chorus of images, like a slide show on fast forward or a time machine at full speed. The sights and sounds frightened and confused me. I felt myself spinning, looking for some frame of reference, as the floor dissolved away beneath my feet. It was impossible to tell for sure which way was up or down, right or left. I could feel myself being swept away, beginning to tumble backward; I suddenly found myself shouting:

"Help! Lord! Please, help me!"

⌘

4

WITHOUT TIME

Eternity is without bound of time or space

Instantly a hand was in mine.

My eyes followed the strong arm upward to Chozeq's steadfast face, suddenly steadied and secure, grounded in a bulwark of stability, even as the images of chaos continued around us.

Somehow I knew we were standing amid swirling time.

"Chozeq!" I said with a desperate sense of relief and trepidation at once; his presence engulfed me, obscuring for the moment all the chaos around us. "I have so many questions," I began... "is this a dream?

It seems so real! I saw him! I saw Pastor Juan in the sub shop... but how... how could he be there and in the hospital at the same time... and I saw him get hurt last week, but he was just getting to the emergency room tonight." I stopped, aware once again of the swirling images surrounding us. "Where is this place? What's happening to me?"

"Place?" Chozeq repeated thoughtfully. "This is no 'place'... it is

without time and place, the domain of angels, the avenue of heavenly messengers across ages of time and distances immeasurable in mortal dimension.

Here we step readily from furthest star to its most distant cousin or from creation's opening light to Earth's final demise, indeed, even to the farthest boundary of infinite eternity."

His words thrilled and frightened me; would I ever see my mother or friends again? I shuddered slightly, asking the question that consumed my conscious mind: "Am I... dead then?"

Chozeq smiled reassuringly, "Nay, lad, but it has been given to thee the great privilege of embarking in the flesh on a journey rarely traveled by other than angelic wings. A privilege it is indeed and wonderful beyond human imagination. But beware, for it also brings thee a burden heavier than any thou hast known. For in opening thine eyes to the unseen truth of our desperate struggle, thou shalt be greatly troubled and buffeted in no small measure by our hideous enemies. In the spirit, the redeemed shall once and for all be free of the curse's wretched shackles, but in the body, ye are still weak and subject to its evil pull. Nary has a son of Adam in all the ages been found without sin's wounding effect, save for One. None in the flesh have prevailed against it – except for that One. It is His rule we earnestly obey, and it is He whose victory has crushed our foe."

"Why?" I stammered, now even more convinced of my own unworthiness... "w-why me?!"

"All shall be revealed, yet now is not the ordained time. Only rest assured that thy faith shall indeed sustain thee. In Him, even the weakest are strong, and the defenseless are unassailably safe. They could not be stronger if they were giants, nor safer if they were in heaven. It is Faith that gives to men on earth the protection of the God of heaven. I assure thee Lad, more ye cannot need and need not wish for.[3]"

"But..," I began again, "what can I, I mean how can I..." the words escaped my grasp as I struggled to comprehend the import of what was happening. "What's the purpose... w-what do I have to do? I-I'm not even sure what you... what He... wants me to do."

He spoke slowly and with great understanding in his voice. "There is nothing hidden that shall not be revealed, but all is not yet prepared in thine heart. Trust only. But heed this carefully! Ye must tell no one of this that thou hast seen nor yet shalt see! Only write what thou seest and most cautiously guard it; for it shall be for a revelation to this final age of man at the appointed time – in the time of His choosing."

As he finished speaking this, I suddenly felt that I was being swept backward again, away from him. I reached out to him but was quickly falling further from his reach. His last words again struck me with great strength of gravity: See that thou tell no one what thou hast seen!

With that, I began to tumble, feeling certain that my feet were high above my head as I rolled uncontrollably downward through the swirling chaos. I closed my eyes and held my arms over my head, sure only that I would soon be crashing somewhere to earth with a frightful impact. The sounds swirling around me quickly began to subside until all grew silent. Instead of falling, I suddenly felt as though I was hanging in a state of suspended time and motion. I opened my eyes... at least I thought I did... all around me was total darkness.

THEN, in the smallest fraction of an instant, a shocking flash of light hit me like a wave crashing over my head. It carried with it a cacophony of jumbled sounds – people shouting and rushing about. I recognized one of the voices, the one screaming my name in apparent anger and frustration – it was Uncle Mike. I felt myself falling back once again, but this time my feet were sliding out from under me, unable to gain footing as they slipped and kicked against the traction-less floor. The room began to come into focus -- Uncle Mike's face was contorted in a mixture of rage, confusion, and then concern as it raced higher and further away. The underside of the shop's counter whizzed past my eyes as my head missed it by mere inches, and a split second later, I hit the floor, bouncing against its thin linoleum and wood planks. My mind was dazed and spinning, but not from the fall.

I felt his hand on my arm, then another on my head. "You awright? What da heck's a madda with you? Jimmy! Can ya hear me? Somebody call'a amulence!"

"No... i-it's OK," I struggled to get the words out, shaking off the dizziness. "I-I'm OK, Uncle Mike." As my eyes refocused, I realized that two people were kneeling beside me, Uncle Mike on one side and, on the other, ... Pastor Juan! My eyes must have grown to twice their size; I suddenly lost my breath again, shuddering in a jolt of surprise.

Uncle Mike noticed my reaction, "Ya know dis guy?" He questioned me, "Ya look like ya seen a ghost."

"No!" I almost shouted, trying unsuccessfully to sound convincing. "N-no... we don't know each other – I-I just saw you coming in before I... I guess I fell." I tried not to make eye contact for fear that he'd somehow see the truth in my eyes.

"Are you sure you're alright?" Pastor Juan asked. "You really took a serious fall there."

"Yeah" – I struggled, looking down at the mess of cold cuts, lettuce, and onions scattered at my feet – "guess I just slipped on the oil there," I said, nodding in the direction of the spill.

He and Uncle Mike helped me up. Mike looked at me close – "you sure you're OK to work tonight?"

"I'm sure, I'm fine," – I reassured him.

"Good," he said with a sudden change in his voice from concerned uncle back to frazzled boss – "in that case, get this mess cleaned up; somebody's gonna get killed slippin' on this!" He headed to the back to get a bucket and mop.

"Hey, we can help you out with that!" Pastor Juan said, motioning to his group.

"No! It's OK, really!" I protested.

Mike didn't like customers behind the counter, especially doing work. He said it would get him in trouble with the Board of Health and some kind of National Labor Relations Board, or something like that. Not to mention the fact that he wasn't insured for that kind of risk.

Sure enough, as soon as a few of them bent down to help, Mike came running from the back, yelling and motioning his disapproval: "Whoa! Hold up! Hold up! Whatcha doin'? Ya can't be back here. Board o' Health regulations!

Customers ain't supposed t' be in my kitchen! I ain't insured in case one 'a you takes a flyin' bounce like twinkle toes here." He threw the mop to me and used his apron to shoo the group out from behind the counter. As I worked on the floor, he returned to the register to write a few more orders.

I couldn't help staring at Juan; he mainly looked the same as in my vision, but a little different somehow... then it struck me – the man standing in the sub shop was younger. My skin was covered suddenly with a rash of Goosebumps; the chill running up my spine made me shudder. Mike watched me from the corner of his eye and stopped what he was doing to come and feel my forehead. "Ya sure you're okay, kid? You're in a cold sweat."

"Yeah, s-sure I'm Ok," I insisted. "Just wet from the rain."

"Great.. all I need's for you t' get sick on me... I'm awready short-handed as it is. Maybe ya should go stand by de oven for a while... you're like a cold fish. Go answer d' phone, will ya?"

The night went by fast for a while after that. The phone orders were still coming in heavy, and Uncle Mike struggled to keep up.

I did my best to do double-duty and cover the register.

GLANCING up from ringing the latest order at the register, I suddenly found myself looking into the eyes of a girl about my age. She didn't seem like just any girl... oh man... was she different! I was suddenly lost in her eyes, just staring, and she was staring back; I felt like our souls were... I don't know... embracing. After a long silent pause, she pulled her eyes away and glanced down at the counter; she seemed to swallow kind of hard.

"I-I w-was wondering if..." she paused, once again catching my eyes, then continued slowly... "if I could get a coke?"

"Y-yeah s-sure," I said, trying to look less shaken.

I fumbled with the fountain I'd used hundreds of times... ice missed the cup and hit the floor. "I'll get it," I said, motioning apologetically to Uncle Mike.

He just shook his head in disgust and kept working his assembly line.

When I returned to the counter with her soda, she was still staring at me, and I noticed the rest of her face for the first time -- she was beautiful! The cup hit the edge of the counter, nearly spilling. I caught it with both hands and held it to the countertop as if it was trying to fly away. "Sorry about that..." I fumbled.

"Thanks," she said, looking at the cup with her hand paused in mid-air – I realized she was waiting for me to let go – I pulled my hands back embarrassedly and put them down to my sides. "You're Jim, right? I heard him call you that..." she nodded toward Uncle Mike.

"Yeah!" I exclaimed with slightly too much enthusiasm, "Jim, that's right... my friends call me Jim-my... guess that's kinda obvious, huh?" I was crumbling in embarrassment at how stupid that sounded.

She smiled warmly and tilted her head slightly to one side... "my friends call me Anna." She leaned forward and put her elbows on the counter, crossing her arms in front of her; "It looks like you've had a tough night." She obviously didn't know the half of it! Her question scared me and warmed me at the same time. I felt myself wanting to talk to her all night and run away out the door all in the same instant.

"Just a little busy – must be the rain..." I said, trying to sound matter-of-fact.

She continued... "Do you work here every weekend?"

"Yeah, usually... it's my uncle's place," I pointed over my shoulder with one thumb at Uncle Mike. Just then, I felt his hand on my shoulder...

"That ice is makin' a puddle, ya planning t' get to it one'a deez days?" Expecting to see him snarling at me, I stepped aside to face him, but instead, he just winked and pushed on my arm with his fist.

I rang up Anna's soda and gave her the change; she raised a finger in front of her as if to say 'just a second'... "I was sort of wondering if you'd like to come to our youth group sometime... Pastor Juan is really cool..."

I swallowed hard and glanced at him. "Yeah, sure..." I said, pulling my eyes back to Anna, "...when do you have it?"

"It's every Friday at 6:00; we just finished before coming here."

"Oh..." I said with genuine disappointment, "...I always work Fridays; I start at five."

"Oh, that's too bad!" She pouted when she said it, with an expression that broke my heart. "Do you go to Bailey High..." she continued... "we have an FCS meeting on Wednesday mornings?"

"FCS?" I said quizzically.

"Oh, sorry... it stands for Fellowship of Christian Students. We just meet to pray and have breakfast together."

"Yeah... I do go to Bailey; I guess I never paid much attention to the clubs and stuff. I didn't know there was a Christian club there."

"It's not really a club," she corrected, "it's a nationwide thing that does stuff with kids in school... we meet across the street from the high school at Carmine's Diner; the owner... Carmine... goes to our church."

"Wow, that sounds pretty cool... wh-what time do ya start?"

"At 7:00." She paused as if deciding what to say next... "You can come and get me at my house if you want and we can walk together... I'm just a block away from there."

My heart was suddenly pounding; "S-sure, what's your address?" Someone behind her was calling her group together to leave. She turned to tell them she was coming, then shot me a smile over her shoulder...

"55 Jessica St., come around a quarter of."

She ran to join her group, and I could see her talking and motioning in my direction.

Pastor Juan smiled and looked over at me, then came walking back to the counter. With each of his approaching steps, my legs grew weaker. I could feel my heart skipping beats as I struggled to hide my nervousness... sure that he'd notice and become suspicious. What would I do if he asked me something I couldn't answer? Could I lie to obey Chozeq's command? That didn't seem right. He was getting closer! As he reached a few steps away, his hand stretched out... I saw my own arm reaching to meet it in a handshake.

"Glad to hear you'll be joining us, Jimmy," he said enthusiastically.

"Us"... the word echoed in my head... Anna didn't mention that he would be there too; I swallowed hard and tried to smile...

"Yeah, thanks," I said.

"See you Wed morning," he continued, then turned to rejoin his group.

ALL I COULD THINK of was what Chozeq had said to me, it repeated in my mind over and over... *see that thou tell no one..*

⌘

5

TELL NO ONE

Faith...tempests are her trainers...

I t was impossible to sleep as I sat in bed on Friday night. My head was swimming with thoughts of the hospital vision and Chozeq's words, they repeated over and over... *"like a broken record,"* as my mom would say, whatever that meant. Praying had been easier since that first night a week ago; in fact, it seemed like I never stopped praying, even when I was doing other stuff. This time, though, I kept seeing Anna's face when I closed my eyes.

'Only write what thou seest and most cautiously guard it...' the memory of Chozeq's words jolted me! Next to my bed, I noticed an empty journal notebook that mom had given me a few months ago. She must have dropped it there today while she was doing some housework.

I grabbed the notebook and began recording everything I could remember, starting with that first vision of Ardent and Chozeq in the city. When I got to the part where Rev Juan was talking to those gang members, I struggled hard to remember his words, but they were oddly out of reach... like a hollow echo. They reverberated in my mind but remained indecipherable. My hands began to shake as I recorded the hellish beasts' angry cries and described their hideous forms. It felt as if the room had suddenly become filled with their blood-red eyes and hot breath. I froze and listened, my heart racing, but I could hear only the faint background noises of our quiet neighborhood outside. Yet, I imagined I could hear the deep low growl of their seething hatred rumbling just below these familiar night sounds. The room seemed thick and foul with their presence.

Anna's face suddenly rushed into my mind again, this time more powerfully than before; it caused me to stop and drop my pen onto the paper distractedly. She was closing her eyes, leaning closer... we were suddenly kissing. The images quickly seized my whole consciousness; my heart was beating wildly, my breathing quickened. It began to accelerate into a flurry of images that seemed completely beyond my control, spiraling downward into lewd impassioned sequences that flashed with shocking intensity. I was embarrassed, stabbed with pangs of guilt, and, at the same time, drawn to the scene like a moth to deadly flames. I couldn't sleep, yet seemed entranced in a dream state that blocked out all around me. The more it raced through my mind, the more hungry I became for it; it choked my conscience, slowly turning my inner man into a shameful beast.

Soon after my soul had given up the last will to resist, there was a loud thunderclap that jolted me from my debauchery. My ears were suddenly filled with a deafening roar of wild carousing. A hot gust of foul-smelling air stole my breath as I opened my eyes and took in the sight of hundreds of gleeful, soul-thirsty devilish beasts surrounding me. They filled the floor of my room, covered every inch of furniture, and hung in the air like ravenous vultures awaiting their victim's demise. For a brief moment, I watched them, dumbfounded and terrified as they conjured their work of deceit and lust. Some threw themselves around the room in celebration of their own wickedness, acting out every imaginable shameful act as if in angry defiance.

Then the scene turned even more terrifying as the realization spread among them that their lustful spell had been broken. A sinister hush fell over the room. The beasts leaned toward me, crowding closely and studying my face. Incredulously noticing how my eyes followed them, my fear plainly obvious.

Ashamed and powerless in the guilt of my recent behavior, terror gripped my heart. I was sure that my soul was left helplessly exposed to these horrendous enemies – certain that God's protection had been lost. How could I expect His protection after such a shameful rush to embrace my sinful nature? One of the beasts looked directly into my face, studying my eyes. Then, with a face contorted with rage, he bared his razor-sharp teeth and roared a ferocious howl – his hot breath and foul phlegm sprayed onto my face. I recoiled in horror and leaned backward, only to press into the jagged and dangerous hoard huddled behind me. They grabbed for my flesh, and I felt one of them sink his teeth into my shoulder, making me scream in agony.

The pain seemed to jolt something within my spirit – I screamed out a rebuke, instinctively calling on the covering of Christ's atoning blood! The display of power that immediately resulted was extraordinary – it was as if a colossal blast emanated from the center of my being and expanded in all directions like a sphere of intense light. It drove the beasts back, hurling them into one another as they were tossed in a disheveled pile against walls, floor, and ceiling.

Instantly I heard the familiar sound of a sheath being emptied and felt the warmth of a giant flaming sword just behind me. I turned, still cowering in guilt and shame, to find Chozeq standing at the ready in my defense. The beasts hissed and screamed their protests but didn't dare to challenge this powerful emissary. The room was soon emptied as they drifted away, still voicing their angry defiance.

I hung my head, shamefully considering the depths of disgrace that I'd anxiously pursued just moments before.

My body still shook with the fear of those terrifying devils; a pain in my shoulder reminded me of the bite one of them had inflicted. I reached for it and saw that my tee shirt was torn – blood emerged from a set of crescent-shaped wounds on the front and back of my left shoulder. I stared in surprise at the blood on my fingertips and turned apprehensively to Chozeq.

"Were they real or a vision?" I asked him, faced with the reality of the answer already evident on my hand in front of me.

"They are no vision," Chozeq replied. "They are more real than any of the temporal things that deck your earthly stage. We have fought them for long ages; they know their time now is growing short." He paused in contemplation, then continued. "Their defiance is increasing, and their hold on mankind is gaining strength."

He lowered his sword to my wound. I grimaced expectantly as I felt the heat of its flame warming the side of my face. Yet, instead of burning, it touched my shoulder like a healing balm that quickly erased the bloody marks from my skin.

Tears began to well in my eyes as I considered my shameful behavior; I stared at the floor, unable to lift my gaze to his face. Chozeq sheathed his sword and lowered himself onto one knee. I felt his enormous hand on the shoulder he'd just repaired – it covered the whole distance from my neck to upper arm and extended partway down my back. He spoke with tenderness in his voice:

"Bear the knowledge of thy weakness carefully and do not lose hold of it," he began. "Delay not to confess and abandon such guilty blemishes at thy Master's feet, for He is faithful always to forgive thee. He will defend thee even amid thy falling if thou wilt but recall His love for thee. Think not that ye must earn His love by thy deeds. There are no deeds worthy of it or by any means able to match its infinite depth –it fills all eternity with its unwavering fidelity. Hold to it in faith!"

I looked at him, wanting to express how weak I felt – how unable...

"LET THIS NOT DISCOURAGE THEE, young one. Thine own weakness is best understood when ye pass through the rivers, and ye would never know God's strength except it support thee amid the water-floods. Consider this," he continued as if making sense of the shame and chaos swirling inside me. "Untried faith may be true faith, but it is sure to be little faith, and so long as it is without trials, it is certain to remain weak. Faith grows most when all things are against her: tempests are her trainers, and lightning guides her way."

He paused and looked at a scale model of a 3-masted ship on my shelf that dad and I built together, using it to illustrate his point... "When a calm reigns on the sea, the crew may spread the sails as they will, the ship moves not; for when the ocean is slumbering, the keel sleeps too. Yet, let the winds rush howling forth, and the waters lift themselves up. Then, though the vessel may rock, and her deck is washed with waves. Though her masts creak under her full and swelling sails, it is then that she makes speedy headway towards her desired haven."

He looked at me again with kindness in his eyes. "Remember always that no stars gleam so brightly as those in the blackest sky. No water tastes so sweet as that which springs amid desert sand, and no faith is so precious as that which lives and triumphs in tribulation." He thoughtfully considered his words before concluding in a quiet and sympathetic voice... "Faith increases in assurance and strength the more it is exercised. So faith is precious, and its trial is precious too.

"Be assured then that the full portion of thy faith shall be measured out in due season. Meanwhile, if thou canst not yet claim the faith of long experience, thank God for what grace ye have. Praise him for that degree of holy confidence whereunto ye have thus far attained. According to that rule, walk, and thou shalt yet have more and more of the blessing of God, till thy faith shall remove mountains and conquer impossibilities.[4]"

His words poured renewed strength into my spirit. I looked up at him, noticing his eyes for the first time as they pierced mine. They were like pools of light, windows to an inner being of pure holiness, yet tender as a father's when he comforts his wounded son. I felt emboldened to ask again the question that screamed within my head:

"Why are you showing these things to me... I mean, why me? How can I be important? There must be millions of people who are better than me...."

Chozeq interrupted me abruptly but with tenderness in his voice:

"Have ye heard none of my words? Better or worse are meaningless peculiarities when all are equally condemned, and all who ask are freely redeemed. Therefore, ye need not question thy Master's leading. Only follow, and be assured that whether He leads thee through blessing or fire, He is thy constant companion and faithful champion.

"Trust Him with all thy soul, and if ever thy trust grows dim, hold in faith to the truth that He remains ever trustworthy."

I swallowed his words like a starving man, anxiously feeding the hunger in my spirit.

I watched his hand move toward me, and he touched the center of my forehead. Immediately I was filled with a feeling of intense peace and calm so deep that it stole my waking, sending me into a deep sleep.

WHEN I AWOKE, it was already late morning. I stared at the bedside clock, struggling for several moments to recall what day it was. Then, finally, remembering it was Saturday as I sat up and rubbed my eyes.

Bright morning light flooded the room, making the night's events even harder to believe. Could I have dreamed the whole episode? The whirlwind of these recent visions had me wondering whether I was losing my mind. Then, Chozeq's words suddenly flooded my thoughts: *"they are more real than any of the temporal things that deck your earthly stage..."*

Looking down at my hand, I noticed a smudge of dried blood on my fingertips.

Instinctively, I reached for my left shoulder; the tee-shirt I'd slept in was ripped and stained – it hadn't been a dream! I jumped out of bed and ran to the bathroom, tugging the tee-shirt over my head. I inspected my shoulder in the mirror carefully; it was perfectly fine, not even a scratch. Holding up the tee-shirt, I studied it again. The tear was clearly outlined with the stains of my blood in a large crescent pattern. I stuck my fingers through the ripped openings; a sudden memory of the pain it inflicted jolted me like an unexpected shock, making me shudder. The memory of the beasts' disgusting breath and touch gave me the urge to wash – immediately! Dropping my face into the sink, I buried it with repeated handfuls of warm water and then lathered energetically with as much soap as I could manage. Still unsatisfied, I hit the shower and scrubbed until the water turned cold.

The shower gave me time to think; my mind was racing as it repeated the events of the last 2 days. Pastor Juan was a real person! The evidence was overwhelming that Chozeq was real also. His words rushed through my head again: "...*tell no one*...."

The hospital scene flooded my mind, then the odd time warp that followed it; Chozeq's words within that chaos echoed inside me "...*this is no place... it is **without time** and place*." It suddenly dawned on me that he wasn't saying that there was *no* time there but instead that it was *outside* of time. "It's the **Old English** use of the word... **without**," I repeated to myself aloud.

A few things began to make sense as I contemplated the significance of this idea. A place where there are no constraints of time – allowing one to move forward or backward, entering time anywhere in eternity! That would sure explain a few things. Like why Pastor Juan looked like he was older in my visions; I guess it probably even explained Chozeq's habit of speaking in Old English!

I was fixated on the question as I quickly dressed and grabbed my dad's old worn-looking Bible from my nightstand. As I sat down, it fell open to Second Kings chapter 2 - Elijah's heavenly translation in a fiery chariot.

"Wow, what a coincidence," I thought aloud to myself. He was caught up to Heaven in a whirlwind; that sounds pretty familiar! With no particular reference in mind, I thumbed randomly forward, landing immediately at Mark chapter 9 – the Transfiguration of Jesus. There was Elijah again, a thousand years later. "Could the whirlwind have been a time portal?" I wondered, "Where was he taken after that meeting on the mount... maybe into the future again... our future?"

As I thought about this, the page slipped, falling open at the eighth chapter of Acts.

My eye caught the account of Philip being "caught away," and the man he was with "saw him no more," as he was transported to another city miles away. As I contemplated this story, Chozeq's words seemed to echo: "*Here we step readily from furthest star to its most distant cousin...*" The words "caught away" struck me... our Pastor is always talking about how believers are going to be "caught up" together in the Rapture that's described in I Thessalonians.

A shiver ran up my spine at this thought – it never seemed more profoundly real to me!

As I returned from being lost in thought, the page had slipped again. Catching it with my open hand, I noticed it had settled on the twelfth chapter of Second Corinthians. I was drawn by the account that Paul wrote there about being caught up to the Third Heaven where "*he heard unspeakable words, which it is not lawful for a man to utter.*" Boy, that sounded familiar. With new interest, I kept reading about Paul's experience, coming to verse 7. "*There was given to me a thorn in the flesh, the messenger of Satan to buffet me, lest I should be exalted above measure.*" I didn't like the sound of that.

I anxiously turned the pages away, landing on John's description of "*a door opened in Heaven*" where he was given his view of the end of the world in Revelation. John's visions in Revelation always scared and confused me. I flipped nervously back to the Old Testament – only to land at Ezekiel's report that the "heavens were opened" when "*a whirl-wind came out of the north,*" leading to his visions of Israel's future.

The coincidence of verses was stunning. I sat with my hands trembling – not only more convinced of the truth of what was happening to me but more shocked and frightened as I realized the company I was in! This didn't make any sense! There had to be some mistake; I really had to be losing my mind. It couldn't be real – not for **me**! The torn and stained tee-shirt came to mind once again; I shook off a chill as the image of that angry beast flooded my memory. As last night's events played on in my mind, I remembered the burst of light that had blasted them all away from me. To my surprise, it had emanated from my own chest. My hand touched my chest distractedly as I thought about it. Just last Sunday, our Pastor had preached about the words Jesus said to His disciples at His last supper. He read about *"the Spirit of truth; ... he dwells with you and shall be* **in** *you,"* and the apostle Paul talked about *"Christ* **in** *you, the hope of glory!"* Maybe I'd underestimated the significance of those promises until now! But what on earth was God doing trying to use a kid like me for something this big and unbelievable?

I picked up my journal; rereading it made me shudder again. After spending the next hour finishing up the story as best I could remember, I looked around the room for a safe place to hide it. A strange thought crossed my mind as I wondered whether the old prophets ever searched the same way for a place to hide their prophetic writings. Suddenly remembering the loose air vent in my bedroom floor, I pried it open and stuffed the book inside.

No sooner had I stood and turned away from it than mom opened my door and peeked in.

"Are you planning to sleep all day? It's after 10:00 – don't forget you promised Kelly's mother you'd help them move today." I had forgotten – I grabbed my sneakers and headed past her, stopping for a second as she kissed my forehead. It made me feel ridiculous, but I guess I didn't really mind.

Heading down the stairs, my attention turned to Kelly's move. Her father had just found a new job on the west coast; they didn't really want to move, but he'd been out of work for almost a year, and jobs around here are scarce.

It would sure be different with her gone.

⌘

6

LOVE'S TRIAL

Our strength is dust and ashes,
Our years a passing hour;
But You can use our weakness,
To magnify Your power.
~ *The voice of God is calling, Holmes/Lloyd*

Our moms always joked that Kelly and I would get married someday. Kind-a weird – we're too close as friends to think about each other like that.

Kelly always did everything I did. We even joined the Little League team together – she was a better pitcher than me, as much as I hated to admit it. I suddenly got a knot in my stomach; I was really gonna miss her after all these years.

I grabbed an apple from the counter for breakfast and headed out the back door.

It was strange; I started noticing things that I'd seen a thousand times and never thought about. Like the old sandbox where Kelly and I played as little kids – it was overgrown with weeds now – and the makeshift pitchers' mound where we practiced together for hours on end. I stood on it, kicking the dirt as my mind drifted. I threw my apple core through the old hanging tire – still had pretty good aim! The knot grew a little tighter in my stomach.

I didn't bother knocking as I walked in the O'Malley's back door – I never did. "Hi, it's me... sorry I'm late," I announced myself.

Mrs. O'Malley stuck her head around the corner, "Hi Jimmy, Kelly's upstairs packing; you can go ahead up." The front foyer was full of boxes, and most of the furniture had already been removed from the living room. It looked strange to see the room empty. I bounded up the stairs, taking them two at a time like I usually do. The upstairs hallway rug was rolled up, and some of the furniture from Kelly's kid brother Ryan's room was waiting at the top of the stairs. The air smelled a little musty, like old dust. I made my way to her room and poked my head in the open door; Kelly sat on her bed with her back to the door as I walked in. She'd been looking through one of our school yearbooks; there were tears on her cheeks as she turned around. As soon as I saw her crying, the knot in my stomach really tightened up, like it was moving into my chest – it took my breath away. Even if I'd been able to think of anything to say, the words wouldn't have come out; my voice was suddenly missing. Looking around for something to distract us, I grabbed a box of tissues from her desk and silently carried it over to her.

She struggled to form a smile as she took them; "Thanks," she said with a sniffle. "I was just looking at our 8th-grade yearbook; remember how much fun we had at our spring dance party?" I just nodded in agreement since my vocal cords were still on strike. Kelly looked up at me; her eyes were really red, and the corners of her mouth were quivering like she was trying to smile, but her face kept forcing her to frown. Then, all of a sudden, she burst out crying and jumped up from where she was sitting, burying her face in my shoulder – her arms squeezed the back of my neck, and she just wept. It took me by surprise; Kelly had never been a person who cries very much. But now, she was really sobbing and shaking. I immediately recognized what she was feeling; I'd felt it before myself. It's the way you feel when your heart is being crushed – when something that means everything to you is being taken away. I cried like that the night before my Dad's funeral. The knot reached my throat and kept going; I could feel tears starting to well up behind my eyes. As I closed them, a few escaped and ran down my cheeks.

I guess this is one of those things that are different about having a best friend who's a girl.

I couldn't imagine any of the guys I know crying on my shoulder – in fact, I'd never thought of Kelly much differently than them; before now. It began to dawn on me how stupid I'd been. Kelly was much more than just a best friend; we were more like brother and sister. As she clung to me, I wondered if it was more than that even.

I opened my eyes in time to catch a glimpse of Kelly's mom in the hall; she was wiping away tears from her eyes too. She quickly turned away as our eyes met, but I could see her dry her face with a sleeve before walking away toward her own room. I patted Kelly's back, which seemed like a good idea at the time, but was probably pretty lame; anyway, it seemed to get her to stop crying. As she lifted her head, she looked at me closely with her wet red eyes. It was an intense look that made me nervous; she looked into me instead of at me – studying my eyes for something.

"Jimmy, there's something I have to tell you." She paused uncertainly and studied my face. "I've been thinking a lot about it... and well... it's gonna sound a little...." She paused, looking like she was going to say something that I'd be shocked by. "I know we've been friends, like forever, but moving has made me think so much about.. you know... us... and it really hit me..." She stopped and looked down at her feet, then up at me, "Jimmy, I love you, I love you so much!" Her face was the saddest I'd ever seen it as she said those words, then she wrapped her arms around my neck again and kept on crying.

Her words were like a flood as they washed over me, taking away the little bit of breath I had left. I had to gasp for air, and the stabbing pain in my chest made it feel like my heart was being squeezed in a vise. I struggled to figure out the wild mix of emotions swirling around inside me – of course, I felt the same way about her... didn't I?

I loved her; there was no question, but was it romantic love or something different? Being apart was going to be like a really close family member leaving – a family member who also happened to be my best friend in the whole world.

Then Anna's face flashed to mind, and my heart skipped a few beats. Meeting her had been like nothing I'd ever felt before.

How could I feel so strongly about Anna when I'd only just met her...? I've known Kelly our whole lives! Boy, was I confused! Talk about an unbelievable few weeks! What was I going to do now?

I knew one thing for sure; I wouldn't hurt Kelly for anything in the world. There's nothing I wouldn't do for her. I'd fight and die to protect her if I had to. Man, fighting and dying sounded really easy right now, compared to this dilemma!

Unable to respond, I stood in silence as her warm tears soaked through my shirt.

After a minute or two, she pulled away and searched my face for the answer she desperately hoped for. I think what she saw in my face was a look of confusion and fear. As she studied my expression, her look of relief at getting this off her chest slowly changed to a look of utter despair. "I'm so sorry!" she wailed, "I shouldn't have said that; please don't hate me!"

I was baffled by the comment, "Why would I hate you?" I protested.

"Forget it!" she said between sobs, "just forget it!"

I held her hands as she tried to turn away; my thoughts were racing for the right thing to say. An incoherent prayer sped through my head, seeking help. "Kelly," I said, getting her to look at me, "you're the most important person in my life; of course, I love you. It's just that... well, I guess I wasn't expecting you to say it.

"You're my best friend... no one means more to me than you do." I paused, watching the dueling emotions of hope and despair reflected in her face. "Why'd you wait until now to tell me this?"

"I don't know!" she gasped the words between sobs; she sat down on the edge of her bed... I followed, sitting beside her. "It's just that leaving made me think of how much I'm gonna miss you." The edges of her mouth curled downward as she struggled to speak... "and I guess I just admitted it to myself." She looked down at our hands, and one of her tears fell against my wrist.

Every guy in school would be more than flattered. Kelly was pretty and vibrant with a friendly personality that everybody loved – she was one of the most popular girls in school. A week ago, I probably would have been overjoyed to find out how she felt... even two days ago! What did that mean, that I really do love her the same way?

This internal struggle was crazy! I didn't even know if Anna *liked* me; how could I be attracted to her after meeting her only once? Still, something had definitely happened in that meeting – it changed me somehow. Everything about this week had changed me! It was like a whole series of new doors were opening for me while Kelly's doors were closing in her face. Her pain tore at my heart, and the fact that I could be the source of some of her hurting made my guilt more intense. I couldn't reject her!

"Kelly," I began, "I really do love you, I do. It's just... I think it's probably best that we not, you know, make it harder... with you moving, I mean. We've been best friends our whole lives – ya know how rare that is? Nobody is ever gonna take your place." She squeezed her eyes shut in painful resolve, releasing a few more tears to splash against our hands.

She shook her head bravely; "You're right," she said, "we have a lot of really good memories together... it's really rare... you're such a close friend." She paused for a moment, then shook slightly as she asked aloud: "why do I have to leave?" She leaned against me, and I wrapped an arm around her shoulder; we just sat there together for a long time while she slowly polished off the box of tissues.

Eventually, Kelly's mom called for her from downstairs; it was time to start bringing her things down. I looked at Kelly; she had her eyes closed, and then she started praying out loud, which was a little unusual for her, but it was her words that really surprised me.

"Lord," she began, "I know you still hold us in your hands, even when it feels like we're all alone, and every door that opens or closes in our lives is part of your awesome plan for us." She paused for a moment and then continued. "I can tell in my heart that you have something special planned for Jimmy; he doesn't have to say anything for me to know that you've given him a special mission. Lord, please give him the strength to follow close to you and do whatever it is that you have for him; I know I can't be here with him, so please bring into his life other strong friends to encourage him. Thank you for the way you're providing for us with dad's new job – please help me accept your path for us and find peace in surrendering to your will."

After she finished, tears were streaming down my face this time – they came out of nowhere and totally surprised me. I knew how hard it must be for her to surrender everything to God that way; it took me a minute to get myself together, and then I prayed for her too.

I held her hands when we finished and looked her in the face – "You know it's not like you're leaving the planet," I said, "We can still talk every day if we want and chat and stuff."

"Yeah," she said through a forced smile, "Ya better."

Kelly's mom appeared in the doorway and knocked; she pretended not to notice our red faces and the pile of tissues but spoke quietly in an understanding tone. "Time to load your things, honey," she explained.

I offered to start carrying boxes down while Kelly finished packing what was left.

As her mom left, I turned back to Kelly, "Thanks for praying like that; it was really amazing."

She just nodded; "yeah," she said.

Mr. O'Malley was quiet when I handed him the box I was carrying; "Thanks Jim," he said as he looked into my red eyes and at the wet shoulder of my tee-shirt. He dropped the box in the truck and gave me an encouraging pat on the side of my shoulder. When Kelly walked down a few minutes later, he slid his arm around her shoulders and gave her a squeeze. She laid her head against him and closed her eyes; a genuine smile came to her face.

Kelly really loved her dad; they had a pretty special relationship, which seemed to have gotten even stronger in the past few years. He and my dad had been really close friends too.

. . .

IT WAS late in the afternoon by the time we finished getting everything loaded. The house looked strange with nothing in it; I couldn't help noticing how much it resembled the way I felt inside. I dropped the last garbage bag on the curb and heard Mom calling everyone over to our house for pizza.

"Hi Jeremy," I said as I met the delivery guy from Uncle Mike's on the porch, "Better weather today than last night."

"That's for sure," he said as he waved back and jogged to his car to head to the next delivery. The phrase "last night" repeated in my head; it seemed hard to believe all that had happened in that short amount of time.

I was the last to sit down at our kitchen table, pretending to steal the slice from Kelly's plate as I slid in next to her. She jammed her elbow into my ribs the way she always did and swatted my hand away. My mother gave me a mock-disapproving look from across the table with that old, "better behave yourself" expression.

Mr. O'Malley said grace with one of his usual long prayers – Kelly & I each snuck bites out of each other's slices during the prayer (she started it.) Ryan thought it was pretty funny.

For a little while, it seemed like just another great dinner with the O'Malleys, but then reality set in again as they all got up to leave. There were suddenly tears on all the women's faces as everyone hugged each other at the front door.

I thought about Kelly's prayer for me as I watched her hug my mother goodbye.

Something about the way she prayed: "...you've given him a special mission," echoed in my head over and over.

I didn't have much time to think about it; the next thing I knew, Kelly had grabbed my hand and quickly tugged me outside. She led me in a run down to the truck and out of sight of the house, where she spun around and surprised me with a hug around the neck... then she kissed me. This was way more than an ordinary kiss. I never knew that a kiss could make you feel like your knees are made of jelly and send jolts of electric shocks up your back. It made the top of my head tingle and the edges of my ears burn!

When she finally stopped, I felt like I had to inhale fast to keep my heart from jumping out of my throat.

I was still trying to calm my racing heartbeat as she leaned close and whispered a timid confession: "I've wanted to do that for a really long time. Think of it as just something to remember me by." I was speechless, but she seemed satisfied with the reply that my eyes gave her.

Ryan came tearing around the back of the truck and crashed his head into my stomach in his favorite football tackle hug. I hugged his head and messed up the top of his hair. "Make sure you write to me," I said to him as he squeezed my waist.

Kelly climbed into the truck with her dad, and Ryan was buckled into the car with his mom. We waved them off as they pulled away and watched until they disappeared around the block. I glanced at their empty house, and a pang of loneliness started to well up inside. I felt my mom's arm around my shoulder. "Thanks for helping them pack up," she said, seeming to understand what I was thinking. It felt like we were really alone now, just mom and me.

The O'Malleys had been like part of our family since I was born – even longer. I realized that mom must be feeling the same way.

"Hey, mom, I'll make you a banana split."

"It's a deal," she said with a smile. We walked back to our house together.

⌘

7

HIDDEN

The secret things belong to Jehovah...
~ Deuteronomy 29:29

S unday mornings have always been my favorite. I watched reflections of the morning sunlight dance across the ceiling, thinking how great it was to lay in bed past sunrise. From downstairs, I could smell the coffee brewing and heard mom starting breakfast. She always made breakfast on Sunday; I loved it. The aroma wafting upstairs revealed that she was making French Toast and bacon – my absolute favorite. My mouth began to water as I slipped out of bed and pulled on the worn-looking robe that was draped over a nearby chair – my favorite robe; it was a thick flannel hand-me-down from dad.

My phone chimed with a text; it was from Kelly. "GMSH," that was her way of saying, "good morning, sleepyhead." It was a pretty lame greeting, but we used it because both of our moms said that when they woke us up as kids. It had become our personal greeting each morning. We'd say "Gamish" to each other on the bus, getting funny looks from our friends. "GMSH," I texted back, "war r u." "Akron," she replied, "drov all nit;" they were making pretty good time. She said they were going to try to make it to Indianapolis before stopping to rest.

Her dad liked driving at night; they made better time that way.

"Kelly says hi," I said to mom, sliding into a chair at the kitchen table and dropping my phone onto the table. "They're around Akron, headed for Indianapolis."

"Wow, already? I hope Ward isn't driving too fast; he's always in such a hurry." Mom would have said that even if they'd only gone 20 miles – she hated highway driving and got nervous when anyone she knew had to do it.

"Seems like they're taking it easy," I said, "they've been driving for twelve hours; I doubt they can go too fast in that truck."

"And what do you know about driving, young man?

Have you been taking long trips lately that I don't know about?" She smiled as she joked; little did she know how close to the truth the answer really was.

I smiled back at her and quickly changed the subject to something that was top of mind: "that bacon smells awesome!" I said, taking a deep breath.

"It's crispy, just the way you like it," she answered warmly. She placed a small pile of steamy French toast on my plate and slid it in front of me.

This is the best meal ever! I'd rather have French toast and bacon than a fancy steak dinner any day.

She sat down with her plate and said a short prayer for the food and the O'Malleys; I could tell how much she was missing them already.

"So tell me what you've been up to this week," she said with her steely gaze fixed on my eyes. I almost choked; I hadn't expected that question. In fact, it was the fact that I hadn't expected it that surprised me most.

I stumbled along with a general answer about being busy with homework and working at the Sub Shop.

"Um-hmm," she said as she chewed her food. "Uncle Mike said you met a girl the other night who seemed to make quite an impression on you." I could feel my face turning red – it never occurred to me that uncle Mike would give mom updates!

She could tell from my expression that she'd gotten her finger on a juicy subject. She casually took a bite and waited for me to continue.

"Oh, he must mean that girl from a youth group that came in Friday night," I answered, trying to sound nonchalant. "She invited me to their prayer meeting on Wednesday morning at the diner; it sounded pretty cool."

"Hmmm," mom said in her classic detective mode. "Is she pretty?"

Usually, I would have blanched in embarrassment and pushed for her to back off at that question, but this time something was different. The answer that started out of my mouth surprised even me: "Yeah, she's really beautiful."

Mom's eyebrows lifted as a smile crossed her face. "Really!" she said in surprise. "Well, let's hear about her; did you find out her name?"

"Just her first name; it's Anna," I answered.

I felt my cheeks flush again as I said her name out loud.

Mom's questions started coming faster… "What's the name of her church… does she live in our town… did she go to Parker Elementary… where are her parents from…?"

"Mom! I was selling her a soda, not getting her life's story!" Mom paused and looked at me, waiting for information. "She lives on Jessica Street; I'm gonna walk to the diner with her on Wednesday."

"You're picking her up?" mom teased with the maturity of a schoolgirl. "Well, when do I get to meet Anna? …she's really beautiful, huh?"

Her next remark stopped me in mid-bite, and I almost choked again: "did Kelly meet her?" She could tell from the wrinkled expression on my forehead that her question had hit a nerve. "Oh," she said with incredible insight, "I guess Kelly doesn't know about Anna – but that's OK; I'm sure she'll be happy that you've met a friend."

I must have looked like a deer in headlights; I felt paralyzed, with no idea what to say next. I couldn't let Kelly find out about Anna from her mother talking to mine – or worse yet, in her own conversation with mom. I needed advice badly; I decided to risk asking mom. She sat waiting for me to speak, slowly chewing a bite of her breakfast; her expression told me she knew I was struggling with something.

"To be honest," I began, "I'm kinda confused about things lately." My heart was beating really hard now – it felt like it would burst out of my chest.

I didn't want to look mom in the eyes – I focused on my fork and took a deep breath, then pushed ahead. "Kelly is... you know... we're best friends. Well... yesterday she said that she felt... sorta different about us – like it might be more than friends if you know what I mean?"

I glanced at Mom, who was listening intently with a super-sympathetic expression that made me even more nervous.

It was the way she looks when she's watching one of those romantic movies that she loves.

My eyes dropped down to my plate; I played with filling my fork before laying it down again and continuing. "Anyway... it was really clear that she feels... that way. Maybe I do too, but maybe for me, it's more like having a sister... I don't know what that's like. Anyway... there's something about Anna that's... I don't know... amazing. I know I hardly know her and everything, but it's like I can't stop thinking about her." I looked at mom for help, "Mom, I don't know what to do! I think it would really hurt Kelly if she heard I was, you know, spending time with somebody else – I don't want to hurt Kelly, I really really don't! But Anna is just incredible..., and I think she might like me too."

Mom put her elbows on the table and laid her chin on her hands, "well, look at you...," she said with a pause, "...a regular heartbreaker. When did you get so grown up?" She thought for a minute before speaking again, "You really like this, Anna, don't you... well, for now, you two are just friends – that's right, isn't it?" She looked at me for assurance, and I shook my head in agreement. "There's no harm in having a friend; just don't rush things – it may turn out to be nothing. My advice would be to just see what happens, just be friends."

Wow, that sounded so simple. "...Okay," I eventually responded, "...thanks." Her answer was just what I needed; I was glad I shared the problem with her. As we went back to quietly enjoying our breakfast, I felt closer to mom than I had in years. It occurred to me that I didn't know much about what she was like when she was my age.

"Hey ma, did you... like... date a lot of guys when you were in school?"

"Who me?! Oh no! I wasn't one of the popular kids; my father was much too strict... truth is that your father was my first date."

"Wow, that's cool. Where did you guys meet?"

"Well, it was through Barbara – Mrs. O'Malley – she had begun seeing Ward and, well anyway, Ward and Vince, ...your father, were best friends. The next thing you knew, he and I were being introduced. After that, the four of us were practically inseparable."

"You kinda still are...." I said, pausing as I thought about dad being gone, but decided not to mention that... "at least, till yesterday," I said instead.

"Oh, a little thing like three thousand miles won't change anything," she said, sounding a little like she was reassuring herself.

I thought about Kelly as she said that.

Mom looked at the clock; "well, speaking of friends, we'd better get going, or we'll be late for church."

THE MORNING in church didn't seem the same without Kelly; it occurred to me that there had only been a handful of times in my whole life when I'd been in a Sunday morning service without her. Our families even took all our vacations together.

We were singing "God Will Take Care of You"[5], and I started to think about the way Kelly had cried about leaving. "Through days of toil when heart doth fail, God will take care of you;" the recent memory brought tears to my eyes as I sang it. I felt mom's arm around my shoulder when she noticed the tears on my cheek. It felt good; I realized that I didn't feel embarrassed by it the way I usually would have – I guess a lot had changed inside me. I glanced at her and noticed she wasn't singing, just looking at me with an expression that reflected everything I was feeling. It struck me that she must feel the same way I did. Probably even more -- Mrs. O'Malley had been her best friend since they were kids – they had become even closer after Dad was gone.

The whole service seemed different like that – *I* seemed different.

When Pastor Wilkes started his sermon, I was amazed at how it seemed like he was speaking directly to me. It was about faith and believing in what was unseen. His words seemed to burn into my mind, answering the questions still swirling inside me:

> *The gravitational pull of the things that are seen is strong, but if God is going to build exceptional faith in us it's necessary for Him to keep us, as much as possible, in the things that are unseen! If Peter was going to walk on the water, he had to walk; if he was going to swim, then he had to swim; but he couldn't do both. Just as a bird must keep away from the trees and trust to its wings in order to fly — if it tries to stay close to the ground, it won't do a very good job of flying.*
>
> *God brought Abraham all the way to old age before fulfilling his promise of a son — forcing him to trust that the promise was God's and therefore it was going to be God's own work. The ability for Abraham and Sarah to have a child was long past impossibility, but that is when he finally looked away from himself and trusted God alone, believing that what God had promised, He was able to perform.*
>
> *Is this what God is teaching you this morning?*

PASTOR WILKES SCANNED the room and I was sure that he stopped to look directly at me.

*God loves to make His work real in **fact** as well as faith. We only have to trust Him and look to Him — He is the one who will do whatever He will choose in the way that He chooses to do it — whether it's impossible or not!*

...Wow

As we drove home, my mind kept drifting back to all the events of the past week. What did Ardent mean when he said Pastor Juan wouldn't *"taste death again before the Lord's return!"* Would he live to old age, or would the Rapture happen right away after that? I wish I knew what year it was in that vision... or how old he was. But, it did imply that the Lord wouldn't return for a while longer – that's more than anyone else knew for sure; maybe that's why I'm not allowed to tell anyone.

But who would ever believe me anyway?

⌘

8

CHASE

As the wild scene ended, I found myself standing over my toppled chair...
rubbing my wounded shoulder.

The house at 55 Jessica Street was a picture-perfect cottage with a white picket fence and manicured lawn; roses bloomed on a large trellis that reached the second floor. It seemed like the perfect fit for Anna. I glanced at my watch; it was exactly 6:45. I nervously made my way up the neat walkway and rang the doorbell. The door opened instantly, and Anna appeared with her backpack over one shoulder. She must have been waiting as anxiously as I was.

She greeted me with a broad smile, "You showed up... I wasn't sure if you'd really come".

"Yeah, but I'm a nervous wreck," I admitted, half-joking.

"Really?" she feigned, "You don't have to be nervous about FCS; the kids are really nice." I didn't want to admit that I was more nervous about seeing her; I just let it go.

She trotted off the porch and started down the walk as I hurried to follow her, already feeling a little like a puppy chasing after its owner. She stopped and waited for me at the gate. "How long have you been at Bailey?" she asked as I joined her on the sidewalk.

"Always," I answered, "I've lived here my whole life... I'm a junior," I added, realizing that was probably what she was really asking. "How about you? I know I don't remember you from Elementary - I would have remembered you for sure."

Anna smiled shyly this time, "That's a sweet thing to say, thanks. We just moved here last fall."

"Was it a job change?" I asked, thinking of Kelly's dad and their move, "where does your dad work?"

Anna looked at me with a timid expression and then looked at her feet as she answered. "We lost my dad two years ago; he was really sick," she said, forcing herself to sound matter-of-fact about it.

I stopped walking and was stunned for a second. "I... I'm sorry," I stammered, "I'm sorry to hear." After an awkward pause, I felt like I had to go on; "I kinda know how you feel," I said slowly, "my dad died too... it was a car accident, it was two years ago next month – May 24th."

Anna's face looked like she was going to cry, but it was more a look of empathy than mourning; a single tear trickled down her cheek. She stared into my eyes with a slightly surprised expression as she answered: "that's the same day... that's the day my dad... that's when we lost him, on May 24th."

I caught my jaw from dropping as I looked at the complicated mix of emotions on her face, completely understanding every detail of her expression. I was pretty sure that every emotion she was feeling at that moment, I was feeling too. In that short instant, we'd suddenly gained a deep bond that neither of us would have chosen, but at that moment, neither of us would have traded it either.

From then on, the rest of the walk had a whole different feeling. We talked about our families, childhood, and the way our lives had changed so much in the last two years. When I asked how she got involved in the FCS group, she told me about her decision to be a Christian – a real Christian, as she put it. It was soon after her father died. I shared my experience, too, telling how I came to Christ at a summer camp with my best friend... Kelly. That led to a half dozen stories about Kelly and me growing up, playing softball, taking family vacations, letting our frogs escape out the window in biology class....

"I'd like to meet her," Anna said sincerely, "I'll bet she and I would be good friends too."

"Yeah, I think you would be...." I said, pausing, "she had to move, though. Her dad got a new job in California – they just left on Saturday."

"You must really miss her," she said, "I'm sure she misses you. I know what it's like to move to a new place with no friends; it's hard."

"I'm sure that wasn't hard for you," I said, but then suddenly felt like it might have sounded like I was dismissing her point... "I mean, I bet you've never had any trouble making new friends... I can see how it would be hard, though," I hurried to add; I fumbled for a different topic... "I'm glad you invited me... you know, to FCS, I mean."

IT SEEMED like we had just started talking when all of a sudden we were at the diner. Anna waited for me to open the door, which I thought was pretty awesome, then she led the way inside and over to a few tables near the back that were full of kids.

"Hi, Mandy!" Anna said above the noise of conversation, holding out her hands to hug her friend. "This is Jimmy, from the sub shop."

Mandy gave Anna one of those schoolgirl looks, letting her eyebrows rise and fall as if she was keeping a secret. "I remember you, Hi Jimmy," she said to me, holding out her hand to shake. "How's your head?"

"My head? ...oh yeah," I finally said, remembering my fall in the sub shop, "it's fine." I could tell I was turning red, I didn't like being the center of attention, and that particular fall was going to be pretty hard to explain.

"Ooo, he's shy...," she said, bumping into Anna, "I think he likes you."

"Oh, stop!" Anna said, gently pushing her friend away, her own face now as red as mine.

Our discomfort was interrupted by a new commotion at the door. "Hi Pastor!" one of the other kids exclaimed. A second later, Pastor Juan was right behind me; I felt his left hand on my shoulder and turned to find his right hand outstretched in greeting.

"It's Jimmy, right?" he said.

"Uh-huh," I stammered.

"I'm really glad you could join us – welcome!" he said with a broad smile.

The conversation around the table was just usual stuff about everyone's lives. Still, Pastor Juan had a pretty cool way of weaving in lessons from his experiences growing up. He told us about times when some verse in the Bible helped him with a decision and about prayers that were answered. Somebody asked him how he ended up being a pastor. He said he wasn't really sure – it just kind of happened over time with lots of little decisions leading him in that direction. "No big visions or revelations or anything," he admitted. He looked right at me when he said that, which made me super nervous – did he know something?

ALL OF A SUDDEN, I felt an intense pain shoot through my shoulder, making me jump up -- knocking my seat over behind me in the process. I recognized the pain immediately – its jagged crescent seared into me as if the devilish beast's razor teeth were being buried in my flesh all over again! This time instead of fear, I felt a flood of outrage. I spun around with a boldness that was unnatural for me; amazingly, I felt like I was ready to blast that disgusting devil back to Hell itself!

To my surprise, as I turned, I came face to face with a scruffy-looking guy in his thirties standing right behind me. His eyes flashed with intense anger as my chair hit the floor directly in his path. It was more than just anger — they bore darkness within them that reflected a deep and overpowering evil. As soon as our eyes met, a flurry of images rushed through my mind. They showed unspeakable crimes. He was inflicting ruthless beatings — I saw him draw a knife and hold it to a cowering woman's bloodied face as she fell to her knees. Something boiled over inside me as my heart filled with a kind of rage. It was a righteous anger that seized me more powerfully than anything I'd ever felt. All at once, I heard myself shouting at him: "LEAVE HER ALONE! YOU CAN'T HAVE HER!"

In a split second, the evil darkness fled from his face, and his expression instantly changed to a look of fear. In fact, it was more than fear – more like terror! He tried to run and tripped over the chair, hitting the floor hard and dropping a knife that clattered across the dining room. It was a switchblade.

A few of the men from the diner came running and held the guy down – they were all shouting as the fallen man tried desperately to get free. He was hiding his face, saying: "KEEP HIM AWAY FROM ME – DON'T LET HIM NEAR ME!"

A cop standing by the counter came running at the commotion just as the man broke free. He lunged at the cop, hitting him in the jaw, but this officer was massive – he just snapped his head forward again with an expression that said: You really shouldn't have done that! The next thing the attacker knew, he was flat on his stomach with his hands cuffed behind his back. The guy was still in hysterics screaming about keeping someone away from him.

It all happened in seconds but seemed to me like it was happening in slow motion. I saw every detail, especially the guy's eyes, when he first glared at me in anger. I recognized those eyes; I'd seen eyes just like them from inches away in my own bedroom. It was like I knew it innately; they looked just like the eyes of those devilish beasts! I suddenly realized he was screaming about me – and he was raving like a lunatic.

I felt someone grab my hand and turned to see one of the waitresses holding it, "Thank you! Thank you So much!" she said with tears streaming down her face. To my astonishment, I recognized her face — I'd just seen it flash through my mind moments before. All at once, three other waitresses hugged her, and all of them were crying.

Carmine, the owner, yelled at the man being escorted by the huge cop and his partner from the diner. "I told you to stay away from my diner! Stay away from Angela!" He spoke with his hands waving, telling the cops: "I press è charges! Lock him up good! I will è testify!"

AS THE WILD SCENE ENDED, I found myself standing over my toppled chair, still rubbing my wounded shoulder. I watched the cops put the attacker in their car, and the waitresses ushered Angela into the kitchen. I gradually became aware of the others at the table behind me and slowly looked back. All of them were staring at me wide-eyed. "I... I.. I'm sorry," I fumbled, picking up my chair and sitting in it as quickly as I could. I glanced at my shoulder to be sure there wasn't real blood this time, finding it untouched. "I don't know what came over me..." I started to say...

"Dude, that was amazing!" one of the other guys said, to a chorus of agreement.

"How did you know?' Anna said, looking at me with an awestruck expression.

"Know what?" I said honestly.

"That was Angela's ex-boyfriend. He's really dangerous; she's had a protection order against him," Anna explained.

"I... I didn't know...." I stammered. I certainly couldn't explain the way that pain in my shoulder made me jump up. No less tell what had happened in my room the other night – especially not here – especially not to her!

"He, like, came out of nowhere!" one of the girls across the table said. "He was heading straight for Angela – I never saw anybody with so much hate in his face. Then you jumped up just in time."

"Yeah, you blocked him," Anna's friend Mandy continued, "Angela might be dead right now if you hadn't been there."

"Oh, I don't know about that!" I objected. I suddenly felt queasy about the whole thing; I could feel my face getting whiter as the blood started to leave it.

Pastor Juan spoke up and waved his hands to quell the rising chatter around the table. "I think we should bow our heads and pray," he said, "Let's thank the Lord for keeping Angela... and everyone else... safe." With that, he began to lead the group in prayer, giving me a welcome respite from talking about what had just happened and from the uncomfortable realization of its implications.

After the meeting, Carmine came and shook my hand. "What you did for our Angela, it was è wonderful!" he said with a grateful expression. "You're a good è boy. Your momma, she must be è proud o' you." He looked at Anna and repeated his point, "he's a good è boy... he's è welcome in my diner anytime. Whatever he wants, it's on è me!"

I felt a hand on my shoulder and turned to see Pastor Juan. "You okay?" he asked, "that was quite a brave thing you did there."

I could feel my face turn red, "Yeah, I guess so... I'm fine, I mean," I said uncomfortably.

He just looked into my eyes, probably seeing my uncertainty and nervousness; "Just give me a shout if you want to talk, okay?" he offered insightfully.

As ANNA and I walked to school, she told me more about the guy – she didn't know his real name, but he was called Chase. He'd been in jail for a year after beating Angela really bad. She met Pastor Juan while she was in the hospital when he happened to visit her hospital room. After that, she started coming to church and gave up drugs, and really changed her lifestyle. Carmine hired her at the diner, and she'd been able to get her own apartment and a decent used car. Chase had warned her that he'd come looking for her when he got out.

"He was terrified of you," Anna said, with a tone that revealed she was more confused than impressed by his strange reaction. "And the way you yelled at him... it was like you were this holy angel about to strike him with lightning or something."

Her description made me really uncomfortable, although, to be honest, that's pretty much how I remembered feeling at that moment. The boldness and indignation that I felt just came out of nowhere.

That was so out of character for me – not that I'm timid or anything, but confronting mean ex-cons with knives wasn't something I made a habit of doing.

"Yeah, pretty crazy huh," I replied self-consciously. Anna gave me an admiring look and smiled with a soft expression that kind of melted my heart. We walked the last block to school without saying anything. Both of our minds were racing with a jumble of thoughts and emotions.

Just before we entered school, she stopped and turned to me: "I'm really glad you came Jimmy, I really liked getting to know you."

"Me too," I agreed sincerely. She made a quick glance over her shoulder at the door as if it was calling us, which it kind of was.

"W-well, thanks for inviting me..." I started to say, just as she interrupted me:

"Do you like rafting?" she blurted out, "the youth group from my church is going to the Water Gap next month."

"Yes, I love rafting!" I said, unable to hide the excitement in my voice that made me sound like I'd just won a prize.

Her face lit up with a wide smile. "Great! I'll send you the sign-up info!" she said as she nodded with her cute smile and turned to leave.

... "Wait!" I said, "What's your number?"

She pulled out her phone, "Give me yours," she said with an efficient mastery, punching in the number as I said it. A few seconds later, my phone chimed with her contact card, including an awesome selfie of her. She flashed a smile as she saw me accept it and spun to run to class.

⌘

9

TEMPORARY

The things which are seen are temporal...
~ 2 Corinthians 4:18

"**D**on't leave your bookbag on the couch!" mom yelled from the kitchen as I entered the front door, stopping me in mid-drop. I still don't know how she always seems to know what I'm about to do from three rooms away. I threw the bag back over my shoulder and made my way to where she was making dinner, dropping it onto a stool beside the counter. I guess there was a spring in my step that made the walk seem shorter than usual. I nudged up to the counter beside mom and stole a carrot from the pile she'd just peeled, snapping off a bite.

"How was your meeting this morning with Anna's youth group?" she asked.

"It was okay," I answered as casually as I could.

"Just okay?" she probed.

"Yeah," I replied, doing my best to sound nonchalant, but then blurted out, "she invited me to go rafting with the kids from her church."

Mom stopped what she was doing and looked at me with a suspicious expression, then continued to peel as she spoke, "you mean a youth group rafting trip? I thought you hated rafting trips – all that splashing and dunking?"

"What d'ya mean? I don't hate it!" I objected.

"Hmmm..." Mom said as if she was a doctor diagnosing a strange ailment. "Will there be adults along on this rafting trip?" she interrogated.

"Sure... I think so... Pastor Juan will be there, I think," I fumbled.

Mom suddenly laid down her peeler and turned to look at me with a serious expression – it wasn't a look of anger or worry, just serious.

"What's going on with you lately? You're... older, all of a sudden." Her eyes scanned my face, searching for the answer to her question. "Has something happened to you recently?"

Her question made me nervous – what did she know – maybe she found my journal! "Wh-what do you mean?" I stammered.

She folded her arms – that was the signal that she had something serious to say. "The police called here today," she began, pausing for my reaction. I'm sure my eyes showed she'd hit another nerve with surgical accuracy; I felt my heart skip a couple of beats. She continued: "The officer said you stopped a very dangerous criminal. He said what you did was very brave — he said you were a hero." I stood speechless; it was obvious to me that I didn't deserve any of those characterizations, but I didn't know how to explain that to mom. "Jimmy, what were you thinking? You could have been..." she couldn't finish the sentence – tears began to well in her eyes, she swept one off her cheek with her fingers. "If anything ever happened to you, I'd ... I-I wouldn't know what... I couldn't bear it." Her tears were a steady stream now.

"Mom, it's okay!" I said with emphasis, trying to be reassuring; I was surprised by her reaction.

"NO, IT'S NOT okay!" she nearly screamed as she lost control and began weeping. "I'VE ALREADY LOST YOUR FATHER... AND

ALMOST LOST YOU THAT SAME NIGHT ... THEN THE O'MAL-
LEYS ... N-NOW THIS!" She hid her face in her hands and wept
openly.

I stood awkwardly in front of her, knowing there was nothing I
could do or say at that moment. The look on my face must have done
a pretty good job of expressing the jumble of emotions I was feeling.
Before I knew it, she had wrapped her arms around me and buried
her face in my shoulder as she cried her eyes out.

I couldn't help thinking about how it was the second time this
week that women had drenched that shoulder with tears; they
happened to be the two most important women in my life. Both were
crying over the thought of losing me... ME! The idea was incredibly
humbling. It oddly made me think about Anna, reigniting the sense of
confusion and guilt I had about my feelings for her.

That thought suddenly brought to mind the memory of what
happened to Anna's father. I began to recall the stories we had shared
of all our memories of things that can never be experienced again. It
struck me how really temporary everything is... how temporary
life is.

Soon mom patted my shoulder gently as she lifted her face away,
turning quickly to wipe her tear-streaked face with a towel. She made
her way to the kitchen table and sat down as she dried her tears. I
slowly took a seat beside her, sitting quietly for several minutes before
finally speaking.

"I found out something kind of crazy about Anna today when we
were talking," I started saying slowly, "about her family, I mean.
Anna's father is... gone too... he... well, they lost him," I said quietly,
pausing as the sound of the words made my throat tighten; I waited
for my voice to return before continuing. "The thing that's really
crazy... is when it happened... it was two years ago... he died on May
24th."

Mom lifted her face and looked at me with a stunned expression,
her eyes searching mine in an attempt to understand what she'd just
heard. "He was sick... for a long time," I continued, "...he died the same
day as dad... the same exact day." My voice choked up a little again as I

mentioned dad. "Mom," I said as I looked down at my hand on hers, "I think maybe you should meet her mom... I think you two should talk."

Mom pushed away from the table without answering. She brushed her hair aside and straightened her apron with her hands as she returned to the counter. I could tell she wanted to speak but couldn't find her voice at that moment.

"I'm, um, going to take this to my room," I said as I stood and grabbed my backpack. Giving her some space seemed like the right thing to do. "I'll be back down for dinner... I have a load of homework tonight." I glanced back at her over my shoulder as I walked away, noticing the way she leaned a hand on the counter, her back to me, and shook slightly in a shudder of small sobs.

I HAD to admit that I was feeling pretty shaken up myself. Part of Psalm 103 came rushing to mind; I must have read it a hundred times in the past two years:

> ...as a father has compassion for his children, So God
> has compassion for those who honor him. For he
> knows our frame; He remembers that we are dust. As
> for man, his days are like grass; As a flower of the
> field, so he flourishes. For the wind passes over it,
> and it is gone; And its place will know it no more.[1]

That old familiar pain stabbed me in the heart again as I thought about how I wished that dad could be here right now... I wished he could meet Anna. "You left us way too soon, dad," I whispered under my breath, "...way, way too soon."

I dropped my backpack on the bed and sat beside it; I couldn't help thinking about the way everything was changing so fast lately. The times I'd been with Chozeq reinforced how much time changes things – the words that Ardent said ...will say... to Pastor Juan echoed in my mind... **the closing days of time...** that sounded so... final. Then it hit me that the only thing really permanent is that... FINAL is permanent... a thing's END is permanent. Everything else is passing... this whole life can be best summed up in one word... *temporary*.

"Time like an ever-rolling stream bears all its sons away; they fly forgotten as a dream dies at the opening day."

~ *O God our Help in ages past, E.Butler*

⌘

10

IN PLAIN SIGHT UNSEEN

...The things which are not seen are eternal.
~ 2 Corinthians 4:18

Mom was quiet all through dinner – it's not like she was sullen or withdrawn or angry or anything like that; she was just quieter than usual. I didn't really have much to say either, we sat mostly in silence as we ate, but I could tell we were both thinking about the events earlier in the evening. I hoped I hadn't hurt her by opening an old wound when I brought up the connection between dad and Anna's father.

"Have you met Anna's mother?" Mom finally asked, clearing her throat as she spoke.

"No, not yet," I answered, realizing as I did how my answer revealed an intention to meet her soon. Mom looked over at me a little nervously as if wondering what effect this strange woman would have on her son.

"Maybe you're right," she said, "it probably would be good for me to meet her... If Anna is getting to be a close friend of yours, well, I think I should get to know her too... and her mother, of course."

I felt relieved as she said that, but also pretty nervous. "Yeah... thanks, mom... that would be good," I said honestly. "I'd really like to know what you think of her... Anna, I mean." Mom's expression softened into a warm smile; seeing it made my heart feel a thousand pounds lighter.

"She sounds like she's very nice," she said, adding, "she has good taste in friends anyway."

"She and her mom are new in town," I continued, "maybe you and her mom could be friends." Mom tipped her head to one side in a slight nod as if to say, "maybe so."

WHEN DINNER WAS FINISHED, I helped her clear the table. She insisted on washing up alone, sending me straight upstairs to do my homework. I struggled for almost an hour with the pile of assignments that I'd earned for the evening; my mind was a jumble of scattered thoughts and distractions. It was a welcome respite when my phone rang, and I saw it was Kelly calling for our nightly catch-up – she hadn't missed a night since she'd been gone.

"Hey, Kell," I said as I answered it.

"Hi," she replied with a hint of concern in her voice, "did you get my text this morning?"

"Um... no... I didn't see...." I stammered in admission as I checked my messages – sure enough, there was her message. It was received at 7:30 am; while I was at the diner.

"Are you okay?" she asked, sounding worried.

"Y..yeah... I'm fine... why are you asking?"

"I had a funny feeling that I needed to pray for you this morning – it woke me up at around 4:00... I guess that's 7:00 your time."

"Oh wow, that's amazing," I said as I connected the dots, "you won't believe what happened." I was glad that I'd already told Kelly about Anna and her youth group; mom's advice had been perfect. "I was at that FCS meeting…" I began, then described what had happened with Angela's ex-boyfriend, Chase.

"Oh my gosh!" Kelly exclaimed, "that's so scary!" I could tell from the short gasp before she spoke that she was concerned.

"Mom was actually pretty upset when she heard," I confessed, "the police called her and told her what happened. She told me it was a really dumb thing to do. I guess she's right."

"She is right!" Kelly agreed, "…what were you thinking?!"

"Those were mom's words exactly," I said, thinking how much alike she and mom really are.

I couldn't tell Kelly why I jumped up, but I felt like I had to describe what I saw in the guy's eyes. "There was something about the guy," I said, "his eyes and face and everything just looked… I don't know. The only way I can describe it is that it was like he had a demon or something."

Kelly was quiet for a minute, then spoke as if she'd just heard something amazing. "That's so weird! That's so much like what I felt when I woke up -- I had the strongest feeling that something… evil was about to face you. I wasn't gonna say it cause it just sounds too nuts." She paused… "Do you really think that's what it was?"

"I do," I answered, although I couldn't reveal to her why I thought so – that would mean explaining the pain in my shoulder or why his eyes looked familiar. "Anna said Chase was a really bad guy; he almost killed his girlfriend Angela before he went to jail and might have really done it this morning… Thanks for praying."

"So…" She said quietly, "sounds like you're getting to know Anna better." Her voice sounded curious, not jealous, but maybe a little nervous.

"…And the other kids in her youth group..," I added, "you'd really like them. She thinks the two of you would be really good friends."

"Oh, you told her about me?" Kelly asked with interest.

"I told her all about you… about all the stuff we did together growing up and everything."

"…Everything?" She challenged; her hinting brought to mind her goodbye kiss.

"Well, maybe not quite everything," I said, "a boy has to keep some secrets."

I paused, thinking about what Anna said about how hard it must be for Kelly, being in a new place with no friends. "How are you doing out there?" I asked with emphasis.

"I'm okay, I guess," she answered, without elaborating. It wasn't like Kelly to be at a loss for words; it made me worried.

"Kel, you know you can talk to me about anything, right? I mean anything at all."

"Uh-huh," she answered... there was a pause, and then she added, "I'm fine, really." It was pretty obvious, however, that she had something on her mind. I also knew her well enough to know she'd talk about it when she was ready.

I thought of telling Kelly what I'd learned about Anna's father but remembered the sound in her voice a minute ago when she commented about me getting to know Anna. Maybe this wasn't a good time to bring that up. I tried putting myself in Kelly's place – she must be so lonely and scared! I changed the subject.

"How's the softball team out there — you gonna try out?"

Her voice perked up a little, but with some trepidation, "Um... I don't think I'll try this year, but I'd like to get involved somehow... it's a good way to meet kids, ya know?"

"Yeah, it definitely is; you should absolutely try out." The conversation turned to how the teams were doing at Bailey. We caught up on what all our friends were doing. We talked for another 30 minutes, and she started to sound a lot more like the old Kelly I know.

"Hey... thanks," she said quietly as we got ready to hang up.

"For what?" I asked, being Mr. Clueless as usual.

"Just for being such a good friend... it really helped me tonight... more than you know."

"That's what friends are for, right?" I said, feeling pretty good that I was able to help a little. "Kelly," I said, leaning close to the phone – as if that made us any closer to each other, "just cause you're out there doesn't change the fact that you're the best friend I've ever had –

you're always gonna be my best friend." There was a short pause, and I heard a sniffle...

"Thanks, Jimmy..." I could tell she was fighting back tears... "that means so much; I feel the same way."

The end of the conversation felt awkward as we both struggled to say goodbye after getting so serious... the words: I love you, seemed to hang in the air, but neither of us said them for fear of complications.

"Hey, take care, okay?" I said.

"You too," she replied.

I couldn't help feeling worried after we hung up – there was something she wasn't telling me, and I could tell it was eating her up inside.

Soon after I hung up, a strong feeling came over me – a deep sense that I should pray. If there was one thing I'd been learning lately, it was that prayer is more powerful than I ever realized. Meeting Chozeq and Ardent had opened my eyes – literally – to the reality of what's unseen around us. The significance of it suddenly struck me — prayer is a direct connection with God Himself. It cuts instantly through time and space and right to His throne... more than that even... to His heart.

It was overwhelming as I considered it. We're so small that if God ever really showed us his greatness without reducing Himself to our humble level, we would be crushed underneath it. He's so vast that he needs to stoop down to view the skies, but he looks on us with so much love that our faintest pain moves His heart.

I felt tears welling up in my eyes as I slid from the chair and dropped to my knees. It was overwhelming to realize that this majestic and awesome creator – the keeper of a universe vaster than we can comprehend – had taken time to intervene for small creatures like us. I was compelled to thank Him, and the immediate response I felt from His Spirit confirmed that He was listening. I broke down and cried.

The burden I was feeling for Kelly and for mom became incredibly heavy on my heart. Then I realized that it was being lifted to His throne by the Spirit Himself. I remembered the burden I had after dad died that was too heavy for me to even raise in prayer – but it was no burden at all for the strength of His arms. I could feel that He was taking it Himself to the throne, carrying it to my great Intercessor. Presenting it to my advocate with the father – my friend.

~ You've known heavy burdens before, and we carried them together; there will soon be others. ~

The sense of these words interrupted my thoughts as if they'd been spoken. They were ominous but at the same time bore a strange comfort – like the security of an unbreakable promise; whatever happened would be under His control. I knew unquestioningly that He would be with me – close to me – through whatever may happen.

Something Chozeq said the other night suddenly came rushing to mind: Faith never grows so well as when all things are against her: tempests are her trainers, and lightning guides her way.

This time those words seemed like a challenge, a call to arms. I felt frightened – this didn't have the feeling of a simple reflection but of a watchman's warning. As I considered what it could mean, Kelly's family came to mind along with something veiled – something dark.

"What is it, Lord?" I prayed, "Please be with Kelly. Please keep her safe! Keep her family safe!" I felt a sense of panic – the feeling of danger was so real. "Lord, you care for us – I know you do! I know you always hear me – you're hearing my prayer now - you've given me this burden for a reason! You have the power to intervene; they belong to you, Lord - they're yours!"

I had tears welling up again as I pleaded for the O'Malley's -- the sense of danger was hanging in the air like a black storm. As much as I prayed, though, it wouldn't go away. I suddenly felt a deep sense of sorrow, as if God's very Spirit was sorrowful, deeply, incredibly sorrowful. My tears flowed harder, and for some reason, my thoughts were filled with the scene in John 11 when Lazarus died… the words from verse 35 hit me like a crashing wave – *Jesus wept.* For a while, I was too choked up to think of anything else. I couldn't find any words that could convey the depth of anguish in my Spirit!

As I became more worried, I thought of Jesus' words in Matthew 18 ~ *if two of you agree on earth about anything they ask, it will be done for them.* I had to tell mom! We needed to pray together!

I RAN DOWNSTAIRS and found mom sitting alone at the table. There were tears on her cheeks, and she held the cordless phone loosely in her hand, having just finished a call. She looked at me with a sad expression and reached out her hand when she saw that I'd been crying.

"I'm so sorry, Jimmy... I guess Kelly told you?" I stopped in my tracks as the sense of foreboding grew even stronger.

"T-told me what...?" I stammered fearfully.

Mom looked at me uncomfortably, "...Barbara said you and Kelly were just talking... I thought she must have told you...."

Mom's face showed a sort of wincing expression as if she was bracing herself to tell me something she wasn't sure she could say. She leaned over to face me and took hold of my hands... "The O'Malleys have been taking Kelly to doctors about her headaches...."

"W-what headaches?" I said in confusion... "she never said anything about having..."

Mom nodded gently to confirm what she'd just said and pressed on, "...the doctors confirmed it today. Kelly has a tumor in her brain...."

"H-how bad... How serious is it?" I asked in disbelief.

Mom looked at me sadly, her eyes jumping back and forth to both of mine, studying my emotions as if trying to figure out how to deliver the news. She briefly squeezed her eyes closed and then stared at me with as much strength as she could muster: "they're not optimistic... they think she has maybe three to six months...."

Before mom could finish, I felt myself gasp a massive gulp of air. My eyes clouded with tears. All the worst fears I was fighting crashed down on me like a cold, angry wave and sent me tumbling in a chaotic churn of emotions. I was bracing myself for bad news, but this was way more than I was prepared for! Mom waited until my eyes cleared, then continued... I struggled to hear her through the noise in my head.

"They want to do Chemo to try and shrink it before surgery," she said carefully. Surgery... my mind repeated... Brain surgery?

"W-why? ...do they think they can cure it?" I asked hopefully.

"Well, ...they want to try," mom said softly.

MOM LOOKED AT ME CURIOUSLY, "Why *did* you come down... it looked like there were tears in your eyes?"

I thought about her question, and the answer now seemed clear: "It was about this...." I said, "about the O'Malleys."

She looked confused, "I thought you said Kelly didn't tell you?"

"It wasn't her... It's hard to explain. While I was praying, I started getting this feeling that something was wrong -- like they were in danger. It was a dark feeling. Then there was the strongest sense that God was sharing his own feelings about them. I suddenly thought about that verse in John 11 where Jesus wept at Lazarus' tomb... I know it sounds crazy, but I felt like I could almost hear Him crying...." My voice cracked as I recalled the feeling... "Mom, I think I heard God cry...."

My eyes teared up again as soon as I said that out loud, and I could see mom's doing the same. From the expression on her face, I could tell that she was suddenly getting the same sense. The feeling of God's presence became so strong in the room, we both just closed our eyes as a flood of tears silently ran down our cheeks. Neither of us could say a word, but it was the most powerful prayer time I can remember ever having, anywhere.

WE WERE LEARNING that sometimes God just cries with us.

⌘

11

SHAKEN

Yet once more will I make to tremble not the earth only, but also heaven...,
that those things which cannot be shaken may remain.
~Heb 12:27

I sat staring in amazement at the words from today's morning devotional, rereading them over and over...

April 20 ~ Do you find yourself in the winter of barrenness and gloom? Is it a dark hour? Remember that it is God who chooses the times for our lessons in faith. Beneath fields of deepest snow, He conceals precious and abundant harvests of unimagined fruit! Even the darkest of nights does not last forever. When morning comes, and spring drives away the barren cold, we will be glad that we did not disappoint our Teacher in our hour of testing. How great will be our rejoicing when the bounty that our faith had already claimed and seen in the distance has become the glad fruition which our sight now beholds!

I YEARNED for these words to be intended for Kelly more than me – the fruits from this trial should be her harvests – she needs to be the one to wake from this night to a morning of healing and life! The message that I was sensing in my spirit didn't affirm that. What was happening to Kelly was a different journey than mine. There was a growing feeling that this message of a coming Spring would not be for her.

I had hardly slept all night, I'd been up for hours begging God to fix this, and when I did try to sleep, I just tossed and turned. The incredible events of the past few weeks with Chozeq have revealed how amazingly omnipotent God is. That only made it harder to understand what was happening to Kelly. He could easily remove this and make her well; why wouldn't he do it? I knew it wasn't because he didn't care or wasn't paying attention; I could still feel the depth of sorrow that his spirit shared with mom and me. But it seemed wrong that he would just use Kelly and throw her life away to teach the rest of us some lesson!

I was still in bed when mom looked in to see if I was getting ready for school. "I don't think I can go today," I said as I rubbed my head, "I had a hard time trying to sleep last night."

Mom didn't argue the point. She sat on the edge of my bed and put her hand on my forehead, checking my temperature. "I know it's hard," she said softly as she finished, "... we have to be strong for Kelly ... she's going to need her friends to get through this ... especially you."

"I don't get it," I said in a thinly veiled complaint, "why is God just letting this happen? He wants everyone to believe in Him, but then He acts like He's hiding and doesn't want to give himself away... why doesn't He answer our prayers?"

Mom sat thinking for a minute, then looked down at her hands as she spoke. "I remember something my father used to tell me... 'God *always* answers our prayers,' he would say, with special emphasis on always. 'We expect that His answer will always be yes, but He has a perfect right to answer with No, or Not yet just the same.' I remember Dad explaining it this way," she said as she looked at me, "a child who begs his father for the car keys might feel like his father isn't being fair in denying him, but he'd be a pretty terrible father if he handed them over before his son was ready to drive."

"I get that," I said, still struggling, "but what harm could come from healing her? It kinda feels like that would be the way to protect her, ya know?"

"Maybe it's not only her that He wants to protect," she said thoughtfully. "I know it's hard to think about right now, but whatever happens, Kelly's life... her real-life... will be a lot longer than her time here – she's an eternal being. God's plan for her is so much bigger than this life. I've had to keep reminding myself of that truth since your father passed on. It was really hard at first, but I know now in my heart that we'll be together again ..." She leaned closer and placed a hand on my arm, "... we'll all be together again."

She was right about it being hard to think about Kelly that way – it was way too hard! I stiffened as I felt the anguish building inside. "It's not right!" I protested, "she's too good... she doesn't deserve this!" I felt my eyes cloud again with tears, and I hid my face, embarrassed at the way I'd been reduced to a quivering child. I hadn't felt this power-less to control my own feelings since I was a little kid... except for when dad died.

Mom sat quietly, seeming to understand my feelings better than I did. "Have you talked to her?" she eventually asked.

"No, not yet," I answered nervously through a sniffling nose, "... I'm not sure what to say, sorry sounds so pathetic, so hollow... it just doesn't come close to how bad this is!"

Mom looked at me with a worried and empathetic expression, but her look didn't give any hint that she agreed with my argument. "You know she'll want to hear from you... you shouldn't wait too long to call her. She'll know how you feel; you don't have to say anything... I'm sure that's the reason she didn't tell you – she knew you'd be hurt."

"I'm not the one who's hurt!" I objected, "She's the one... s-she's the one who's d-dying," I complained, struggling with the words.

Mom didn't answer. She just rubbed my shoulder for a minute and then got up, tucking the covers around me as if I was eight years old. "Try to get some rest," she said, then left, quietly closing the door behind her.

I WOKE about two hours later, surprised that I'd actually fallen asleep. The clock read just after nine-thirty... that would be around six-thirty where Kelly was, I reasoned. I sat up and looked at my phone on the nightstand, finally fighting up enough courage to pick it up. That's when I noticed a text waiting... "call me," it said... it was from Kelly.

There was no avoiding it any longer. I hit the call button beside her message and listened to the phone ringing on her end.

"Hi," she said quietly as she answered.

"Hi," I said. I'm sure that my voice gave away how guilty I felt for not calling; "Sorry I didn't call you sooner..."

"Don't be sorry," she said sincerely, "I know I should have told you... I just couldn't talk about it... I'm not really sure I believe it yet myself...."

"H-how are you feeling? Mom said you're getting headaches?"

"I'm fine; it's okay," she said. There was a silent pause; I guessed we were both thinking the same thing... that she's really not okay... it's not okay.

"What are you gonna do?" I asked quietly, "I mean, are you gonna take some time off from school?"

"I hadn't really thought about that..." she confessed. "I guess I'll have to be out a lot when the chemo starts..." her voice trailed off as if she was deep in thought.

The frustration I was feeling began to bubble up inside... I guess the honest word for it was anger – I was starting to feel angry at God for what Kelly was going through. We talked for another half hour and somehow managed to not say much of anything. Kelly sensed that I was struggling.

"I have to finish getting ready; my bus comes soon," she said finally. "It must be getting late there… you probably need to get to class." I was embarrassed to admit that I was staying home, especially when she was going in herself.

"It's okay, I have time," I said, not quite lying.

"Hey," I said in a sober tone of voice, "… I'm not gonna stop praying for you – God is gonna get tired of hearing me."

"Thanks… I'm counting on it," she answered with the hint of a smile in her voice.

Once we had hung up, it was all I could do to keep from throwing my phone at the wall. I sat on the edge of the bed and pounded the mattress with my fists as I groaned like a wounded bear. I had never known that God's choices could seem so unfair! I wasn't frustrated because I didn't believe he could heal her. It was because I knew he could! And I knew… somehow… that he wasn't going to. It seemed that something else had changed about me in the past few weeks. I couldn't say if it was a result of jumping through time, but for what-ever reason, it suddenly felt like I was able to sense certain things in the future. Kelly's fate was already crystal clear… as much as I fought the feeling, I knew already that she wasn't going to make it.

⌘

12

A CONSUMING FIRE

Wherefore, receiving a kingdom that cannot be shaken, let us have grace, ...
with reverence and awe: for our God is a consuming fire.
~Heb 12:29

Each night that we talked it seemed like Kelly was adjusting a little better to her new reality; although I couldn't say the same for myself. I hadn't told her what I was sensing, of course.

Anna took the news about Kelly almost as hard as I did. Not that she had the same sense as me about her future; I think it brought back a lot of painful memories about her dad's fight with cancer. Her mom made us dinner, and they brought it over, using the opportunity to introduce themselves to my mom. Mom insisted that they stay and eat with us and the two of them seemed to hit it off the way I knew they would. By the time they left, both our moms were hugging and had tears in their eyes. That seems like the universal sign of female bonding.

Pastor Juan set aside the FCS group's Friday night meeting to have a prayer vigil for Kelly. They all stopped in at the sub shop afterward to lend me their support. I couldn't help thinking about the prayer Kelly had prayed for me the day she left and how God had so incredibly answered it, giving me more support than I could have dreamed of. The thought made me feel guilty as I wished the tables were turned.

Our church set up a care fund to help the O'Malleys with Kelly's expenses. Everyone was deeply affected by the news; the O'Malleys had been part of our church for such a long time. Word spread around school literally overnight, and kids and their families started arranging fundraisers of their own to contribute to what the church had set up.

Kelly's first chemo treatment was scheduled for Monday morning. On Sunday night, she was feeling nervous, so we prayed together about it. It was humbling and heartbreaking to hear her praying for me, still so concerned about my feelings and friendships even in the face of her own unspeakable tragedy. I felt more and more dismayed as I prayed with her for her healing, while the sense of foreboding kept growing stronger each day. I had to stop a few times to stifle tears, not wanting to give away my growing hopelessness.

On Monday night, Kelly didn't answer when I called. Instead, I got a call back from her mom a few minutes later; she explained that the chemo had made Kelly really sick – too sick to talk. I remembered Kelly saying that the first dose would be especially strong – it was supposed to shock the tumor, at least that's what the doctors hoped. I couldn't help thinking that it seemed like the opposite of medicine – their goal was to kill something, not cure it. Mrs. O'Malley sounded exhausted; she promised to tell Kelly that I'd called.

"How's Kelly?" I heard Anna ask as I answered her call a few minutes later.

"Hi…" I said sadly, "She's not doing so good… she was too sick to talk tonight; the chemo was really bad," I explained.

"I'm so sorry," she said sympathetically, "that part is really hard; I remember my dad going through it."

"Will it always be like this? Does it get better after a while?" I asked, still shaken by the way Kelly's mom described its effects.

"Not really...," Anna said quietly.

KELLY'S TREATMENTS were every Monday, and so we skipped Monday night calls. Even Tuesdays were really hard for her, and she had to end the call early most of the time because her stomach was too upset and she was getting migraines. What Anna had said about it not getting easier turned out to be very true. On many nights Kelly just cried on the phone. She was broken-hearted when her beautiful long hair started to fall out in huge clumps, and she cried about how lonely she felt not knowing anyone from her new school. She tried returning to school for just a day or two each week after starting chemo but soon became too weak and sick. She said it made her really self-conscious to see people looking at her like a pariah, especially when she started losing her hair.

At least the one good thing I could share with her was the way everyone who knew her back home was thinking about her and working together to raise support. I told her about how they were having a moment of silence before each of the school softball games and the way the team retired her jersey and hung it on an empty chair whenever they played. After hearing her talk about how lonely she was, I started asking kids to send her messages and cards. The school even let me make an appeal over the school PA system during home-room. Pretty soon, Kelly's mailman was bringing bundles of cards and letters. Some of the kids in Anna's youth group set up a blog page, and almost overnight, it was filled with messages and pictures from kids at school and from both our churches.

Even more amazingly, the FCS group was growing like crazy. So many of the kids who admired Kelly had begun flocking to the meetings and were giving their hearts to Jesus. The group was practically taking over Carmine's diner on Wednesday mornings. Kelly was especially moved by that, more than anything else. She told me that her illness was worth it if it brought just one person to Jesus. I struggled with her words, finding it harder and harder to accept the degree of sacrifice that she was so freely willing to make.

The doctors were being honest with her – Kelly made her parents promise that they wouldn't hide anything from her about her condition. In spite of all the treatments, her headaches continued to worsen, and the doctors admitted that the tumor wasn't getting any smaller.

JUNE 14TH WAS MY BIRTHDAY – I was finally turning seventeen. The FCS kids surprised me with a birthday cake at the breakfast meeting; Carmine made the cake himself and served slices to everyone — no charge. As had become the habit recently, I spent part of the meeting sharing how Kelly was doing. Then we all prayed for her together.

Mom surprised me by picking me up after school. She had taken the afternoon off from work to bring me to the DMV for my driving test. Somehow, I passed on the first try. Although, the cones in the parallel parking space suffered some extra wear and tear.

Almost seven weeks had gone by since Kelly had begun treatments, and her condition wasn't improved. In fact, it seemed worse each day. I could hear the weakness in her voice, and her perpetual optimism had begun to dim. It was incredible that she was able to be optimistic at all, I silently admitted.

ON SATURDAY, the FCS rafting trip arrived, and the crowd of kids was huge. It had been the group's idea to document it on Kelly's blog, and everyone was wearing tee-shirts that said *"Kayaking for Kelly!"* Most of the kids were in rubber rafts and not kayaks, but no one seemed to care about the difference. Each raft was given a waterproof sport cam. A few of the kayakers wore helmet cams; there were also kids from the school's video production club stationed along the shoreline taking video. All the footage was being collected to make a documentary so Kelly could experience it as if she was actually there herself.

I had to admit I was pretty overwhelmed. Anna sat next to me in the first raft with her friend Mandy and some other kids; Mandy had the cam and suggested that I say something on video for Kelly. It took me by surprise, but I managed to say something – it spilled out pretty naturally… "Hey Kel. We're making you this video at the Water Gap cause we know how much you love rafting." (That was true, she really loved rafting but rarely went when we were together because she knew I didn't like it as much.) I pointed to my tee-shirt and explained that the FCS group was dedicating the day to her, and then I stood up and shouted: "EVERYBODY WAVE TO KELLY!"

Mandy stood and panned the camera across the entire group behind us. More than 70 kids were climbing into rafts and gathered along the riverbank, all wearing Kelly tee-shirts; they waved and shouted like crazy. When the cam pointed back to me, I blurted out the next thing that came to mind, leaning in close to the camera as I spoke. "It's amazing Kel, it's like everybody we know is getting saved. All these kids here are coming to FCS and have started going to church – our high school Sunday School class is up to like 40 kids now, and the high school class at Anna's church is even bigger."

Describing what was happening reinforced to me the realization that God is using Kelly's illness for exactly this – to bring so many of our classmates to Him. The thought struck me with mixed emotions – I wanted there to be another way… another person!

"I wish you were here, Kel… I'd give anything for you to really be here…." I started to get emotional as I paused… "We all really miss you a lot…."

My voice cracked, and I could feel my eyes starting to get wet. Mandy saved me from embarrassing myself by spinning the cam around and holding it over her head for a selfie with the crowd shown behind her. "LET'S GO RAFTING!" she shouted as the group erupted in a loud cheer.

At that, our raft was shoved hard into the river current, and we started paddling frantically to steer around the rocks in our path. In minutes we were all drenched and laughing hysterically. I glanced over my shoulder at the amazing sight of a river filling with kids behind us and caught Anna's eye as she beamed a wide smile at me. Pastor Juan came paddling up alongside in a kayak and smiled at us, just in time to be nailed with a bucket of water by one of the guys in our raft. He grinned and returned the favor, smacking the water with his paddle to douse us in an ice-cold spray.

It's a good thing the sports cams were waterproof, Mandy was more drenched than anyone, but she didn't stop recording for a second. From the way she was laughing, I was pretty sure the sound-track from her footage was 90 percent giggles. I can honestly say that I enjoyed rafting for the first time in my life – I really, really enjoyed rafting!

IT WAS dusk when the buses pulled into the church parking lot. The kids were all singing worship choruses and clapping their hands like a bunch of "wild Pentecostals" – I liked kidding with Anna by describing her church that way. Our own church was more "grounded" in their worship, but we were still deeply moved in our own way. Still, I couldn't remember the last time I felt so free and genuinely joyful.

Stepping off the bus, I noticed that Mom and Anna's mom were both waving their arms for us to come immediately. They both had somber expressions on their faces. As I got closer, I could see that mom looked like she'd been crying. "It's Kelly..." mom said in an urgent tone, "she's suffered a ruptured aneurysm – we have to get to the airport... I'll take you home to change... hurry!"

The feeling of joy that I'd been basking in moments earlier disap-peared as quickly as the blood that was leaving my face. I looked at Anna and saw her holding her hand in front of her mouth in shock; neither of us spoke as I jumped into the car and mom sped off.

⌘

13

GOD'S MOTIVES

As often as I'd spoken with Kelly and thought I knew what she was going through, nothing could have prepared me for what I saw when we entered her hospital room. I barely recognized the girl in the bed. I would have looked for Kelly in another room if not for her parents sitting beside her. Her head was completely bald, and she was so skinny that the bones in her shoulders and arms poked out sharply. Her lips and fingertips looked blue despite the oxygen line nestled beneath her nose. Several tubes and wires attached her to an array of tech gear, which beeped intermittently with worrisome-sounding alarms.

Mom rushed to Mrs. O'Malley, who stood immediately to greet her, and they hugged for a long time as I heard them stifling small sobs. Mr. O' stood and offered his hand, thanking me for making the trip on short notice. I could see from his red eyes that he'd been crying recently and likely hadn't slept much in days.

"I-is s-she..." I started to ask.

"She's asleep," he interrupted, "the doctors stopped the bleeding, but there's still pressure on her brain... they have her sedated for now." I looked over at her and stared, still barely able to recognize the specter in front of me.

The trip had taken us most of the night, but it was still just 2:00 AM Pacific time. My growling stomach gave away the fact that I hadn't eaten in over 12 hours, not counting the bag of peanuts they'd offered on the plane. "Hungry?" Mr. O' asked, "there's a semi-decent cafeteria here. Can I get you a hot dog or something?" He didn't wait for me to answer, turning instead to the women and announcing that we were going down to bring back some dinner.

As we rode the elevator alone together, he put his hand on my shoulder, "I've been hearing a lot of good things about you, Jim," he began, "you're becoming quite the young man... your dad would be proud of you, son." His mention of dad sent a subtle chill through me, but it was a good feeling.

"I think mom would like me to be a little less grown-up," I said, feeling safe sharing my feelings with him.

"Ah, that's just your mom being a mom," he said. "Deep down, she admires what she sees you becoming." His words weren't profound, but hearing them fed some deep need inside me, another chill ran up my spine.

The doubts I was feeling about God's motives boiled to the surface, and I struggled with whether to share them. We stood silently as the elevator announced each passing floor with a chime, and my resolve slowly grew. Mr. O' waited quietly as if sensing that I had something on my mind.

"Uncle Ward?" I finally said, using the name I've called him all my life. "I've been kinda struggling with something lately... with what's happening to Kelly mostly... it's... well... do you think God really cares about us – you know, as people, I mean?"

Mr. O' didn't say a word or look me in the eye, but the way his hand clenched my shoulder told me that he registered my question. Once I'd opened up, the words began to flow out on their own in a way that even surprised me with what I heard myself say:

"I mean, He always talks about how we have to die to self and deny ourselves and take up our cross and about suffering and abandoning father and mother and all that. It's like He doesn't care about who WE are or any of OUR dreams. It's like He USES the people who love him the most in terrible, tragic ways. Like Kelly... she didn't deserve what's happening to her; even if it serves a greater purpose... she doesn't deserve to die!"

I saw Mr. O' bow his head forward and clench his eyes closed as a few tears ran down his face. I caught myself and suddenly felt terrible about what I'd said... about Kelly dying. "I-I'm sorry," I stammered, "I didn't mean she's going to d--,"

"It's okay," he cut in, "...you're right," he added sadly, "I know what you meant... her chances honestly aren't good."

He turned toward me and looked me in the eye, his own eyes wet with tears, "Jimmy, Kelly's illness doesn't mean that God doesn't care about her." His voice grew quiet, like a friend sharing a deeply personal lesson. "I've lived long enough to know that there's more to life than just the dreams that we have for ourselves. The reason He wants us to surrender ourselves to HIS will is because His dreams for us are hugely larger than any that we have for ourselves. You're right that God doesn't think about us in human terms... that includes our human limits and weaknesses... He sees us as much more than human. You could say that we're like squirming caterpillars that can't see past the next leaf when God already sees us as butterflies."

Although he was speaking quietly, there was a deep intensity in his words... and his eyes. I could see that he emphatically believed it. I wanted to believe it too... I desperately wanted to... I needed to believe it to get through what was happening to Kelly. But the thought of how she looked laying in that hospital bed came flooding to mind, and I felt my stomach tighten and my fists clench. A voice in my head screamed: who cares about childish butterfly stories when something this terrible is happening! God isn't perfecting Kelly... He's killing her!

The elevator chimed for our floor, and the doors opened. Mr. O' could sense from my body language that I was still struggling with the question. He didn't try to argue his point; he just rubbed my shoulder as we walked out together.

· · ·

THE CAFETERIA actually wasn't bad; he'd been right about that. Compared with most hospitals, considering that it was after 2:00 in the morning, the hot food looked pretty good. Of course, that might have been because I was so hungry I would have eaten almost anything. I filled a tray, and he got a hot dog and coffee and then suggested we sit down and eat there. We picked a table by the windows in the vast empty room, and he bowed his head to give thanks. His prayer was short for him but clearly heartfelt.

"Lord, you understand that we sometimes need to see the love you have for us with not just our faith, but sight as well. Please use whatever means necessary to do that and make your plan visible so we can truly understand that all things work together for good to us. We humbly confess that we need to feel your embrace in this difficult time."

That was it. No thanks for the food or request to heal Kelly or declaration of faith in God's invisible sovereignty. It was a simple prayer of surrender.

I just looked down as he finished, feeling ashamed to look him in the eyes. He was going through so much; who was I to say that I felt the pain of Kelly's loss more than he did? I didn't want him to see any of the doubt in my eyes, or worse yet, the anger that I could feel welling up inside me. We sat quietly as he watched me eat for a moment and then glanced over at the TV on the wall, pretending to be interested in whatever it was showing.

The worst of my feelings slowly subsided as I finished my meal, although the deeper doubts remained. I looked up at him, a little embarrassed: "Thanks for letting me vent. Sorry for the way it came out."

He looked at me with a mien that revealed he completely understood; I could tell that he genuinely grasped what I was going through.

"It's okay," he said softly, "you're not the only person to ever have doubts about God's motives. Just do yourself a favor, remember to give Him the benefit of the doubt too – maybe He does know what's best for us."

I forced a laugh – realizing that there was actually a lot of wisdom in his comment. I felt really grateful, at least for the way he let me share my true feelings without judging me for them. "Umm… could you not tell my mom what I said?"

"Don't worry about it," he assured me, "– it's safe between us."

We picked up some food and coffees for mom and Mrs. O' and headed back to the room. Mom was sitting by Kelly's bed and holding her hand – she asked me to take her place when we entered; I sat down cautiously and carefully took Kelly's hand. It felt cold and limp, almost lifeless; I instinctively placed my other hand over it to warm it. The voice inside my head seemed to wail in a mournful cry: oh Kelly… what has He done to you?! I felt tears starting down my cheeks and dried them quickly against my shoulder.

It wasn't long before fatigue overtook me, and I fell asleep leaning on the bed with my head resting on my arm, still clinging to Kelly's hand. A nurse woke me a while later; she apologized and said she needed to take Kelly's blood pressure. Mrs. O' suggested that it was a good time to take our suitcases to their house and get some rest – Mr. O' insisted on staying with Kelly.

The drive wasn't very long, about 20 minutes maybe. Mrs. O' offered Kelly's room, and mom suggested I take it. I managed to convince her that I preferred the couch, which was actually true – there was no way I could have slept in Kelly's bed. Mrs. O' suggested I sleep in Ryan's room instead - he was staying with some friends who'd offered to watch him for a few days; they had a son of their own who was Ryan's age. As it was, I tossed and turned for more than an hour before finally falling asleep from pure exhaustion.

⌘

14

MERE HUMANS

When my heart is overwhelmed: lead me to the Rock that is higher than I.
~ Psalms 61:2

Early morning sunlight was beaming through the blinds when I awoke. I could hear someone in the kitchen making breakfast — the smell of French Toast with bacon was unmistakably mom's. It filled the house, along with the smell of fresh coffee, making it impossible to sleep for a second longer and reminding me that it was Sunday.

"I've always loved your Sunday morning breakfast tradition," I heard Mrs. O' say to mom sadly, "If I had it to do over again, I'd copy that."

"Hi," I interrupted, trying to break the sudden gloom in the room. "Don't worry, Mrs. O, Kelly, and I ate enough Sunday breakfasts for all of us. You never had a chance; she was always at our house, usually still in her pajamas."

They both laughed, and Mrs. O' nodded to me: "That's true, thanks for reminding me," she said appreciatively.

"Go get washed up," mom instructed, "these will be ready when you get back." It occurred to me that I still had river water to rinse off from the rafting trip; a shower sounded great.

Mrs. O' was hanging up the phone when I returned, explaining that they were taking Kelly for an MRI and CT scan to see if the swelling in her brain had gone down. "They might decide to operate," she added nervously. "Ward said they told him they wouldn't schedule surgery until tomorrow unless it was an emergency. He said that we shouldn't rush back. It will be a while before they know anything."

Mom placed a plate full of my favorite meal in front of me and went to console Mrs. O'. I suddenly had no appetite.

The two of them finally sat down at the table, and mom lifted her hands in a gesture that invited us all to hold hands. She looked at me, "Would you like to ask the blessing, Jimmy?" I froze and subtly shook my head no, with a pleading expression on my face, no doubt. Mom shifted her head in that small sideways gesture that she makes when something surprises her and then got a worried expression. "I'm sorry honey, you usually want to… It's okay, I'll say it," she said. I felt both of them squeeze my hands reassuringly as mom prayed, making me realize that my refusal had revealed more about me than I'd wanted to.

The breakfast was delicious, as usual, but I struggled to finish it. When I refused seconds, mom knew for sure that I wasn't my normal self. "What do you say we head back to the hospital now?" she offered.

On the ride there, my phone chirped, and I pulled it from my pocket to see a text from Anna; it just read: "Ok?"

I replied with a quick: "Please pray."

She responded right away with:

"we R!
Had an FCS vigil since the bus.
Prayed all night!"

I STOPPED and reread her message a few times, then typed back: "All night? Everyone?"

"YES!" she replied.

I quickly typed: "TY!!!"

We got to the room just as they were bringing Kelly back. We watched as they wheeled the bed carrying her motionless body into the room and hooked her back up. Mr. O' looked at all of us, getting our attention; he looked utterly spent and exhausted.

"They think the swelling has gone down enough to let her wake up. They're going to stop the sedative but keep her on pain medication," he explained. "It might take an hour or so for her to wake up on her own."

"Oh, that's good news," Mrs. O' responded anxiously, "What did they say about surgery?"

Mr. O' took his wife's hand as he answered, "Nothing's been scheduled for now..." he paused as the silence conveyed what he couldn't bring himself to say, "– they think it'd be best to wait... as long as possible."

Even I knew that meant the surgery was too dangerous to do until it was the last resort. Mrs. O' put her head on his shoulder and turned to hug him – I could hear her sobs even though I didn't want to look. Mom sat down in the chair across from me and hid her face in her hands.

I felt the most intense sense of hopelessness I've ever known. A flood of memories washed over me of times when Kelly had come to help me when I'd been hurt. When I broke my arm, she wouldn't leave my side, even insisting on riding in the ambulance with me. She was beside me each time I needed stitches and stayed at the hospital when I had my appendix out. She stayed with me through high fevers when I stepped on a hive of yellowjackets. She was even there for me when I hit my head on that school locker and ended up in the nurse's office. In all those years, I didn't remember her ever needing me to help *her*.

Now she needed me… really badly… and there was nothing I could do to help her… there was nothing *anyone* could do.

At least nothing that mere humans could do….

A sudden pang of bitterness filled my soul at the thought that the one who really could help her was refusing to. I needed to get out of there; I had to get away from this! I took off, running from the room and down the hall, past the nurses' station and out to the elevator lobby. I pushed the button five or six times and punched the elevator door. Then punched it again… and again and again as the tears that flooded my eyes obscured everything around me. Someone put their hands on my arm and shoulder – I recognized her through my tears as the nurse who woke me at Kelly's bedside – she had tears in her own eyes as she looked at me. That's when I broke down and collapsed to my knees, crying out in an anguished wail and pounding the doors with both fists. This was worse than any pain I'd ever felt in my life!

Mom and the O'Malleys were around me immediately. I grabbed mom as she knelt next to me, and this time it was my turn to soak her shoulder with tears. When I'd recovered enough composure to get up, the nurse insisted on checking my hands, which were bloody and swelling. They led me into a small room near the nurses' station and cleaned the cuts, then wrapped a bandage around my knuckles.

Mom brought a cool, wet towel to wipe my face – typical mom, who knows where she got it from, but it helped. We sat there alone together for a while as she silently rubbed my back and brushed the hair from my face; I hardly noticed.

"Mom, did you get mad at God when dad died?" The question took her by surprise; there was a long pause before she answered.

"Yes," she finally said truthfully. "I guess I was mad at Him for a long time… sometimes, I still am. I think what made me the angriest was having to watch you grow up without your father."

"Do you think God could have saved dad if He'd wanted to?" I asked.

Another short pause… "Of course, yes, I suppose He could have," she answered honestly.

"Then why did He let him die?" I said, turning to look at her. Her expression was a jumble of sadness and pain mixed with uncertainty.

"I don't know…" she said softly. Then suddenly, something changed in her, switching her expression from uncertainty to resolve. She took my hand, "But someday you'll know why," she said quietly as if she was sharing an important secret. I looked at her, confused.

"There's something I need to tell you…," she revealed. She paused and took a deep breath, then looked at me carefully as she continued: "I prayed for weeks after the accident. I was so hurt when God took your father that I could barely get through a day. I could hardly eat and was praying almost constantly until one night I had a …visitor." She looked at me with an odd expression, as if to say, you're not going to believe this, then she glanced around to make sure we were alone. "It was an angel… I saw an angel Jimmy! It sounds incredible, I know. I've never told anyone about it before… but something makes me feel like it's time for you to hear it."

She stopped and looked me in the eye to gauge my reaction – if she only knew the things that I'd been doing myself with angels recently, she would be the one looking at me strangely.

"He said that one day you would know why your father died… it would all be clear to you one day. He even told me his name, I'll never forget it… he said his name was Chozeq."

When she said Chozeq's name, the shock literally jolted me from my seat. I landed on one knee; judging by how faint I felt, my face must have turned completely white. I held my head in my hands until the dizziness passed; everything in me wanted to tell her that I'd met him too, but the echo of his words to me flooded my mind… *tell no one…!* I just knelt frozen in place and looked at her breathlessly.

"Jimmy! Oh my gosh! Are you alright?! Please don't think I'm crazy. It's incredible, I know, but please, believe me, it's true!"

"I believe you, mom, I do. I believe what you're saying; it's just so amazing." I slowly climbed to my feet and started to pace restlessly back and forth; "Why did he say I'd know why dad died?"

"I don't know," she admitted, "that's just what he said – that it would all be clear to you one day."

I suddenly thought of something Chozeq said: *"There is nothing hidden that shall not be revealed, but all is not yet prepared in thine heart."*

I sat down and looked at the floor, fighting back a wild range of emotions. Now I felt like I really had to tell mom what I knew about Kelly – it hadn't been part of what Chozeq showed me, so it wasn't technically forbidden, I reasoned to myself. I didn't really know how I knew it, to be honest. I just knew that keeping it inside was eating me up; I knew I could trust mom with this much....

"...GOD PLANS TO TAKE KELLY," I blurted out.

"W-WHAT?" Mom said in surprise. "Well, I guess that's what the doctors think, but we have to keep hope... We have to have faith...."

"NO..." I interrupted, "...I knew it even before today... I knew it the night we heard... even before we heard that she was sick."

Mom looked stunned, "That's why you were crying when you came downstairs that night..." she recalled. "But how... why?"

"I don't know...." I said as I started to tear up again, "...I really don't know."

There was a knock at the open door, and we looked up to see the nurse.

"I wanted to let you know... Kelly is awake now if you'd like to go see her."

We stood immediately and started for the room.

⌘

15

HIGHER THOUGHTS

My thoughts are not your thoughts...
~ Isaiah 55:8

My nerves were wrecked – I was emotionally drained from all the events of the last 2 days but thought that I had finally gotten it under control. However, when Kelly saw me come into the room, her reaction nearly put me down for the count. She burst out crying and tried to get up, holding out her arms to me. I lost it and started to tear up myself as I made my way to her. When we hugged, she squeezed me so tight that I almost couldn't breathe – I just closed my eyes and wished it could never end. As soon as we parted, her mother gently reminded her that she needed to stay still, carefully helping her lie back.

She noticed my bandaged hands and looked at me curiously; "Nothing serious, just an accident... I did something stupid," I explained as I wiped the tears from my face on my sleeve, quickly changing the subject:

"I got a text from the kids at FCS – they had an all-night prayer vigil for you last night." I looked at mom and added: "as soon as they saw us leave, they started praying, and they never went home."

"Oh my goodness, the whole night!?" Mom exclaimed. Mr. & Mrs. O' were duly impressed as well, repeating how thankful they were for everyone's concern and prayers.

"You wouldn't believe how many people are praying for you," I said as I held Kelly's hand. "Between all the kids at FCS and their churches, it's hundreds – there are hundreds of people praying for you."

"Oh, and you should have seen what they did on the rafting trip!" mom added, "The whole thing was in your honor."

"You went rafting in my honor?!" Kelly said, teasing me. "You hate rafting!"

"Why does everyone say that?" I protested. "Well, maybe I do a little bit, but this was really cool – we had tee-shirts printed for everyone with your name, and they took video – it'll be on your blog as soon as it's ready."

"OH! That's so cool! I can't wait to see it!"

"You're gonna love it," I promised, as I started to describe the day and began telling her more about all the kids who'd started coming to FCS since they heard she was sick. As I went through the names of friends we'd known all our lives, she sat with her mouth open in astonishment. I noticed tears welling up in her eyes and stopped to see if she was okay.

"It's so... incredible... and so humbling," she said as she was moved to tears. "Whoever would have thought that all those people would be saved because I got sick? God is so amazing!"

I glanced at Mr. O' as he met my gaze – he didn't have to say anything to make his point; he just bowed his head with a subtle nod. I had to clear my throat as I pretended to agree with her. On the inside, I was being torn up, wrestling with God over his choice of tools.

We talked for an hour as Kelly laughed and joked – it was the happiest I could remember her being in months. It was so great having the old Kelly back for a little while, at least to see a glimpse of the beautiful personality I'd known for so long. Pretty soon, she grew tired and then became more and more exhausted. We all decided it'd be best to let her sleep a while.

SINCE IT WAS LUNCHTIME, I offered to show mom where the cafeteria was. This time the elevator was full of people, so we couldn't pick up on our earlier discussion there. The cafeteria was getting crowded too, but we managed to get a table away from the others near the windows where we could talk.

"So, the Angel... Chozeq... did you ever see him again?" I asked, trying to sound as mystified as possible.

"No," she answered sadly, "that was the only visit, at least that I know of."

The last part of her answer, "...that I know of..." made me look up, wondering if it was a hint that she suspected anything more.

"Was that all he said, just that one sentence?" I probed.

"Well, I suppose there was a little more... He told me his name and said God had heard my prayers." She paused, thinking about something else, but then it looked like she decided not to share it; "... that's all really," she confirmed instead.

After that, she got kind of quiet and stared out the window as she ate her lunch, obviously deep in thought. Of course, there was plenty for me to think about too. I wondered if Chozeq would tell me what he meant or reveal any more of what he told her. I was also feeling torn about whether my premonition about Kelly was really true. I could never have imagined that so many people would be praying for her. Maybe that would move God's heart after all. She seemed so much better this morning.

MY PHONE CHIRPED with a text from Anna: can u call me? it said. "It's Anna," I said to mom. "It's fine... call her back," she encouraged.

I tapped speed-dial and held the phone as I listened to it ring....

"Hi, how's everything going?" Anna asked as she answered. I told her how well Kelly was doing and how grateful she had been for everyone's prayers. Anna promised to share Kelly's thanks with the group.

"The rafting video is ready," she said excitedly, "wait till you see it. They did an awesome job!"

"Wow, already? They must have worked on it for half the night!"

"The whole night, actually, she said with a chuckle. It's really amazing. Check the blog. There's a link on the home page."

"Anna, you guys are incredible. I'll never be able to repay you for everything you've done."

"Get out! We're the ones repaying you! You're the guy who saved Angela's life, remember?"

I looked at mom uncomfortably. "That was different. It just happened... spontaneously." Mom's expression told me she'd picked up on the subject of the conversation – the incident at the diner was still a sensitive topic between us. "Hey, I have to go, but THANK YOU so much! I'll call later."

"What was that all about?" Mom asked suspiciously.

"They finished the rafting trip video...." I said, avoiding the diner reference, "the group worked on it all night. Anna said they did an outstanding job. I can't wait to show Kelly!"

"Well!" She said, slowing me down, "Kelly's asleep, remember? But I'd love to see it. How do we watch it?"

"On this," I said as I pulled my tablet from my backpack and flipped it on. "Oh, sweet!" I noted, "the hospital has WiFi; I won't have to use the hotspot."

"Are you even speaking English?" She asked with a confused expression.

"Forget it," I said as I opened the blog and stood the tablet up at the end of the table. The home page had been filled with pictures from the rafting trip along with a prominent link that said Watch the Video. I tapped it and waited a few seconds for the link to load.

THE OPENING SCENE was of me saying what I said on the raft. It was embarrassing to watch but made me kind of choked up anyway, especially when it got to the part where I almost started to lose it. Mom instinctively touched my arm in a sympathetic gesture. Once past that, the rest was pure action!

The whole thing was set to music with some pretty cool choreographed timing and well-placed screams and laughter. The opening scene of everyone waving to Kelly looked incredible. They started with the slow pan that Mandy shot and then cut in a half dozen views from wild angles from some of the other cams. It was timed to music with an awesome heavy beat. The river footage was like watching a roller coaster ride with giant water splashes, kids getting knocked overboard, and even underwater shots from upside-down kayakers. There were a few frantic episodes from our raft where I looked like I was trying to save us from certain death on the rocks. Every scene was full of tee shirts emblazoned with Kelly's name. She was going to love it!

As the rafting ended, the video cut to scenes I wasn't expecting – it looked like they were recorded back at the church. It started with Peter Murphy looking into the camera. He was a year older than me but had been a classmate of ours since elementary school and had always been a tough guy. I guess you could say he was the class bully – he and I had our share of run-ins over the years. He was from a rough home situation and the last two years for him were especially bad -- full of drugs and trouble with the police. His message floored me....

"Hi Kelly, this is Pete Murphy. I wanted you to know that I've given my life to Jesus, and it's mostly because of you. All the years I've known you, I was always amazed at how you lived your faith no matter what happened around you. I know I gave you and Jimmy a pretty rough time when we were kids... I finally realized that a lot of that was because I was jealous of you guys because of what you had. I guess I was jealous of your friendship with each other and your dedication to what you believed in. When I heard you were sick, it woke something up inside me – I realized that none of us is promised a tomorrow. That's when I took Jimmy up on his invitation to go to an FCS breakfast and saw how the kids were totally committed to Jesus – all-a-sudden it became real. Man! God just got ahold o' me!

"And Jimmy, I gotta say you got some serious spiritual mojo goin' on lately – God is using you, brother! Anyway, Kelly, I wanted you to know I'm a Christian now and to thank you for being a big part of that. We're really praying for you."

Peter's clip was followed by one from Chrissy Mathews, one of the girls on the softball team. She'd been one of Kelly's biggest rivals and never missed a chance to make herself look good at Kelly's expense. I always felt kind of bad for her; she had parents whose expectations were impossible.

Chrissy's comments started like Peter's: "Hi Kelly, thanks to you, I've given my life to Jesus! I wanted to say I'm sorry about how I've acted for, like, our whole lives – God has started helping me be better. You're the role model that I want to be like someday. Thank you for letting His light shine through you for all those years… you have no idea how much of an impact it made. We're all praying hard for you to get better!"

The testimonies went on – one after another, as person after person proclaimed their new faith and thanked Kelly for being a major part of their decision. There were more than a dozen testimonials. Then at the end of the video, they had a scrolling list of kids' names who said Kelly had been part of their decision to accept Christ. It showed the date that they were saved, and it scrolled for three or four minutes with over fifty names, all with dates in the past month! It was overwhelmingly powerful.

I had to admit that I was stunned. I never imagined that this many people could be touched like that by what was happening to Kelly. It clearly never would have happened if she hadn't gotten so sick. I felt a faint hope that maybe all these people praying so earnestly would make a difference.

Maybe God would change his mind.

⌘

MY WAYS

...Neither are your ways my ways
~ Isaiah 55:9

J ust then, Mr. and Mrs. O' walked over and joined us at the table with their trays. Mr. O looked exhausted, but they both seemed more relaxed and almost upbeat as they sat. Mrs. O hugged me gently, "I'm so glad you came, Jimmy," she said sincerely. Mr. O nodded in agreement and smiled, "We haven't seen the old Kelly in months; it was so good to see her laughing again."

Mom chimed in, "The kids in the youth group have made a fantastic video from their rafting trip! You have to see it!" She looked at me expectantly as she signaled that I should start it again.

"Well, do they want to see...?"

Mrs. O cut me off, "Yes! Please! I'd love to see it!" Mr. O nodded and agreed.

As the video played, both of them smiled and laughed and were obviously enthralled. When the testimonies began showing at the end, they both became quiet, and I could see them glancing at one another.

They reached across the table and held hands as Mrs. O wiped a tear from her eye. After the list of scrolling names ended, they just sat staring at the black screen. I wasn't sure what to make of their reaction. Their silence made me a little nervous. Then Mrs. O hugged me again and leaned her head on my shoulder as she fought back the tears... "That's amazing... That's the most amazing thing I've ever seen...."

Mr. O grabbed my hand and looked me in the eye: "God's plans are so much bigger than ours, aren't they?" I nodded uncomfortably at his reference to last night's conversation. I certainly couldn't refute his point.

For a while after that, I stayed quiet as the three of them talked, and Mr. and Mrs. O finished their lunch. It was my turn to stare out the window, deep in thought about whether the outcome for Kelly would change. As anxious and hopeful as I was, I still couldn't say for sure that I was feeling any assurance she'd be okay.

Mr. O eventually placed his hand on the table, "You all can stay here and talk. I'm going up to the room in case Kelly is awake."

"Good idea," we all agreed, "we'll come with you."

SHE WAS STILL SLEEPING when we returned, which gave me a chance to figure out how to connect my tablet to the room's big flat-screen TV. I'd finally gotten it working when she began to stir. Her parents offered me the chair beside her bed, and I sat quietly as she calmly opened her eyes and looked at me; a smile came to her face.

"I must look terrible," she said self-consciously as she rubbed her face and moved her hand up instinctively to adjust her hair. The feeling of her bald head seemed to catch her by surprise. "Oh, I guess I don't have to worry about messy hair anyway," she said softly with an embarrassed smile.

She kept her hand on her head a little longer and closed her eyes. "How are you feeling, sweetheart?" her dad asked.

"A little bit of a headache," she admitted.

He checked her forehead to gauge her temperature, and she

winced a little in pain as he touched it; he pressed the call button for the nurse.

"Can she have something for pain?" he asked as the nurse arrived. She looked at the clock and agreed that it was time for Kelly's next dose of pain meds. She returned a moment later with a couple of pills and a cup of water. Kelly was guarding her movements carefully to avoid any sharp motions. She asked for the lights to be lowered as she swallowed the pills, and the nurse took her blood pressure. After the nurse was done, Kelly closed her eyes and leaned back; it was clear from the way she focused on her breathing that she was in a lot of pain. It was such a contrast to the way she'd seemed earlier that it made us all a little concerned.

To our relief, after fifteen minutes or so, she began to look like she was feeling better. She motioned for her mom to come nearer and whispered something in her ear. Her mother smiled and nodded, then turned to us; "Ward and Jimmy, would you mind stepping outside for a minute?"

"No problem," Mr. O said, "we'll go grab some coffee for everyone. Can I get you anything, sweetheart?" he said to Kelly.

"No thanks, dad," she said with an appreciative smile.

IT WAS all small talk as we made our way down to the cafeteria. I asked him how he liked his new job, and he asked about our hometown sports teams. "That youth group at school sounds amazing. How long has that been around?" he asked.

"It's not really at school," I explained, "it meets at Carmine's diner once a week and at the First Avenue Assembly on Friday nights."

"Sounds like it's been growing quite a bit lately," he noted; "that's nothing to take for granted." He glanced at me with a friendly but serious expression. "You may not be old enough to fully appreciate it now, but movements that bring large numbers of people to Christ are a rare thing. God is doing something very special; just remember that."

I knew that he was talking about the way God is using Kelly's illness; I appreciated how he didn't make a big deal of pointing it out to me. It was starting to seem like maybe it wasn't such a bad thing if Kelly was recovering after all – maybe that's what God planned all along. I pushed the darker premonitions out of my mind.

WHEN WE GOT BACK to the room and confirmed that it was safe for us to enter, we were surprised to see Kelly dressed in jeans and a nice shirt and sitting in one of the cushioned chairs. She wore her favorite baseball cap on her head. "HEY! Look at you!" her dad exclaimed. She smiled at him and then looked at me as if seeking my approval as well. I was thrilled – my face must have shown how much I loved the way she looked because she smiled back and laughed like a flattered schoolgirl.

She stood as I walked closer: "I wanted to give you a real hug," she said shyly; her eyes were an ocean of swirling emotions: full of vulnerability, uncertainty, hope, but mostly love. Her hug felt so good as her arms squeezed my back and her chin pressed hard against my neck. It fed my soul in surprising ways that flooded me with something I desperately needed but hadn't admitted until then. She felt so good in my arms; I didn't want to let her go... ever. We both just stood like that silently with our eyes squeezed closed – probably for much longer than anybody expected. No one interrupted; no one in the room said a word. Kelly buried her eyes against my shoulder as she ended her embrace and slowly slid her forehead against me as she backed away. The baseball cap slipped off her head and hit the floor behind me, but she hardly noticed – I could see her eyes welling up with tears, but she remained strong and smiled at me. My hands instinctively held her head, and we gently let our foreheads touch. I can honestly say that our silent exchange conveyed more between us than we'd ever shared in seventeen years of life.

I wrapped one arm around her shoulders and slid alongside her, turning toward the others. Both our moms had tears streaming down their faces. Her dad's eyes were a bit glassy with moisture, too – he reached over and handed her the baseball cap, and she quietly said thanks as she put it on.

"Hey! We have the FCS video ready to show," I said, "want to see?"

"Oh yes!" she said enthusiastically.

I started the video -- relieved that it worked just fine on the big TV, then hurried back to the chair beside Kelly as the opening music played. She leaned closer and took my hand, then smiled at me when she saw my opening comments.

"Oh, that's sweet!" she said when I started to get teary-eyed. Her dad laughed at the way I winced when she said that.

I watched her from the corner of my eye as the rafting scenes played – she was enthralled and deep in the action, shifting and ducking at the wild scenes. It did look pretty awesome on the big screen – it had my heart racing even though I'd been there in person! She laughed and squealed as kids went overboard and ducked when huge splashes doused whoever had the cam.

"Is that Anna?" she asked warmly as we watched one of the scenes.

"Yeah, it is – how did you know?" I said, honestly impressed but also slightly nervous.

"Just a guess…" she said with a smile, "she seems really nice."

Just then, the raft bumped a colossal rock, and Anna went overboard. "Nice driving!" Kelly joked with a giggle, "I can see why you don't go rafting much."

"Hey! The river was trying to kill us; what can I say!" Kelly giggled and joked for the rest of the whitewater scenes as she smiled from ear to ear.

When the testimonies began, she quieted the same way her parents had, and she squeezed my hand. She looked at me in amazement when Pete spoke, then exclaimed, "Oh my gosh! That's Chrissy!" putting her head on my shoulder as she watched in shock.

She looked at the others silently, intent on hearing every word. Her silence was interrupted only by short gasps of surprise as she recognized kids she would have never expected there in a million years. She couldn't imagine how she'd had any impact on their lives, let alone the profound changes they all described. Soon I could hear sniffles as their overpowering messages struck home.

She watched the scrolling list of names intently, reading each one and adding gasps as she recognized more surprises. She looked at me with wet eyes as the list finally ended; "Oh – my – gosh, Jimmy!" she said with a stunned, serious expression. "All those people! It's amazing! But, how… why…? What did I ever do?"

I wasn't sure how to answer. I knew what her father probably wanted to say but felt like I'd be a hypocrite if I just claimed that God was using her illness for good – I still felt more like He was using *her*. No matter how special the purpose, it still made me angry. It crossed my mind that if Jonah could be mad about a dying gourde plant that was giving him shade,[1] then I certainly had a right to be even madder about a dying friend! It's crazy what goes through your mind when you're mad at God.

So I didn't answer. I just hugged her close.

⌘

17

A PRAYER ANSWERED

Though he slay me, yet will I hope in him...
~ Job 13:15

The rest of the afternoon was about as perfect as it could be, all things considered. Kelly was happy and peaceful and seemed really, truly contented. We went for a walk – at least I walked; the nurses insisted that Kelly stay in a wheelchair. The hospital had a picturesque rooftop garden that was the perfect place for a casual afternoon of relaxed conversation. For a while, the insanity of her situation seemed forgettable.... Except for the facts of her wheelchair and the longing she felt for her beautiful hair. Especially her hair; it was clear that that was a stabbing reminder that pierced even the most incredible abundance of contentment she might otherwise be feeling.

After two of the swiftest hours I could remember ever living, it was time for us to head back. She was looking tired, and it was clearly becoming harder for her to ignore the relentless pain that hounded her. Gratefully, the nurse was watching the time and had Kelly's pills ready for her the moment we got back. Mr. O' and I took another walk as they helped her get changed for bed. She was fast asleep when we returned.

WE TOOK turns going down for dinner, not wanting her to be alone. When mom and I came back from eating, we were pleasantly surprised to find Kelly propped up in bed holding the tablet with the video playing.

"It's her third time through it," her dad explained, "I think it's a hit."

She was smiling like a kid on Christmas morning. "I'm getting in years of rafting time," she joked while tilting the screen back and forth as if it was a video game. She laid it down and looked up at me as we walked in, "I really love it," she said softly.

"If I'd known how much you loved it, I would have gone with you more," I apologized, feeling a pang of guilt. "You've always sacrificed your own feelings to make other people happy... especially me. I was always so selfish that I never appreciated it until now."

"I meant the video...," she said with a smile and an amazing insight into what I was feeling. "Forget about the rafting, don't feel sorry about that!"

I SAT down on the edge of the bed beside her without a word, and she held out her hand for me to hold. She paused thoughtfully for a moment and then looked at me with an intensity that cut right through me. It was calm and loving and not judgmental at all, but it honestly felt like she was looking directly into my soul. She sighed sympathetically, "I know this is really hard for you," she said, "but please don't be mad at God for what's happening."

I glanced at her father, but he looked at me surprised and shook his head to say that he never told her. She gently squeezed my hand and continued. "It's easy to see it, Jimmy. What God is doing is a lot bigger than either of us." Her words echoed another comment that her father made. His face showed that he was just as shocked as I was to hear her saying that too. "What He's doing through what's happening to me is amazing Jimmy, it's unbelievable and humbling… I wouldn't trade one of our friends who've been saved for a hundred years of life." Her words cut through me like a sword, making me wince in guilt, while at the same time, I felt my soul rear up in defiance against the unthinkable transaction that God had ordained.

Kelly pulled on my hand and lowered her voice, even more, making me lean close to hear her, "…What He's going to do through you is even more incredible," she said in a thrilled tone. She lowered her voice to a whisper as she looked into my eyes and continued… "Your special mission is SO important, Jimmy! No matter how hard it gets, you have to keep going – there are so many at stake!"

I looked at her in surprise as a chill ran up my spine. I started to ask her to explain what she meant – but she interrupted me by touching my lips with her fingertips. Her expression changed, growing intensely earnest, and she looked into my eyes with a mix of emotions that was too complex for me to interpret… "I was so blessed to have you…" she said in a half-whisper, "I always loved you… my whole life."

JUST THEN, she closed her eyes and leaned her head forward as if she was getting dizzy, and then her head jerked back as her eyes rolled upward, and I felt her hand go limp -- she sank back onto her pillow. The monitors on the wall started blaring a series of alarms, and the steady blip of her heart rate flatlined. I gasped in shock and urgently called her name as her parents rushed to her side and leaned over her, trying to get a response.

The nurses rushed into the room and swept everyone back from the bed, drawing the curtain around it as a pair of interns raced in pushing a crash cart. We heard them work frantically, and then someone yelled "CLEAR!" followed by the crack of a Defibrillator firing. The sequence was repeated two more times before the heart monitor picked up a faint heartbeat. They continued to work fever-ishly as one of the nurses ran urgently from the room. We heard her voice on the hospital loudspeaker a moment later, calling for Dr. Ernhart to report to Kelly's room number …STAT!

The doctor was running as he entered the room and joined the team at Kelly's bedside, where he quickly invited her parents to join him. His examination led to a rapid and urgent diagnosis – she needed surgery right now!

Kelly's mom and dad gave their consent immediately, and in the briefest of moments, they were wheeling her bed from the room. Mr. O' put his arm across my shoulders, sensing how shaken I was, and invited me to follow. The four of us chased the bed as the interns nearly ran her to a waiting elevator, and we jumped in behind them. Kelly's heart monitor revealed her heart's weak and intermittent beats; in my mind, they seemed to echo the last words she said to me. I kept hearing them repeat over and over in my head.

When the elevator opened, Kelly was taken through a set of double doors, and a nurse led us to a nearby waiting area. I grabbed my phone and texted Anna: "Need prayer now!!!" She responded immediately: "OK, spreading the word!" Mom came alongside me and put her arm around my shoulders. I showed her my phone's screen, "Anna is asking everyone to pray."

I knew if I turned to hug mom, I'd totally lose it, so I just stood still and stared at the door they'd taken Kelly through. Soon Mom turned to the others; "You haven't had any dinner… we'll go and bring something up." We all knew she was really just making an excuse for us to take a walk together; the elevator was empty and quiet.

Mom spoke gently, "I think you should know that whatever happens to Kelly, God isn't throwing her away; this is what she prayed for."

Tears welled up in my eyes, and I fought them back; "What are you talking about?" I asked in a tone that revealed some of the bitterness I was feeling toward God at that moment.

"Barbara shared with me that the day Kelly learned about her tumor, they prayed together," mom explained. "Kelly didn't pray for healing; she prayed that God would use her illness for good. She wanted her life to count for something special. She never changed her request; every time they prayed, she asked the same thing."

I struggled hard to stay strong but felt a couple of tears escape my eyes as I squeezed them shut. Mom seemed to understand how hard I was struggling to keep it together. She kept a little distance, somehow knowing that I'd crumble if she put her arm around me. As I thought about what she'd said, it occurred to me that it had been the same whenever Kelly and I had prayed together too. She always asked for God to use what was happening for a greater purpose. I always thought of it as just her way of keeping her hopes grounded; in fact, I secretly rejected the idea each time I heard it.

"God has answered Kelly's prayer... You showed her that yourself with the beautiful news about what's happening in the FCS group."

"Why does it have to be one or the other?" I managed to say as I fought my emotions, "W-why couldn't He let her live too?" I knew, of course, that mom didn't have an answer to my question, and she didn't try to offer one. She just looked at me silently with an expression that showed she understood everything I was feeling... she'd been through it before herself.

⌘

18

UNBEARABLE

...We carried them together

We returned from the cafeteria as fast as we could, bringing back a couple of sandwiches and cups of soup for Kelly's parents. Not that we thought they would really have much of an appetite. The hospital was pretty huge and confusing. We ended up on a different set of elevators than the one we'd taken down. Stepping off, we noticed a set of doors that said **Chapel**, which we hadn't seen before.

"So that's where they put the chapel," I noted to mom. "It's no surprise that it's here next to the O/R. I guess God prefers using tragedies... that seems to be how He works," I said, revealing more of my disapproval than I intended to.

Mom looked at me with the benefit of her hard-won experience and gently made the point that it's people who most often turn to God when tragedy hits. It's the way people are – not the way God is. I was forced to admit that was true.

"I guess you're right," I confessed, "it does make sense for Him to know that and to be waiting." I understood it all logically, but my Spirit was still raging.

The surgery lasted for hours. Every hour or so, one of the doctors would emerge to give an update. They explained that Kelly's aneurysm had reopened, and the tumor needed to be removed to allow normal blood flow. It was located in her brain stem, where the body's basic functions were controlled, like movement, breathing, and heartbeat. There was a high likelihood that Kelly would be paralyzed as a result... or worse. They also explained that her heart was already fragile, and they feared that resuscitation may not be possible.

Mr. O' pulled his chair around to form a circle and suggested that we pray together, taking his wife's hand and mine – I held mom's, and she grabbed Mrs. O's. He started with a prayer of thanks, which kind of amazed me under the circumstances.

"Lord," he began, "besides your amazing grace, Kelly is the most wonderful gift that you've given to us. Thank you so much for entrusting her to us to be her parents for the past seventeen years. Thank you for all the joy and wisdom she has brought to our lives. You are using her life so profoundly to show others your love and to draw so many to you. We know that was...that is... her prayer, and we thank you for answering it."

Kelly's mom could be heard sniffling, and mom handed her some tissues. Mr. O continued... "We know you feel the pain that we feel at this moment and that you love Kelly even more than we can comprehend. We desperately want you to heal her... We ask you humbly for mercy and pray that your hand would give healing in this desperate hour...."

Mr. O's voice cracked, and he had to pause to get his composure.

BEFORE HE COULD CONTINUE, we heard footsteps, and I opened my eyes to see Dr. Ernhart kneeling down on one knee beside our chairs. He placed his hand gently on Mr. O's arm and had a sorrowful look on his face.

"I'm very sorry...." He said, "I'm afraid Kelly didn't... we lost her... I'm so, so sorry...."

Kelly's mom immediately fell onto her husband's shoulder and wailed in a mournful cry. I suppose it was the sound of her inconsolable sorrow that affected me even more than my own – I buried my face in my hands and felt my body shake violently as the sense of loss overtook me. Mom wrapped her arm around my shoulders and did her best to comfort me.

I could hear Kelly's dad trying to thank the surgeon for all that he'd done to try and save her, but he broke down before he could finish. The doctor understood and said he'd be nearby when they were ready to talk.

"Can we see her?" Kelly's mom suddenly asked through her tears.

The doctor nodded, "Of course." They huddled together as they stood, and he quietly explained that Kelly's surgical wound was visible. He wanted to be sure they were prepared for that. They nodded as they visibly braced themselves and followed him.

I was beside myself; I had to get up and walk, hardly realizing that I pushed mom away as I jumped up – I paced back and forth, holding my hands on my head and shaking it in disbelief. All the dark premonitions I'd had since that first night came flooding back in an unwelcome confirmation that they'd all been right. I suddenly remembered the chapel doors. I began to run toward them without a second thought, leaving mom alone as I burst inside.

It was a small chapel, probably able to seat a few dozen people. It had a small altar area in front with an altar rail and a lectern with a single stained glass window behind it with a nondescript design. The room was empty and quiet. I ran straight to the altar and fell to my knees – too conflicted to cry or pray; I just knelt there with my clenched fists pressed against my head.

My swirling thoughts and emotions flowed over me as if I was being pulled down into a violent whirlpool, chaotic and raging. I felt like I was drowning. The words I had heard impressed on my Spirit in my bedroom on that first night reemerged: "you've known heavy burdens before, and we carried them together...." This time my soul reacted with the raging accusation that had been welling up inside me: "YOU KILLED HER!" I wanted to shout, "How can you speak of comforting when you didn't even want to save her!"

The Spirit grew silent within me as I began to feel like the ceiling was made of lead, blocking any attempt to pray. Clouds of despair hung overhead, thick and cold. I pounded my fist against the altar rail and bent to the floor, dropping my head into my hands.

Just then, the floor began to swirl, spinning me around and making me feel weightless as if pulled through space. By now, it had become a familiar feeling, but this time felt more ominous than before. I held my eyes closed tightly, too afraid to open them as it occurred to me that I might soon meet the one who was the object of my rage and defiance – the thought terrified me!

⌘

19

BETWEEN THE BEFORE AND THE AFTER

...but Moses said, If your presence does not go with me, carry us not up there.
~ Exodus 33:15

In an instant, I heard a cacophony of strange sounds, people talking... arguing, actually... and some kind of livestock... sheep and goats! A mix of scents struck me; spices, animals, smoke, maybe it was incense... and a strong odor of other less pleasant things... it all surrounded me. A hot wind struck my face, causing me to throw open my eyes in confusion. Like a man awakened from a deep sleep, I struggled to make sense of my surroundings. A searing sun nearly blinded me as I tried to look up.

I was kneeling in the dirt – on my hands and knees. Looking down, my eyes focused on my hands but struggled to make sense of the sight; they looked like the hands of a young child! I flexed my fingers and grabbed a handful of sand, letting it pour to the ground, feeling its warmth in my palm, and inspecting its grit between the tiny fingertips.

A tug on my arm suddenly yanked me to my feet. A woman's voice was speaking sternly in words I didn't recognize at first. She grabbed my hand and wiped the dust from it against her robes; I studied in amazement the sight of her hand more than twice the size of mine and rough with calluses. Still, it held me gently as it engulfed half my forearm. Shielding my eyes from the sun with my free hand, I strained to look up into the face of this strange benefactor. She wore a scarf around her head, but I could see her face, marked with the lines of premature aging and darkly weathered. Her lips were cracked and dry. As I studied her face, her expression softened, and she smiled down at me, grabbing my chin playfully. Her eyes were warm as she spoke again, "Little Simeon, you worried Mama! Don't you ever run off like that again! "

Simeon? Who's Simeon? I looked around me and then back to her; she was speaking to me.

Her words sounded strange and foreign, yet I understood them just fine. She held my hand as we began to walk. The road was hot under my bare feet, causing me to dance along anxiously beside her. It was a narrow road, really more of an alleyway, and crowded with merchants' carts full of unfamiliar-looking things. Rough-looking fabrics could be seen hanging from poles. Some were being inspected by women who argued with their peddlers in animated exchanges. Tables full of clay pots and other utensils were mixed together with baskets of odd-looking fruits and dried herbs. Live animals were everywhere, braying goats and sheep and cages made from sticks full of strange-looking birds. We maneuvered past Donkeys loaded with huge burdens and gigantic-looking camels who blew indignantly at passersby and spit into the dirt. The road widened as we neared an intersection and soon emptied us onto a larger avenue that bustled with faster moving carts and a crush of people.

"So many people!" I heard the woman say, "Even more than normal for a Passover feast! It's because of that miracle worker. That's why they've come; they think he's a prophet; they hang on his every word. Your father the most of all – he follows that man all over the country to who knows where! My goodness, you'd think the man was God Himself the way your father adores him."

Her words made me pause; I stopped and looked at her, then at the scene around me – could it be? She tugged impatiently on my arm, "come on, Simeon, you can't be tired already. Just a moment ago, you were running off like a branded ewe; so full of vigor you are!"

I followed along again, now looking around me in all directions, anxious for clues to this growing mystery. From behind us, there came a sudden racket of clanging chains and horses' hoofs. The crack of a whip cut the air. A rugged-sounding voice yelled for people to clear out of the road – it was a voice of authority, a harsh-sounding voice. We rushed out of the way as he passed, and my jaw dropped at the sight. He was riding in a chariot! I stared at his clothes as he rode away – he wore an army uniform that I recognized – the uniform of a Roman centurion!

The woman who'd called herself Mama tugged me forward again, seemingly unfazed by this amazing sight, as if she'd seen it a hundred times. She spoke to no one in particular as we walked: "If it weren't for your grandpapa, we'd likely starve, imagine him still out fishing at his age! What choice does he have?! With your father and your uncle Andrew both off wandering the countryside! And now dragging us all the way here from Bethsaida…."

She kept talking, but I didn't hear anything else; I just stared at her – trying to digest what she'd just said. Fishing... Bethsaida... grandpapa... Uncle Andrew! The only thing she hasn't said is that she's married to Simon Peter! Her words broke through my distraction again.

"Everything about him has changed, he sleeps in the wilderness, and he even wants to be called Cephas instead of Simon…."

The words struck me like a blast of wind, the kind so strong that it takes your breath away and leaves you gasping. Now I was looking around in all directions, trying desperately to figure out where we were. We were approaching a large gate in a stone wall that was so long it seemed to go all the way around the city. Up ahead, I could hear a considerable commotion – it sounded like thousands of people screaming and cheering. I guessed we might be heading toward a big stadium.

All of a sudden, a flood of people began streaming through the gate toward us. They were waiving coats and looking backward through the gate, then they started laying their coats in the road and bowing down – some of them had tears running down their cheeks that made long stains in the dust that covered their faces.

We were quickly engulfed in the throng, which was gathering from every direction. Some young men had begun to pull branches off the nearby palm trees and wave them in the air. They dropped them on the road and bowed low to kiss them where they lay.

That's when I saw Him! The colt he rode was small but seemed to move with a regal air as confidently as a thoroughbred horse. I knew immediately who He was! I stood in shock as the people in front of me seemed drawn to their hands and knees, and a surge of emotion flooded my eyes with tears. For several moments I saw nothing else except His face as He looked at me – He looked at me! Out of all the throngs, he found me! His eyes were full of immense power – I was drawn into them as they expressed an infinite volume of meaning, which seemed to pour into my soul. I could somehow feel his sadness so deep that it shook the depths of my soul. Yet it was matched with an equal measure of joy and purpose, echoing like the fulfillment of an eternity of planning. Surrounding it all was a love so overpowering that it consumed Him – it washed me away in its wake!

I was sobbing uncontrollably as Mama swept me up into her arms. I buried my face against her shoulder and wrapped my arms tightly around her neck; my small body shook violently. This kind woman could not have understood the eruption of emotions in my soul; indeed, even I couldn't fathom them! She rocked me in her arms until the outburst subsided, no doubt thinking her small child had been merely frightened by the crowds.

I looked up through eyes awash in tears to try and spot him further ahead. Jesus disappeared in the throng that pressed against him and soon closed in behind his procession.

I felt a strong hand on my back, and Mama shifted me in her arms. Looking around, I saw a dark-haired man with a thick beard; he kissed Mama on her forehead and rubbed his thick hand through my hair. His face was filled with jubilation as he spoke, "Don't be afraid young Simeon, this is a great day! Our King has finally come! The Messiah of Israel has finally been revealed, and all the nation has accepted him!" He looked at Mama, "Even you, Salome, I can see it in your eyes; you know that he is truly our Messiah!"

"Oh, Simon! I do! I see it! What will become of us now, she asked, will he be crowned King? Will he break the bands of these Romans?"

"Soon, my dear, I feel it will be very soon! A few days ago, I witnessed the most remarkable sight – he was transformed before our eyes on the mountaintop, revealing His true glory! And we saw Moses and Elijah with him – talking to him! We shook with such terror that we fell to our faces. He is more than just a king – he is the Son of God! His very words are eternal life!"

I shuddered as he spoke. He touched my cheek and placed his hand on my head; "how fortunate you are to be starting your life at such a glorious time for our nation," he said with a mix of joy and certainty. "I must be going; the Master will be seeking me." He kissed Mama again on her head and ran ahead to rejoin the other disciples.

Most of the crowd had moved along following Jesus as well, soon Mama stood nearly alone in the dusty road, still rocking distractedly and staring toward the distant throng. She didn't speak a word, quietly turning toward the gate and continuing on.

As soon as we walked through it, everything changed again. This time the throng that I saw in front of me was angry, holding their fists in the air and shouting hatefully. Others in the crowd seemed broken-hearted and despondent, and many of the women were weeping bitterly. I realized that the kind woman I'd called Mama was gone… and that I was no longer a small child. In fact, I soon understood that I appeared to be invisible to the crowd around me. My first instinct was to search for Chozeq and Ardent, but they were nowhere to be found – I was alone.

A swell of loud shouting from the crowd made me turn to look toward the focus of their angry gazes – back toward the gate. There, emerging from inside the city, was a large group of centurions surrounding a few prisoners. The condemned men were severely beaten, especially one who was so bloody and disfigured that he was unrecognizable. I knew him quickly by the thick ring of thorns that was pressed cruelly into his head and the grotesque cross of timbers that he struggled to carry on his back. His brokenness was a dramatic contrast to the immense power that he'd emanated earlier; he stumbled and collapsing to the ground. Sand and sharp gravel stuck in his open wounds as the heavy timbers crushed him down into the dirt road. I watched as a rugged-looking man was yanked from the crowd and forced to carry the gruesome cross; traces of flesh and blood from its surface were smeared into the man's robes. "Simon of Cyrene," I said under my breath in astonishment.

With enormous difficulty, Jesus lifted himself onto his bloody knees and then climbed unsteadily to his feet. He had a fiercely resolute look on his face as he forced his battered body onward. That's when I began to notice the hideous creatures that were mixed among the throngs surrounding him. Their hate-filled eyes and sharp jagged teeth were all too familiar. Their talons squeezed and shoved the centurions and onlookers that were in their grasps, who reacted by striking out at Jesus, hurling at him handfuls of dirt and hate-filled curses.

Others among the crowds wailed in sorrow and screamed at the sight of him. "Daughters of Jerusalem," I heard him cry out to them, "don't weep for me but weep for yourselves and for your children. ... For if they do these things in the green tree, what shall be done in the dry?[Luke 23:28]"

Clouds as dark as smoke gathered overhead as the small band of condemned men was led in a grueling climb up the hill. The heavy crosses were dragged into place and dropped onto the ground... then two of the condemned men fought against the soldiers, who stretched them across the cruel timbers, while the third man... Jesus... laid his body down voluntarily. I saw the long metal spikes being driven through his hands and feet – the gathering clouds grew thicker overhead with each blow of the soldiers' heavy hammers.

"FATHER... FORGIVE THEM..." he screamed as the nails tore through him, "THEY DON'T REALIZE WHAT THEY'RE DOING...." I could see His words radiate invisible waves that moved out in all directions and struck me with the force of a hurricane, shaking me to the core of my being.

As they lifted his cross and dropped it roughly into place, the air began to fill with the screeches and profane roars of a vast gathering of Hellish beasts. They joined the human throng in mocking him, growing thicker in number with each passing moment. I heard the crowd around me mock him and scream in angry defiance – "He saved others, but can't save himself! ...If you're the son of God, come down from the cross!"

A voice could be heard above the others. It boomed like an echo from another place: "YOU KILLED HER! YOU DIDN'T EVEN CARE ENOUGH TO SAVE HER!" My heart stopped as I recognized my own voice!

I looked down and saw that my clothes were thick with putrid filth; the crushing guilt was overwhelming. Then my eyes began to notice other souls that were also gathering... human and immortal. They wore tattered clothes as filthy as mine that bore features of every country, social class, and age of time from all history. Many wept bitterly while others prostrated themselves or screamed out with cries begging for forgiveness. The cacophony of their cries was deafening, together with the mocking shouts of the crowd and the beasts' screams and profane roars; I tried to stop my ears with my hands, but the sound could not be dimmed.

As I watched the horrifying sight, the throngs grew larger and larger. Still, nowhere could be seen any of Ardent's angelic hosts. The darkness became thick, and the concentration of evil was so heavy that it nearly crushed us – but it was far heavier at the central point of its focus – at the cross. Jesus steeled himself against it as he bore the unfathomable weight; his entire being was wrenched in an expression of pure and utter agony.

In the swirling chaos, a black rain of horrible stench raced toward him from all directions. Jesus shuddered as it struck him and gasped in excruciating pain as it pierced his soul. To my horror, I realized that its source was from my own filthy clothes – and from the ragged stains of all the countless others gathered there. I began to weep in remorse and fell to my knees.

The horrifying scene bore on and on for hours—each moment seeming to Him like an eternity of horrible anguish. As the darkness reached its blackest pitch, the sickening black rain finally ended – he had taken it all. Jesus suddenly cried out in an agonizing cry that was shocking in its intensity: "Eloi, Eloi, lama sabachthani![1]."

His life had been poured out. His body was completely spent. Jesus looked upward and spoke in an anguished voice: "Father, into your hands I commit my spirit."

Then I saw him close his eyes, and His whole body tensed as if he was mustering His last ounce of strength. Then He screamed out with an emphatic cry that sounded like a warrior dealing a death blow to defeat his ferocious foe with his last enormous gasp of pent-up strength:

"IT… IS… FINISHED !"

AT THE EXACT moment that He shouted, the ground shook violently, and I saw a blinding flash erupt, sending a brilliant shock wave outward from the cross in all directions. It washed over the throng of souls in a cleansing wave, transforming our filthy rags into robes of shining white. I wept in joyful relief at the overwhelming feeling of forgiveness! My angry defiance was gone; in its place, there was a deep sense of utter joy in my spirit that made me spontaneously shout in praise! Watching through tears, I saw the scene all around being breathtakingly transformed as the wave of light spread outward as far as the eye could see. It suddenly illuminated the darkness with millions of shining garments, all brighter than the sun! The hellish hosts began to panic and scrambled in all directions, shielding their eyes from the brilliant onslaught.

I looked at the cross and saw Jesus' broken body begin to glow with a light more brilliant than any of those that surrounded him. Then I gasped as I saw the spectacular glory of his true form emerge from its impossibly small human containment.

I bowed my head to the ground in awe-inspired reverence but could sense that His gaze spanned the entire sea of immortal faces. He was conveying a personal message of forgiveness and drawing our eyes to look on Him freely. It thrilled my soul so completely that I struggled to catch my breath. He then fixed his attention downward beneath the earth and instantly vanished from sight.

⌘

20

ETERNITY

Here lies the purpose of our struggle!

I n the next instant, I found myself standing before a massive set of doors that had been flung open. Above them were carved ancient words that read DEATH and SHEOL. The enormous doors were broken from their hinges. From inside, there arose a gigantic cheer of victory that shook the cavernous depths.

Then I recognized Jesus emerging in joyous celebration with throngs of ancient saints all wearing white robes. They were singing and clapping, and He was dancing as joyfully as King David bringing home the holy Ark. His face was filled with pure joy as he stood outside the fallen gates and looked back at his rescued prisoners, and then he waved his hand upward in a guiding gesture. When I turned to see what he waved toward, my eye caught sight of Chozeq and Ardent standing at the vanguard of an angelic legion too large to number. Their familiar faces were bowed as they accepted an order from Michael, their commander, who in turn was bowed low in a welcoming greeting to Jesus.

Jesus smiled broadly in return and then repeated his guiding gesture. One after another, the white-robed saints were announced by name and then were met by their angelic guides and escorted away, disappearing in flashes of light. I saw Jesus embrace many of them like dear friends when they approached… hearing their names called out: Abraham, Jacob, Moses, Joshua, David, Shadrach, Meshach, and Abed-nego, who lingered with their Lord sharing fond remembrance of their ancient times together.

Finally, after what must have been days of elapsed time, the last man could be seen approaching. He was hesitant and seemed fearful and ashamed to come near, but Jesus went to him and threw his arms around the man, then walked with him together toward the gates. I overheard Jesus say how good it was to walk together once again – he called the man his old friend, a comment that filled the man's eyes with tears of joy. They declared the man's name: "Adam, "as Jesus hugged him again, and he was escorted away.

When the procession of souls finally ended, he looked directly at me and held out His hand with a smile. His look burned through me with such a thrill that I shuddered and collapsed to my knees in over-whelming emotion. When I looked up again, he glanced behind him and then back to me with a nod of His head toward the sight behind. His expression suddenly showed deep agonizing sorrow; then, he was gone.

CHOZEQ WAS IMMEDIATELY STANDING CLOSE beside me. The questions that I hadn't been able to ask while watching the epic scene flooded my mind. I looked up at my angelic guide, slightly confused; "All those people who Jesus embraced… I knew some of their names – they lived long ago… I read about their lives in ancient times. But they looked like they knew Jesus – like they'd met Him before."

Chozeq smiled as he considered the meaning of my question. "Our Lord did not first appear in your earthly history as a babe in Bethle-hem," he explained. "When the world was set upon its axis, he was there. There were many times before his incarnation when he descended to this earth in the similitude of a man. In Eden's garden, on the plains of Mamre,[1] by the brook of Jabbok[2] beneath the walls of Jericho,[3] and in the fiery furnace of Babylon,[4] the Son of Man has always visited his friends. Because his soul delighted in them.[5]"

Despite the profound comfort in his words, Chozeq's countenance seemed changed as he considered the next thing he was to show me. He looked immensely saddened. "Arise, lad, there is somewhat more to show thee here still," he said, waiting for me to climb to my feet. I followed his long strides as he led me to the edge of a terrifying precipice and pointed across it. There on the other side of the vast chasm, I saw an enormous gate behind which, teeming millions of desperate souls writhed in horrible agony, seeking escape. Terrible bursts of flames could be seen rising high behind them as they were seized and tossed back into the horrific inferno. I knew what I was looking at immediately and fell again to my knees as the horror of it robbed me of strength.

"Look well... here lies the purpose of our struggle!" Chozeq cried urgently. The seriousness and power of his booming voice were as terrifying to me as the sight itself. His flaming sword pointed toward the horrendous gates as the smell of sulfur nearly overcame me. "Gaze ye upon the terror of the universe... a tragedy more severe than any in all the realms of creation or the heavens. Mark it well and lose not the image of it from thy earthly mind!"

As he said that, the searing image of Hell's agony burned into my consciousness like a vivid nightmare, never more than a hairbreadth away from reemerging to full view. I was shaking as we finally turned to leave, and I followed Chozeq closely as the burning image made my knees weak. The terror of the sight had robbed me of strength... and words.

We made it back to the place where Jesus had been. Although the place itself was stark and barren, the memory of His presence here filled it with comfort. The memories it offered were a stark contrast to the terror I'd just witnessed.

I looked at Chozeq feebly, struggling with the overwhelming reality of my own failures and unworthiness; they were too many to count! I thought of the way I'd so recently defied and challenged the Lord with my angry doubts. "I deserve that place... I deserve it too!" I said, dropping to my knees.

Chozeq knelt on one knee beside me, and I felt his massive hand on my shoulder. He spoke with tenderness in his thunderous voice: "Didst thou not see that thy name is graven on His hand,[6]" he said softly. The memory of Jesus holding out his hand toward me moments earlier flooded to mind, and I was suddenly able to see what Chozeq was talking about. It brought an incredible thrill to my soul as my eyes clouded again with tears.

"Forget thy doubts and give ear only to the promise of his still small voice saying 'Fear not, I am with thee.' Look upon him who is the great Surety of the covenant, faithful and true. Know that He is bound and engaged to present you, the weakest of the family, with all the chosen before the throne of God.[7]"

Suddenly a loud trumpet sound echoed through the cavernous place, shaking it to its foundations – it was unmistakably the heralding of a tremendous victory.

"What is that?!" I asked in surprise.

"AHH! He has risen! He is risen from the dead!" Chozeq declared, raising his hands in spontaneous praise as he jumped to his feet. Then in a sudden flash, we were gone from there.

———————

WE WERE IMMEDIATELY IN A WIDE, open place. Warm sunlight bathed my shoulders, and a comfortable breeze blew gently across my face, bearing the scents of fruit blossoms and clean, pure air. We looked over a panorama of indescribable beauty with crystal clear rivers and expanses of lush forest. The sights were so spectacular it was like seeing things illuminated for the first time after never even knowing that I'd been living in darkness my whole life. Every earthly color I'd ever seen was merely like black and white in comparison! I noticed that the street beneath my feet was smooth and shined like a golden plate.

"Jimmy?!" The voice that called from behind me sent an impossible thrill through my soul. I spun anxiously around and met the most beautiful being I'd ever seen; she took my breath away. "Jimmy? Is that really you?"

The excitement continued to steal my breath as I looked at her face... "K-Kelly?" She was dressed in brilliant white, with long flowing hair, and wore a crown with hundreds of star-like gems that sent beams of light wherever she turned.

"Jimmy, you're still..." she began to say as she looked at my human form "...How are you here?" There was such joy in her voice that the sound of it triggered laughter inside me. She was standing outside one of the gates of a fabulous city that shined like the sun. She was so beautiful... everything was so beautiful! I was powerless to speak.

She stepped closer and hugged me; her touch felt like my soul was being bathed in pure water. "Your time here now may be short, but we'll see each other again," she said, "your mother was right about that – we'll all be together again."

My heart jumped when she said that, and I followed her gaze as she turned and looked to someone behind her. I recognized him instantly.... "DAD!" I cried out.

My sight of him came just in time to see him run to me and throw his arms around me; "I love you, son!" he said as he wrapped his arms lovingly around my neck. I held onto him for as long as I could. His embrace was like a refreshing drink to a man who had been dying of thirst.

When dad and I finally ended our hug, I felt Kelly's hand on my back; "it was your father's passing that saved me..." Kelly said softly.

I looked at her in shock; "W-what did you say?" I stammered. Dad nodded to her approvingly with a humble expression on his face.

"You need to know," she explained, "I'm sorry I never told you. I was so afraid it would have changed the way you felt about me. The night that your accident happened, I was at a concert with people I thought were friends. I got myself in trouble, pretty bad trouble; your dad was coming to get me - that's why he was driving so fast. Jimmy, I hid it from you then, but it was a time when I had completely turned my back on Jesus."

I remembered – we had drifted apart that year. She had a boyfriend at school and was starting to fight with her parents constantly. Looking back, I couldn't believe that I'd never seen it before.

"I could have died that night from the overdose... I shudder to think where I'd be right now..." she continued.

The searing image of those desperate souls clawing at Hell's gates flashed through my mind – the thought of that being Kelly's fate chilled my soul.

"The Ambulance reached me in time ...but it was your father's death that woke me before it was too late. It changed... everything, it led to the healing of my family... and it brought the two of us so much closer... it saved me."

I know there aren't supposed to be tears in Heaven, but my eyes quickly clouded. It explained so clearly why she had wanted her own death to be used to save others, just as his had saved her. I looked at Dad, who just nodded gratefully.

I finally gained enough composure to ask Kelly the question that burned on my soul. "What did you mean... you said I had a special mission... and that I need to keep going – that there are so many at stake?"

She looked at Chozeq as if sharing unspoken words, then back at me with a maturity that seemed vastly beyond her age when I knew her. Yet, she spoke with the same love and tenderness as always: "I think you already know the answer to your question," she said with an understanding smile.

Dad put his hands on my shoulders; "I'm so proud of you, son. Someday you'll be able to understand just how proud I am." He patted the sides of my shoulders, "But now you have important work to do." He hugged me again, giving me a hearty pat on my back, then smiled; "Tell your mom I love her... and give her a message for me, tell her that Daisy made it, tell her she's beautiful and can't wait to see her mom again."

I looked at him in shock... "Wait! W-what? D-do I have a sister?"

He just nodded and looked to his side as she came closer and took dad's hand; "Hi," she said as she smiled at me -- she looked a lot like mom... and dad.

THE SCENE QUICKLY FADED, and I found myself once again amid a swirling whirlwind of chaotic images. I knew the place... instead of panic, this time I closed my eyes and held out my hand, waiting for Chozeq's firm grasp. His grip was as sure as ever, and it immediately stilled my tumbling.

"This is **Without Time**," I said, glancing around. "That's what you called it; I remember being here." Chozeq nodded silently. A flurry of questions ran through my mind, but I realized that somehow I already knew the answers to most of them. One did confuse me still; I looked at Chozeq curiously and asked what most worried me.

"In all these journeys, you have always been with me... until now. Why couldn't I find you this time?"

He looked at me as though I'd asked the wisest question he'd ever heard – though I didn't suspect for a moment that that could be true. His words burned through me as he answered:

"The pillar of fire and cloud that guided Israel was not an angel, but the presence of the Lord Himself. God has likewise not left thee in thy pilgrimage to the guidance of a mere angel. At thy hour of greatest need, it was He Himself who shepherded thy path."

Still holding my right hand in his, he placed his left hand on my shoulder and looked me in the eye emphatically. "Remember lad, though ye may not see Him in a fiery pillar, He is indeed always with thee. Infinite and unmeasurable is the faithfulness of His promise that He will never forsake thee."

WITH A HUGE GASP OF BREATH, I was suddenly aware of my surroundings, lying face down on the chapel floor.

"Jimmy! Jimmy! Are you alright?" I heard mom asking urgently as she shook me. "I was just about to go get a nurse... are you alright?"

Turning with a start, I saw her kneeling on the floor beside me; I nodded my head, yes, still struggling to get reoriented. She studied my face carefully with a worried look in her eyes and then started to ask again how I was feeling. I interrupted her as I blurted out the message that was burning inside me – "I saw Kelly! ...and Dad!" I exclaimed, surprising and probably frightening her as I turned toward her on my knees. "She was beautiful, mom – so beautiful! Her crown was filled with spectacular beams of light, and her whole being was like pure joy!"

Mom looked at me confused, and then her expression turned to sadness. She was probably thinking how sweet it was that I had dreamed about Heaven. Yet her look said that she was worried I would soon come crashing down when I returned to the cold reality of what had just happened.

"That sounds so nice," she said honestly; I could sense the pain of her own deep sadness. She rose from the floor and sat down on the front pew.

I straightened up and looked at her thoughtfully, pausing for a minute to figure out how to say what I was thinking.

"I know why dad died; I understand it now," I said. Mom's face twisted in a curious expression that revealed that a sudden realization was sweeping over her. "I saw him, mom... I spoke to dad." Her eyes began to tear up as she listened, not daring to let herself believe what I was saying. "He ran to me and hugged me – it felt so good! I didn't know what to say... I was so overwhelmed!"

Then I told mom the story that Kelly had shared – the reason that God let dad die had all become so clear to me! The look in Mom's eyes showed that she was having a harder and harder time dismissing what I was saying as just a dream - she was fighting back the tears as she listened.

I paused and quieted my voice; "Dad said he was proud of me...

and that someday I'd understand how proud he is," a tear ran down mom's cheek, and she brushed it off with her hand, still staring at my face. I looked at her and leaned forward – "He asked me to give you a message, mom; he said he loves you, and he wanted me to tell you that Daisy made it and that she can't wait to see you again."

Mom suddenly raised her hands to her mouth in shock, and her face filled with a look of overwhelming emotion and astonishment – she couldn't speak. She looked at me shaking her head and trying to form the word HOW?

"You never said I had a sister…." I said softly, "she's beautiful — she looks just like you."

Mom leaned forward sharply and lost her balance, slipping from the pew onto her knees as she staggered like she'd been hit with a knockout punch. She finally sat on the floor with her legs at one side and leaning on her hands. Her eyes were squeezed closed, and I realized she was crying so hard that all the air was gone from her lungs. She suddenly gasped and drew in a long gulp of air, making that inhaling crying sound that people make when they've completely lost control, and then she let out a long wail and wept. I crawled over to her, and she wrapped her arms around my neck and squeezed me hard. In all the times I'd known mom to cry, I'd never before seen her cry this hard. When she finally regained control, we sat on the floor together while she kept gasping in short wrenching breaths and wiping the flowing tears from her eyes. Eventually, her crying stopped, and we just sat side-by-side for a long time without speaking.

Mom finally spoke after the long silence; her eyes were fixed straight ahead with a distant look.

"Daisy was born prematurely…." She looked over at me uncomfortably, then added, "…before your father and I were married. She lived for a month before we lost her," mom said quietly as she brushed the tears from her cheeks. "We never talked about her because… well… it hurt too much, I guess." She looked over at me, slightly embarrassed, and confessed, "There was something else that Chozeq and I talked about that day… I asked him if Daisy was in Heaven… did she make it? I said – I used those words." Mom wrung her hands together as she recounted Chozeq's answer. "He said that eternity would tell… and then he added that the answer to my question would one day become be clear to you." She looked at me with an astonished expression "… that's what he said. I never knew what it meant… how would you know something that could only be known in eternity?"

There was a great deal more to that answer than mom could have dreamed; I just sat silently and nodded my head.

AFTER SITTING QUIETLY for a while longer, I looked around at the small chapel, remembering what I'd been thinking when I first came in here blaming God for Kelly's death. "Remember what I said before about why I thought God put this chapel here?"

"Um-hmm," mom acknowledged.

"You were right," I admitted, "about the way we… the way people… tend to turn to Him mostly when there's a tragedy. But I was wrong when I thought that God knew that and waits for us …I was so wrong about that. He doesn't wait for us at all…

"…HE NEVER STOPS CHASING US."

⌘

21

LEGACY

Believers, look up - take courage. The angels are nearer than you think.
~ Billy Graham

Our family's church was packed for Kelly's Memorial service. Practically everyone from our church was there, along with half the school, most of the town, and a crowd from Anna's church. It really brought into focus how profound the impact was that Kelly had had on our community.

I looked around the auditorium as I sat waiting for my turn to say something, seeing so many faces that I'd known all my life and many more that I'm not sure I'd ever met. Most of the girls were sniffling into tissues, and many of the guys had stunned looks on their faces. None of us ever expected to be facing the fact that a friend our own age had already met the end of her own mortality.

Anna and her mom were near the front. Mom was sitting with Mr. and Mrs. O' and little Ryan. I was surprised to see Sean Daniels, the kid who had been Kelly's boyfriend a few years ago. He was sitting with his latest girlfriend, who had a bored expression on her face. The look on his face was anything but bored, however. He was almost ashen looking.

The Pastor made his remarks and introduced each of the people making comments. Mr. Wilson, Kelly's favorite Sunday School teacher, spoke first. Then other friends told about how they knew Kelly and shared simple but amazing stories about her.

Mom spoke just before me. There wasn't a dry eye in the building when she finished telling how Kelly had become such an encouragement to her after Dad died.

Then it was my turn.

Everyone knew how close Kelly and I had been, and there was complete silence as I stepped up to the mic. I got the feeling that everyone was holding their breath, hoping I'd be able to make it through without losing it. I looked down at the notes I'd scribbled and tried to clear my throat as quietly as I could before starting.

"I actually don't know when I met Kelly," I began, "I just don't remember a time when she wasn't in my life. Many of you probably remember that when we were kids, people assumed we were brother and sister because we were always together. We attended church here every week for sixteen years and, until two months ago when she moved, I hadn't been in this building without her more than two or three times in my whole life."

I took a deep breath and paused for a minute to calm my racing heart. "No matter how well I knew Kelly, though, she always surprised me. That was especially true over the past few months – she surprised me with some genuinely incredible lessons in those months. They were the most profound lessons of all.

"Of all of those, the most amazing was her sincere desire to see something important come from her illness... Something eternal. While we all prayed for her healing, she never once asked God for her own healing; she wanted something even bigger." I looked over at Kelly's dad, who was nodding in agreement through his tear-filled eyes. "The thing that she desperately wanted most of all was to see others find peace with God. If her illness could be used to help make that happen, then she accepted her own fate gratefully.

"In fact, we saw her moved to tears when she heard about the friends who had decided to follow Christ. I remember what she said to me just before… she….." (I had to stop and choke back a few tears, skipping the word I couldn't say as I rephrased it.) "One of the last things she said was that she wouldn't trade one of our friends who've been saved for a hundred years of life."

I choked back the swelling emotion in my chest again and cleared my throat, then pressed on: "The most earnest prayer of Kelly's life was answered."

I looked down at the church, filled to capacity, and suddenly went off my script with a surge of deep emotion stirring inside me. "He answered her prayer in the same way that He always delivers – He did it big! How many are here today as believers because of her prayer!"

I meant it as a rhetorical question but noticed hands being spontaneously raised all over the church. Pete Murphy stood to his feet, followed immediately by Chrissy Mathews and then other kids from school. Soon, nearly 100 kids were standing. Many of them were crying; some had their hands raised in thanks as they stood with their eyes tightly closed.

I was blown away and finally lost it as the tears began flowing. All I could think of was how overjoyed Kelly would be to see the incredible sight in front of me; I hoped that she was seeing it, in fact! The sense of God's Spirit was so powerful in the room that you could almost see the cloud of Shekinah glory descending. Kelly's mom leaned her head on Mr. O's shoulder as they both hugged and cried together.

I HAD REGAINED my composure by the time the spontaneous outpouring subsided, and everyone was seated again. The room was silent with anticipation, and a sudden unction seemed to fill my Spirit as I looked over the audience.

"There's a Psalm that says: Precious in the sight of the Lord is the death of His saints.[1] I struggled recently to understand how anyone's death could be precious – God had to show me that there are things bigger than this life… eternal things." I caught mom's eye, and she nodded slightly in a way that conveyed our shared secret.

"I've learned lately that God's plans are much different than ours – His are much bigger… and they lead to the most spectacular outcomes, even when we doubt what He's doing. I know now that His outcomes are spectacular beyond anything that we could imagine.

"A good friend of mine told me recently that God does not leave us in our life to the guidance or protection of mere angels: Jesus Himself leads the advance guard… He's the one who is the closest to us in our times of most desperate need.

"I believe that Jesus is here in our midst at this moment… He has come with a challenge -- He calls on us to answer His challenge!

"He is challenging us to embrace what He is doing in our lives through these events… to embrace the words: 'Thy will be done!'"

The memory of Heaven's glory and seeing Kelly's face of ecstatic joy suddenly filled my mind; the joy that was bubbling up inside me began to flow out uncontrollably.

"ANSWER THIS!" I practically yelled, "…what reason can there be for us to be mourning today instead of rejoicing? Why should we give in to gloomy views of the future? Who told us that this night would never end in day? Who said that the winter of our pain would last from snow and ice to deeper snow or never-ending storms of despair? He hasn't told us these things; in fact, he calls us to remember that day follows night, that spring and summer come after winter!

"We should Hope then! We should always hope! God doesn't fail us. Could we honestly believe that God doesn't love us in the midst of all this? Mountains, even when they are hidden in darkness, are as real as in the daylight. God's love is as true now as it has been in our brightest times. We will yet climb Jacob's ladder with angels, and behold the one who sits enthroned above it - our covenant God – our advocate with the Father – our dearest friend!

"Believe me when I say that the indescribable splendors of eternity will make us forget the trials of time, or only remember them enough to bless God for leading us through them and for using them for our lasting good.

"It's because of this that we can sing amid our deepest trouble and rejoice even while passing through the furnace. We see the day coming when He will again make our wilderness blossom like the rose! He will cause the desert to ring with our exulting joys because this earthly pain will soon be over, and then 'together forever with the Lord,' our joy will never end!²"

The church practically exploded in instantaneous response to the message that the Spirit impressed on all of us. People began to shout in praises while many bowed low and others stood to their feet. Some wept while others prayed through tears of joy.

THE FERVOR that had come over me continued to swell inside. I leaned close to the mic to be heard above the noise. "There are some here who haven't heard God calling before, but you're hearing Him right now!" The room quieted as people began to pray silently, among the sounds of many crying. "He has destined this hour – this is the moment in all eternity that He has determined to meet you. He has thrown open Heaven for you – come and meet Him here now!"

Sean Daniels bolted from his seat and staggered to the altar in a mad rush, falling to his knees as tears streamed down his face. Pastor Wilkes quickly knelt beside him and began leading him to the Lord. Then a surge of others from school began filing forward. The Pastor waved to some others to come and help pray with them as he stayed with Sean. Pastor Juan was soon helping as well, along with others from both churches who met the swelling crowd of desperate souls. They were weeping in a miraculous flood of Godly sorrow – we could literally see the Spirit working repentance everywhere we looked. Kids from FCS soon gathered around those who'd come forward, and everyone was crying and praying for their friends.

I saw Mr. O' make his way to Sean and kneel beside him, and they hugged, with tears on both their faces. Mom and Mrs. O' were hugging and crying uncontrollably.

As I stood in the pulpit with my head bowed, I suddenly heard

Kelly's voice -- so clearly that my eyes opened in surprise. "Your special mission is SO important, Jimmy!"

Immediately I became aware that a whole host of angels were in the room with us - I could see them! They were ministering to the kids who had come forward and delivering comfort to weeping souls all over the sanctuary. A pair of beautiful cherubim stood with their hands-on mom and Mrs. O' as both women cried tears of joy.

Then I felt a familiar touch on my shoulder as Chozeq's huge hand covered it. We shared a glance; the look of pure joy reflected in his face made my heart leap inside me. He didn't say a word but nodded in thankful approval at the incredible scene.

⌘

22

THE VOICE

I was in prison and you came to me

P astor Juan surprised me with a hug as the crowd was filing out of the auditorium. His eyes were still wet from crying, and his face beamed like a lighthouse.

"Thanks for sharing what God put on your heart; you know He really used you today, right?" He looked into my eyes closely to see if I understood what had just taken place.

I nodded and smiled as I answered, "I'm just the vessel, man!" I said honestly.

"You've got it, brother!" He said with a smile as he put his arm around me with a supportive squeeze. "I've been trying to get to some of these kids for over a year. This is the hand of God; it's totally awesome!

"...I know this has been a rough time for you," he added with a shift in his voice that conveyed his sincerity. "I'm around if you ever want to talk, okay?"

I nodded gratefully, and we shook hands. He paused as he began to walk away and then turned back with an earnest look.

"Hey Jim, I think I could use your help with something if you're willing?"

"Sure... I think so; what is it?" I answered. He looked at me for a minute like he was trying to decide whether to ask and then slowly continued.

"It's okay if you say no; I know it's kind of a lot to ask... It's just ... the way he reacted to you before, I think maybe...." He scratched his chin as he collected his thoughts, giving me the impression that this was apparently a spontaneous idea. "It's Chase – the guy from the diner – you know, Angela's ex-boyfriend?"

"Yeah, I definitely remember...," I said tentatively. I had the feeling that whatever he was about to ask was not going to be an easy sell to mom.

"I've been visiting the prison, trying to get through to him. Something is blocking it with him, something really dark... I think you know what I mean."

I gulped as I thought about that encounter at the diner – I knew exactly what he meant. "Yeah... I think I do," I said quietly, trying not to show how little enthusiasm I had for the idea. Despite all I'd just witnessed, the thought of confronting that demon again sounded a little too Indiana Jones for me at the moment.

"Well... Just pray about it. Let me know how you feel next Wednesday at FCS." I nodded, feeling like I'd just been drafted for a mission behind enemy lines.

I didn't mention his request to anyone else, but it weighed on my mind the rest of the morning. Prison was one of those places I knew existed but hoped to never visit. More than that, I had zero desire to meet Chase again; I distractedly rubbed my shoulder as I thought about the pain that had jolted me that day in the diner. I could almost feel it.

Without warning, a vivid memory suddenly flashed through my mind — it was of the view across that terrifying chasm. It came over me like an electric shock as I remembered looking down the length of

Chozeq's flaming sword toward those horrendous gates. The clear memory of those terrifying flames and terrified souls made me shudder.

Anna and some friends from FCS walked up to me as I was standing there deep in thought. "You okay?" Anna said softly. Her question jolted me back to the present.

I took a deep breath as I saw her, and my heart calmed; I didn't need to fake a smile. It came naturally as I looked at her and the others.

"Yeah, I'm fine, thanks... thanks to all of you. Everything you did... that video, the blog, all your prayers... it's just really, really appreciated."

WHILE I WAS STILL TALKING, Pete Murphy came walking up with his eyes red from crying and threw his arms around me; "Man... I'm so sorry about Kelly," he said sincerely.

To say that Pete could be an intimidating guy was a gigantic understatement. He looked like an NFL linebacker with arms the size of chimneys and tattoos all over. In pure body mass, he was twice my size. I did my best to hug him back.

"Brother, that word you gave hit me so hard... I cried for like an hour!" he confessed amazingly.

Seeing him made the reality of what God was doing suddenly hit home.

"I am SO happy to see you here, Pete!"

"Yeah, you and me both!" He responded, "It's so amazing what's going on. I never thought I could feel like this... And in church no less!"

Anna and the others laughed and agreed – it kind of occurred to me that the depth of this feeling was new to me too.

Pete leaned his head forward and lowered his voice, "Hey uh... can we talk? There's somethin' I gotta ask ya... in private-like."

I looked at the others, "Excuse us for just a second," I said while Pete and I walked over to an empty spot by the windows.

He looked nervous about what he was going to say next and continued.

"This is gonna sound crazy... it's like, got me thinkin' I'm nuts or somethin', but here goes... when I was prayin' in there, I heard somethin'... a voice. It was as clear as day, but when I looked around, nobody was there. It said: 'I was in prison and you came to me.' I'm telling ya, it made my hair stand up... I figured I just imagined it, ya know? It was noisy with everyone upfront praying and stuff. Then I heard it again a second time... The same words, 'I was in prison, and you came to me.' It was so clear I knew I hadn't imagined it that time – I was startin' to freak out. Everybody from my pew was upfront, so I got down on my knees and just listened – then I heard it again, 'I was in prison, and you came to me.' Three times, just like that! Then I was just holdin' my breath – I was afraid to even breathe!"

Then Pete looked at me with an astonished expression; "That's when the voice said, 'Go to Chase with Jimmy....'"

Pete looked bewildered.

"What d'ya think it means? ...chase what? What's it got t'do with prison?"

This time it was my hair that was standing on end. "Come on," I said, "We have to find Pastor Juan!"

WHEN WE WALKED DOWNSTAIRS to the fellowship hall, people were mingling around tables for the buffet lunch that the church had provided. Mom was standing near the doorway with Mr. and Mrs. O' as they greeted people; they grabbed me and asked me to join them. I tried not to look reluctant as I agreed, turning to Pete and pointing out Pastor Juan on the other side of the room.

"Tell him what you told me," I whispered to him, "... don't tell anyone else."

"What was that about?" Mom asked.

"Just helping Pete – he was looking for Pastor Juan," I said carefully. Thankfully, there wasn't time for her to grill me further; there was a line of people anxious to greet us. I watched Pete approach Pastor Juan and then saw the two of them head upstairs.

The next thing I knew, Anna was standing in front of me with a 'remember me?' expression on her face.

"You're a busy guy today," she said sympathetically.

"I'm SO sorry!" I apologized, "I meant to come right back...."

"It's okay..." she interrupted with a smile, I totally understand."

Since we were in a greeting line, I leaned toward her to hug her, and she kissed my cheek as she hugged my neck, catching me by surprise. It was the first time we'd been closer than a handshake, and it made my heart jump. I found myself lost in her eyes momentarily when she backed away – she seemed to have that effect on me when I least expected it.

I caught sight of Mandy standing nearby with a Cheshire Cat grin and felt suddenly embarrassed, straightening up again. "See ya later," I said quietly to Anna, who nodded, looking slightly embarrassed herself. Mom took Anna's hand in both of hers and warmly thanked her for everything the FCS group had done. She introduced her to the O'Malleys, who shared their genuine appreciation.

Mrs. Mirabella, Anna's mom, came by soon afterward with some friends from their church, and mom invited her to join us at our table.

AFTER THE BUFFET lines had finished and everyone was seated and eating; mom reminded me that I'd promised to introduce the rafting video. Talk about having nothing to say and too much time to say it... my mind raced as I walked to the front of the room, trying to come up with a good intro. I stood behind the lone mic stand and collected my thoughts.

"A few months ago, my life was going along pretty much the way it always had, and a very special friend was in the middle of everything I did. I assumed then that things would always continue just like that. God had different plans about that. In fact, as I think back on the events of the past few months, God has had his hand in almost everything. I remember so clearly the prayer that Kelly prayed on the day she left for California. As hard as it was for her to move to a new place, her prayer was for other friends to support me. Since meeting the kids at FCS, Kelly's prayer has been answered in ways I never could have imagined. Kelly seemed to have a particular inside track with her prayers, as a matter of fact. Most of the people in this room are a living testimony to that.

"This video was filmed on a rafting trip just last week that was held in Kelly's honor. She watched this over and over again with a range of emotions, from laughter to tears of joy. I think that image of her said the most about the kind of heart she had – I hope watching this with that in mind conveys a little of who she was and how she should be remembered."

I caught a glimpse of Kelly's mom when I walked to my seat as she wiped the flowing tears from her cheeks. Mr. O' stood and grabbed my hand as I walked past, giving me a hug. The lights dimmed as the projection screen showed the opening scene. I whispered to mom that I needed to use the bathroom and then snuck out.

I WASN'T LYING about visiting the bathroom, but as soon as I came out of it, I went looking for Pete and Pastor Juan. I found them in the sanctuary, sitting right where Pete said he heard the mysterious voice. Pastor Juan was showing Pete the verses in Matthew 25 where Jesus said the exact words that Pete had heard spoken.

"Jesus was making the point that anytime we do things for someone in need, it's just like doing it for him," he explained. "There's something else," he said, "a lot of times when God wants to show that something is significant, he repeats it." Pastor Juan turned to Acts chapter 10 and read the account where Peter was shown his vision of unclean foods and told to eat.

"Hey, same name!" Pete joked, pointing his thumbs at himself.

Pastor Juan laughed and then explained the key point: "God repeated the vision 3 times to convince Peter that it was important. I think that's why the voice you heard was repeated three times."

"Yeah, but what's it mean?" Pete asked, "Go to chase something with Jimmy…? That makes no sense."

Pastor Juan looked over at me to see if I'd made up my mind yet about his request. I nodded yes. At this point, I didn't feel like there was any real choice. Then he looked at Pete; "right before you told Jim what you'd heard, I had just finished asking him to visit the prison with me… To see a man there named Chase. I think it's pretty obvious that God wants you to come along on that visit too."

Pete's eyes grew large. "You mean, like, God is sending us on a mission!?"

"I guess you could say that, yeah," Pastor Juan agreed. "You should know that Chase is a dangerous guy… more than just physically." He looked over at me again to make sure I was really okay with the idea.

"Who am I to disobey an audible voice from God?" I said, stating what seemed to be the obvious takeaway from all this.

"I'll make arrangements for the visit," Pastor Juan said, "let's plan for next Saturday morning."

⌘

23

THE HEAVENS

...as high as the heavens are above the earth, so great is His lovingkindness
~ Psalm 103:11

M r. & Mrs. O' stayed at our house for the night; they were going to be flying back to California in the morning. The two of them looked so brokenhearted – I wished that I could tell them about seeing Heaven and meeting Kelly. I know that one glimpse of the joy in her face would scatter all their sorrow, the way it had scattered mine. The image of that beautiful hillside in my Heavenly vision filled my mind, making my spirit surge with amazement. An idea suddenly hit me.

We were all sitting in the kitchen as Mom and Mrs. O' worked together making dinner. It was a beautiful June evening, right at the beginning of summer. "Hey, I have an idea!" I said, "let's take dinner to Lookout Point and have a picnic by the lake." They all looked at me in surprise – that had apparently been the last thing they would have thought of doing, especially this late in the day. "I'd really like to... can we?" I pleaded. I looked down for a second at my folded hands on the table... "There's a place there where Kelly and I used to go to watch the sunset... I'd really like to show it to you."

Suddenly the mood in the room changed – there was a silent pause, and then all of them nodded and agreed. Mom pulled the picnic baskets from the pantry, and Mrs. O' began to load them while Mom went for an old blanket. Mr. O' and I dug a few folding lawn chairs out of the basement and helped load everything into the car.

It was a short ride over to The Point, as we called it. There were one or two other cars in the gravel parking lot, but it wasn't crowded at all. We grabbed the baskets and gear and started out; all of them headed for the main trail... "Not that way," I explained, "over here." I led them in the opposite direction up the hill. The grass-covered path curved around until we could no longer see the parking lot and then opened up into a broad grassy field. I took them to an old apple tree near the top. The view from there overlooked the lake about a quarter-mile below. It offered a panorama of the forested vistas to the west. Everything was in bloom, and the gentle breeze felt amazingly refreshing. It was about as close a sight to Heaven as I could think of.

THERE WAS a flurry of activity as everyone was busy setting up. I played catch with Ryan ...sort of; he hadn't quite mastered the catching part yet... until it was time to start dishing out the food, then it got quiet as we silently looked at the beautiful view. The summer evening was slowly surrendering to the night as the sky changed from blue to orange and purple. Soon sunbeams could be seen bursting through a low pack of fluffy white clouds along the horizon, and a tapestry of orange-pink sky and wispy clouds stretched all the way over our heads. Soon the darkening sky gave way to a few bright stars that were beginning to peek through. It was incredibly peaceful as the tranquil quiet of the evening crept over the scene.

"Kelly used to say how mind-blowing it is that God puts on this show every single night, and most of the time, we just ignore it," I shared.

"It's spectacular," Mr. O' said, sounding like he was truly seeing it for the first time in his life. I saw Mrs. O' put her head on his shoulder and wipe a few tears.

"This looks a little like a reflection of Heaven, except the real place is a thousand times more beautiful," I said.

"You say that as if you've been there," Mr. O' joked, "but I'll bet you're right," he added. Mom rubbed my shoulder, silently acknowledging our secret.

As we watched the breathtaking sight, I could hear the muffled sound of Mrs. O' crying softly and detected Mr. O' sniffling as he held his wife and she hugged Ryan close.

The memory of Chozeq's words unexpectedly came to mind: *At your hour of greatest need, it was He who shepherded your path.* I realized then that it wasn't a vision of Heaven that they needed most. It was simply a view of the One who is the source of all comfort. I silently prayed that God would help them with this impossible burden – just like He'd helped me. We carried them together – the reassuring words swept through my mind once more.

The Psalm that had been such a comfort to me for the past two years came to mind, and I pulled out the small Bible I'd carried along.

"Kelly and I used to like to take turns reading a Psalm or something just before the sun went down; this one is my favorite." I read aloud.

Bless the Lord, O my soul: and all that is within me, bless
  his holy name... Bless Jehovah, O my soul, and
  remember all the good that He has done for us: He
  forgives all our sins; He heals us and redeems our
  souls from terrible destruction; He crowns us with
  loving-kindness and tender mercies; He is the one
  who satisfies us with good things so that our youth is
  renewed like the eagle's.
Jehovah is merciful and gracious, slow to anger, and
  abundant in mercy. He hasn't dealt with us the way

our sins deserve; nor rewarded us according to our
iniquities. For as high as the heavens are above the
earth, so great is His love for us. As far as the east is
from the west, so far has He removed our sins
from us.

The way a father loves his child is the way He has loved
us. Because He knows our frame; He remembers that
we are dust. As for man, his days are like the grass; as
flowers of the field, so we flourish. For the wind
passes over it, and it's gone; and the place where it
was knows it no more.

But the lovingkindness of Jehovah is from everlasting to
everlasting upon those who love Him, and His righteousness is unto children's children;

Jehovah has prepared His throne in the heavens; and His
kingdom rules over all.

Bless the Lord, all you angels of his that excel in
strength, that carry out his commands, listening to
the voice of his word. Bless the Lord, all his hosts; the
ministers of his, that do his pleasure. Bless the Lord,
all his works in all places of his dominion: bless the
Lord, O my soul.[1]

———

IT WAS silent as I closed the Bible and sat quietly. The atmosphere was
filled with emotion. "Would it be okay if I prayed?" I asked. They just
nodded their heads, still unable to speak. I knelt between Mom and
the O'Malleys and put my arms out to touch their shoulders – they all
did the same with me, and we locked arms. I paused silently for a
moment; the thoughts of that first night when mom and I cried came
flooding to mind and now seemed incredibly comforting. The feelings
that I felt that night about God's vastness seemed especially fitting
here on the hilltop.

"Father, the glory you show us in creation is just a dim reflection of your true glory… when we think of the true vastness of who you are, we can't help but be amazed at your love for us. We're so small that if you showed us all your glory, we would be crushed underneath it. You need to stoop down to view these spectacular skies above us and bend to see what angels do, yet you turn your eye even lower and look on us with so much love that our faintest pain moves your heart. Your ear is always open to our cries.

"We remember that You endured the cross because of the joy that was set before you. We can't help but think of how Kelly was so freely willing to accept your will because of the joy set before her. We know that she is rejoicing tonight in your presence, and we rejoice with her.

"Still, we miss her, Lord. We pray that you would be all the comfort we need – remind us of the joy that is set before us also and of the day when we will all be together again, forever in the Lord."

After I finished, no one said a word, but I could hear the faint sound of crying in the darkness. I finally climbed to my feet, and mom stood up beside me, giving me a big hug – she just held me for a long time.

⌘

24

MISSION

Behold, I send you forth as sheep in the midst of wolves.
~ Mat 10:16

As the week went on, I was feeling more and more nervous about the prison visit. Mom was surprisingly fine with it when I told her; I guess she figured there'd be plenty of guards around, and at least none of the criminals would be wielding knives. To be honest, it wasn't knives I was worried about. At the Wednesday morning FCS breakfast, Pastor Juan quietly pulled Pete and me aside to let us know that the prison would expect us at 8:00 AM. We didn't get a chance to talk much about what to expect with the other kids around.

By Friday night, it was all I could think of. I was haunted by the memory of all those terrifying devils that had filled my room, and the pain of that beast's razor-sharp bite still seemed fresh on my mind. I couldn't help recalling the blood on my fingertips; it made me feel terrifyingly vulnerable.

The more I thought about it, the more I doubted my ability to help

Pastor Juan. That confrontation in the diner had been as big a surprise to me as everyone else, I admitted.

I anxiously prayed and did my best to reassure myself. I repeated Chozeq's words about Jesus being the one who leads the advance guard, but it didn't help; I was physically shaking. I finally decided that I couldn't go through with it and picked up my phone to text Pastor Juan.

Just as I did, I noticed something in the mirror that startled me – my reflection showed a misty-looking figure just behind me. Suddenly the same pain that I felt in the diner shot through my shoulder again, causing a reaction in my spirit that completely shocked me. Rather than fleeing in terror, I was instantly filled with an unnatural and intense boldness.

I spun around and shouted at the figure, demanding that it show itself. It instantly materialized, revealing a hellish minion. This one, however, was a ghostly grey-white, unlike the others I'd seen who had been dark red or pitch black.

"TELL ME YOUR NAME!" I demanded, not knowing quite why I was asking.

"TERRORE !" it screamed in reply as its mouth stretched grotesquely huge, I AM TERRORE, ...FEAR AND COWARDICE WIELD I!" It shrieked as it leaned toward me and reared upward.

THE PIERCING PAIN in my shoulder intensified as it spoke, and the creature's threats somehow only seemed to embolden me further. "YOU CANNOT STRIKE FEAR IN THE LORD'S ANOINTED," I heard myself shout – the words surprised me, "IN THE NAME OF THE LORD OF HOSTS I BANISH YOU TERRORE! I COMMAND YOU IN JESUS' NAME TO LEAVE HERE … AND NEVER AGAIN RETURN!"

. . .

THE DEMON LOOKED surprised that its spell had been so quickly shattered. Then it shrieked loudly in a long agonized wail and was suddenly pulled backward and dragged roughly through the window. Its deafening screech was louder than sirens in a five-alarm fire, echoing off of the neighboring houses. I watched as it was thrown from the 2nd floor onto our front lawn, where it continued to screech in an ear-splitting wail as it was sucked under the ground. Finally being silenced as it was pulled beneath the green turf.

I stood staring out the window in shock. My first thought was, how will I ever explain this to the neighbors and mom!

THERE WAS a knock at my door, and I gulped, then cleared my throat and said "c-come in," in as normal a voice as I could manage.

Mom brought in an armful of folded laundry and laid it on the bed. I waited for her to ask what just happened, but she didn't say a word. "D-did you hear anything a minute ago, like a lot of …noise?" I asked carefully.

"No, nothing I can think of," she said. She looked out the window, "Was it from outside?" She asked.

"I guess so… guess it was nothing," I said quickly. She gave me a kiss on the forehead and turned toward the door; "don't forget you have that prison visit in the morning," she said matter-of-factly as she walked out.

PASTOR JUAN RANG my bell promptly at 7:30. Pete was already with him in the car. The prison was called Stockslock Maximum Security Penitentiary; most people called it the Stockslock Pen. It was a half-hour ride from town, which gave us a chance to finally talk about what we'd be doing there.

I was still feeling elated by my victorious encounter with Terrore.

At least my butterflies were gone. In fact, I was actually feeling anxious for the next opportunity to do it again, forcing me to remind myself that I shouldn't get cocky. The worst thing I could do would be to rely on my own strength, I kept telling myself.

"Chase has agreed to meet with us in the prison chapel," Pastor Juan said. "I thought that'd be the best way to get close to him," he explained. "I know one of the guards. He's a solid Christian – he'll stay with us."

"What do you plan to say to him?" I asked.

"Figured I'd leave that up to the Spirit," Pastor Juan said with a smile.

"Why are you so interested in gettin t' this guy?" Pete asked.

"Not really sure," Pastor Juan answered, "seems like God is the one who's the most interested – you can attest to that yourself. It's not every day He tells us to visit someone in an audible voice."

We prayed together in the car before getting out, then headed to the enormous front gate. I couldn't help feeling intimidated by the imposing sight of tall iron bars topped with razor wire. It suddenly reminded me of the terrifying memory of Hell's enormous gates. A low-pitched horn blared as the gate slowly opened to let us in.

Getting through security took less time than I expected. The guards all knew Pastor Juan, and I guess I didn't look like much of a threat. Pete did attract more attention, but Pastor Juan vouched for him, and they let him through. I wondered if getting out would be any harder. Pastor Juan introduced us to Mitch Washington, the guard he told us about. "Thanks for visiting today, guys," Mitch said as his colossal hand shook mine. He was a giant, about 6'6" and at least 290 lbs – all muscle. "I'll show you where the Chapel is; I don't know what God has in mind, but this guy Chase definitely needs it. He's really out there... even the other tough guys leave him alone."

Mitch led us down a wide corridor with blank white cement walls to a set of double doors with a simple label painted on them: Chapel. The room inside was bare except for a dozen pews and an old beat-up-looking lectern. There were windows on one side covered with bars, along with frosted glass with chicken wire inside like they use in the school gym. We didn't have to wait long. Just a minute or two later, the doors opened again, and three huge guards led Chase into the Chapel; his wrists and ankles were cuffed, with a chain connecting both.

He had a cold, arrogant expression on his face as he looked at Pastor Juan as if daring him to take his best shot at converting him. His eyes glanced over at Pete and barely registered his presence, quickly ignoring him. Then he looked to where I was standing on the opposite side of the room. His expression changed dramatically – there was a flash of what appeared to be fear in his eyes, but then his face hardened, and he glared at me with a look of pure hatred. Mitch noticed it too and stepped forward instinctively to protect me.

"Thanks for coming, Chase," Pastor Juan said as he invited him to sit down. Chase kept staring straight at me as he walked to the front and sat on the first pew.

Mitch nodded to the other guards to let them know they could go; "Just call if you need us," the first guard said as he tapped the radio on his belt.

Chase and I continued to stare at each other. There was something about his eyes that gave him an especially evil look; I knew what it was. Something was different this time, though – it didn't seem like exactly the same presence I'd met in the diner. Unlike then, this time, his cold hate-filled stare gave me the sense that he'd rip me apart with his bare hands if he got the chance. Every natural part of me told me to be terrified and intimidated. Still, something else within me countered with a deep sense of calm and a completely unnatural confidence. The look in his eye, in fact, looked no different to me than any of the other hellish beasts I'd seen before in even more frightening forms.

That's when it struck me... I knew the creature I saw in Chase's eyes – it was exactly the same beast who had stared into my eyes that night in my room – the leader of that devilish hoard.

"Well," Chase said in a mocking tone, "if it isn't little Jimmy Mathew Moretti."

Mitch looked at Pastor Juan in surprise and then at me. "We didn't give him any names," he said sternly, "he has a habit of just knowing things like that."

Pastor Juan registered what Mitch said and looked back at Chase. "Do you know why we're here?" he asked him.

"Who knows why any of you ####-'n Preacher freaks do any ####-'n thing... leave me the #### alone."

"God sent us here, Chase; He has a plan for you... He's going to save you."

"Are you out of your ####-'n mind! God has a plan for me?! What, like He wants me t' do a job for 'im? Maybe he wants me t' rid da world of creepy hypocrites like you. ...Right, Jimmy-boy?"

"GOD DID SEND US... IT's TRUE!" Pete piped up, "I heard Him! I heard a voice from God telling me to come here!"

Chase rolled his eyes; "Like I'm gonna believe that..." he mocked. Then he focused on Pete for the first time; "Hey, I remember you – we've had some real good times together. Do yuz guys know whut Petey here has been up to?"

"THAT'S ENOUGH!" Pastor Juan yelled – he was holding a small vial of anointing oil that he had dabbed on his thumb; he reached out and placed it on Chase's forehead. "IN THE NAME OF..." he began...

Chase's reaction was instantaneous and shocking. Before Pastor Juan could finish his sentence, Chase reeled back and stretched his legs out straight, snapping the chain between his wrists and feet. He reached up and grabbed Pastor Juan's arm and twisted it – we all heard the sickening sound of the bone snapping as Pastor Juan screamed in agony.

Pete responded in a split second, landing a massive sidewinder punch on Chase's face that knocked him backward with a dizzying blow. The punch made Chase let go of Pastor Juan's arm, freeing him to stagger backward. Pete immediately went to help the Pastor as he crumpled to the floor in terrible pain. Chase sat dazed for a moment, then he reared up again and climbed to his feet in a rage. Mitch blocked his path and shoved him backward, but it was like he was pushing on a brick wall - Chase didn't budge. Instead, he swung his handcuffed fists upward, striking Mitch in the chin with such force that it lifted the huge guard off his feet and sent him flying backward – he was out cold.

CHASE STARTED toward Pastor Juan and Pete with murderous rage in his eyes. That's when the searing pain in my shoulder flared the most intensely, causing me to shout at him in a voice that thundered like it had come from Ardent himself:

"STOP!"

Chase immediately froze, then turned to face me with even more rage. He started to step toward me, and I heard myself demand:

"TELL ME YOUR NAME!"

A pair of deep voices came from Chase that seemed to growl like raging beasts:

"EMINOR... EXITIUM !" they screamed. There were two of them!

"UNHOLY BEASTS OF MENACE AND DESTRUCTION – I BIND YOU BY THE POWER OF THE LORD OF HOSTS... THE COMMANDER OF HEAVEN ORDERS YOU TO COME OUT OF HIM!! COME OUT IN JESUS' NAME!"

JUST AS IT had that night in my room, the mention of Jesus' name triggered a blinding flash that erupted from the center of my chest, striking Chase and snapping his head backward. The blast went right through him, sending both of the hideous demons hurling into the air in plain sight. They shrieked, spraying their foul phlegm over the floor in front of them, and then they reared up, ready to attack me with their huge talons bared.

"I BANISH YOU EMINOR AND EXITIUM FROM THIS PLACE AND FROM THE HUMAN REALM FOREVER!"

IN A SINGLE MOMENT, the creature's faces shifted from rage to defiance and then rebellion before being filled with terrified denial. They screeched in an ear-splitting cry as they dropped like stones to the floor, flailing wildly as they were dragged downward until they had vanished completely.

Chase staggered and collapsed to the floor, unconscious. Immediately the doors burst open, and a small army of guards swarmed in. Several grabbed Chase, discovering that he was out cold, while a few went to help Pastor Juan and Mitch. They all looked at me with perplexed expressions — I was the only one in the room still standing.

⌘

25

SAVED

You've been called out of darkness into His marvelous light!
~ 1 Peter 2:9

An hour later, Pete and I sat in a waiting room in the prison hospital while Pastor Juan was having his arm set. Mitch was resting in a curtained area off to one side while Chase was strapped to a bed nearby, sporting a pretty massive black eye from Pete's knockout punch. He was awake and kept looking at me and repeating, "I'm sorry, I'm so sorry! ... They're Gone! I can't believe they're gone! Thank you! Thank You!"

The guards standing around shook their heads and could be over-heard talking about him: "That guy is totally gone... he's off to the Psych Ward for sure." "Yeah... good riddance, as far as I'm concerned...."

Pete hadn't stopped talking about what had happened – I kept reminding him to keep his voice down. "Is this what bein' a Christian is like?" he whispered in astonishment, "I never knew this stuff really happens! Man! Have I been blind all my life!"

I tried to explain that this was kind of unusual, but he pressed me, "Is this the first time you ever saw something like this?!"

"...Well, not exactly," I had to admit.

It was a welcome respite from his interrogation when Pastor Juan finally emerged in a cast from his wrist to his shoulder. He looked humbled and a little embarrassed as he walked to where I was sitting and put his free hand on my shoulder, then patted it as if to say thanks and well done. "Is Mitch OK?" he asked as he looked into the area where he lay resting.

"They said he'll be fine – they just gave him something to make him sleep until his headache clears," I said.

Pastor Juan nodded and then turned his attention toward Chase. "Can I talk to him?" he asked the guards.

"Suit yourself, Reverend," they said, waving him past.

The moment Chase saw Pastor Juan, he started apologizing profusely. Pastor Juan reassured him and patted his shoulder until he calmed down, then spoke to him quietly. "Do you remember what I told you when I said that God sent us to see you today?"

Chase nodded as tears began to well in his eyes. "You said God was gonna save me...."

Pastor Juan waved for Pete and me to come to join him. We gathered around the bed, placing our hands on him as Pastor led us in a prayer of thanksgiving, then he looked at Chase; "Do you know what the word Savior means?" he asked him. Chase shook his head no with an uncertain, pleading look. "It means 'one who saves from danger.' The name Jesus is translated from the name Yeshua — it's a Hebrew word for Savior; He saves us from our sins and the penalty they carry. Are you ready to turn away from the sin in your life and be saved?" Chase broke down as he shook his head, yes, begging for God's mercy through his sudden tears.

Pastor Juan led Chase in a simple prayer of confession – the 'Sinners Prayer' as we loved to call it. It's a prayer that every genuine believer has prayed – continually prays. Hearing someone pray it for the first time always brings a warm thrill to my spirit. Chase was barely able to get the words out as he wept bitterly and repeated them anxiously; his whole manner emitted a spirit of pure contrition.

I couldn't help noticing that all the guards had gathered and were staring in awe at the sight of the most feared man in the prison, now weeping in repentance and giving his life to Jesus.

WHEN THE PRAYER WAS DONE, and Chase had regained his composure enough, Pastor Juan explained what had just happened and welcomed Chase to the family. "You've been called out of darkness into His marvelous light![1]"

"I can feel it! I can actually feel it!" Chase exclaimed with a gigantic smile – his face practically glowed with a look of wonder and amazement.

Pastor Juan pulled his own small Bible from his jacket pocket and told Chase he could have it. Chase's hands were still strapped to the bed. Pastor Juan walked over to one of the guards – a guy he recognized as a friend of Mitch. We could see the guard agreeing to make sure Chase got the Bible as he took it for safekeeping.

Chase turned to me – "I don't know how to thank you for what you did," he said. "I don't know how ya done it... I ain't never seen anything like that..." he struggled with words, then looked at me curiously. "Did it hurt when he did that?" he asked.

I looked back at him, confused – "When who did what?"

"He must'a been an angel... he had t' be," Chase explained. "That big guy who was right behind you back in the chapel... he was at the diner too... he was huge! He kept jabbin ya on top of the shoulder with that giant sword – it was on fire, and it flamed up each time he touched ya. Sounded like a blast furnace or somethin. Looked like it must've hurt, man! -- every time he did it, you winced like you was in pain and shouted. It made those... things in me... it made 'em shake and get real mad. Then all-a-sudden they was gone... that's all I remember, 'cept wakin up here."

I looked over at Pete – he shrugged his shoulders apologetically and signaled that he hadn't seen anything like that.

Pastor Juan came back and promised Chase he'd be back to check on him and told him to start reading the Bible – "Start with the book of John," he advised him.

WE MADE our way out to the car feeling elated over Chase's conversion. Watching the huge prison gate open was like a symbol of what had just happened in his soul.

Pastor Juan was in no condition to drive – besides the cast, they'd given him something for pain that he said was making him sleepy. Pete and I looked at each other; I had my license but hadn't ever actually driven anywhere yet. Pete was a year older and didn't own a car. Still, at least he'd been behind the wheel a few times. Pastor Juan handed him the keys.

We could hear Mrs. Rodriguez's voice over the phone when Pastor Juan called to tell her what happened. I'm pretty sure I picked up the words "loco..." and "insano..." in her reaction as they talked in Spanish. She didn't sound too pleased with Pastor Juan, but the words "te amo..." (I love you) came across clearly at least a half dozen times. The poor guy looked really discouraged when he hung up the phone. He just bowed his head.

"Hey, Pastor... what you did today was awesome...." I said quietly as I leaned forward from the back seat. He shrugged once in a dismissive laugh as if that was the furthest thing from the truth. "I'm sorry about your arm. That wasn't your fault," I said. "It was really brave." He subtly shook his head to say he disagreed.

"It's true, man – that was heroic!" Pete chimed in.

"What was heroic was you guys!" Pastor Juan said earnestly as he looked over at us. "Pete, if you hadn't done what you did, I probably wouldn't be alive right now. And Jimmy!" He shifted in his seat to turn and look at me... "you did exactly what I thought you would." He studied my face for a moment, "I saw it in you the first time we met."

Pastor Juan and Pete both looked at me silently for a second. Their faces had gotten serious – these weren't 'great job buddy' expressions. They were more like – 'wow, this guy is different.' I could tell they were both a little intimidated by what happened – maybe a little scared.

"W-what'd ya see? …today, I mean?" I asked them; I wasn't sure which parts had been perceived or invisible. They both looked at each other, then Pastor Juan looked at me.

"I have to admit," he said, "I've never seen anything like it before. Those demons that were blasted out of Chase… we saw them! We heard their screeches… the way you talked to them… the look of eternal damnation on their faces when you banished them." His eyebrows lifted as he remembered another detail; "They knew your name as soon as they saw you!"

"W-well…" I answered uncomfortably, "…Mitch said Chase did that a lot, remember?" "He might have known me from the diner, maybe."

"He knew you at the diner," Pastor Juan explained. He took a breath and sighed, "I probably should have told you, … I'm sorry, I should have told you. When I first went to visit Chase at the jail, he mentioned your name. I figured that he'd just heard it when they were arresting him but couldn't remember anybody saying it as I replayed that morning in my mind. Then I heard later from Mitch that your name was kept from him for your protection – I guess that's standard protocol with guys like him." Pastor Juan looked down as he thought, "It wasn't just that he knew your name, though. It was the sound in his voice when he said it – it's hard to describe, it was like hatred and fear all mixed together."

"Yeah, I can see why!" Pete chimed in, breaking the tension." I'm tellin' ya…" he added with a smile as he raised his voice, "…if I was a demon, I know I'd be stayin way clear 'a Jimmy-Boy – that's for sure!"

I couldn't help laughing but looked at the floor and shook my head to disagree. None of this had anything to do with me – I just happened to be the guy in the middle of something unbelievable that God was doing!

I looked back at both of them with a smile; "We make a pretty good team, don't we?"

"You said it, brother…" Pastor Juan agreed. "And we have a team

Captain who's invincible! I think we should thank Him right now."
Pastor Juan bowed his head and led us in prayer.

I FINALLY GOT to work around 1:30, jumping out of the car as Pete
dropped me off on the way home. Uncle Mike wasn't real happy
about me being a few hours late, but at least I made it before the
dinner rush.

By the time mom came for me at 11:00, I was exhausted. Of
course, she wanted to know how everything went at the prison. I'll
admit that I left out a few things – like the demons and Pastor Juan's
broken arm. I didn't want to get her upset… and I wasn't sure exactly
how to describe it anyway. Instead, I shared that Chase had been
saved and told the way he wept as he gave his heart to Christ.

"REALLY?!" Mom said in surprise as a huge smile filled her face. "I
thought he was a pretty tough guy?"

"Yeah, he was… God is pretty amazing," I said.

As soon as we got home, I headed straight upstairs for the night.
Before getting ready for bed, I grabbed my journal and sat down to
write, but then I laid it aside and opened my Bible to the first chapter
of John instead, thinking about Pastor Juan's advice to Chase. The
opening words of that book always gave me a thrill. After reading
them through, I closed my eyes and breathed a prayer of thanks for
what God had done.

"YOUR LORD IS HONORED by these growing virtues…." The sound of
Chozeq's familiar voice beside me made me open my eyes – I saw him
on one knee beside the bed, resting both his hands on the handle of
his giant sword. I smiled at him, and he smiled back. "Faith within
thee grows stronger with its exercising," he said approvingly.

"I have a lot of help…." I said, feeling humbled by the compliment.
"Thanks for being there with us today." He just nodded.

My mind was racing with the events of the day, and looking at

Chozeq's sword reminded me of Chase's comment about seeing him behind me in the chapel. "When Chase saw you," I asked carefully, "... he said you were touching my shoulder with your sword... is that the pain I keep feeling?"

"Nay lad, the pain is thine own – a reminder of thy weakness that God hath given to thee. He instructs me only to salve it, that it be not too great a burden for thee."

I thought about that and remembered the Apostle Paul's words about being given a thorn in the flesh. Far from creating dread, the realization brought a deep appreciation for how much God genuinely cared for me. I blinked to clear the sudden mist in my eyes.

I glanced over at the journal lying beside me and thought about all the incredible experiences it recounted. "Mr. O' told me that what God is doing here is something special... he said I shouldn't take it for granted. He doesn't even know about half of everything that's happened." I looked at Chozeq, "Is this really as rare as it seems – am I the only one seeing these things? Are they happening now for a reason? Like, because the end is coming soon?"

"Ye ask many questions, lad," he looked at me kindly as he sheathed his gleaming sword and then crossed his huge arms as he sat back on his heels. "The Master's work is flourishing all over this world. His Spirit is moving in every land." He smiled at me, "...and yes, that which is happening with thee is rare... rare indeed."

I thought about today and last night; "Those... demons... are they getting more hostile? It seems like they're everywhere."

"Aye," he said, leaning forward, "though their numbers are not increased, they increase in defiance the more that men's rebellion grows against their creator. There have been many times in earth's history when they have grown defiant indeed – defiant but not strong."

HE LOOKED at me with a fire in his eyes that burned equally with joy and confidence.

"Remember that the servants of the Most High can look with calm

contempt upon their most haughty foes, and thus can ye. Know that
our enemies are attempting impossibilities. They seek to destroy the
eternal life, which cannot die while Jesus lives; they strive to over-
throw the citadel, against which the gates of hell shall not prevail.
They kick against the pricks to their own wounding and rush upon
the bosses of Jehovah's buckler to their own hurt."

HE LEANED on the hilt of his sword and looked at me kindly, taking
me into his confidence.

"We know their weakness. What are they but fallen and powerless
creatures? They roar and swell like waves of the sea, foaming out their
own shame. Yet when the Lord arises, they fly as chaff before the
wind and are soon consumed as crackling thorns in the fire. They are
so utterly powerless to do damage to the cause of God that the
weakest soldiers in Zion's ranks may laugh them to scorn."

THEN HE PUT his strong hand on my shoulder and looked me in
the eye.

"Come what may, forget not that the Most High Himself is with
thee -- when He dresses in arms, what enemy can stand? They are as
mere potsherds who cannot long contend with their Maker when He
arises from His place. His rod of iron dashes them in pieces like a
potter's vessel, and the very remembrance of them perishes from the
earth."

A BRILLIANT SMILE came over his face.

"Away, then, all fears!" he said as he gave my shoulder a firm grasp,
"...the kingdom is safe in the King's hands![2]"

⌘

26

NEW THINGS

... New things I now declare; before they spring forth I will tell you of them
~ Isaiah 42:9

Crowds at the breakfast meetings at Carmine's had been getting bigger and bigger over the past few months, but after Kelly's Memorial service, they became really packed. Pastor Juan moved the starting time a half-hour earlier, and the group still continued to grow. There weren't any tables left for regular diner customers most weeks, and kids were still standing. Carmine said it was the best thing he ever saw – he started hanging a "Closed for Business" sign on the door to make sure we had the whole place to ourselves. What was really impressive was that the school year had ended, and everyone was still coming. In fact, the kids begged for more meetings, so Carmine offered to host the group on Mondays and Fridays in addition to Wednesdays.

Some of the kids started bringing their guitars and leading the group in songs – the singing soon lasted for over an hour. Carmine was just fine with it and was right in there singing along. He even had a small piano brought in. It turns out that Angela is incredible on the keyboard! Someone brought their drum set in the next meeting, and a few others brought their horns and even a fiddle.

The warm summer mornings allowed Carmine to open all the doors to the patio area, and the crowd soon overflowed into the parking lot. Pastor Juan used a guitar amp as a makeshift PA system to give a short devotional, and kids started using it to give their testimonies. Those became the most fantastic part of the meetings, as kids took turns at the mic to tell how they'd met Christ and to talk about how He was changing their lives. In every meeting, more kids came forward in sincere repentance. God continued to add to His church daily... well, I guess it was technically every *two* days.

All the excitement attracted the town's attention, of course. A few police officers started showing up to help direct traffic and keep an eye on things. I recognized Sheriff Flanagan; he had been a friend of my dad since they were kids. He shook my hand with a smile and gave me a pat on the back when he saw me.

BY THE END OF JUNE, it was clear that Carmine's diner was simply becoming too small. Attendance had grown to the point that half the group was standing in the parking lot, and the growth showed no sign of slowing. Sheriff Flanagan approached Carmine after the Monday Meeting with a look on his face that signaled bad news; he was accompanied by the Fire Chief and the Health Commissioner. Carmine looked crestfallen when he came to tell Pastor Juan the news that they had delivered – the FCS group would have to find someplace else to meet starting next week.

The church buildings were a possibility, but both our churches were pretty far away, and most of the kids had been walking or biking to the diner. We knew they'd have a hard time getting to either church.

Poor Carmine looked devastated as he sat beside the piano with his head in his hands. A small group of us were still hanging around, and Pastor Juan gathered us together for prayer.

"Lord, this is not our work; it's yours," he began. "We're truly grateful for your provision until now and for Carmine's willingness to serve you in the way that he has. We know that today's news is not news to you. You've known all along that your work would outgrow this meeting place – you knew it even back when the possibility was still inconceivable to us. We also know that you will provide for your great work, and even though we don't know how that will happen, we trust you for it. Father, we agree together in faith, touching Heaven, and thank you for the answer that is already speeding on its way."

Afterward, I walked Pastor Juan to his car. "You sounded really confident when you prayed," I said honestly, "where do you think we'll meet next week?"

"I haven't got a clue!" he said. "I just know that what God is doing is way too big for it to end because of this."

He gave me a nod and raised his eyebrows in a gesture that said: Please pray! Then he climbed into his car.

I COULDN'T STOP THINKING about that silent request for prayer the rest of the day. It seemed like every minute that I wasn't talking, I was silently praying – through my whole shift at the Sub Shop. Uncle Mike got a little annoyed at me for being distracted – or spending the day in La La Land, as he called it.

When Mom picked me up, I shared the news about Carmine's; we sat at the table and prayed about it together when we got home. It was after 11:00 PM, too late to call anyone right then, but she offered to call Pastor Wilkes in the morning to ask the church to pray too.

As I headed up to my room, it was still impossible to focus on anything else. As much as I tried, though, I couldn't seem to form a coherent sentence that meant anything – every stream of thought sounded like gibberish when I tried to vocalize it. Still, it was gibberish that felt like it wanted to pour out of me more earnestly than any prayer I could remember. The feeling of the words reminded me of the sense I had on that first night after meeting Chozeq – the night I heard my name spoken. I knelt beside my old wooden desk chair and started to whisper the words that wouldn't stay silent. They felt so familiar – like a forgotten language that was still understood somewhere deep inside.

THAT'S when the atmosphere in the room changed abruptly – I was surrounded by sounds; it was like the sound of a vast crowd of people. One voice was much louder than the others... directly behind me. I recognized the voice, but not the words – the voice was Anna's. She was crying and shouting out an incredibly earnest message, but the words were indecipherable. They were in a language I couldn't understand – just like my whispers.

The sounds were so real that I opened my eyes immediately and was taken aback by the scene around me. I was kneeling on a rough wooden platform that was surrounded by people. Everyone was praying – many were kneeling, and behind them, many more were standing with hands raised and tear-streaked faces. I recognized many of the kids from FCS, but there were many others who I didn't recognize... and many who were older – college-age and other adults of every age.

Anna was standing at the front of the platform with her hands raised and tears streaming down her face as she cried out in a loud, clear voice. Her words carried an intense force that thrilled and yet disturbed the soul. As soon as she finished, she melted to her knees as if the message had taken every bit of strength she had.

There was a moment of quiet as a hushed silence swept over the crowd, then a voice could be heard calling out from off in the distance, this time in words I could understand. It was Chrissy Mathews' voice, but she spoke so loudly and with such forceful authority that it was entirely out of character for the Chrissy I knew.

She cried out urgently.

"Where does the fighting within you come from? Isn't it from your own desires that war inside you? You lust, and do not have: you harbor violence in your heart and covet, but cannot obtain: you fight and war; yet you have not, because you ask not. When you ask, you do not receive, because you ask amiss, that you may spend it in your own pleasures.

"Oh faithless generation, don't you know that your attachment to this world separates you from Me? Whoever is a friend of the world makes himself an enemy of my Spirit. Do you think that my Word speaks in vain? I have made my Spirit dwell in you; is it My Spirit that fills you with worldly longing and envy?

"You are weak, but it is in your weakness that I will give more grace. Humble yourselves, therefore, for I resist the proud but will give grace to the humble. Submit yourself to My Spirit; resist your enemy the devil, and he will flee from you. Draw near to Me, and I will draw near to you. Cleanse your hands, oh sinners, and purify your hearts, you double-minded. Be troubled and mourn and weep: let your empty laughter be turned to mourning and your vacant joy to heaviness. Humble yourselves in the sight of the Lord, and then I will exalt you.

"Come! Come unto me all of you who labor and are heavy laden, and I will give you rest! Drink of the water that I give you freely, and it will be a wellspring of refreshing joy, springing up unto everlasting life![1]"

I SAW Chrissy collapse into her seat as she finished, just as Anna had.

Everyone fell silent again, and then a spontaneous outburst of weeping began to sweep over the crowd. It was quiet at first and then grew louder and louder as different people throughout the audience seemed to surrender all fear of what those around them might think. They were focused solely on the burden of their own pricked conscience. They cried out in repentance, begging loudly for mercy with such humility that those surrounding them were drawn to confess their own grave sins.

All of a sudden, this Spirit of God-breathed repentance swept through the place with such force that I could literally see it moving like a wave over the sea of crying faces. Some fell to the ground like they'd been knocked unconscious, while others dropped to their knees with pleas for mercy on their lips.

My eyes suddenly began to see images surrounding each person as I looked at them. The images looked like projections of rings of people, one ring after another in endless concentric circles. They were all being influenced by this event in that central person's life. Dozens of different concentric circles projected from each person that I looked at. I heard Chozeq's thunderous voice speaking in a hushed tone beside me: "Every life touches many others," he said, "the Spirit's move this night is going to ignite a fire that sweeps from here, spreading over the land with such revival as has not been seen since the days of your forefathers.

"This night's coming is foretold to you," he said, looking at me like a captain giving orders, "so that you may do all to ensure its arrival."

He placed his massive hand on my back, and I felt myself grow weightless and begin to rise into the air. I noticed for the first time that the floor beneath everyone's feet was green grass. As we rose higher, I could see that the ceiling was oddly shaped and covered with some kind of fabric – like canvas. It suddenly dawned on me that it was a tent – an enormous circus-sized tent. We floated straight through it into the dark night, rising higher until I could see that it stood in the center of a large field. The light pouring from inside revealed crowds overflowing from it on all sides; they were falling to their knees in an expanding wave as I watched the scene. Beyond them, I could see a large area of fields where hundreds of cars and buses were parked. Beyond those, I suddenly recognized the familiar sight of Carmine's diner and the lights of the other businesses along Main Street.

"This is it!" I exclaimed excitedly, "This is God's answer! It's been right here in front of us the whole time!"

⌘

27

VAN CLIEF'S FIELD

...it will happen soon... right out there

I barely slept the rest of the night. As soon as morning broke, I called Pastor Juan and asked him to meet me at Carmine's; "It's urgent!" I insisted. He was waiting at a table when I arrived.

He looked surprised when instead of joining him, I walked from the front door straight to the back of the diner and looked out the open patio doors. The sight brought a thrill to my soul. Pastor Juan walked up beside me with a curious look on his face.

"I know where we're meeting next week," I said excitedly and nodded toward the field, "there."

"In the field?" he asked skeptically.

"Yup," I answered confidently, "In a tent."

Pastor Juan patted my shoulder to humor me, "Is this the urgent emergency you wanted to meet about? You think we should get a tent?"

"Not just any tent," I said, "a circus tent... it needs to be gigantic!"

Pastor Juan made a dismissive gesture, "Yeah – Right," he said.

Then he looked at me again with a quizzical look; "You're really serious, aren't you."

"Look, Pastor Juan, I can't tell you how I know it, but God is about to do something incredible here... really incredible! I know we have to get a tent... it will happen soon... right out there," I said, pointing into the middle of the huge green field in front of us.

Pastor Juan was suddenly looking at me with a strange, serious expression. He stood silently for a minute, just staring at my face – I could see his eyes searching mine. Then he looked out at the field. He distractedly pulled out a chair and collapsed into it; I sat down next to him.

"I-I h-had a dream last night..." he began explaining quietly. "I can't really remember much of it, but I saw people getting saved... hundreds of people... like... an amazing number." Then he looked up at me with an incredulous expression, "The last thing I remember was seeing you... pointing just like that and saying: ...*it will happen soon... right out there*. It was exactly like you just said it ...exactly the way it just happened. Then I woke up."

I felt a thrill up my spine, not because I was surprised, but because of how cool it is when God orchestrates things.

Carmine came from the kitchen to greet us; he still looked heartbroken over the news from the town. "Mr. Giovani," I asked anxiously, "do you know who owns the field right there?"

He answered in his usual partly-broken English: "Quello? il è Van Clief's farm... what-for do you ask?"

"That's where we have to meet," I blurted out, "we have to put up a tent!"

Carmine looked at me like I had lost my mind, then he dismissed my suggestion with a wave. "Old è Van Clief he'd never allow it – he guards è dat land like è fortress."

"But he doesn't even farm it anymore," I insisted. "Maybe if he knew why we wanted it, he'd agree."

"That's gonna be de last thing that would è make him agree. I don't remember him ever stepping è foot in è church... an' he has even less use for è school kids."

Pastor Juan was sitting quietly as we spoke, then he looked at the field and then back at both of us; "It couldn't hurt to ask him," he said.

Carmine was taken aback by his comment; he stopped and just looked at Pastor Juan with a disarmed expression. "Be my è guest!" He finally said as he lifted both hands in surrender, "but it's è pointless if you ask è me."

To my surprise, Pastor Juan got up from his chair immediately; "Coming?" he asked me with a smile. I nodded and quickly followed him toward the door, noticing Carmine's shaking head as we said goodbye.

THE ENTRANCE to Van Cliefs farm was a mile up the road; I never noticed before how really big the place was. Pastor Juan turned his car into the long dusty driveway and slowly navigated a maze of potholes toward the old farmhouse, pulling up within a few yards of the front porch. The minute we stepped out of the car, we heard a gruff voice shout, "Stay right there!" Looking up, we saw Mr. Van Clief on the porch with a shotgun in his hands. Pastor Juan and I instinctively put our hands up and stood beside the car.

Pastor Juan looked over at me and then back at Mr. Van Clief; "We've come to talk to you... I'm Pastor Rodriguez... from the Wells Avenue Assembly. This is Jimmy Moretti."

"Hello, Sir," I said as respectfully as I possibly could.

Mr. Van Clief lowered his gun and looked at me. "You Vince Moretti's boy?"

The question surprised me, "Y-yes, sir," I answered nervously.

"Git over here, so's I kin git a better look at ya," he ordered, thumping the barrel of his gun against the porch and leaning on its stock, using it as a cane.

I cautiously walked toward him – "Come on! Come on! I ain't got all day, especially at my age!" he said, waving his hand at me in invitation. I stopped at the foot of his porch steps, and he leaned down for a closer look. "Well, sure as shootin', I kin see the resemblance. Was a darn shame, your dad's passin'... a darn shame."

He turned and hobbled toward a wooden rocker, one of several lined along the old porch, and climbed into it. "Come on up here and sit down," he said, pointing at the rocker next to his, "... you might as well come too," he yelled to Pastor Juan.

"You knew my dad?" I asked as I cautiously sat down.

"Sure did... and your grandpa an' great grandpa too; great men, all of 'em."

I just sat and stared at him, hoping he'd say more.

"Your dad was a big help t' me here on the farm years back – he used t' work fer me in his younger days. That's before he went off and married your mother – a fine girl she was... knew her grandpa too. How is your ma?"

"She's fine, thanks."

"Yeah..." he said with a sigh, "can't run this place no more by myself. Sure hurts t' see it all layin' fallow and run down like it is."

I could see the pain in his face as he looked out over the empty land; it was more than just disappointment – his look carried a lot of other pain too.

The apparent effects of years of wear made me think of the farm's long history – it must have carried a lifetime of memories for the old man. His comment about knowing my great-grandpa piqued my interest; I'd heard a few stories about him but never thought to ask dad about him when I had the chance. Mom didn't know much – just that he'd died in the war.

"What was my great-grandpa like?" I asked, breaking the silence. Mr. V looked down at' the floorboards and thought for a minute.

"Lou, and me, well... we was best friends, closer'n bark on a tree; done pert-near everything together when we was kids." He looked up and waved toward the fields as he continued... "This-here was my pa's farm. Your great-grandpa Lou showed up with his folks t' work it – migrants, they were; he couldn't o' been more 'n eight years old at the time. They was jus' in the country a short spell... new immigrants, ya know. Anyways, Lou and me was the same age, an' we hit it off real well from the git-go. My ma insisted that he go t' school – he'n I used t' walk together up t' the old schoolhouse… guess we did that fer 'bout ten years together."

He was smiling as he described their childhood; I got the feeling there were many great stories that he could have told about those days. Then he abruptly ended the conversation and sat quietly.

"What happened after that?" I asked with keen interest.

"Well – the war happened!" He snapped back. "I ain't talkin' about that no more," he added.

I swallowed kind of hard, guessing why he didn't want to talk about it. Then questions about grandpa started to flood my mind.

"I guess my grandpa was born before that, then… before the war?"

His brow furrowed and he shrugged slightly; "guess you could say that. Lou married Lucy right out 'a high school. They had that summer together before we wuz both drafted off t' service that same fall. She didn't find out she was pregnant until after he was already gone off to boot camp."

I wanted to ask him how great-grandpa died but thought I'd better not. "When did my dad start working here?" I asked instead.

Mr. V pulled off his hat and scratched his bald head for a second as he thought about that. "Around age fifteen, I reckon… least he was in high school anyways. He stayed with me a good ten years – till he married and opened his garage. He was a fine mechanic… could fix near-about anything with a motor in it."

Mr. V slapped the arm of his rocker suddenly to change the subject. "I don't reckon you came up here t' ask me 'bout yer family tree… what is it you came fer?"

Pastor Juan and I looked at each other, and he quickly nodded for me to ask since I seemed to have a rapport with the old man. As I looked around at the old farm, an idea suddenly came to me.

"Yes, sir…" I began nervously, "…we were wondering if we could make a deal with you." I glanced at Pastor Juan, noticing his worried expression, then I continued. "We'd like to use one of your fields – the one up by Main Street …in exchange for helping you with your farm."

"What d'ya need the field fer?"

"For a tent... that is, I mean, we want to put a tent on it... to have meetings in."

"What, like a camp or somethin?"

"Well, sort of...." I said, looking at Pastor Juan. "I guess you could call them camp meetings... I like that, actually."

Mr. V sat quietly and scratched his chin as he thought it over. "How big a tent do you have?"

"W-well, we don't actually have it yet... but it'll be big -- we're going to need one that's really big, you know, like a circus tent size."

Mr. V took off his hat again and scratched his head, looking like he'd just heard the craziest thing in his life, but he didn't question us about it at all. After a long silence, he looked at us both with an expression that was all business.

"I need that-there tractor repaired first thing," he barked, "it's too late in the season fer plantin' corn, but the fields could use a dose o' barley ... the seed's there in that smaller silo -- they need plowing and planting. The irrigation needs repairs. Think ya kin handle all o' that?"

I looked at Pastor Juan, thinking about all the kids we could get to help. He looked back with a slightly astonished expression and slowly nodded with a slight shrug that said he thought so.

"Yes, sir, it's a deal," I said as I held out my hand. Mr. V shook it with a grip that was surprisingly strong for a man his age.

"That's a fine handshake you got there, son... kin tell a load about a man from the kind o' handshake he's got."

THEN HE CLIMBED out of his chair and leaned his shotgun against the house, grabbing the walking cane instead that was leaning beside it. "Follow me," he said as he turned and started down the stairs into the yard. We looked at each other curiously and followed along behind him as he slowly made his way to one of the two large barns. He picked a key from the ring on his belt and unlocked the padlock on its door, shoving it open. "Come on," he ordered as he walked inside.

He led us over to a set of stalls and pulled open the gate in front of them, then pointed his cane at a bunch of large wooden crates that were stacked neatly inside it. The boxes were numbered and on the side of each one was a label that had been stenciled onto it – our mouths dropped open as we read what they said: C.I.R.C.U.S. T.E.N.T.

"It's been takin' up space in my barn fer years," he said matter-of-factly, "think ya could use it?"

We were speechless. We both looked at him with a shocked expression that screamed our unspoken question: *...You have a Circus Tent?*

"Yer both lookin' at me as if I was P.T. Barnum or somthin'..." he said as he saw our expressions. "It ain't as mysterious as all that. Back in the day, we used to have a big Harvest Festival here. Biggest in the county... even the State probably. All the farms would bring their produce an' livestock... ever-body 'round these parts looked forward to it. Leastwise, that's whut we done when there was other farms 'round." He peeled off his hat and rubbed his head a few times as he sighed. He smacked the side of one crate lightly with his cane: "It ain't been raised since I sold off the land there on Main Street – most o' the ol' festival grounds is built up with stores an' such nowadays.

"Tell ya what," he said. "That ol' house o' mine ain't had a fresh coat o' paint in 30 years... if ya could do anything 'bout that – the labor, I mean, I'll buy the paint — then I'd be obliged to lend ya this here tent fer as long as ya need it."

I was stunned! In my enthusiasm, I wrapped my arms around old Mr. V and hugged him like he was my long-lost grandpa! He cleared his throat two or three times and then awkwardly raised one hand and patted me on the back.

When I stepped back from him, he had a slightly flustered look on his face. "I reckon that'll do as well as a handshake," he said with a slightly disapproving expression.

Pastor Juan looked like he was going to pass out. This was too much for him to take in all at once. He tried to extend his broken arm to shake hands and then quickly switched to offer his left hand. "This is very generous of you, Mr. Van Clief, thank you... thank you very much." He paused uncertainly and then continued, "I don't suppose you also know how to put up a circus tent... do you?" he asked the surprising old man.

"Well, o'course I do... I own one, don't I? It jus' takes ten or twenty strong-bodied men an' a tractor... like ol' Bessy there."

I turned and followed his gaze, noticing the old tractor; "You seriously named your tractor Bessy?" I blurted; my overwhelmed brain seemed to have left my mouth on autopilot.

Luckily, Mr. V wasn't offended; he responded with a slightly self-deprecating smile and shrugged. "I'll admit it ain't original, but it seems t' fit 'er," he said. "Did ya happen t' git any o' your pa's talent with fixin' motors?"

"Maybe a little," I confessed. "Dad practically raised me in the garage. Got any tools?"

He nodded toward the wall behind me, and I turned to find a whole mechanic's garage worth of tools, all neatly organized, with compressors and air wrenches... the works!

'OLD BESSY' was parked outside the barn under an overhang that kept it out of the rain; it wasn't in bad shape, considering its age. I pulled off the tarp that covered it and unclipped the hood panels to look at the engine.

We spent an hour oiling things and re-gapping the plugs, tightening the belts and wires, and getting the gum out of the old carburetor. Then we used Pastor Juan's car to give its battery a jump. It started and ran roughly, then quit again after a minute. I sniffed around underneath the tractor then hollered up to Mr. V.: "You don't happen to have a spare fuel pump around here, do you?"

"Matter-a-fact... I bought out the stock 'a parts for her from the dealer back when they quit makin' em. Good thing too... that dealer's been gone fer a spell-a-years now his-self."

That did the trick; pretty soon, we had Bessy purring like a big old lion.

As I jumped down off the seat, Mr. V slapped me on the back a couple of times in congratulation. I thanked him and shook his hand.

"Can we start tomorrow?" I asked excitedly.

He nodded with a sober expression, back to being businesslike. "Farm work is early work... usually starts afore 6:00, but I'll give ya till 7:00... sharp."

CARMINE ALMOST FELL over a chair when we got back to the diner and told him the news. He stood looking out at the vast field, already calculating the logistics. "We're gonna need lots o' parking... an' it'll need electricity – I'll call my è brother Enrico... we can take it from my è diner."

I enlisted Anna to help spread the news that we needed anyone who could help with the farm work to meet at Van Clief's farm in the morning. She posted a request for help to explain what was happening and had confirmations from more than a dozen kids within an hour – everyone was incredibly excited!

MOM WAS SHOCKED when I told her what happened. "Mr. Van Clief did that?" she exclaimed in amazement.

"So, dad worked for him before you guys were married?" I asked her. "He told me how he was friends with great-grandpa. He said he knew Gramps Farro too."

Mom was quiet for a minute. "I never knew that... that he knew my grandfather; funny that they never mentioned that. What did he say about Gramps?"

"Just that he knew him; he said that you were a *fine girl*," I added with some dramatic effect.

"Oh really? A fine girl, eh? I'm not sure he felt that way back then; he thought Vince was just marrying me because of, you know... cause of Daisy. I can't believe I'm saying that to you!" Mom was red-faced.

"It's ok, mom," I said quietly, "I've met her, remember?" A tear escaped from mom's eyes as that memory flashed across her face.

"Did he object to your marriage?" I asked carefully.

Mom took a minute to recover and then answered with a sniffle... "Oh yes, he did... big-time... he told Vince to leave his farm and never come back. It broke your father's heart; Mr. Van Clief had been like a father to him."

I thought about the way dad never knew his real father... I couldn't believe I was hearing all this for the first time! "So, you guys never talked again... in all these years?"

"Well, no, they talked... after a few years, your dad offered to do some odd jobs for him... your dad kept that old tractor of his running practically single-handedly. But they were never close after that... Mr. Van Clief can be a pretty stubborn man."

"I can see that!" I said in agreement. The thought that our families had once been so close, and I never knew it shocked me... "Did he come to dad's funeral?" I asked curiously.

"Yeah...yeah, he did. Ward said he saw him sitting way in the back... he was all alone. He was at the graveside too but stood way back by the road."

Mom suddenly straightened in her chair, as if that thought had triggered something inside her; "I think I want to help you tomorrow -- I'm going to take the day off and help."

⌘

28

DAYLIGHT WORK

We must work the works of him that sent me, while it is day
~ John 9:4

Pastor Juan and I pulled into the long driveway at 6:00 AM the following day – we figured we'd get there early to prepare. The first thing we noticed was that the potholes were gone – the driveway was graded smooth and had a fresh coating of gravel. I saw Ol' Bessy parked with its bucket on top of a recently cut pile of stone near the barn.

Our first reaction was to worry... what if Mr. V had given himself a heart attack! We parked near the house and started toward the front door, only to see him already out on the porch sipping coffee from a tin cup.

"Yer early... I like that in a farmhand," he called out in a voice that signaled he was making a joke.

"Did you grade the driveway?" I asked him.

"Yup – spent yesterday... felt good t' accomplish somethin'. Bessy did just fine – ya done a good job on 'er."

"But… what if something had happened like it rolled over or …a heart attack?" I stammered.

Mr. V dismissed my concerns – "Dyin's a certainty at my age… I kin think o' worse ways. Don't be badgerin' me like an ol' hen… I might reconsider our whole arrangement."

Pastor Juan nodded toward me with a look that suggested I should drop it.

"Speakin' o' hens… go fetch a basket o' eggs from the hen house fer us… bring all that's there. I got the griddle heatin'."

By the time the first car arrived, the table had been set up buffet-style out on the big wrap-around porch. Pastor Juan was in the kitchen scrambling eggs while Mr. V flipped flapjacks and bacon on his huge griddle. The table was loaded with pitchers of fresh milk, homemade butter, and mason jars of strawberry jam.

Pete Murphy climbed out of his mom's old Buick with a car full of other kids – they all jumped out excitedly. Right behind them, mom pulled in – she had Anna and her mom with her, along with Mandy and a couple of other kids that they'd picked up. "My mom is gonna help too!" Anna shouted to me – "she grew up on a farm."

Pretty soon, a half dozen other cars had pulled in, all loaded with kids and, in some cases, parents who wanted to help. Finally, a dozen more started arriving on bikes. There were over forty people altogether!

"Well, I'll be…." Mr. V said as he walked onto his porch and saw the crowd. "Looks like I'll be makin' a few more flapjacks."

"I ah… think there's probably enough already…." I said as I looked at the large piles of them already on the table.

"Well… maybe so, but enough plates is gonna be a problem," he noted, slightly embarrassed.

"HERE!" Mrs. Mirabella called, holding up a giant stack of thick paper dinner plates, "…we brought them for lunch, but there's plenty!"

Pastor Juan came out onto the porch behind Mr. V, wearing a lady's apron that gave the kids a good laugh. He smiled and then waved his good arm to quiet everyone and turned to Mr. V.

"We want to thank you for your hospitality Mr. Van Clief. This is an amazing breakfast and very generous of you. With your permission, I'd like to ask God's blessing on the food and today's work?"

"Suit yerself," Mr. V answered politely.

"Lord, we're grateful for your amazing provision and guidance in bringing this group together in this place and in your perfect timing. We know your methods are always with a purpose and your blessings are always bigger than we expect or deserve. Please guide the work today and keep all safe from injury. Bless this amazing breakfast and use it to give strength for a full day's work. We gratefully receive it in your son's precious name. Amen."

"I reckon it can't be a bad thing havin' a minister to kick off a good day's work," Mr. V said to me with a wink.

Pastor Juan lined everybody up for the buffet table – it didn't take much coaxing. Everything smelled so delicious. I don't know if it was the farm air or just the fresh food, but it had to be just about the best breakfast I ever tasted.

ANNA and her mom took charge of washing up and drafted Sean Daniels to wash the pots. Mr.V. Laid out the game plan for the farm work. Pete and I were given the job of repairing the irrigation sprinklers. Meanwhile, he showed some of the men how to hitch the plow on Bessy and load the seed hopper. Pastor Juan got the rest of the group started scraping and prepping the old house; luckily, Mr. V. had plenty of ladders and scaffolding in his barn. Once all of that was in motion, the two of them got into Mr. V's old pickup truck and left to go buy the paint.

Pete and I surveyed the sprinkler system – it was pretty stiff from not being used for a few years, but nothing that some oil and elbow grease couldn't fix. By noontime, we had the mechanical sections working and then set our sights on the water flow. By the time we got back up to the house for a lunch break, the north side of the farmhouse was already half painted. The two south fields had been plowed, and ol' Bessy was working on the west one, which was the biggest.

As we arrived, I noticed Mr. V standing in the barn doorway, looking around as if he was seeing a scene from another universe. 20 kids were swarming over the outside of his farmhouse on ladders and scaffolds with scrapers and paintbrushes. Two men were replacing the front porch steps, and a group was trimming bushes and clearing out flowerbeds. Anna and her mom were leading a team cleaning out the chicken coops and straightening up the barnyard. Mom walked around with a pitcher and plastic cups offering drinks. She approached Mr. V and offered him one; it seemed pretty certain that he hadn't realized who she was yet. He turned to her with a confused look on his face and a burning question on his mind.

"Who are you people anyway?" he said to her.

"I'm sorry... what?" she stammered, confused by his question and wondering if he'd recognized her.

"In all my born days, I ain't never seen a bunch o' folks actin' like you all. Is this some kind o' government youth program or somthin?"

"Oh no, we're not with the government... this is our church... several churches, actually," she replied. The tone of her voice revealed that she was almost as amazed about what she was seeing as he was.

"Well, I ain't never seen any church doin' nothin' like this," he answered.

"Yes, sir... to be honest, neither have I," she responded as she joined him in looking around. He looked over at her with a surprised look. "...Oh, uh, until recently, that is," she quickly added. "This is part of something amazing that has just started... something that God is doing – all these kids just started coming to church in the past few months... most of them had never been to a church before."

"What made 'em come?" he said as he looked at her. There was a searching look in his eyes. Like someone standing on the outside looking in at the greatest mystery of his life.

She looked momentarily taken aback by the question, then gathered her thoughts and attempted to answer. "I guess it started with Kelly... the O'Malleys' girl... she grew up with most of them... she died recently of cancer – a brain tumor."

"Her dying made 'em start going to church? I woulda figured it'd do the opposite."

"Well, I guess that's what you'd expect normally, but Kelly was a very special girl; she had an amazing effect on people."

"What kinda effect?"

Mom thought for a minute...." The kind that makes you feel privileged to have known her... and that forces you to think about what's really important... about how short life is."

"Ahh," he uttered, "I sure know somethin' about life bein' short... can't hardly believe mine's about finished up."

"Oh, don't say that! You've got years ahead of you!"

"Hardly likely. But even so... I figure I better take 'em a day at a time."

Mom looked at him, thinking how different he seemed compared to the tough-as-nails and bitter man she'd known for so long. At least, that's the way she always thought of him. "Life here really is short," she said carefully, "...but that's not all there is. The chapter after this lasts for eternity... I think you sense that, don't you?"

He looked into the dirt, then cleared his throat; "Suppose so," he barked. Mom caught his signal that he didn't want to talk about that anymore. She looked down, slightly embarrassed, glancing at the pitcher in her hand.

"Iced Tea?" She asked, holding out a cup.

THAT'S about the time that Pete and I walked up to the two of them.

"Hi mom, whatcha got in the pitcher?"

Mr. V suddenly looked at mom as the connection finally dawned on him. "Well, I'll be hornswoggled..." he said as he looked at her more closely, "my apologies Mrs. Moretti, you must think I'm a senile ol' coot."

"Please... Call me Maria! It's perfectly alright... I'm sure I don't look the same as that young girl you remember."

"You wuz a pretty young girl as I recall... that's whut Vince saw in ya, that's fer sure. But you're a fine-looking woman too, jus the same, if I may say."

Mom blushed noticeably; "Well, thank you, you may say," she joked.

Mr. V looked down a little awkwardly and shoved his thumbs into the front pockets of his overalls; "I gotta thank you most of all... Maria... fer comin' here an' helpin' out. After all that's happened... it shows a real bit o' Christian charity, that's fer sure."

Mom shook her head no and motioned that she wanted to apologize too, but he dismissed the need for her to with a wave, then turned toward me. "You raised a fine boy here... spittin' image of his dad. He done fixed ol' Bessy as quick as a wink," he slapped his hand on my shoulder, "...your dad would be proud of ya' son." Mom and I shared a glance as we thought about that – he is proud, I know, I thought to myself but didn't speak it.

"We got the gears moving on the sprinklers," I reported, "I think it's just the water flow that needs regulating now."

Mr. V smiled; "Already, eh?" Then he rattled off a series of things for us to check before testing the system with water, listing the sequence as if he'd started the system a hundred times, which of course, he had. "That kin wait till after lunch," he finally said, "you boys are probly famished – a good day's work'll make ya hungrier'n a bear in a vegetable patch."

Just then, the sound of kicked-up gravel announced someone pulling up the long driveway; I turned to see the van from uncle Mike's sub shop pull up to the house. Uncle Mike himself hopped out and pulled open the van's rear doors, hoisting out a big box. "Ay Jimmy!" he yelled to me, "grab that other box, will ya?"

I could tell from the smell of oil & vinegar wafting from the box that it was filled with his specialty; he must have worked half the morning making an order this size. I picked it up and followed him onto the porch where he was laying out the contents of his first box into piles labeled Turkey, Ham & Salami, Tuna, Meatball, and Cheese. Mom came alongside uncle Mike and gave him a kiss on the cheek; "Thanks again for doing this," she said. "No sweat, Sis... jes, don't expect dinner too," he added with a smile.

Everybody gathered around, and PJ said grace, then we dug in. Mr. V was right about farm work giving you an appetite – I was starving.

THE AFTERNOON FLEW past even faster than the morning had. The fields had all been plowed by day's end – except for the one on Main Street – and the house painting was nearly done. Pete and I had gotten the irrigation repaired, primed, and ready.

The whole gang of us gathered together at the house and agreed on the game plan for tomorrow; not everyone could come back – mostly the adults couldn't – but the kids all said they would. PJ laid out what still needed to be done on the house. Mr. V picked Pete and me again to work together and assigned us to get the hopper hooked to Bessy for laying seed.

Finally, Pastor Juan bowed his head, and everyone grew quiet. "Lord, we thank you for the work that's been done here today... for the visible work that you've used our hands to do and also the invisible work that you've done in hearts and minds with your own hand. We're truly thankful for Mr. Van Clief and his generosity and hospitality today; we earnestly pray for your blessing on his life and your touch upon his heart, as well as on our own. We stand in awe at how you plan our destiny and provide for your work in ways that also help others and ourselves – we cannot outgive you. Your blessings are pressed down, shaken together, and running over."

After we said amen, Mr. V stood silently looking at the ground for a little longer than usual, then he cleared his throat and looked up as if catching himself. Pastor Juan offered his left hand to shake and thanked him again as Mr. V did the same in return. The old man looked at mom and me when we came over to say goodbye. I could see something in his face that I hadn't seen before; it was a look of gratitude but seemed mixed with something else... the shadow of deep regret. He thanked mom with a tip of his cap, then put his left hand on my shoulder as he said goodbye, offering me his right hand to shake. I ignored his hand and put my arms around him, giving him a quick hug instead.

The instant I did, the scene I saw around us unexpectedly changed in a flash of light. I was hugging a much younger man, a younger Mr. V. Then I realized we weren't hugging – I was lifting him, dragging him. We were in a muddy field, and I could hear the sound of explosions and what I guessed were bullets whizzing past. I was pulling him toward a line of soldiers who were waving me on anxiously – two of them grabbed him as we reached them. Pulling him to safety. It was at just that moment that I looked down and saw my chest explode as a stream of bullets cut through me from behind! It was like watching a movie... I could see and hear everything but felt nothing. I saw myself drop to my knees and looked at the face of the man I'd just saved – it was twisted in anguish and horror as I heard him scream: "NOOOOO! LOUuuuuuuuu!"

I fell forward to the ground as a flurry of images began speeding along in a blur that I could barely interpret – just able to make out a few fragments. In some of them, Mr. V seemed to be cursing God; the scenes were of happy and sad times... a wedding, a child's birth, then flashes of funeral images – his parents, a child, his wife. I saw my father as a young man angrily jumping from the front porch and throwing a tool belt to the ground. Finally, I saw the clasped hands of an old man, nervously seated across from a doctor who was speaking words that reverberated. "You should get your final affairs in order..." the doctor said.

THE SCENE MADE me shudder like I'd been hit with an electric shock. Mr. V searched my face as I stepped back, and I could see the pain of all of the scenes I'd just witnessed reflected in his eyes. His expression hinted that he detected something new in my eyes as well, and he looked at me with a questioning-and-then-fearful look. He was clearly flustered as I stepped back.

Mom picked up on the exchange and looked at both of us with a concerned expression, "What's wrong?" she asked.

"N-nothing…" I assured her, "j-just feeling kinda tired, is all." She didn't offer a response but just looked at me silently for a moment, then glanced back at Mr. V with a worried expression.

The flurry of activity around us broke up the surreal exchange as everybody helped get things put away for the night and mom rounded up the group riding with her. The driveway finally emptied as the cars all drove away. Pastor Juan and I were the last to leave. As we headed down the long driveway, I looked over my shoulder at Mr. V standing alone in front of his house, watching us go. There was a preoccupied look on his face.

"I THINK Mr. V was pretty impressed by today," I said to Pastor Juan as he pulled onto the main road.

"Are you kidding? He was blown away!" Pastor Juan answered. "This is totally amazing -- it's incredible what God is doing… I can hardly believe it myself; it must seem crazy to him!"

"Yeah…" I said distractedly, finally taking my eyes off the old man; I couldn't stop thinking about the scenes I'd just witnessed when I hugged him.

Pastor Juan looked over at me – "what's going on?" He asked, "… I've seen that look on you before -- it's a lot like the way you looked after stopping Chase that day in the diner."

His comment jolted me back to reality, "OH… Sorry! It's nothing like that… I guess I'm just tired from working all day, that's all."

"Uh Huh…" he said skeptically. There was a silent pause for a minute or two, and then he continued: "How did you know, by the way?"

"What do you mean?"

"The tent… when you told me about it yesterday, it wasn't like it was a new idea… you said it as if it had already happened."

My face turned red… I hadn't given much thought to how that announcement might have come across… it really did seem pretty remarkable given the way things were turning out. I did my best to explain it without giving too much detail: "You had a dream the other night, right?" I reminded him, "Well, it was kinda like that for me too... except it wasn't a dream actually... I just knew it... I knew it'd be a tent... that's all I can say."

"You're giving me goosebumps, man," he said with a smile.

"Just wait," I said, "I have a feeling that God is about to do something incredibly, amazingly awesome... right here... in that tent."

Pastor Juan shook with a shiver as a chill ran up his spine. "Praise God! I feel it in my spirit, man! It's true!"

WE WERE JUST ABOUT to pass Carmine's as he said that, and he suddenly hit the brakes and turned into the parking lot; "I think there's something we have to do," he said as he pulled his car to the back of the parking lot. He stopped for a second, then pulled forward onto the grass and kept driving until we were in the middle of the grassy field, where he shut off the engine and jumped out of the car. I followed him, confused as he walked a few yards further through the tall grass and then dropped to his knees. That solved the mystery of what he meant about there being something we needed to do; I ran up and knelt beside him.

He knelt silently, praying for several minutes, and I did the same. I couldn't help recalling the scene from my vision and imagining where everything had taken place in relation to where we knelt – I could practically see the image of the tent top as I floated above it, with its vast overflowing crowd spilling out from all sides... right here in this field.

"Lord, we kneel in awe before you and claim this ground for the work that you're about to do here," Pastor Juan prayed aloud. "We consecrate this place... this field... to you. Please confront everyone who ventures here. May they experience a powerful encounter with you... stir hearts!... shake lives!... we pray that none who come here will ever be the same! May they be forever changed for having met you face to face... here on this hallowed ground!"

. . .

As we continued to pray, we were overcome with the sense of expectation for what God would soon do – it was so palpable we felt like we could just open our eyes and see it! A familiar touch on my shoulder made me quietly look up to see Chozeq kneeling just behind me to one side. He made a gesture instructing me to keep silent. The field was bathed in the golden light of a brilliant sunset. I followed his gaze across it to see, first one powerful angel and then others, standing at the corners of the expansive grounds. Their swords were drawn and held above their heads pointed skyward as they stood with wings spread wide, vigilant, and ready to defend God's hallowed ground.

"Our Lord has heard your prayer," he said in his booming angelic voice. Pastor Juan bent forward, touching his forehead to the ground, and began to cry, as if Chozeq's unheard words had washed over his spirit in a powerful wave of confirmation.

⌘

29

HERO

The next morning almost everyone was early getting to the farm. Carmine had heard about Mr. V's breakfast and insisted on bringing today's. It was a good thing because I'm pretty sure we'd cleaned out Mr. V's pantry already. Mr. V looked at Carmine suspiciously when he first arrived, then seemed humbled and slightly embarrassed as he saw the spread of food. He cleared his throat nervously as Carmine approached him; "God, He is using you, Mr. Van Clief... Grazie, for what you're è doing!" he said as he held out his hand to shake. Mr. V nodded with a gesture that conveyed he felt he wasn't really doing all that much and shook Carmine's hand. I wasn't sure what the history was between them, but the way they looked at each other made me guess that this was kind of a break-through... like a momentous event.

Right after breakfast, Pete and I got busy gassing up the tractor and loading the hopper with barley seed. Mr. V insisted on making the first run himself to show how it's done, then handed it off to Pete.

Pastor Juan had the painting crew organized like a fine-tuned machine – they were well underway by the time I joined them. He was barking out orders to different kids, using their initials as short-hand: 'AM' for Anna, 'MJ' for Mandy Johnson, 'CM' for Chrissy Mathews, 'SD' for Sean Daniels, etc. I listened to him for a few minutes and then shouted: "What do you want me to do, PJ?"

He looked at me confused, "PJ?" he asked.

"Yeah... Pastor Juan... PJ," I explained. The other kids laughed and immediately started calling him PJ too. He just smiled and told me to get to work.

The ground floor siding and porch railings were finished, so I was given the job of painting the porch deck – battleship grey.

BY LUNCHTIME, Pete had planted the two south fields and was halfway through the big west field. The painting crew was putting the finishing touches on the eves and window trim; it was clear we'd be finished with everything in a few more hours.

"It looks like we'll be done around here today," I noted to Mr. V. "Would it be alright if we worked on putting up the tent tomorrow?"

"I reckon that'd be alright," he answered without hesitation as he continued to watch Pete. "Need t' prep the field first... it'll need mowin' at a minimum. Takes near a day t' lay the tent out first... might need sum mendin' in a spot 'r two."

He glanced over at me for a second and then looked back straight ahead toward the tractor as it moved across the field in the distance. "It's sure ironic," he said, "seems like everything good that's happened in the last two days has come from things I done threw away or wrote off."

"What do you mean?" I asked.

"I've been a damned bitter man, son," he said. "Ain't been able t' see past the rough parts o' my life t' see the good. I reckon I've been drivin' folks away fer most o' my life. Then here you-all show up doin' all this... Guess I'm feelin' damned guilty, that's all."

"I know what you mean... about the rough parts of life, I mean. At least, I think I do... I lost a really close friend just recently – guess you could say we were close as bark on a tree."

He smiled and nodded at my reference to the phrase he'd used to describe him and great-grandpa. "Yer ma told me about that... the O'Malley girl was it? You were close, eh?"

"Yeah, real close... we were best friends our whole lives; we did practically everything together."

"Tough break, son, that's a real tough break. Guess ya kin say that fits the kind o' rough times I was talkin' about."

I looked at him as he kept staring into the distance, noticing that his eyes weren't following Pete anymore. He was just staring straight ahead. The images I'd seen when I hugged him flooded my mind.

"My great-grandpa saved you, didn't he?" I blurted out, not really thinking beforehand.

He looked over at me with a surprised expression that showed the same hint of fear I'd seen yesterday right after we hugged. Then his face turned ashen, and he suddenly grasped his chest and staggered back to sit on the open tailgate of his truck. "My Nitro... Nitroglycerin pills," he stammered, "...on the kitchen counter... hurry 'n git!"

I took off running as fast as I could, praying a plea for Mr. V with every bounding step. I found the bottle of tiny pills beside the sink and sprinted back to the yard.

"Open it... git me one... quick," he said breathlessly. I handed the pill to him, and he slipped it under his tongue, then leaned back against the side of the truck bed.

"We should get an ambulance! I'll call 911..." I said as I reached for my phone. He grabbed my forearm and stopped me. "I don't want no damned ambulance... it'll pass, jus' give it a short spell, that's all."

I sat catching my breath – my own heart was racing too; bringing up the war had obviously been a bad idea. "Mr. Van Clief, I'm sorry," I said, trying to calm my voice, but my words came out in a jumble; "...I shouldn't have brought that up... it was just that I guessed maybe... I thought,...maybe my great-grandpa was a hero, that's all...."

I felt him squeeze my arm, and he closed his eyes, then opened them and looked at me with a sad expression. "He was a hero... don't ever think otherwise," he said softly.

After a few minutes of sitting silently, he pulled on my arm; "Help me up," he requested as he struggled to sit straight. "Take my cup there an' fetch me some water from the well, will ya?"

I was tempted to argue that the faucet would be better but decided not to. The old pump handle on the well worked smoothly, and water poured out on the first pump, showing how regularly it was still being used. I held his tin cup underneath the flow, which filled it instantly.

He took the cup from me as I returned and drank a long draft from it, then wiped his mouth on his sleeve. "Sit down," he ordered, pointing his thumb toward the tailgate next to him. I obeyed, bracing myself for a talking-to.

Instead of scolding me, he began a story - surprising me.

"WE WAS in the 88th Infantry ...it was my idea to get Lou and me assigned to the same unit; that was my first mistake." He paused for a minute, deep in thought.

"We was takin' a ridge that had an MG34... a mighty big machine gun... atop it. It was first light... my job was t' crawl 'bout halfway up an' try t' take out the gunner with a grenade, which I done, but it turned out that jus' stirred up a hornets' nest from over the other side. Anyways... I turned t' hightail it an' got m'self shot in the leg – found later that the bullet hit the bone an' went clear through... it hurt sumthin' awful. I laid there like a damn fool bleedin' to death."

Mr. V looked at me uncomfortably as if he was confessing to a horrible crime, then continued. "Next thing I knew, it was Lou grabbin' me 'round under my arms and dragging me back t' the wall where our unit was hold up. He got me over...."

I could see the anguish in Mr. V's face as he recounted the scene – it was the same look that he had in my vision... it still affected him the same as when it first happened.

"H-he got me over..." he repeated as a tear ran down his cheek. "Then we heard the MG34 – my grenade hadn't taken it out," his hands were clenched tightly into fists as he struggled to continue, "... Lou......Lou, he didn't make it over." He looked down at the dirt.... "If I'd dun a better job, Lou'd a made it home," he said as a few more tears rolled down his face. He looked at me. "If I hadn't insisted on him bein' in the same unit, he never would'a been there in the first place."

He wiped the tears off his face with his sleeve. "I never had the guts t' tell yer pa or grandpa 'bout that... jus' couldn't look 'em in the eye with 'em knowin' the truth about it. Cause it was my fault... I'm the reason he got killed. But I couldn't keep it secret no more – I had to let ya' know he was a hero... your great-grandpa was the biggest hero I ever knew... still is in my mind."

I was suddenly struck by the words that Kelly had shared at my father's side... how she'd been afraid to tell me about what happened when dad died – afraid it would change the way I felt about her.

"It wasn't your fault," I said, looking at his tear-streaked face, "... nothing you did caused it."

"Well, if the fault's not mine, then whose? ... the soldier that shot him was jus' savin' his own skin... he ain't t' be blamed."

"Maybe it wasn't anyone's fault... maybe God just had His own reason... for saving you, I mean. You wouldn't be here today if great-grandpa hadn't saved you, right?"

"What's yer point? My life's near over an' I ain't dun nothin' worth being saved for. I wish it was me stead'a him; you don't know how many times I've waked up wishin' Lou'd jus' left me there stead'a savin' me."

"I don't know why God did it," I answered, "but He always has a reason."

I looked up and saw Pastor Juan walking toward us. It was evident that Mr. V had been crying, but Juan didn't mention it.

"Everything okay?" he asked with concern.

I wanted to reveal the scare we just had with Mr. V's heart trouble but instead sat quietly glancing over at him to see if he'd bring it up. Mr. V saw me looking and got the message; "Well, I might'a had a little flair up o' heart trouble... it aught'a be no surprise I got a bad ticker. But no worries, Jimmy done got me my nitro pills."

Juan flipped over an empty five-gallon paint bucket and sat on it. "I guess life has a way of catching up with us, doesn't it?" he commented as he waved his broken arm and smiled. "I suppose that's God's way of getting our attention as we get older."

"Well, if that's the case, He sure knows how to git it... jus' wish He could do somethin' ta' undo sum o' the messes we made over the years."

"That's actually something he does especially well," Juan answered without missing a beat. "The Bible is full of promises and stories of how God wipes away sin and washes away our guilt. What's really amazing is that He doesn't say he just overlooks our sins... He says he makes it as if we never sinned. He couldn't do that without changing the past."

Mr. V looked at Pastor Juan as if he was out of his mind; "You ain't makin' no sense. It ain't possible to change the past."

"He's God; what makes you think he can't? I don't think it's any coincidence that the very first miracle that Jesus did was to change water into wine... and it was especially good wine. How do you suppose he did that? Wine is only wine when it's aged, but that wine had no past for it to be aged in – it needed to be given a past... a new past that He created. It stands to reason that if God can give a past where there was none, then He can remove a past where there is one." He paused and looked Mr. V in the eye as if gauging whether what he was saying was making sense to him. Mr. V stared at him, obviously struggling.

"Here's the really important point," Juan continued. "God doesn't just forget our sins or pretend they aren't there. He wipes out our sin. It's not just that everything is the same, and we're forgiven despite it. He says it's just as if we never sinned in the first place. Think of that... He says that when a person is redeemed, the truth becomes that they have no sin... which means they've actually never sinned. In salvation, God does the impossible. The guilty become actually innocent. Impure sinners become as holy as God Himself — beloved offspring of a pure God. Pure, as in: 'never sinned,' and our sinful souls as red as crimson become as white as freshly fallen snow. Utterly free of all guilt for all eternity!"

There was a silent pause as Mr. V stared at Juan, then he dropped his head and looked down at his folded hands. "I ain't been much fer church talk... but if I was, I'd be likely checkin' out yer church."

Juan smiled and nudged him in the arm. "I'd love for you to check out our church anytime," he said with a smile. He stood and put his hand on Mr. V's shoulder – "Church or no church, I'd like to pray for that bad ticker if you don't mind."

"Well, sure... 'preciate it," he answered. Juan nodded to me, and I hopped off the tailgate to stand next to him as we both put our hands on his shoulders -- Pastor Juan started to pray.

"Father, we thank you for Mr. Van Clief's life and are truly grateful for the help he's giving to your great work. We know that your interest in him didn't just start this week... you've had your hand on him for his entire life. Everything that's happened in his life until now has borne the mark of your guiding hand and protection. You've brought him to this point in his life with your strong hand of mercy and for your own noble purpose. We ask now for you to touch his body with healing and the strength to fulfill that purpose...."

I felt Mr. V's body shudder, and he suddenly sat up straight as if he'd been startled. Juan kept praying, "Even more, Lord, we pray for healing in his spirit and renewal in his soul. May he sense at this moment the unfathomable love that you have for him. You love him just the way he is, just the way he has been, and you will love him without reservation until the last of his appointed days. In faith, we thank you for healing his body... thank you for touching his soul... thank you for opening his eyes to the depth of your love for him. We commit him to your sovereign care and mighty power in Jesus' glorious name."

Mr. V shook again with a slight shudder. I noticed that his face was wet with tears. We stood quietly in silent prayer as we waited for him to get his composure; finally, he looked up, slightly embarrassed. "Guess I'm turnin' soft in my old age," he quipped as he wiped his eyes.

"That's the first thing that God does when he draws us to himself," Juan said, "he starts to soften our heart."

Mr. V put his hand up to ask him to stop. "I 'preciate all yer prayers, Reverend, but I don't think God's lookin t' save the likes o' me..." he paused with a distant look in his eye, "... there's some things in life whut can't be undone." Juan decided not to press him about it; it was clear that a seed had been planted, now it was God's job to make it grow.

WITH THAT, Mr. V rubbed his sleeve across his face and climbed to his feet. As he stood up, a surprised look suddenly came over his face; "Well, I'll be..." he said distractedly.

"What's wrong?" I asked him.

"Reckon it's the first time in near 70 years I ain't had a pain in that leg standin' on it." He shifted his weight to it and hopped slightly... "Well, I'll be...."

"What'd I tell you!" Juan said with a smile, "God always gives more than we ask – we prayed for your heart, and he healed your leg too!"

Mr. V took a deep breath and rolled his left shoulder a few times.... "Come to think of it," he said with amazement, "I ain't feelin' no pain in my chest neither." He looked at Pastor Juan, surprised, "You folks are sure differnt from church folk I'm accustomed to... I'm near inclined t' be joinin' ya if I ain't careful."

"I hope you aren't careful then!" Juan joked.

⌘

HINDERED

"Did you hear that?
~ Pete

On Friday morning, I was more excited than ever to get to the farm – it was time to start putting up the tent! The plan was to prep the field in the morning and then uncrate the tent and get it laid out on Friday afternoon. The 'tent raising' was planned for Saturday morning. We already had a small army from both churches who'd volunteered to help on their day off.

Pete was here to help with preparations, along with a half dozen others. Pastor Juan greeted everyone and thanked them for helping again - we'd gotten used to calling him PJ, so everyone kidded him about that. Mr. V showed us how to hitch the mower on Bessy, and then Pete headed for the North field. I checked on the irrigation systems that had been started up the night before; they were all working perfectly, watering the newly planted fields.

With that done, we began to take stock of the tent gear. It was obvious that Mr. V had been meticulous in packaging things; even though it had been stored for decades, it didn't look like a thing was missing. We loaded the crates onto a trailer. The three long telephone pole-sized center poles were secured to it, with a set of wheels attached to the other end.

It was after eleven o'clock AM when we finished. I exited the barn and looked out toward the north. We could just barely see the tractor a mile away in the distance. The panoramic view of the open field made me recall the sight that Chozeq had shown me of God's angelic guardians. If only Pete knew the company that he was in, I thought to myself with a sense of awe.

About thirty minutes later, we saw Pete riding Bessy up the dirt road toward the house – he was singing at the top of his lungs, and there were trails of tears streaking the dust on his face. He jumped down from the tractor, beaming like a lighthouse, and hugged me.

"You okay?" I asked him curiously.

"Yeah, I must look crazy," he answered unapologetically as he wiped his face with the bottom of his shirt. "Don't know what came over me... when I was down there mowing, it just felt like this awesome presence of God came around me... I can't explain it." He thought about it for a second and added, "I had such a strong feeling that God is getting ready to do something here... something amazing!"

I shuddered slightly as that familiar chill ran up my spine; I looked over at PJ, and he looked back with the same reaction and then smiled with a subtle nod.

Mr. V. walked out of the barn just then with a brisk swagger in his step; he hadn't used his cane all day. "Guess the mowin's done okay," he commented as he saw the tractor, "we kin hitch up the trailer soon's we eat."

There was something different about Mr. V. It was more than just his improved physical condition; he was like a man with a mission all of a sudden. The look in his eye was earnest and purposeful. I couldn't help thinking that he reminded me of a commander preparing the bulwarks for battle.

"We'll lay out th' poles' n check the ropes' n canvas this afternoon," he directed. "The more we have ready fer tomorrow th' better." He squinted at the western sky... "I'm a mite worried 'bout that sky there though... could be some rain comin'."

I looked up at the sky, wondering whether he could really predict the weather with nothing but a glance. Mr. V. just rubbed his chin as he studied the horizon... "I think ya may's well shut down th' irrigation after lunch," he decided. "Fact is, from the look of it, we may need t' be postponin' that tent raisin'," he added. "It won't do t' be tryin' that in a muddy field... no sir... that won't do at all."

I looked at him, stunned. "B-but, we'd have to wait a whole week before we'd have the help we need again," I protested.

"Can't be helped," he insisted, "would never git th' traction to raise 'er if it's muddy," he explained as he pulled off his cap and scratched his head, staring toward the north field.

THE SOUND of a car pulling up the long drive made us turn to see Sean Daniels park and climb out with a large bag from Carmine's; "Lunch is served!" he announced.

I turned and looked back at the sky with its darkening clouds; my spirit was feeling like a balloon with the air gone out of it as I slowly followed everyone else toward the porch.

I had no appetite as I sat on the porch looking out at the darkened sky. PJ had used the blessing for the food as an opportunity to pray that the storm would miss us, but it didn't look like it was going anywhere.

While I sat there quietly staring, a thought suddenly filled my consciousness – in fact, it was more like a voice; it startled me with its clarity. The words were unmistakable... just as if they'd been spoken aloud. I felt Pete's hand grip my arm and turned to see him looking at me with a shocked expression. His face looked like all the blood had drained from it.

"Did you hear that?" he asked in an awe-filled voice. I nodded yes, momentarily unable to speak. PJ looked at both of us apprehensively, "What's wrong?" he asked, his face revealing his confusion.

Pete didn't answer. Instead, he stood to his feet and looked out toward the tractor; I immediately stood up alongside him. "I-it's t-the voice..." he said to me in a hushed whisper, "...the same voice I heard at the chapel." He looked at me with a thrilled expression, "Did you hear the same as me... did you hear what he said to do?" I nodded, still unable to talk. The words repeated in my mind...

IT'S NOW TIME... Hitch the trailer.

A LOUD THUNDERCLAP suddenly shook the house, making everyone duck for cover. The air turned wet and cold as if a tremendous downpour was about to fall. The sound of the thunder was still echoing off the barns as we heard the voice speak again....

ONLY TRUST... Hitch the trailer.

PETE and I looked at each other wide-eyed and started walking toward the steps. "What's going on?" PJ asked... "you guys look like you've seen a ghost."

"Heard, actually," I said, leaning to speak in his ear. He looked back and forth between Pete and me as the realization dawned on him. "Y-you? You both heard it?"

"Whut in blazes is goin' on with you people?" Mr. V. said as he watched the three of us.

His words were interrupted by another tremendous thunderclap – this one even louder than the first.

. . .

IT's TIME... NOW! the voice commanded urgently.

AS EVERYONE DUCKED for cover from the frightening sound of the thunder, Pete took off running, surprising me. I chased after him, catching up just as he bounded down the porch steps, and I jumped right behind him. The instant that our feet touched the ground, a third enormous clap of thunder shook the air; it made my hair stand straight, and I spun around looking to see where the lightning had struck.

Instead of lightning, however, I saw the scene around me suddenly freeze. Everything was standing motionless like it was frozen in time. Pete hung suspended in midair between steps, and the air became utterly still. I looked up at the blackened sky and realized that the clouds were still moving; then, I began to see that their blackened bellows were filled with a vast sea of black-winged creatures. The sharp edges of their jagged wings could be seen undulating like a massive swarm of angry bats – so many that their numbers obscured the sun.

No sooner did this realization strike me than my attention was drawn to a flash of bright light. I recognized Ardent as he materialized on the porch roof in front of me. While I watched, he raised his blazing sword above his head, sending a beam of blinding light skyward that cut through the black hoards above. Immediately the sky was filled with bright flashes as a legion of angelic warriors appeared. They cut the sky open as they swept the hellish beasts aside, causing the black clouds to split apart and roll back like a giant curtain opening above us. My heart was beating wildly as I watched the incredible scene.

THEN, more quickly than it had begun, it was over. I stood looking up into the bright sunny sky as black clouds continued to roll back in the distance. Pete stopped in his tracks and looked up in surprise, watching the sight with his mouth hanging open. PJ and the others ran down from the porch and stared into the sky in amazement. To them, the transformation from cold darkness to warm sunshine had been instantaneous, making them gasp in wonder.

"Well, I'll be..." Mr. V. said as he stared upward from the porch steps.

I looked at him awkwardly, hoping to avoid having to explain what had just happened. "W-we... It's... N-now is... I mean... we should hitch the trailer now..." I stammered, pointing toward the tractor. Pete looked at me and swallowed hard, concealing our shared secret, then he looked at the ground and continued on toward Bessy.

⌘

GUARD DUTY

The tent was in better shape than we could have dreamed. It honestly looked practically new as we stretched it out in the open field and drove a few large stakes into the ground in the places Mr. V designated. We followed his directions to roll it up in preparation for the morning. With his guidance, we laid the center poles in position and secured the tether ropes used to stand them in place. Mr. V. took a final inventory and looked into the evening sky. "If this clear weather holds, we should be in good shape fer morning," he said.

We scanned the field full of gear, and a thought occurred to several of us at the same time: "Think this stuff will be okay out here all night?" Pete was the first to ask it.

"We could ask the police to keep an eye on it," I suggested.

"They can't spend all night watching one place," PJ reasoned.

"I'll stay," Pete volunteered.

"You can't stay here all alone," PJ cautioned.

"I'll be fine… the cops can check on me once in a while…."

"I'll stay," I interrupted him. "I can stay with you. I'll just call mom and let her know."

Mom had no problem with the idea; she offered to dig out the camping gear and soon arrived with a pair of sleeping bags and a lantern, along with a pile of snacks to hold us over. Mr. V offered us some of his firewood to build a campfire, and Carmine brought out a few thermoses full of chicken soup, coffee, and hot cider. It was a fantastic clear summer night – the moon wasn't full, but the stars looked close enough to touch.

As we lay looking into the night sky Pete broke the silence... "Mind if I ask you a question?" he said.

"Sure, what is it?"

"Since I've become... you know, a Christian, things have been pretty wild. Like with hearing those voices and that stuff with Chase at the prison and what happened today... I'm starting to realize, though, that stuff like this isn't really normal... not too common, I mean... I mean, it's kind of unusual... right?"

"Yeah, you could definitely say that."

"Yeah, well anyway, I keep noticing that it's mostly when you're around that stuff happens. What is it about you... is that like a special gift you have or something?"

The question was completely unexpected and made me uncomfortable – I was glad that it was too dark for him to see my face turning beet red. "Wow..." I said in genuine surprise, "I-I guess... so... I mean, it's not me... it's got nothing to do with anything I'm doing."

I took a deep breath and let it out slowly – the question I'd asked Chozeq about this very thing was fresh on my mind. "God's not only doing things here in Center Springs; his work is flourishing all over the world," I said, trying to paraphrase Chozeq's answer. "His Spirit is moving like this everywhere." I thought for a minute and then added, "There are certain times when He does things that are really special... really amazing. I think we're lucky enough to be living in one of those times... He just happens to be letting us be part of what He's doing."

"I'm kinda new at this," Pete said, still staring into the sky, "but I don't think luck has anything to do with it... I think He knows exactly what He's doing right now... and who He's doing it with... it's for a reason." He rose up on one elbow and looked at me: "What do you think the reason is?" he asked.

Pete's question suddenly pierced me like an arrow... what do you think the reason is? It instantly triggered the most horrific memory of my life. Chozeq's terrifying words echoed in my mind: "...here lies the purpose of our struggle!" The image of what he showed me when he spoke them filled my consciousness. I could see his flaming sword pointing toward those gates teaming with human souls... utterly hopeless as they writhed in excruciating agony. I could suddenly smell the sulfur and hear their terrified cries. Chozeq's words seared themselves into my mind all over again: "Mark it well and lose not the image of it from thy earthly mind!"

I gasped as the horror of it filled me, and I rolled onto my side as if I'd been kicked in the stomach. My heart was racing fiercely, and I struggled to catch my breath as tears flooded my eyes.

"Jimmy! What's wrong?!" Pete yelled urgently, "...are you alright?!" I felt his hand on my shoulder as he knelt next to me; "What is it, man? What's wrong... are you hurt?!"

I shook my head no, doing my best to calm down and catch my breath. I lay staring into the campfire, projecting the terrifying images in my mind onto its white-hot flames and bright red embers. The fact that the campfire was tangible seemed to help – I slowly drew my gaze away from it, leaving the horrific scene behind.

I looked up at Pete slowly, noticing how the light from the fire reflected in his face and danced against the white lettering on his sweatshirt. I had to swallow a few times before I could talk.

I pushed myself away and sat up, looking over at the confusion and concern on his face." T-There's only one reason..." I said softly, "... it's the same reason He does everything here ...on earth, I mean. It's the reason Jesus came ...the reason He died."

Pete studied my face, noticing the tears; the concern in his expression changed to something else – a reflection of something the Spirit was doing in his heart. I saw him swallow hard; he watched me intently as I continued.

I grabbed a split log from the firewood pile beside me and touched it to the fire but didn't put it in. Words seemed to want to flow from somewhere deep inside me as I started to talk, beginning with a verse that came rushing to mind: "Hell has enlarged herself, and opened her mouth without measure.[1] Those are words from the book of Isaiah," I said. Pete's eyes grew larger, and he swallowed again. "Hell is real, Pete. It's even more real than us sitting here right now. Everything we see and experience here …this whole life, it's just temporary… it's gonna be gone soon. But Hell is eternal… it's not gonna end… ever."

A fearful expression briefly crossed Pete's face, but then his expression changed quickly to sadness. I noticed the hint of a tear in his eyes as they became glassy in the reflected firelight.

"You said it this morning yourself…." I said. "It feels like God is about to do something here… right here in this field… something totally unbelievable." A breeze suddenly blew across the field as if the Spirit was adding confirmation to those words. It sent a thrill through my Spirit. A few more tears ran down Pete's face as he scanned the land and nodded in agreement.

"The reason He's going to do it…." I heard myself continue, "isn't just to make the church bigger, or even to make the world better. He's doing it for just one reason – the same purpose that He has planned for and poured His entire soul into since the Garden where Adam fell. It's the thing that He cares about day and night …the thing He can't stop thinking about for even an instant."

I leaned forward and poked the fire with the log I was holding, then drew it back. "It's to save as many souls as possible. To save them from the greatest horror in the universe - something that's so much worse than death." I tossed the log onto the fire, releasing a cloud of sparks that flew upward; "Pete! Believe me when I say it's an eternal destiny more terrifying than people could ever imagine!"

Pete wiped the tears that were welling up in his eyes and looked down. "That's powerful stuff… makes you wonder why nobody talks about it, you know? When you talk about it, it's almost like you've been there and seen it." He looked up at me, "That's a gift. Sometimes, when you talk about stuff like that, people can practically see it. How do you do that?"

"I guess I didn't know I was doing that... it's just how I feel mostly... and look who's talking about gifts -- who's the one hearing supernatural voices?"

He looked up at me and raised his eyebrows, "Based on what happened today, you're apparently doing that now too," he answered with a nervous smile.

IT WAS AROUND 3 AM when I awoke with a funny feeling... it was hard to explain at first, a vague sense that someone was watching us. The campfire had died down to just some glowing embers. I got up and pulled a few logs from the woodpile and put them on top of some thinner sticks, on the red coals, carefully arranging them and blowing until I'd gotten a flame started.

I sat with my back to the fire to fight off the night chill, just staring into the darkness at nothing in particular. Pete was sound asleep with just the top of his head poking out of his sleeping bag.

As my eyes adjusted to the dark again, I noticed something glowing out near the edge of the field. It was a pair of reddish dots just about a foot off the ground – I stared at them, trying to figure out what they were... or if I imagined them. Then they suddenly began to move... rising another foot or two higher, and I heard a snarling growl.

The realization struck me... I'd been staring at a wolf! Judging from the sound of its growl and the height of its eyes, it was an enormous wolf! Something my father taught me years earlier came rushing to mind.

Never stare a wolf in the eyes, he once told me on a camping trip. Direct eye contact is confrontational to wolves, and they'll want to prove their dominance.

Oh great, I thought to myself – and here I've been staring it down for the past five minutes!

It also occurred to me that wolves are pack animals – that meant that either this one wasn't alone or, if it was alone, that it was probably sick or rabid. Neither possibility sounded very good!

I could hear it slowly inching closer, snarling louder and louder. It was close enough to now be seen in the dim firelight, especially its white fangs as it bared its teeth. I thought about waking Pete but was afraid that the wolf could interpret his surprise as fear and then attack. Regardless, however, it wasn't backing down... it just kept getting closer! In another half-minute, it'd be in pouncing range.

I grabbed a burning stick from the fire and slowly rose to my feet, carefully placing the flame between us. Bad idea that only seemed to challenge it – it bared its fangs even wider. It growled harshly, then let loose a barrage of loud ferocious barking that made the most vicious junkyard dog sound like a pound puppy.

Pete's head popped out of his sleeping bag, and I heard him scream in surprise – so much for the plan not to wake him. Just as I feared, the wolf immediately attacked – I watched it bounding toward us with a look of blood lust on its face. I stood frozen – there wasn't time to do anything but cry out in an incoherent prayer, and even that sounded more like a scream of terror!

The next thing I knew, there was a bright flood of light and the sound of a gunshot! I looked toward the source... in Carmine's parking lot to see a policeman standing in the light of his car's headlights, holding his pistol in the air. The wolf jumped straight in the air as if he'd been launched by a giant spring and then took off running in the opposite direction.

I bent forward, catching my breath as I tried to calm my racing heartbeat. Pete was on his feet, holding his head in his hands and pacing back and forth. I heard Sheriff Flanagan's voice and realized that he was just a few yards away, walking toward us. "You guys alright?" he asked, "Good thing I happened along just then."

"Wow, you're not kidding...." I said in a breathless voice, "...you saved our lives!" Pete and I looked at each other... "At least, his life," I joked nervously, "... I'm pretty sure I could have gotten away while it ate Pete."

"Thanks, buddy," Pete retorted, "good to know you had my back." We both laughed in relief, and he slapped me on the back; "glad you're okay," he said.

Sheriff Flanagan holstered his gun and aimed his giant flashlight around at the surrounding fields. "It's pretty unusual to see a wolf around here... especially alone; they usually stay clear of people," he noted. "There haven't been any other sightings reported... it must've come straight here from the state park -- that's a good 20 miles. I'll call in an APB."

Another patrol car pulled up as we finished giving the sheriff our report. "I've stationed a patrol here for the rest of the night," the sheriff said, "just in case that wolf gets hungry again." We laughed at his joke, grateful for the protective gesture.

"Thanks again, sheriff," we both said, shaking his hand.

PETE and I sat down by the fire. "This makes two crazy things that have happened today," Pete noted. "I guess something doesn't want to see God do what He's planning here," he concluded.

"Something or someone," I added. "That was pretty scary, I have to admit... but we don't have anything to worry about – God's in control. There's nothing that any enemy can do to stop what He's planning."

"I get that," Pete said, "I just wonder if he needs us to still be around when He does it."

I laughed at his joke nervously. To be honest, I hadn't ever seen either one of us in any of my visions of future events.

⌘

STAND

Stand and See the Salvation of the Lord!
~ Exodus 14:13

W e never made it back to sleep. Before we knew it, the early summer dawn was lighting the eastern horizon, and soon after that, we heard Carmine arrive to open his diner. He greeted the patrolman on duty and then walked out to say good morning to us.

"The officer told me what'a happened… a wolf?" he exclaimed, "that's the first I ever hear of è wolf here!"

I nodded to confirm what he'd heard. "The Sheriff said it came from 20 miles away; I guess it must have smelled your chicken soup," I joked.

"You like my soup! I give you all the soup you è want! Come and have some breakfast. I make somethin' è special for you boys."

We followed him back to the diner, taking the opportunity to wash up while he got started in the kitchen. As we sat at a table, Angela arrived, surprised to see us inside. She smiled as she greeted us, and we suddenly had placemats and silverware, as if by magic. "How does she do that so fast?" Pete asked, turning his head to watch her walk away. There seemed to be a little extra interest on his part that I hadn't picked up before. I noticed her look back over her shoulder at him – she smiled when she caught him looking at her. I registered the interesting encounter with a smile but didn't mention it.

It seemed like Carmine's breakfast would never end... it might not have if we hadn't thrown our hands up in surrender. I lost track of how many sausages, pancakes, and omelets we put away, but if that wolf had eaten this much, he wouldn't have been hungry for a week.

"What d'ya say we go raise a tent?" Pete said as he pushed back from the table. "Now you're talking!" I exclaimed.

PETE WAS THINKING ALOUD that he should take his car to pick up Mr. V when we noticed him driving Ol' Bessy up the dirt road from his house. Pete glanced at his watch; "It isn't even six o'clock yet!" he noted – amazed how early the old man was out and about.

"That figures..." I said with a smile.

"Thought sure I heard a gunshot las' night," Mr. V said as he climbed off the tractor. We brought him up to speed on the events of the night. "Ain't never seen a wolf in these parts b'fore... not in all my days," he said, scratching his head as he considered the mystery. "Ya say it was alone, eh? That might explain why it attacked... probly rabies."

"Well, Sheriff Flanagan put out an APB to see if they can catch it before it hurts anyone," I informed him.

TWO MORE CARS pulled into the parking lot just then – one was PJ's, and the other was Mrs. Mirabella with Anna and Mandy. "Wow, you're early!" I said to Anna as she ran over to say good morning.

She smiled and handed me a cup of hot cocoa, "We brought you breakfast!" she said, beaming proudly as she waved toward her mom with a few foil-covered plates. I didn't have the heart to tell her we'd already eaten a week of breakfasts. Especially since they'd obviously gotten up at the crack of dawn to do it. I looked at Pete with an expression that begged him to play along....

"Thanks! That was so thoughtful of you!" I said.

Pete caught my hint, "Oh, yeah, thanks, that's awesome," he said, doing his best to conceal a slightly apprehensive look.

PJ whispered in my ear, "you guys ate already, didn't you?" I pretended to ignore him and just smiled at Anna. The smile on her face was worth forcing a few extra bites of food. I walked with her to thank her mom and Mandy while Pete took PJ aside and quietly brought him up to speed on the night's events. Pastor came to the same conclusion that we had… something was trying hard to prevent us from continuing.

BY SEVEN O'CLOCK, the lot was practically full of cars. Not only did we have the original group of 40 people from Wednesday, but there were at least two dozen more who had come to help as well.

Mr. V. approached us with a concerned look – he was pointing to the sky again. We followed his gaze to see that the western sky had become filled again with thick grey rain clouds, and we could hear the rumble of distant thunder. The breeze carried air that felt moist, although the morning sun was still shining on us from the east. I studied the clouds for any sign of the same enemies I'd seen yesterday, but they looked like typical rain clouds this time.

"I just got a thunderstorm warning on my phone… Anna said as she walked up to us, looking up at the threatening sky." She showed me her weather app with a radar map – it looked like the storm was headed straight for us. I looked at PJ, concerned – there was no doubt in my heart that we had to go ahead. We needed to get this tent raised now!

PJ gathered everyone together in the field beside the waiting tent and thanked them all for coming, explaining how important it was that we get the tent up before the rain hit. He led the group in prayer.

"Lord, this is the day we've waited for… we've been thrilled to witness the work of your own hand in providing a place for us through Mr. Van Clief's generous offer to let us borrow his tent and the field we're standing on. We know that there are forces at work that have tried to stop what you're doing. Thank you for the way you have provided what's been needed at every turn. We now agree together in asking your blessing on this consecrated ground and jointly dedicate this field and this tent to you... make it a place of blessing for countless souls... and most importantly, a place where many will come to find your grace and forgiveness. In faith, we trust that you are about to do a great work on this very spot – like Moses and the rescued children of Israel, we hear you telling us to simply Stand and See the Salvation of the Lord!"

A HUGE BREEZE blew across the field from the east as PJ finished praying, blowing against the storm front as if adding a dramatic endorsement to his words. I looked across the large group, seeing many with hands raised and tears in their eyes. It occurred to me that the earnest prayers of this same group were responsible for the way God was moving in our small town. Prayer moves the hand of God, I whispered to myself, echoing a small voice within my spirit.

PJ finally handed it off to Mr. V, who greeted the group cordially. "I gotta say," he admitted, "I feared we might not get 'nough folks to handle what's needed... I shoulda known there'd be plenty o' y'all." Everyone laughed. "Well, that thar storm is fixin' ta mess things up pretty good, so we better git movin' in a hurry." Then he split the group into work teams and handed out mission instructions with impressive efficiency, proving once again that there was more to Mr. V than met the eye.

He designated PJ, Pete, and me as group leaders – Pete's group was tasked with raising the huge center poles while our teams were told how to anchor the ropes along the back and sides of the long tent. We unfurled the huge canvas, and Pete's team slid the center poles into position at their tent mounts and attached thick ropes to their tops. The ropes were threaded through pulleys attached to deep stakes we'd driven the day before on the other side of the field and then connected to Ol'Bessy.

On Mr. V's signal, Pete started driving the tractor slowly forward while his team anchored the large poles and the rest of us stretched out the sides and stood up the side poles. The enormous tent rose perfectly off the ground and opened outward like a gigantic flower as the main poles lifted to their standing positions. It was amazing how smoothly the whole thing went – even Mr. V called it a miracle. He nodded toward the storm with concern: "If the wind catches 'er b'fore she's tied, it'll rip 'er t' shreds," he said nervously.

The storm was nearly on top of us as men from the church frantically drove stakes to anchor the ropes that folks were holding. I could see the rain coming across the land to our west, moving fast and getting closer. I closed my eyes and breathed a plea for God's help; at the other end of the tent, I could see PJ facing the storm and closing his eyes in prayer as well. As I prayed, I could hear the rain, so close now that it seemed like it was already on top of us; then, a loud thunderclap forced me to open my eyes.

WHEN I DID, I was suddenly able to see the angelic guardians once more. They were standing at the edges of the field facing outward toward the storm with their mighty hands raised. I looked around in amazement as I realized that the rain was all around us – completely encircling the field – yet not a drop had fallen anywhere inside its borders.

Winds were swirling as everyone was scrambling to secure the ropes – it took an hour or so to get all the sides staked and tightly tied. Soon after it was finished, the storm finally cleared, rolling off to the east.

Everyone cheered as the last stake was driven and the final rope was anchored. I looked toward our guardian protectors and smiled, bowing my head in thanks.

"Well, if that ain't the darndest thing I ever seen...." Mr. V said as he walked up behind me and scratched his bald head. I turned quickly, half-expecting him to say he'd seen the angels. "Did I jus' see it rainin' all around an' not a drop on us?" he asked, staring at the storm moving away.

"I think so…" I answered honestly, in relief.

"Yep… sure 'nough… darned if didn't…" he repeated in amazement. He looked over at me and scanned the rest of the group… "Guess the man upstairs is lookin' out fer you folks," he concluded with a tone that revealed it was more than just an expression. I nodded my head in agreement and smiled.

Just then, he noticed someone trying to hang one of the side curtain flaps… "That's upside down!" he shouted as he quickly walked off to show them how it's done. Soon he had a pair of teams trained and working on hanging the rest of them. Meanwhile, a group of carpenters began pulling lumber from a truck for the central platform inside.

The tent was completely assembled by lunchtime, and Carmine's brother Enrico arrived with his crew to install the lights. The sight of the enormous tent actually standing there in real life seemed surreal.

THEN, just as I thought things couldn't get any more unbelievable, PJ and I turned to see an 18-wheeler pull into the lot. The driver walked right up to us with a clipboard in his hand; "Reverend Rodriguez?" he asked.

"Y-yes…?" PJ answered uncertainly.

"I have a load here for you," he said as he handed him the clipboard. PJ's eyes opened wide in stunned amazement as he read it and then looked at the driver… "REALLY?" he asked.

"That's what it says…" the driver confirmed, "…and that's what's in the truck, sure as morning."

A crowd had gathered around at this point, curious to learn what this was all about. PJ followed the driver to the back of the 40-foot trailer and stood back as the doors were opened. There inside, stacked neatly from floor to ceiling and filling the trailer entirely from front to back, were seats – folding theater seats, to be exact.

"There are a thousand of them!" PJ yelled to the crowd around him. "Here's the letter that came with them," he said as he climbed up onto the tailgate and read it aloud:

Dear Rev. Rodriquez

These seats have been salvaged from the auditorium at Point West Theological Seminary. Please accept them as a donation to God's work in Center Springs with the university's permission. We ask that they be dedicated in loving memory of Kelly O'Malley.

Signed,

Edward G Johnson

President, Johnson Engineering.

TEARS STARTED to well up in my eyes when I heard Kelly's name, and I looked up at PJ.

"...How?" I mouthed silently.

Mom walked up beside me and put her arm around my shoulders. "That's the company Mr. O'Malley works for now," she explained, beaming. "They heard about what was happening here a few days ago, and the timing couldn't have been better. Ward said everything just fell into place -- his boss even paid for the truck to deliver them."

I looked back at her, completely speechless, then turned and hugged her tight.

⌘

PREPARING

The effectual fervent prayer of a righteous man avails much.
~ James 5:16

I t honestly felt like I was dreaming as I stood at the back of the enormous tent, looking over the rows and rows of seats toward the front platform. The seats were empty, but I knew they would soon be filled – I felt confident there was no stopping God's work from going forward now.

It was after dark on Saturday night, and everyone had gone home – everyone except PJ, Pete, and me, that is. The tent glowed brightly under Enrico's excellent lighting setup. He even added extra plugs for the guitar amps and PA system with Ground Fault circuits and surge suppressors to keep things humming static-free. The seats had all been neatly laid out in rows and sections; it was fantastic how perfect their condition – they were worn looking, but not one showed any sign of damage.

However, something had been troubling me for a few hours, and I had no idea what it was. As much as I struggled to remember my vision, I couldn't recall any hint of what we might have missed; still, the feeling was relentless that there was still unfinished work.

I wandered toward the platform, looking down at the ground, as the burden in my heart just seemed to grow heavier. When I reached the front, it finally overcame me. I dropped to my knees at the makeshift altar and was suddenly overwhelmed with a burden so heavy that I struggled to even breathe. I laid my forehead against the altar and began to cry.

PJ and Pete were standing outside and happened to notice me there. "Is everything alright, Jim?" I heard PJ say as they came alongside me. I couldn't answer. Both of them knelt and put their hands on my shoulders, then began to join me in prayer. The more we prayed, the heavier the overwhelming burden grew. It wasn't dark or oppressive – just the opposite; it was like the presence of God Himself was pressing on top of me.

It was impossible to form words, but inside my spirit, I was pleading. Images and emotions surged through my mind, and the impression of God's closeness made me feel a crushing sense of my own guilt. Chozeq's words from months before echoed through my mind:

"...All are equally condemned, and all who ask are freely redeemed."

Searing images of Hell hung ever-present in my consciousness – they blew against me like a terrifying tempest of scorching heat.

At the same time, cutting through all the chaos were vivid scenes from that astonishing vision of the cross... I saw the earth-changing blast when Jesus cried:

"...It is Finished!"

The glorious brightness of a million redeemed souls thrilled me as I recalled seeing Hells' hosts scatter and my own robes being made a blinding white.

A sudden awareness of Kelly's amazing words made me flinch as I remembered again how she'd whispered them in my ear:

"...Your special mission is SO important, Jimmy!"

In my mind's eye, Dad's face came clearly into focus, bringing to mind all the joy I'd felt in that moment of reunion. The words he said when we parted seemed to reverberate over and over:

"...Now you have important work to do!"

Everything pointed to something... some mission... an urgent commission... but I still didn't know what it was! I felt a sense of panic as if a million people were waiting for me to answer a question that I couldn't hear and had no idea how to answer. All I could do was plead... and cry.

PJ and Pete were praying more and more earnestly beside me – I could hear their tear-filled cries as they struggled with the same growing sense of need for God's leading. Then gradually... imperceptibly... their voices faded, seeming further and further away as they grew fainter until I suddenly realized that I was enveloped in silence.

THEN CHOZEQ'S booming voice shook me, making my eyes snap open. We were high in the air, looking down on the lighted tent below us. "...Trust...."...that was what he had said. If I'd been in a less troubled state of mind, I might have seen the irony in being told to trust by an angel who was suspending me in midair.

"What have we missed?!" I begged, "... we've done everything you showed me... the tent is ready... I've done all to ensure its arrival, just like you said. But it feels like something's missing?"

He looked at me kindly, "Ye have indeed done well Lad, I need not tell thee that our Lord is pleased – already in thine heart ye know that He is." He looked down at the empty tent below. "What was revealed to thee has not yet been fulfilled. The night that ye witnessed has not yet arrived... all has not yet been done to ensure its arrival," he noted.

"But everything is in place... everything is ready," I argued.

"Nay, all is not ready. The most difficult preparations are still to be made – it is a great work that must yet be done here." Chozeq lifted his gaze and looked out across the lighted shops along Main Street and then nodded toward the scattered lights of homes beyond. "Although His work will be revealed here, His true work is not done in this tent, but in the hearts of restless souls."

"But only God Himself can change hearts," I said in dismay.

"Tis true indeed, Lad. The Lord himself must open the heart; He alone can put the key into the lock of the door and open it and get admittance for himself. He is the heart's master as he is the heart's maker. But it is the earnest prayers of the righteous that move His hand."

I knew he was right... I guess I'd always known that was true, but I still struggled. "Why?" I said carefully, "He's God; why does He need us at all? I mean, He's the only one who can soften people's hearts, and only He can bring people to the true repentance that saves them... He's the one who draws all men to Himself."

"Aye, ...if He is lifted up," Chozeq reminded as he added the rest of Jesus' words. He paused for a moment and then looked at me probingly, "Why does He appoint farmers to plant and harvest when He alone causes the bountiful yield?" he challenged. "Why is a child entrusted to a loving family when God alone makes them grow?"

I knew the answer to both of those, of course... it was because of weeds and droughts and for protection from things that cause harm. Children need to be taught and loved and nourished; it's not just growth that matters.

Chozeq simply looked at me as the answer to my question finally dawned on me. "That's why He says it's earnest prayer..." I repeated as it struck me. "The reason our most earnest prayers move His hand is because it's in those times when we're anxious and concerned that we're most willing to give care and nurture and protection to it." He nodded in confirmation with an approving smile.

"But, how can we provide nurture or protection for something invisible that the Spirit is doing?" I worried.

"Concern thyself only with earnest prayer," Chozeq said reassuringly, "...forget not that it is God who works."

"So... prayer is the preparation that's still missing," I said as I finally understood what he'd been revealing. "How long?" I asked, "... how much longer until the vision is fulfilled?" Chozeq nodded his head forward slightly with a look that said I should know better than to ask that. Then he gave my shoulders a firm encouraging grasp, and I saw him spread his enormous wings behind him.

"Soon Lad, it will be very soon…". The next thing I knew, he was gone, and I was kneeling again at the altar.

I JUMPED IMMEDIATELY to my feet, surprising PJ and Pete. "It's prayer! We have to pray!" I nearly shouted.

"Y-yeah… that's what we *were* doing…." Pete said in surprise, slightly confused.

PJ just looked at me curiously, then got up and leaned back to sit on the altar rail, crossing his arms without a word.

"We're not done with our preparations…." I said to him excitedly, "We need to have a prayer vigil… that's what's missing! We need everyone! We need to rock Heaven for revival!"

PJ uncrossed his arms and smiled. "Wow… Yes!" he said with a mix of relief and conviction on his face, "You're right!" He stood and paced as he thought it over. "That can be our first service here… a dedication service. We should do it tomorrow night at 6:00… I'll announce it in church tomorrow morning; we should call Pastor Wilkes to help too… a prayer vigil at the tent to pray for Center Springs!"

I AWOKE Sunday morning to the incredible smell of French Toast and bacon. The past few weeks had been such a whirlwind that mom and I had hardly spoken; I guess she sensed it too and decided it was time for us to reconnect.

She smiled at me as I slid into my usual chair at the table. "Your French Toast is almost ready… I'll bet you're starved after all that farm work this week and sleeping outside." I didn't have the heart to tell her how much I'd eaten at Carmine's the previous morning. I could probably go another day before feeling very hungry. But, I can always make room for her French Toast, it's still the best… although, Mr. V's might be a real close 2nd place, I thought to myself.

"Your father got this recipe years ago from Mr. V," Mom said matter-of-factly... I think his are still a little better – that breakfast on Wednesday was so good!" she admitted. That revelation dropped into the pile of information about our family's past that had accumulated lately – I smiled at how cool the picture was becoming.

"Uncle Mike is anxious to have you back at the Sub Shop," she said.

"Oh yeah," I said, realizing that I'd almost forgotten about work, "I guess I can start back tomorrow. Tonight's gonna be a dedication service at the tent."

"Oh, okay," she said as she slid my plate in front of me and sat down with her own. She sat quietly, looking at me for a moment after we finished saying grace. It was as if she was mentally comparing me with her memories of the boy she knew me as a few months ago. "I'm so proud of you... the way you've handled every-thing the past few months... and what you've been able to do with Mr. Van Clief and that tent... I hardly recognize you... you've grown up so much."

"I haven't really done anything. Pastor Juan and everybody at FCS have done most of it," I argued with a slight blush.

"Um-hmm..." she said, unconvinced, as she sipped her coffee. "The sign of true humility is sharing credit," she said with the admiring look of a doting mother. I furrowed my brow in uncomfortable dissent, and she smiled.

I decided to change the subject. "Mr. V told me about how great-grandpa Moretti died," I said, figuring that would divert the conversation.

Mom nearly dropped her fork, and her eyes opened wide, "HE DID?!"

She listened intently as I told her the story, and then she sat silently for a moment, deep in thought. "You have no idea how many times your father tried to get him to tell what happened... the poor man, it must have been such a burden for him all these years." She looked up as another thought struck her; "Did he say anything more about how he knew my grandfather?"

"No, just that he knew him."

"It's just odd that Gramps or Dad never mentioned it," she noted thoughtfully.

"Did Great-Grandpa always live in Brooklyn?" I asked, trying to help solve the mystery. I never knew Gramps Farro; he died before I was born.

"Yeah," she confirmed, "He never visited here as far as I know. Even if he had, it doesn't seem likely that he and Mr. V ever met, at least, not that Mr. V would be likely to remember after all these years."

The question sort of hung in the air unanswered; "maybe I can ask Mr. V how they met," I offered.

"Oh no, don't bother," mom insisted, "it's really not important."

We let the question drop and moved on. "How are the O'Malleys doing?" I asked.

"As well as can be expected," she replied, "They haven't stopped talking about what a comfort you were."

"Me? You mean like when I was beating up the elevator and dealing with my anger issues?" I half-joked.

Mom gave me her classic 'Stop it' look... "No... you know what I mean. They were impressed with how much of a young man you've become – I'm not the only one who's noticed how much you've grown up; they noticed it too."

I was tempted to prove her wrong by crossing my eyes and sticking out my tongue or something but figured I'd just accept the compliment and move on. Maybe I really was growing up.

"Those seats that Mr. O's company sent us are amazing – "I said, switching the subject again, "they're practically in perfect condition. Did Mr. O think of that?"

"No, actually, it was Mr. Johnson who suggested it. He was at Kelly's Memorial service, you know. Ward says he hasn't stopped talking about how impressed he was with the service and all Kelly's friends. Ward even caught him watching the video on Kelly's blog again after they got back."

"Wow," I said, "The service didn't scare him or anything? It was pretty intense," I worried.

"Oh no, he loved it! He's a committed Christian… that was one of the reasons Ward wanted to work for him."

"Oh wow, that's pretty cool," I said.

There was a silent pause for a minute, then mom picked up the conversation again; "So tonight is a dedication service?" she asked.

"Well, yeah, that's what Pastor Juan is calling it… we weren't sure what to call it really… we just know that we need to pray for Center Springs. I mean, really pray."

Mom looked at me thoughtfully as the idea seemed to soak into her spirit; "That's a really good idea," she agreed, "that's exactly what we need."

⌘

DEDICATION

Let them make me a sanctuary; that I may dwell among them...
And there I will meet with you...
~ Exodus 25:8,22

Word about the dedication service spread fast. Practically everyone from the FCS meetings at Carmine's was there, plus most of the people from both our churches. Even with all those people, though, the tent was still just a third full.

One person I really hoped to see, Mr. V, was nowhere in sight. I promised myself that I'd make it my mission to get him to come at least once.

PJ and Pastor Wilkes were both on the platform; Pastor Wilkes opened the service and greeted everyone, then PJ opened in prayer. From the very start, we could feel that something would be different about being here; it seemed like a powerful Divine presence filled the place. PJ had only just started praying when someone broke down crying, and then soon, there were two or three more that were openly weeping along with her.

His prayer never really ended... at least he never said amen. He paused with his eyes still closed and started to sing a slow chorus. The instruments picked it up, and everyone joined in. That song led to another, and soon PJ was leading us in an intense worship service.

We sang like that for almost an hour. As the last chorus was being sung, PJ quietly walked down to where I stood in the front row and put his arm around me. He didn't have to say anything; the Spirit was already pulling on my heart so hard that it was beating out of my chest. He just looked at me, and I nodded back, then we walked back to the platform together. He walked me to the mic and then stepped aside as I stood looking at the crowd. The faces were familiar -- I'd known many of them all my life. Others were new friends from FCS, and most of the rest could be recognized from Kelly's memorial service. Some were still swaying with their eyes closed in worship; many of them had tears on their faces.

I took a deep breath to still my racing heartbeat and said a silent prayer, then began to share what was being impressed on my heart.

"It wasn't even a week ago that we found out we couldn't meet at Carmine's anymore... on account of how big this has grown. Now here we are in this..." I waved around at the amazing tent, and the crowd applauded. "I think God is telling us something!" Everyone celebrated again as shouts of worship and amen erupted throughout the audience.

I felt the Spirit's message bearing on me and grew serious as I looked out over their faces. "It's been pretty obvious that the enemy... you know the one I mean... he has tried hard this week to keep this from happening. I think that means we're doing something really important." More shouts of amen repeated through the crowd.

"The reason it's important is that there are lives at stake... more than lives even... there are souls at stake. God wants to rock Center Springs with a revival... he wants us to claim this city for his kingdom! As a few of us were here praying last night, we received a strong confirmation that this is the moment that he has decreed for something amazing to happen. I believe that with all my heart." There were more shouts of amen.

"...But before that can happen, we need to pray...." I caught Pete's eye as he looked at me and nodded back in earnest agreement. "We need to pray as hard as we can for as long as it takes until God starts changing hearts all over this town! I don't think the enemy who has tried to stop this is going to quit trying, so we need to do all we can and pray as hard as we can for God to do what only He can!"

I stopped and looked at PJ and Pastor Wilkes, "God's calling us to more than just a prayer service; I think He's calling us here to a prayer vigil.... We need to take hold of the horns of the altar and not let go until He pours out the blessing that He wants to give this town! People! ...there are souls at stake! The souls of people you see every day... people you work with and shop with... people you live with – who you love!"

I looked toward the back rows of empty seats and pointed, beginning to shout as the fervor of the Spirit's message seemed to lift me outside myself. "God has a name assigned... a soul destined, for every one of those empty seats... I don't think there's a single extra seat here – every one of them is here for a reason, and very soon, we're going to see them filled with transformed lives. In fact, this is only the beginning... the revival that starts here is going to spread across our country...!"

People were raising their hands and shouting in thanksgiving. The same promise was being confirmed in hearts all over the crowd.

Angela was sitting at the piano and suddenly shouted emphatically into her microphone....

"*IF MY PEOPLE...*" she began with her eyes squeezed closed, as a hush came over the crowd, "*...which are called by my name, ...will humble themselves and pray, ...and seek my face and turn to me....*"

People were holding their hands in the air with faces turned upward streaming with tears; each of her words seemed like it echoed in our hearts with the confirmation of the Spirit's voice.

The words washed over us with powerful force; "*...then I will hear from heaven... and forgive their sin, and heal your land. ...Now is the* *appointed time... Behold, My eyes are open, and My ears are attentive to your prayers from this place. I have chosen and consecrated it so that My name may dwell here; My eyes and My heart will be here at all times.*[1]

Seek Me while I may be found... Turn earnestly to me right now, and I will pour you out a blessing... pressed down, shaken together and flowing over. Ask now, and I will send upon you the latter rain that has waited until this appointed time. It will be a blessing so great that it will overflow and sweep across your land, bringing a mighty harvest of souls. Pray for your friends and your neighbors... pray that the Lord of the harvest will send laborers into fields that are white unto harvest! Ask earnestly and seek my face, for I am not hidden from you... ask freely, and it shall be freely given to you!"

THE SENSE of God's presence among us was so strong that no one dared speak... most of us hardly breathed as solemn awe fell over us all. I felt a sudden unction in my heart and spoke softly into the mic.

"The work that God has started doing is personal... He's doing it deep in the hearts of men and women... not just here in this place, but all through this city. His work in our city has begun... it's started... at this moment he's beginning to make himself known in every receptive heart."

I hardly realized that my voice began to rise louder as the fervor in my heart filled me. "Now is the time to pray for those you love who don't know him yet – lift them up before the throne – ask him to work his mighty work within their hearts!" My voice grew even louder as the message burned inside me... "There are no hearts in this city too callused or hardened for him to change... he stands ready tonight even to melt hearts of adamant! – He will break bars of iron! – He'll snap chains of bronze! He will lead those who are captives tonight into the broad open air of his freedom and fill them with joy that's unspeakable and full of glory! Tonight we must begin to pray for their souls... pray for their freedom... pray for their salvation! Pray that they find their way here to this place... this is their meeting place with the Lord of Life! He's waiting for them... He's been waiting for this moment at this place since the foundation of the world! This moment when His divine movement begins... when those living throughout Center Springs... and then our nation... begin to rush into the arms of Christ!"

I WAS SO CAUGHT up in the message that God was pouring into my heart that I barely noticed the steady stream of people who had begun to rush from their seats to the altar and fall to their knees. They filled the front, surrounding the platform, as more continued to file forward. Those who couldn't fit turned and knelt in the nearest rows of seats. People were pouring out their hearts in intercessory prayer, weeping and imploring God for the souls of friends and neighbors.

The power of their prayers was like a tremendous whirlwind that had the deafening sound of an enormous locomotive, and it was sweeping up everyone in its path. Even in my most astonishing vision, I'd never experienced anything quite like it. The move of the Spirit that it generated felt like it could blow away the entire city!

There were no more words that could match the intensity of what God was already speaking in every heart. I fell silent and staggered backward as a flurry of images rushed through my mind. They were faces of people I was being compelled to pray for. Teachers and coaches from school, checkers from the supermarket, kids from classes, people who had come into the sub shop, officers on the police force, inmates, and guards at the prison. I didn't even know most of them by name, but I could feel God's tremendous love for them and sensed the approaching horror of their eternal destinies. The ever-present memory of Hell's image burned in my mind as it waited for them like a relentless and terrifying predator. The crushing burden of that reality pulled me to my knees, and I found myself weeping and pleading for their salvation!

Mr. Van Clief's face came to mind, and just then, I heard one of the kids at the altar call out his name in her prayer. Her plea for his salvation was echoed by others all around her as they lifted their voices in agreement. "Yes, Lord!" "...please save him!" "...we lift him to you,

Lord!" An image instantly flashed through my mind. It didn't play like a movie but simply appeared like a memory of something that had already happened. I saw Mr. V. enter from the back of the tent; the seats were completely filled, there was no place for him to sit down. I saw him walk further and further down the aisle, and the closer he came to the front, the more his eyes filled with tears; he reached the front row and kept walking as his eyes overflowed, now tears were streaming down his face. He reached for the altar rail like a desperate man and collapsed to his knees.

I opened my eyes and looked at the place where I'd seen him kneeling, but it was filled with the girls who were lifting him in prayer. I glanced back at the rows of seats – all of them were still empty. I knew that it was more than just a dream – what I witnessed hadn't happened yet... but it would!

The implications of the lesson I'd been shown became clear to me. I looked over at PJ and Pastor Wilkes, who were both kneeling at their seats praying together, and made my way over to them. "We need to lift up their names!" I said urgently as I nudged their shoulders, "...I think we should all agree together ...about each name ...each person!"

Both of them stopped and looked up at me as I saw what looked like a deep burden being lifted from their furrowed brows – they smiled and nodded in agreement, and PJ jumped to his feet and hugged me. He nodded back to Pastor Wilkes, who had climbed to his feet and moved toward the mic. Pastor Wilkes began with a prayer that echoed the deep intercessory yearning surging around us. Then he quoted Matthew's Gospel where Jesus said that "if two of you shall agree on earth touching anything that they ask, it will be done for them of my Father who is in heaven. For where two or three are gathered together in my name, there I am in the midst of them.[2]"

He quietly invited anyone with a burden for someone to speak their name, offering to join together in praying for that person. Jillian, one of the girls who'd recently joined FCS, immediately shouted out through sobs. "My mother! ... she's got cancer... stage four... and she doesn't know the Lord..." she broke down weeping as she pleaded "... Please! ...please! pray for her! ...her name is Mel ...Melanie."

As Pastor began to pray for her, the surge of the Spirit's moving suddenly felt like a Saturn Five rocket was lifting off in our midst. Jillian and a ring of others kneeling around her collapsed to the ground as if stricken unconscious. I was physically jolted by an image of a woman I didn't know. She suddenly lurched from her seat as her body shook and then straightened – leaving her standing with a shocked look on her face. Her expression quickly turned from surprise to gratitude, and then she began to weep, crumbling to her knees beside the couch in desperate prayer. I felt a burning need to make my way to the altar rail and leaned over just as Jillian began to stir...

"Your mother has been healed... she's on her knees seeking Christ right now – go home to her!" She looked at me in shock, and then her face filled with an expression of overwhelming joy; two of her friends took her by the hands, gasping through their tears, and they ran out together.

The place erupted in waves of praise as word spread about what had happened. "Please pray for my brother Barry...," "...for my uncle Jay," "...for my father Sam," "...for Jen, my sister...." The rounds of requests and prayers continued as the powerful surge of the Spirit intensified and incredible deliverances began to unfold. People arrived to pick up sons or daughters at the exact moment that their names were being raised, only to stagger stunned and weeping to the altar as God took hold of them right then and there.

We had no sense of time passing; it was after midnight when I finally glanced at my watch, yet the power and presence we felt among us hadn't diminished in the slightest. If anything, it had grown stronger. The group had barely thinned, and there were still hundreds praying and weeping as names continued to be called out. Each time starting the amazing cycle of weeping, miracles, and praise all over again!

⌘

LENA'S VISION

Its power was frightening and awesome, but it was so incredibly beautiful...
~ Mrs. Mirabella

t 2:00 AM, a crowd of over a hundred people was still earnestly praying. I was kneeling with some of the FCS kids and felt Mom's hand on my shoulder. When I looked up, I saw her standing beside me with Mrs. Mirabella; their faces were wet from crying. Mom motioned for me to stand, and they both looked at me with uncertain expressions.

Mom spoke first: "Lena has something I'd like you to hear... something I think you might be able to help with," she said as she looked over at Anna's mom. Mrs. Mirabella looked at me nervously, glancing back and forth between Mom and me a few times before speaking.

"I saw something while I was praying... I don't think it was a dream...." She spoke slowly, as if still in awe of the sight she described. "Your mom thought that maybe... well, maybe you could help me understand it."

Mom looked at me and nodded expectantly — she didn't divulge what we'd shared back in the hospital chapel, but the look in her eyes told me that was why she had come to me. I swallowed hard and waited for Mrs. M to continue.

"Well... when it started, I remember seeing a huge field of golden grain...." Mrs. M began, "...it stretched as far as I could see in all directions. It was endless. The sky was crystal clear and vivid blue... so blue that it was awe-inspiring... and the air was perfectly still and calm. As I watched, a commotion appeared in the center of the field — it was small at first, like a gentle rustling, then it grew into a swirling breeze that was just barely strong enough to move the tops of the grain, tracing a circular pattern across the surface. Pretty soon, the wind grew stronger until it created what looked like a whirlpool in the center of the field, making the grain stalks bend low as they were touched by the wind. It was odd; the stalks weren't beaten down by the wind... it was more like they were bowing as it touched them.

"The swirling wind kept expanding larger and larger, filling more and more of the field, and the wind swirled faster and faster. It began pulling the grain off the stalks and sending it flying into the air, where it formed a huge funnel cloud... like a tornado. It stayed in one place, just growing larger and larger... swallowing more and more of the field. As it grew, it came closer and closer to where I stood. Then when it was nearly upon me, I could see that the grains of wheat had become sparks flying upward... it was beautiful. I could see them gathering into a giant pillar — like a pillar of fire. It was loud... like a tornado, but with the sound of a raging inferno... its power was frightening and awesome. Still, it was so incredibly beautiful," Mrs. M added.

"Then it suddenly just exploded outward, almost instantly consuming the entire field for as far as I could see," she explained. "It was so amazing! It filled everything with swirling light and warmth. It made me tremble and gasp ...its beauty thrilled my soul with overwhelming joy -- it was astonishing!

"It burned like that for a while, but not very long..." she continued as her expression turned crestfallen. "Pretty soon, the surrounding sky started to turn cold and dark, and an icy, freezing rain began to fall. At first, the fire drove the rain back, but a cold mist crept over the ground, slowly killing the stalks of wheat and causing the fire to shrink smaller and smaller. Finally, I could see the last of the sparks flying away upward — disappearing through the shrinking blue opening in the darkened sky. As the fire retreated, the rain and ice beat the field harder, eventually crushing what was left of the wheat until the entire field was left frozen and lifeless. As I watched it, I was struck by a deep feeling of despair. The sight of everything frozen and dead made me feel sick and heartbroken, and the cold made me shiver terribly. I collapsed to my knees and wept so hard. When I woke, I guess I was kind of hysterical; that's when Maria saw me crying." She wiped tears from her cheeks as she recounted it.

Mom looked at me, "Do you think it means anything?"

I wanted to go get Pastor Wilkes and PJ, but they were both seriously occupied praying with people. What she described somehow resonated within me, as if the Spirit was confirming the vision she'd seen; but what did it mean? Without saying a word, I just dropped to my knees and started to pray; Mom and Mrs. M followed, kneeling beside me. Almost instantly, I was jarred by the sound of a voice... THE voice... I immediately recognized it from the other day on Mr. V's porch — it was the same voice that had spoken my name months before. It was gentle but emphatic as it clearly said: "The vision is a sign of that which has begun..." I instinctively opened my eyes, even though I already knew there would be no one there — as I did, I could see Mrs. M looking around with a surprised and fearful expression; she caught my eye, and I nodded to acknowledge I'd heard it too. We looked at Mom kneeling between us, but she was praying with her head down as if she hadn't heard anything. Just then, it spoke again: "The fields are white unto harvest, what has begun cannot be stopped... doubt not... but, be strong and of good courage."

Mrs. M's eyes widened in astonishment as she stared at me, and I nodded that I'd also heard it again. She looked all around, confirming that no one else was speaking to us. She frantically shook her head in a gesture that said she didn't understand — it echoed the question in my own heart. Surely, God was revealing this for a reason... what did

He want us to do? As we listened intently for more of the message, there was only silence, except for the noises of everyone praying around us. Then we heard the voice again, more softly, but just as clear: "Look to what Matthew has written... it will be as I have told you."

JUST THEN, Mom bolted up straight and opened her eyes with a gasp, surprising both of us. She looked at Mrs. M with a wide-eyed expression and then glanced at me, holding a hand below her neck as if she was catching her breath. "I-I saw it..." she said breathlessly as she looked at Mrs. M. "The field... the fire... the rain... everything... It was beautiful... and terrifying... just like you said." Mom looked over at me and then back at her, speaking to both of us: "...there was something else — it floated down from the sky just as everything was dying around me. I caught it in my hand... it was a small scroll. When I stretched it out to read it, it was blank, but then words appeared as I looked at it. They burned across the surface in golden flames, leaving the message behind in burnt lettering... so beautiful." She paused with an awestruck look as she remembered it.

"W-what did it say?" I asked anxiously.

"It was a reference... to the Bible," she said, pausing as she recalled it, "...Matthew 24:4-14." Mom looked at us curiously, wondering what it could mean.

I saw Mrs. M's mouth drop open, and the hairs on my neck stood straight as the chill up my spine made me shudder. I jumped to my feet and ran to the platform to get a Bible; the two of them met me at the platform's edge, around to the side near the back, away from everyone else. I sat on the edge of the platform and opened to Matthew 24, reading it out loud:

And Jesus answered and said to them, Take heed that no man deceive you. For many shall come in my name,

saying, I am Christ; and shall deceive many. And ye
shall hear of wars and rumors of wars: see that ye be
not troubled: for all these things must come to pass,
but the end is not yet.

For nation shall rise against nation, and kingdom against
kingdom: and there shall be famines, and pestilences,
and earthquakes, in divers places. All these are the
beginning of sorrows.

Then shall they deliver you up to be afflicted, and shall
kill you: and ye shall be hated of all nations for my
name's sake. And then shall many be offended, and
shall betray one another, and shall hate one another.

And many false prophets shall rise, and shall deceive
many. And because iniquity shall abound, the love of
many shall wax cold.

But he that shall endure unto the end, the same shall be
saved.

And this gospel of the kingdom shall be preached in all
the world for a witness unto all nations; and then
shall the end come.

ALL THREE OF us sat staring at the open pages, feeling the weight of
their implications. "Wow..." I finally said.

I didn't mention it to them, but I was beginning to understand the
gravity of what was really happening. Everything I'd been going
through... everything I'd been shown. It was becoming clear that it
was all part of God's preparation for this very thing — for what's
beginning here. His last Great Awakening. The truth of it was
looming before me like a titanic, obliterating wave; it meant that the
world's final chapter had now really begun, ...*the End of the Age*.

⌘

MARANATHA

Come quickly Jesus!

By 4:30 AM the mid-summer sunrise was already casting long shadows across the surrounding field. Inside the tent at least 50 people still remained; some huddled together in small groups as they joined one another in lifting up their endless list of urgent burdens, while others prayed quietly or drifted in and out of sleep.

Mom put her hand on my back, and I looked up. "I have to start work in a few hours — I'm going to head home for a little sleep," she explained. "Do you want to come home?"

I was actually feeling pretty exhausted. "I guess so, sure," I answered, slowly climbing to my feet and following her to the parking lot. Almost as soon as the car started moving, I was out cold. Mom shook me to let me know we were home, and I staggered upstairs, then just kicked off my shoes and collapsed on top of my bed.

It must have been about four hours later when mom stuck her head in to say she was leaving for work; it felt like no time had passed at all. I rolled onto my back and lay there thinking about everything that was happening. Despite all that I'd experienced, I still could hardly believe it. Words from the passage in Matthew hadn't stopped echoing in my mind since I'd read them. *The sign of your coming and of the end of the Age....* It reverberated, **the end of the Age...** repeating over and over in my head.

AFTER GRABBING a quick shower and a change of clothes, I decided to head back to the tent to see what was going on. A note on the frig from mom pointed me to breakfast and a lunch bag that she'd packed for me. I devoured both of them before making it out of the house — I was starving.

As I headed down the driveway on my bike, I made a quick decision to take the long way around — passing by Van Clief's farm. I figured I'd stop in and see how the old man was doing. Mr. V was using Bessy to move some rocks as I peddled up the driveway. He waved to me and parked the tractor as I leaned my bike beside the porch.

"Well don't you look a sight," he said in his usual abrupt style, "was ya up all night?" He pointed over his shoulder with a thumb toward the tent in the distance... "It looked like that tent was lit up the whole blasted night." He said it as if the lights were likely to wear it out.

"As a matter of fact, yeah, we had a prayer vigil till sunrise," I said, feeling a little like I was bragging. "You must have been up all night yourself if you noticed the lights?" I added curiously.

"When ya git t' my age, sleep has a way o' decidin' when it comes an' goes."

He waved at me to follow him as he headed inside the house, "Come on an' get a drink, ya must be a thirstin' after ridin' that bicycle clear 'cross town." I followed him into the kitchen, knowing that it didn't pay to argue with him. He poured two glasses of cold lemonade and invited me to sit down at his sturdy old kitchen table. He gave me a piercing look as we sat.

"What was ya praying fer all night long?" he asked with a hint of wonder in his voice.

"Well, for people mostly... family, friends... we prayed for you," I added with a smile.

"Fer ME?" he said in surprise, "I told ya b'fore, God ain't interested in an ol' mess like me."

"Yeah, I think you said that right before he healed your bad leg," I reminded him.

"Well, that ain't the same," he objected, sounding more like he was trying to convince himself than me. I briefly saw a desperate look in his eye as if he remembered something traumatic. He stared out the window for a minute, then finished off his drink and let the glass smack the table roughly. "Finish up yer drink, I kin use yer help outside if ya got th' time."

"How's Bessy doing?" I asked as we stepped off the porch.

"Jus fine - don't make 'em like her anymore. Noticed a leak in the hydraulics though, maybe ya kin check it out."

I found the leak in one of the fittings and tightened it up, which seemed to do the trick.

"What are you doing with the rocks?" I asked.

"Been fillin' in the drywell out near th' irrigation overflow; it was gettin' mighty muddy out there." He rubbed his head, looking out toward the spot he was talking about, and then pulled his hat back on. "Could use help spreadin' rock if yer so inclined?"

The work didn't take long. Mr. V had finished most of it with the tractor already. I got the feeling that he mostly just wanted company. Something was definitely eating at him.

I glanced at my watch... "I think I need to get going — have to be at work by noon," I explained. He nodded back.

"Thanks a heap Jim, ya been a great help t' me," he looked around at his freshly painted house and repaired irrigation system and the fresh-plowed & planted fields and nodded his head again. "Yup, a great help," he repeated.

"Hey, think you want to come to the tent meeting tonight?" I asked him hopefully.

He looked at the tent in the distance with a furrowed brow; "I ain't much fer church meetins," he said apologetically. "Maybe some other time."

I remembered the image I'd seen of him walking up the aisle and just smiled at him; "no problem, maybe sometime soon."

WHEN I GOT to the tent, I was surprised to see a dozen people still there. They mainly were reading their bibles or napping but had clearly stayed all night. Pete was one of them. Some empty food containers suggested that Carmine had brought over breakfast.

I sat down next to Pete in the first row, and he looked up at me, then quickly waved for me to follow him as he stood and headed for the back, inviting me to sit down in the last row. He spoke quietly, "Everybody's talking about the vision," he said mysteriously.

"W-what vision?" I stammered, unsure which one he was referring to.

"The one Mrs. M saw," he explained, "Mandy heard her talking about it last night." He looked at me with a serious and almost frightened expression and leaned forward: "I looked up the verses," he said,"...Matthew 24 — it's about the end of the world, isn't it."

I looked back at him and swallowed kind of hard. "Yeah... yeah, it is. But it's a good thing... it's amazing." I stopped and looked at him, remembering that he didn't know what I did about pastor Juan's future. Those events could still be years away. "Look, the important part of what she saw was what comes first — a revival... an incredible, world-shaking revival!"

Just then, Pastor Juan walked up and grabbed a seat next to us; "Hey guys!" he said in greeting. "I overheard what you're talking about; sorry, didn't mean to eavesdrop." He leaned forward and looked at us both; "Remember Angela's prophesy last night about God telling us to ask for Him to send the latter rain... He said it has waited until this appointed time? The latter rain is in the Bible." PJ opened his Bible and looked up the book of James, thumbing through it until he found what he was looking for... then he read it out loud to us:

> Be patient, therefore, brethren, until the coming of the
> Lord. Behold, the husbandman waits for the precious
> fruit of the earth, being patient over it, until it
> receives the early and latter rain. Be ye also patient;
> establish your hearts: for the coming of the Lord is at
> hand.[1]

"The outpouring that happened at Pentecost didn't finish there," he continued. I felt my heart racing as I considered what he was telling us; "The book of Joel says that when the last days come He'll pour out His spirit on all flesh... I think that's what's happening here — I think this is the start of the Latter Rain! There have been other outpourings before... other revivals... but this time is different- I just feel it!"

He paused and looked at the uncertain expression on Pete's face. "There are things that you already know, Pete," he continued, "... things you've seen and heard - like God's audible voice and what happened at the prison; things that nobody else knows but us. You know what I mean, right?"

He nodded at me; "y-yeah... I haven't told anybody," he assured us.

"Well, I'm not sure how I know this, but God is doing something here — right here... something incredible! We just have to keep doing what we're doing and make sure nothing gets in the way. There are souls at stake... thousands- maybe millions of souls!"

"I'm gettin a chill up my spine, man!" Pete said. "I'm on-board with that; I definitely am!" He thought for a minute.... "What about that other stuff in Matthew - about us being killed and hated and stuff?"

"Yeah, I know, that sounds really hard — that happened in the early church too," PJ continued. "We just have to look around the world; that's already happening. Maybe not here in America yet, but in lots of places. It's already mostly the Christians who are being targeted. It's going to get a lot worse, according to the Bible. Still, it also says that where sin abounds, grace abounds much more. We have to remember that the worse the darkness gets, the more brilliant the light becomes."

The things Chozeq had told me flooded to mind - about trials being trainers and how sweet the water tastes in a desert. I knew that we were in a war, and God wouldn't be unopposed in what he was doing, especially now as the enemy's time was coming to a close. Even though I should have been nervous or even fearful, I wasn't… not in the least. Instead, I felt a sense of excitement, and words bubbled up in my soul, spilling out just as Pete blurted out the exact same thing — we said it in unison: "Come quickly, Jesus!"

We looked at each other in surprise and high-fived. PJ smiled; "In the Early Church, they had an expression that meant exactly that… *Maranatha*, from two words, *marana-* and *tha*… it means Lord come!" Pete and I looked at each other; "…Maranatha Bro!" we both said in unison.

UNCLE MIKE SAID he was happy to have me back at work. It turned out that the dinner rush started early — it was a madhouse from 4:00 until 6:00, and then business practically disappeared after that. The thought crossed my mind that maybe the tent meeting had something to do with that, but I dismissed it as wishful thinking.

As it turned out, maybe it wasn't so wishful after all; the tent was definitely fuller — nearly half full as a matter of fact! I hadn't realized how many people came and went during last night's meeting, but now all of them were back at the same time. Many of them had brought friends! Even Jillian's mom was there, which made the crowd explode in a wave of praise!

⌘

AN OLD MAN'S DREAM

...and your old men will dream dreams
~ Acts 2:17

I t was another late night before the crowd thinned out, leaving a small contingent of kids and some church elders who stayed straight through the night again. I had dozed off sometime after 3:00 AM and then woke at around 5:00 and wandered outside. I had a strange feeling that I needed to go see Mr. V for some reason.

Walking up the dirt road toward the farmhouse, I noticed him on his porch; he sat quietly and watched me coming as he rocked slowly in the porch rocker. It didn't look like he was in any hurry to get to work today, which was unusual given the way he always insisted on starting his farm work early. As I finally climbed the steps and neared him, I thought I saw traces of tears on his cheeks... he was still looking toward the tent, just staring at it as if his thoughts were a million miles away. I walked past him and sat down in the next rocker, where I was in his line of sight.

I didn't say anything, waiting for him to speak first with some witty remark or at least a characteristic howdy. After sitting silently for a moment or two, he shifted his gaze away from the tent and toward me; "Saw a mighty big crowd o' folks out there las' night... stayed pretty late too. Wut'd ya have a concert or sumthin?"

"Just a service," I answered, "...we prayed mostly."

He bobbed his neck backward slightly as he nodded as if to say he wasn't surprised. He glanced back at the tent again, staring at it as if it was an alien spaceship or something.

"Is anything wrong?" I said, interrupting the silence. It took a moment before he answered....

"Don't suppose so," he said with a slightly embarrassed tone, "... jus' me, I guess."

I sat quietly for another minute before speaking, "You should come and see for yourself... it'd be great to have you join us sometime." I waited, but he didn't respond. "We're seeing some amazing things happening! Mrs. Andersen was healed of stage four cancer... her daughter Jillian was praying for her and asked us all to pray and the next thing...."

"Ya ever had a dream?" he said suddenly, cutting me off as if he hadn't heard a word I was saying. "...I mean one that seems so clear ya'd swear it was real an' no dream at all, 'cept fer the way it repeats over an' over?"

I stared at him dumbfounded, wondering if he somehow knew about what I'd been experiencing. However, I had no idea how he could. Or was he talking about himself? I didn't answer.

"Somethin' tells me ya probly have," he added; "There's somethin' 'bout you... 'bout all you folks. Yer a differ'nt bunch, that's fer sure. Things ain't stopped bein' differ'nt 'round here since ya'all showed up."

"What's it about? ...the dream, I mean." This time I was the one interrupting.

He looked down at the floor, deep in thought, as if deciding whether to share it or not. "Guess it ain't nothin' much," he finally said, "just a dream... it ain't nothin' but a dream."

"Yeah, but what was it? I'm curious," I prodded.

"There ain't nothin' to it," he insisted, "dreams is dreams, an' that's all."

"Maybe so," I said, probing, "but it looks like it bothered you... sure you don't want to talk about it?"

"Forgit it!" he answered, suddenly sounding irritable. "Talked about it plenty already — I ain't got a mind t' talk 'bout it no more!"

Whatever it was, it sure had him spooked; he'd clenched his fists and straightened in his chair like he was physically shaking the image from his mind. We sat quietly again as he glanced back at the tent, deep in thought. The silence was awkward - he obviously hadn't stopped thinking about the dream, whatever it was.

"Looks like it'll be a nice day...." I finally said, falling back on the tried and true weather topic. He looked at the sky and over at the horizon.

"Yup, sure does," he agreed. He kept his eyes on the horizon as he rocked slowly in his chair.

"Well, guess I better be getting back," I said, feeling like he preferred to be alone.

"Had any breakfast?" he barked, still looking straight ahead.

"N-no, ...you offering?" I asked. "My mom is still using the French toast recipe that you gave dad years ago."

"Is, is she? Bet she's better at it 'n me, I don't make 'em much these days."

"She makes them great, but I have to admit those flapjacks you made us last week were great too."

He half smiled, still not looking toward me, "secret's in the milk 'n eggs, he confided, "gotta be same-day fresh... none 'a that pasteurized an' half-froze stuff from the supermarket. ...Go fetch us some eggs," he ordered as he pushed himself up from his chair, "I'll light up the griddle." My stomach started to growl as I suddenly realized how hungry I was.

For a dozen hens, they sure can lay a lot of eggs, I thought to myself as I collected a dozen or so. He had the mixing bowl and milk jug out on the counter when I got to the kitchen, and I could smell the old griddle as it began to heat up. I watched him slice off a few wide strips of fresh bacon and crack a few eggs into the bowl. He slid the bowl toward me, "beat 'em nice an' even," he instructed. Next he slid the fresh milk jug over... "jus' pour enough t' whiten 'em a mite," he said. I had no idea how much a mite might be but poured slowly until he yelled stop.

"Now a splash 'a vanilla an' a pinch o' cinnamon," he explained, sprinkling the ingredients into the bowl in precisely unmeasured amounts.... "Then a good pinch o' salt. Now here's the secret ingredient," he confided, splashing a few spoonfuls of pure maple syrup into the mix.

Next, he carved off a few slices of homemade bread — he really did have an aversion to the supermarket variety. Before long, a half dozen slices were sizzling on the griddle. The smells wafting through the room made my stomach growl with anticipation.

There was no question that this was absolutely the best-tasting breakfast I'd ever had. Mr. V sipped his coffee with a bemused look on his face as he watched me eat; it made me wonder whether I reminded him of my dad doing the same thing at my age.

After we cleaned up the kitchen, I followed him outside. I had to admit I really enjoyed farm work, or maybe it was just that I liked spending time with the old man. His mood was a lot more upbeat than it had been when I first arrived; so was mine.

Despite all that, though, I hadn't slept much the past few nights, and it wasn't long before the lack of sleep began to catch up with me. Mr. V noticed that I was dragging and suggested I rest for a while in his porch hammock; I barely remember laying down before I was out cold.

WHEN I AWOKE, I was surprised to see that it was dark out. I glanced down the road toward the tent and could see it lit and glowing. The distant sound of music drifted across the fields, but it wasn't what I expected. This sounded like music from a radio playing some old classic 50's songs over the loudspeakers. In the dim light, I could see Ol' Bessy parked up the dirt road and figured Mr. V must have ridden it there. It surprised me that he hadn't awakened me sooner.

The closer I approached, the more out-of-place things seemed. I could see people milling around the tent. Young kids were running around - it looked like they were playing games. I couldn't hear any singing or anything that sounded like a service going on. A sudden gleam caught my eyes, and I turned to realize it was from lights reflecting off of Bessy as I approached. The shine made me realize this must not be Bessy after all - this tractor was brand new; it looked like it had just rolled off the factory floor.

Standing beside it, I looked toward the tent at a scene that completely confused me. The kids running around were chasing something… piglets! As I scanned the grounds, I realized that there were animals with ribbons and people clapping. People were eating corn dogs and watermelon, clustered in energetic conversations. The tent's side flaps were rolled up, revealing tables loaded with produce and booths that were grilling and selling food. One section was roped off where some older kids were leading animals around in front of judges.

It finally dawned on me that I was looking at a Fair… the Harvest Festival! A look toward Main Street confirmed my suspicion. There was no sign of Carmine's diner or any other businesses; they hadn't been built yet!

Once I made that connection, the scene made more sense, although it didn't explain why I was seeing it. I looked for Chozeq but didn't see him anywhere. Yet, judging from the way everyone ignored me, they couldn't see me either. I scanned for something… anything… that might explain why I was here.

That's when I saw them, seated on a bench deep in conversation. Mr. V was probably in his early thirties, but I recognized him just the same. The man he was talking to was about the same age — I knew him immediately. Even though I'd only seen black and white pictures of him, I knew who he was. It was my great grandfather, Farro, without a doubt!

⌘

PURSUED

...even if it takes a lifetime!
~ Matt Farro

G ramps Farro looked out of place in his shined shoes and suspenders, with a white shirt and bow tie, although his sleeves were rolled up and his curly hair was askew, making him look at least half a farmer. Mr. V, in comparison, was in his trademark overalls and was sucking on a corncob pipe. The most striking things about them both, though, were the expressions on their faces; they appeared to be having a deadly-serious conversation - maybe even an argument.

I cautiously drew closer, still not entirely sure that they couldn't see me. Just to be safe, I stood with my back to them while I tuned in to their conversation, pretending to watch the kids who were racing each other to catch piglets. Grandpa Farro's thick Brooklyn accent made it easy to pick out his voice above the din of noise all around us.

"I'm tellin' ya Jim, it's not helpin' you to be mad at God. What happened to Clorinda was a terrible tragedy, but it doesn't change the fact that God loves you!"

"Well, it changes it fer me!" I heard Mr. V snap back. "I ain't got no use for a God who lets tragedies happen without liftin' a finger! It ain't just Clorinda... she was the jus' the latest... look what happened to Lou... an'... our little Abi..." his voice cracked as he choked up when he said that.

Gramps was quiet for a moment, then continued with a gentler tone in his voice. "Look, I know it's been rough... I don't even know what I'd do if I had to go through what you have. But that's exactly the reason you have to give God a chance — if ya want to see Clorinda and Abi again...."

Mr. V cut him off with an angry retort: "Don't give me any o' that horse s***! Religion is always promisin' some grand reunion in the clouds or somethin' — I ain't buyin' it! If God was real, an' half as lovin' as you claim, then he wouldn't o' let 'em die— plain 'n simple!"

I looked over my shoulder and saw gramps dragging both his hands through his hair as he struggled for a way to get through to his old friend. He raised his eyes toward Heaven, obviously not seeing me as he looked straight past and into the starry sky. I could see a prayer in his eyes. He looked back at Mr. V and spoke softly again.

"Remember how we used to have talks... Lou and you and me... when we were on the front. Remember how he used to say God had us in his hands?"

I saw Mr. V stiffen; "That example ain't helping yer case, Matt," he said with a pained look on his face.

Gramps pushed the comment aside and pressed on. "The part that always stuck with me was how he'd always say that being in God's hands meant we were holding onto each other - cause we *were* God's hands." Gramps leaned forward and put his hand on Mr. V's shoulder; "Lou proved he believed that Jim.... If I'd been the one on that hill, it would've been me he saved... it would've been any of us!"

Mr. V angrily pulled away and jumped to his feet, throwing his pipe into the dirt. "HE SHOULDA LEFT ME THERE!"...he shouted loud enough for everyone around to turn and stare, "g-d damn it, I wish he'd left me there!"

He used his sleeve to wipe an unwanted tear from his cheek and looked around self-consciously at the crowd. Then he turned and briskly walked away, limping toward his tractor as fast as he could move. Gramps stood up and watched him go, breathing a prayer out loud; he was standing so close to me that it was as if he was whispering it in my ear.

"Dear Lord, Jim needs you more than any man I know - from this moment on, please pursue him with your love... don't let him out of your hands. Please find a way to get through to him, even if it takes a lifetime!"

The prayer sent a chill up my spine. At the same time, hearing him say Mr. V's first name suddenly struck me as the dots connected — realizing that dad must have named me after him.

I turned to look back at gramps and nearly bumped into someone else standing directly beside me. I shifted aside instinctively, even though I knew they couldn't see or feel me, and was jolted in surprise when I got a look at who it was. Mr. V... old man Van Clief... was staring at gramps. I could see tears on his face as he considered the prayer that had just been prayed.

This was it! This is the dream he said he kept having; this must be why he kept staring back at the tent that way when we were on his porch.

As I watched him, the scene suddenly dissolved around us. I saw Mr. V squeeze his eyes closed trying to block out the images and sounds that quickly surrounded us next — as if he'd seen them before and dreaded them terribly. They swirled around us... scene after scene in which he rejects and curses God in angry outbursts... scenes of pain and tragedy.... I saw dad again as he jumped from Mr. V's porch and threw down his tool belt... an exchange flashed between Mr. V and Carmine as he angrily rejected an invitation to church... I recognized images of dad's funeral and could feel Mr. V's intense sorrow over the loss. Then the images intensified with memories of other funerals... his young daughter... his wife... as gramps' words echoed: "...if ya want to see Clorinda and Abi again...". Suddenly we were standing in front of a set of horrendous gates — gates that I recognized too well! We saw them open as he was dragged forward — he screamed in horror as he watched his arms burst into flame!

I was jolted from sleep at the shock of the horrible sight, falling from the hammock as I heard myself screaming, "NOOOOOOOOO!"

"WHAT IN BLAZES!" I heard Mr. V say as he stood to his feet, nearly knocking the rocker over behind him. The bright sunlight made me shield my eyes as I struggled to get my bearings. It took a minute for my heart rate to slow enough to catch my breath. I looked up at him as my head cleared.

"I-i-is it morning... did I sleep all night?" I asked in confusion as I squinted into the sunlight.

"All night? Ya barely been layin there an hour," he answered in surprise. "What'd ya do fall out? Guess it takes some practice t' sleep in that thing."

I barely heard what he was saying — the intensity of the last image I'd seen was still seared on my consciousness. I wanted to talk about the dream but wasn't sure whether I should... I wasn't even sure if it was really something God was revealing or just my own imagination running wild. I thought again about the vision I'd seen of him coming to the altar... that one was real; I was sure of it.

I climbed off the porch floor and dusted myself, looking around at the old homestead as I did. It looked about the same as in my dream, although that scene was admittedly dark. I thought about how Mr. V had lived here for so many years and made my way over to the rockers where he was standing.

"I guess you've lived here your whole life, right?" I asked as we both looked out over the surrounding scene; "pretty much..." he said as he nodded. I looked at him and thought for a minute about how to ask the question that was burning on my mind, then carefully asked, "You were married, right? ...Years ago? What happened?"

The question caught him off guard. He looked at me strangely, then stared off into the distance at nothing in particular and sank back into his rocker with a sigh. "What'd ya wanna know fer?"

His question threw me a little. I fumbled for an answer.... "I — Uh... well, I think I saw her picture in your living room... figured it was your wife."

"Yup... sure was," he said, making it sound like an unfinished sentence. I stood quietly to see if he'd go on; when he didn't, I sat down in the rocker next to him; my heart was pounding.

"Her name was Clorinda, wasn't it?"

His head turned with a start, and there was a brief glimmer of fear in his eyes. "How'd ya know?"

The pounding of my heart made me stop and catch my breath before answering. I quickly decided to be honest with him about my dream. "I-I heard my great-grandpa say it... in the dream," I explained. "You called him Matt, and gramps called you Jim... I got the feeling you fought together in the war... you mentioned a daughter too... Abi."

His face was ashen as he sat silently and stared at me. I leaned toward him and gulped, trying to calm my nerves, then went on: "I saw the rest of it too," I added as gently as I could, "...all of it."

A single tear ran down his cheek, but he still didn't say a word. He seemed frozen in place, except for his eyes that kept desperately searching mine for some natural explanation. I sat back, frantically hoping that I hadn't done the wrong thing in telling him.

Remembering the way he had been staring at the tent, I looked toward it....

"That's why you keep staring at the tent, isn't it? It reminds you of that night." I looked back at him, noticing his hands shaking as they gripped his rocker's armrests. "It's ok..." I tried to reassure him, "it's not the first time I've seen dreams like that. How many times have you had it - the same dream, I mean?"

There were a few tears on his cheeks now as he struggled to answer. "Suppose it's been every time I fall asleep... started the night that tent was raised."

We sat quietly, and I could sense that his heart was racing as much as mine. There was no doubt that the dream meant something... it was God's answer to my great-grandfather's prayer.

"I heard what gramps prayed... you heard it too, didn't you." He didn't answer but nodded in agreement.

"Remember that friend I told you about? ...Kelly — the one who... well... who passed away?" He nodded slightly, just enough to signal that he remembered. "I was mad at God when it happened... really angry. I felt like he didn't care... like he was just using us, ya know?" I saw him swallow hard as his eyes told me that he knew the feeling. "It turned out that He was really doing something more incredible than I could ever have imagined. I've realized that it was part of something so much bigger... something that's saving hundreds of lives... maybe even thousands."

He still didn't talk, but I could tell from the tension in his hands and face that he wasn't ready to agree with me yet about that — at least not for his wife and child.

After another minute or two of silence, I quietly cleared my throat... "does the dream always end the same way?" I asked. He couldn't find the words to speak his answer; he just nodded yes. The mix of emotions in his eyes revealed a lifetime of regret and hopelessness. I thought for a second as an idea seemed pressed upon me... upon my spirit. "That's not an irreversible view of the future... not yet... it's a warning," I said, sharing what I was feeling. "God is giving you a chance to change that ending."

Another few tears rolled down his cheeks as he struggled mightily to hold it together. He shook his head no as if trying to echo what he'd said before about it being too late for him.

I looked away, wanting to give him his privacy as he wiped the tears off his face. Looking down at my hands, I continued:

"I DIDN'T KNOW your name before I heard gramps say it in the dream... your first name, I mean. It made me realize... dad named me after you." I looked up at him, continuing, "He did that years after the two of you had your falling-out. I think that was a sign that mistakes can be undone... forgiveness changes the past." The words that PJ had shared a few days ago came to mind: "God doesn't just forget sins or pretend they aren't there. He wipes out our sin by changing our past." Somehow I could tell that Mr. V remembered those words too.

The look on his face revealed a monumental struggle going on inside him. I thought about what Chozeq said about God being the one who unlocks the heart — I breathed a silent prayer for Him to do that for Mr. V.

"SOMETIMES IT FEELS BETTER to hold onto pain than to let it go," I offered as I related to what he was going through. "But the freedom that comes from letting it go is a thousand times better than holding it. As much as you might think you deserve it, God's not offering you judgment... not right now... He's offering you freedom."

⌘

39

ATTACKED

Wednesday night brought an even larger crowd as convoys of cars from other area churches began to arrive. The news was spreading, especially among the church youth groups, and they were coming in droves. Many of the kids were bringing their instruments — the music was incredible as they rocked the place in heartfelt worship! Wednesday night's service started out in just about the same way. This time, a friend of Pastor Juan -- the youth minister of an inner-city church -- opened the service. Sure enough, what began as a prayer turned into an incredible time of worship. Two hours later, that church's senior pastor, Bishop Bradley, finally made it to the platform to preach. His church had a great name: the Mount Zion Fire Baptized Gospel Lighthouse. Not surprisingly, the altar was soon packed once again with desperate people seeking God.

As I sat on the edge of the platform at 2:00 AM, it occurred to me that the tent hadn't been empty since Sunday — someone or other had been here around the clock for more than 72 hours straight! Glancing out over the rows of seats, it didn't look like that was changing anytime soon. In fact, there were more people now than there had been on any of the previous nights. God's presence still felt so strong — it was like a portal had been opened here directly into Heaven!

I somehow made it by on only the couple of hours of sleep that I caught in the mornings before starting work at the Sub shop. Incredibly, I didn't feel tired. I suppose that even if I were, the services were so riveting that I couldn't imagine sleeping if I wanted to. So many people had been healed of severe illnesses that it was beginning to feel almost commonplace. Common, that is, except for how incredible the miracles were. Last night we even saw two young kids with MD jump from their wheelchairs as their parents wept in awestruck gratitude! In addition to the healings, the number of people who continued being saved was staggering. Since Sunday, it was well into the hundreds.

By Thursday night, the convoys of cars were joined by buses as church groups from even further away arrived. The nightly events had become the talk of the entire town, and the local paper had included a front-page article in Thursday's edition. It recounted eyewitness testimonies of miraculous healing, marriage reconciliations, and the stories of some of the FCS kids who had been delivered from drug addictions.

One of the area's major network news channels dispatched a reporter and cameraman to investigate first-hand. She seemed skeptical at first as she began to interview many FCS kids but gradually became more nervous and uncertain as the service began and she witnessed what was unfolding around her. A small group of firebrand seminary students ended up leading her to the Lord while the astounded and surprised cameraman captured her tear-filled conversion on live TV.

. . .

"Saw the news las' night," Mr. V said as we sat at his kitchen table on Friday morning. "Looks t' be a mighty unusual bunch o' happenins goin' on out there. Ain't seen nothing like it... leastwise not since I was a young-un... Nope, ain't seen nothin' like that in more'n eighty years."

He had confessed to me earlier that the same relentless dream was still repeating every time he tried to sleep; he looked exhausted. My heart went out to him as I pondered the torture he continued to endure; if only he would just surrender to God's forgiving arms! Mom was right; he really could be awfully stubborn. I knew that this was much deeper than just stubbornness, however. He was honestly unable to forgive himself and still couldn't conceive that God could forgive him either.

My thoughts shifted back to his last comment as it finally registered in my mind. "There was a revival like this eighty years ago?" I asked curiously.

"Revival?" he repeated, sounding slightly confused by the question. "Don't know if it was a revival or not — it's jus' how folks wus." He thought for a minute and sipped his coffee... "As kids, we went every week up to the old Methodist church — yer great-grandpa Lou and me. Called 'em the shoutin' Methodists in them days. Lou caught religion more than I did... it set real well with him; I reckon he might'a been a preacher if it hadn't a been...." He stopped talking and sat quietly without finishing the sentence.

"I like it when you talk about the old days," I said after a short pause, trying to liven the conversation again. "I never heard about the shouting Methodists before... that's pretty cool."

He shrugged. "Suppose so."

"Did you always go to that church?" I asked.

He looked a little embarrassed but answered honestly, "Never been back since the war ... 'cept for my weddin' day ... an' funerals."

His answer didn't surprise me, but I kind of regretted asking it. I realized the risk in asking a question like that to someone his age; there are bound to be bad memories along with good ones.

An idea suddenly came to mind as I thought about the way he had been so close to Great Grandpa and Dad... "Would you mind if I call you Uncle Jim," I asked him. "It feels like we're kinda like family, ya know?"

His serious expression gave way to a smile, and he messed up my hair, "Yeah... that's jus' fine Jimmy, I reckon I'd like that."

THE CROWDS CONTINUED GROWING throughout the weekend, with endless moves of the Spirit sweeping over everyone there. I stood at the back of the tent watching cars arrive for Sunday night's service. The parking area was already packed, and the line of traffic waiting to park stretched all the way up Main Street; this was by far the largest crowd we'd seen. The seats were filling quickly — it looked like we'd definitely be at capacity before all those cars parked. I looked at the clear night sky, trying to match it with the scene that Chozeq had shown me... I couldn't tell for sure if this was the night I'd seen, but I couldn't help feeling that something noteworthy was about to happen. Oddly enough, I had a slightly ominous feeling, too — one that was a lot like what I felt the night we learned about Kelly's tumor. I did my best to push that thought out of my mind.

Anna and her mom walked up to me; "What are you, the greeter?" Anna joked as she shook my hand with an exaggerated formality.

"How do you do, madam?" I said with my best Cary Grant impression as I smiled back at her. "Can you believe the crowd tonight? I asked. It's got to be over a thousand people!"

"Wow, yeah," she said, looking around, "It's incredible!"

"Should we save you a seat?" she asked hopefully.

"I think PJ wants me up at the platform," I answered, feeling disappointed about passing on her invitation. The way she pouted at my answer made me feel terrible, even though I knew she was mostly kidding around. I walked with them up the aisle until they found seats and then waved goodbye as I headed to the front.

. . .

As I TURNED to watch where I was going, I nearly walked straight into a man who was standing in the aisle. The look on his face made me stop immediately — he was sweating profusely and stared at me with a desperate look in his eyes. I guessed he was probably in his late thirties; he had unkempt hair and seemed out of place wearing a heavy raincoat.

"A-Aare y-you Jim M-Moretti?" he stammered.

"Yes… what's wrong?" I answered. An uneasy feeling crept over me as soon as I heard him speak.

"I-I'm s-sorry… they're making me… they won't leave me alone…" he cried in a pleading voice.

I SAW him lift his arm from inside his coat and realized that he was aiming the barrel of a sawed-off shotgun straight at me. I saw his expression change and watched his eyes suddenly darken into a cold stare that emanated more than hatred — it was pure evil. It was the last thing I expected right then and caught me entirely by surprise — before I could say a word, **he pulled the trigger.**

THE BLAST CAUGHT me in the chest at point-blank range — the barrel was almost touching me. I remember being thrown backward by it several yards as everything around me slowed to a crawl. I heard Anna scream my name and saw men jumping the man with the gun and tackling him before I hit the ground. I realized I wasn't gasping… I wasn't breathing at all.

I looked up through eyes that wouldn't move and heard Mom's screams as she collapsed to her knees beside me and began to wail — "N-NO! OOHH NNOOO… OH GOD, PLEASE NOOOO!"

Someone knelt next to her beside me, announcing that she was a nurse. In seconds, two more men arrived, explaining that they were EMTs as they helped the nurse rip open my blood-drenched tee shirt. They wadded something up and pressed it against the wound, holding it there as they began CPR.

The scene grew darker as I struggled to hang on — I heard PJ kneeling at my head, talking to me, telling me to hold on. The next thing I knew, I was looking down at myself, watching them work on my limp body. I could see Anna screaming and crying hysterically as her mom tried to console her and keep her in her seat. Mom was kneeling beside me, gripping my hand so tightly that her fingers were white. Her eyes were awash with tears, but her prayers were streaming like a mighty torrent aimed straight toward Heaven... I could see them!

I BECAME aware of Chozeq directly beside me and turned to him. "I didn't think it'd be like this," I said in confusion. "It feels the same as the other times... I thought dying would be different."

He looked at me with an understanding expression, "Tis because ye haven't died, Lad," he explained.

"Thy great mission is still before thee."

He nodded toward the ground behind me, and I followed his gaze to see the man who shot me being hauled to his feet by Sheriff Flanagan and a deputy. Looking down at the man, I could see a blur covering his face as if it was obscured by something... or, more accurately, a series of somethings. I soon recognized them as the flashing and morphing faces of a demonic host... a legion, I thought to myself.

I suddenly feared for the Sheriff and his deputy.

"Those cuffs won't hold him!" I exclaimed in concern.

Chozeq drew his sword but stood powerless to intervene. He could see from the look in my eyes that I didn't understand why he didn't challenge them!

"Angels have no dominion here... it is the realm of men," he explained, looking me in the eye with a gaze that conveyed the importance of what he'd just said. It could not have been clearer if he'd issued a direct order.

I looked desperately down at my shattered body — "But how?" I asked urgently, "...How can I?"

Instead of answering my question, he placed his huge hand on my chest and lowered his sword to the wound in my body below.

IN AN INSTANTANEOUS FLASH, I gasped a huge breath and looked up into the faces of those kneeling around me. As soon as I breathed, I began to cough, spitting up wads of blood.

PJ and the others were telling me to lay still, staring at me with astonished expressions. I ignored them, raising my head in time to see the possessed man snap the chain between his cuffs and throw the deputy into the air, sending him crashing into a row of chairs. Unable to stand, I looked up at him, and he caught my gaze, staring back with a dismissive scowl. I knew what I had to do — the pain in my shoulder was throbbing even more intensely than the stabbing in my chest. I drew as deep a breath as I could and tried to shout...

"L E G I O N..." I cried, but my voice was barely a whisper. I fixed my gaze on his eyes, which looked like vacant black sockets, and mustered all the strength I could find, crying out again — this time with a voice that made him shudder...

"L E G I O N !" I shouted, gasping for another breath, "...JESUS,"... *<gasp>* "...WHO I SERVE,"...*<gasp>* "...COMMANDS YOU,"...*<gasp>* "... TO LEAVE HIM!"...*<gasp>* "...BE CAST,"...*<gaaaasp>* "...FROM THE REALM OF MEN!"

THE MAN'S head snapped back and shook from side to side so rapidly that it became a blur, then the beasts let out a blood-curdling wail that sounded like a pack of vicious animals tearing their prey to pieces. His mouth stretched impossibly wide, and I saw the swarming mass of hideous creatures emerge into the air like a cloud of foul mist. The man collapsed to the ground as if he'd been beaten within an inch of his life. I looked up at Chozeq, who stood with his sword at the ready, and then noticed with him the other powerful guardians who had been standing as the protectors of God's hallowed ground. They surrounded the swarming beasts as Chozeq sentenced them: "Foul creatures, thy time has come to its end - thy chains await thee!" The angels' swords ignited, bathing the creatures in flaming light and sending them crashing to the ground, shrieking and wailing as they were dragged into the earth.

My head collapsed back onto the ground as I lay spent, drifting out of consciousness.

⌘

40

WHITENED HARVEST

Lift up your eyes, and look on the fields; for they are white already to harvest.
~ John 4:35

I woke in a hospital bed hours later... it was morning.

"Hey there..." Mom said quietly as she leaned closer and squeezed my hand. She looked elated to see me awake despite her apparent exhaustion.

"Hey," I said, then immediately regretted it — the unexpected pain took my breath away.

"Shhhh," she said to silence me. "You have a few broken ribs and some bad internal bruising, but other than that, you're fine. The doctors say you're a miracle." I flashed my eyes and nodded yes, wishing I could speak. She squeezed my hand and looked me in the eye closely, "You can tell me about it later," she whispered. She glanced toward the door and back at me, "You have some visitors, feel up to it?" I nodded.

Anna peeked her head in and waved timidly; I smiled back and waited for her to come in. She looked like she hadn't slept all night either, but her face absolutely glowed as she said good morning. She took my hand in hers and asked how I was feeling.

"He's not supposed to talk," mom interjected protectively as I nodded that I was okay.

Anna's mother entered behind her and greeted mom, then Pete poked his head in and waved.

"Thought you might want this," he said, holding up a bag from Carmine's, "...Bacon, egg, and cheese on a roll; it beats hospital food."

The four of them made small talk as I took a few bites and happily listened. Pete was the first to mention last night's service - he looked at me and shook his head as if in disbelief.

"Last night... whoa... you did it again, Bro!" He caught himself and looked around the room, slightly embarrassed that he might have said too much, then he continued. "I think everybody saw it... you did it in front of like a thousand people!" He stopped again and looked at Anna — she shifted her gaze downward as if she was suddenly embarrassed herself. "You should have seen the rest of the service! What happened to you was like a match in a tinderbox — it ignited something amazing!"

I immediately recalled the words that Chozeq had spoken in my vision: "...the Spirit's move this night is going to ignite a fire that sweeps from here...."

Anna and her mom had a look of awe on their faces as they nodded in agreement. Pete began describing how as soon as the ambulance took me away, everyone started to pray for me. "As we prayed, there was a feeling like I never felt before, even more than any of the other nights. It was like we were all together, ya know. Like we were ONE — a thousand of us! Man! It was incredible!"

He looked again at Anna, and she lowered her eyes shyly; "God used Anna," he said, as a chill ran up my spine. "It blew me away... she stood up there in front and let God talk... PJ said it was Tongues, just like the book of Acts!" I looked at her face — her expression showed no embarrassment or boasting... it was pure wonder; the thrill of it still showed in her face. "Then it was Chrissy who got up," Pete continued. "PJ called it the interpretation; he said it was a kind of prophecy. You shoulda heard it, man!"

I just listened in amazed silence as I pictured the exact scene he described... I hadn't missed it... only I'd seen it a few weeks early... God had worked it out so that I hadn't missed a thing!

"After that, things just went crazy," he continued, "I mean, crazy in an excellent way. Everybody there started cryin' an' askin' forgiveness... I don't think a single person could've left without bein' saved last night!"

Just then, Anna's phone chirped, and she checked it. "Can we put on your TV?" she asked as she looked up. She tuned to the local network news, and we all watched — it was a story about last night. We recognized the reporter as the same woman who'd been saved the night before. She looked into the camera with tears streaming down her face as she described a profoundly personal experience...

"What's happening here is like nothing I've ever experienced," she said as she wiped a tear from her cheek. "Not many know publicly that my husband is a wounded warrior. He suffered a head injury that left him without the ability to speak or to use his right arm and leg — he's been in a wheelchair for two years." She wiped more tears from both her cheeks as she continued, obviously struggling to hold herself together. "The footage we want to show you is real..." she cried for a second with a few gasps of joy and then managed to continue, "...I want you to see what just happened..." She lowered her mic and nodded to the crew to play the clip.

The scene showed the camera panning across the expansive crowd as everyone prayed. Many people were crying and lifting their hands when it suddenly looked like a wave swept through them, knocking many of them to the ground or their knees. I recognized it as the wave I'd seen in my vision. As the camera followed what was happening, it panned toward a man in a wheelchair near the back. He had a deeply remorseful expression on his face and sat with one arm raised and the other lying limply in his lap. When the wave struck him, he fell from his wheelchair onto his knees. Then he could be seen looking down in surprise at his legs and suddenly raising and moving the fingers in his limp arm. He grabbed his disabled leg with both his hands in shock and then climbed to his feet and stood, then began clapping his hands and leaping and praising God....

"I-I CAN WALK! P-PRAISE GOD I CAN WALK!" The reporter ran into the scene and threw her arms around his neck, screaming and crying in joy as he spun her around and around.

The broadcast cut back to the studio as the news program's familiar anchor picked it up. "That was the scene last night in Center Springs as our own Caden Koller captured a truly remarkable experience." He turned to his right, and the camera zoomed out to show Caden and her husband both sitting beside him. "Thank you for sharing that very personal moment with our audience," the anchor said sincerely. Seated to one side of the Kollers was a man who the anchor introduced as their doctor, and on the other side was Pastor Juan!

"AM I INTRUDIN?" a familiar voice called from the doorway, interrupting the TV. I looked over to see Mr. V standing with his hat in his hands and smiled at him. "The Reverend came by an' told me you was here... told me wut happn'd." He looked over at mom and nodded in thanks, "He let me know you sent him, Maria. I truly 'preciate that... much obliged."

Mom smiled back... "Thank you so much for coming!" The fact that he had visited a hospital — much less come to see me was a really big deal.

I could see the way his eyes scanned my face and the bandages around my chest — I couldn't help thinking that maybe the sight reminded him of my great-grandpa. He stood quietly for a moment, just looking at me. "Guess you, Moretties are all heroes," he finally declared with a tone that was as serious as it was honoring. I was in no condition to talk, or I would have insisted that all I'd done was stand in the wrong place.

He approached my bed and stretched out his hand, holding a small box. "Brought ya somethin' I figured you'd get a kick out of. I've been holdin' onto it fer years."

I took it from him and opened it. "It's yer great grandpa's high school class ring," he said, clearing his throat. "Lou... yer great-grandpa... gave it t' me fer safekeepin'. I think he'd approve o' me givin' it t' you."

I stared up at him in surprise, watching the mix of emotions in his face. I knew this ring had to have meant a lot to him for all these years. "It's a real hero's ring," I said, choking back a swell of emotion, not to mention the pain in my chest. The words flowed out naturally and irresistibly... "This really means a lot... thanks, Uncle Jim."

I saw mom wipe a tear from her cheek. Mr. V cleared his throat to keep from becoming emotional himself. "Don't go an' lose it," he barked. I couldn't help laughing out loud at his dry humor, then immediately winced in pain. "Oh, er... sorry about that," Mr. V said as he saw me stiffen painfully.

He glanced back at the TV, hoping to change the subject. "They've been playin' that all mornin'," he noted as he watched the Kollers' doctor describe the unexplainable miracle. "This thing's gettin' a life of its own — the news is full o' stories today 'bout folks wantin' to go back an' start meetins like yer's all over the state." He paused thoughtfully for a minute... "I reckon I may have t' git down there m'self an' check out what's goin' on." We all looked at each other in surprise. "Well... it *is* my property, after all," he added defensively.

"You'd better get there early, or you won't find a seat," I said, smiling to myself. I was remembering my incredible vision of seeing him searching for a seat all the way down the aisle to the altar.

If Chozeq was here, I'd be giving him a high-five!

⌘

41

STERLING

The Lord is not slack concerning his promises... but is
longsuffering... not willing that any should perish
~ 2 Peter 3:9

The room was dark as I lay awake, alone in my hospital room. The events of the past week were racing through my head. The way that God had been moving was like a whirlwind in more ways than one — it was overwhelming. I thought about Mr. V's promise to attend tonight's service, and my heart leaped — I just wished that I could be there to see it really happen! I lay my head back and carefully breathed a long sigh, trying not to stir the searing pain in my chest . . . .

No sooner had I closed my eyes than my surroundings completely changed once again. The change didn't surprise me, but the timing did... making me wonder what God could be wanting me to do in this condition. The first thing that caught my attention was that my bed was gone - I was floating! Along with that came a welcome realization that the pain in my chest was gone too, at least for the moment. As my eyes adjusted to the darkness, I found myself looking up into the night sky's tapestry of stars. I could feel a calm breeze, along with the reassuring touch of Chozeq's hand on my back. Sounds of music and singing drifted into the air from behind me, catching my attention; I turned to look and smiled at the familiar sight of the giant glowing tent below us.

The crowd that I saw gathered this time made me gasp... it was staggering in size. People were standing shoulder to shoulder like a vast sea of humanity, surrounding the tent and nearly filling the field. I looked back at Chozeq, and he nodded with a brief smile, then took us lower until we had drifted inside the huge tent's canopy once again.

Chozeq pointed to a place at the back of the tent, where I saw Mr.V, standing — he was staring in wonder at the sights around him. It looked like the service had been going on for a while... maybe even all day. So many people had already been healed that the aisle was littered with discarded crutches and wheelchairs. People were weeping and rejoicing everywhere. But I could tell from the look on Mr. V's face that something was holding him back. He couldn't bring himself to venture inside.

"Why won't he go in?" I asked Chozeq, unable to understand his hesitation.

Chozeq didn't answer but simply placed two of his fingers on my forehead...

THE SCENE SUDDENLY CHANGED... I was looking at a young Mr. V, but not as young as he'd been in his dream of the Harvest Festival... we were in a place I didn't recognize — it was a crowded city. That's when I noticed that he was talking to Gramps Farro and reasoned that we must be in Brooklyn.

Gramps was older too, of course; I guessed they must both be in their late forties. Their conversation was heated — Mr. V was yelling at Gramps. I could see that there was a lot of commotion going on around them... like celebrating. People were toasting each other and talking about some parade they'd just been to. I turned just in time to see a hawker nearby hold up the next day's bulldog edition of the newspaper, and I read its headline: *JOYOUS WELCOME FOR ASTRO-NAUTS!* The picture on the paper's front page showed three men waving from the back of a convertible in a blizzard of ticker tape.

The sight made me freeze... I knew very little about my Dad's father, but one thing I did know was that he had died in New York on the night of the Apollo 11 Astronauts' ticker-tape parade. I looked around urgently, scanning the crowds for any sign of... then I saw them! I could tell it was my Dad's parents from their wedding picture on our fireplace — they looked practically the same age as in their picture, in their early twenties. They were standing across the road from Mr. V and Gramps ... they seemed so happy. I saw Dad's father buy a paper and show it to his wife... Grandma — it seems funny to refer to them as my grandparents; they were so young. She was pushing a carriage with a baby inside... it was my father. I watched them kiss like they were oblivious to all the people and chaos around them....

THE SCENE CHANGED AGAIN, and I was back at the tent. Old man Van Clief had started down the aisle... tears were welling up in his eyes. I could hear him speaking under his breath... somehow, I could hear his words. He was broken-hearted, apologizing... "I'm sorry fer it all, Lou, so sorry... Sorry fer what I got ya into... sorry fer what I done t' yer boy..." I could see a steady stream of tears flowing down his face as he stopped in the aisle and buried his face in his sleeve...

SUDDENLY, I was distracted from that amazing scene by loud shouting beside me. It was the younger Mr. V's voice... as I turned to look, the scene instantly switched back to 1969. I'd never seen Mr. V so angry. He grabbed Gramps Farro by the shoulders and then shoved him backward, knocking him to the ground along with several others standing behind him. The ruckus attracted the attention of a group of policemen standing up the road, and they started making their way closer. I looked back at where Dad's father had been standing and saw him shaking his head at Mr. V and waving urgently. Mr. V saw him, but dismissed his petition with an angry wave of his hand, then moved toward Gramps, who was staggering to his feet.

"Jim, Wait!" my Dad's father yelled from across the street — then he started to run; his eyes were fixed on Mr. V as he held up his hand, imploring him to stop and wait. I heard his wife... my Grandma... scream his name, ...LOUuuuu! and an instant later I heard horns blaring and brakes screeching and then the horrible thud as he was thrown to the road....

I COVERED my face in shock at the horrendous sight... when I lowered my hands, I was back in the tent. Old man Van Clief was weeping steadily as he staggered forward. "Forgive me... oh Lord forgive me... I ain't worth Savin'...I know I ain't... my past is beyond changin' — the hurt I caused ain't forgivable."

He was nearing the front row of seats. The congregation was standing, and PJ was leading the singing — he watched him move closer with a compassionate expression. I heard a few of the girls nearby mention his name in prayer as tears filled their faces. A powerful spirit of intercession permeated the air...

MY YOUNG GRANDMOTHER'S screams drew my attention once again — as I turned toward them, I was back in 1969. Mr. V tried to run into the street, but he was pushed back by one of the policemen. He watched helplessly as they lifted Grandpa into an ambulance... with the sheet pulled over his head. Grandma was helped into a police car holding Dad as they placed her baby carriage in the trunk. She was weeping as they drove away behind the ambulance.

I saw Gramps Farro approach and try to comfort him, but Mr. V's face hardened, and he held up his hand in a signal for him to keep away. "It's all yer fault!" he shouted at Gramps, "You an' yer meddlin' in my life is done... you keep away from me! I never wanna see you again!"

"Jim... what are you sayin? Gramps objected, "We've been friends for 20 years! I've only wanted to help...."

Mr. V cut him off in mid-sentence, "You ain't no friend o' mine, far as I'm concerned!" he said bitterly. His eyes burned with anger as he looked at Gramps for the last time in his life and then turned his back and shoved his way through the crowd...

As I FOLLOWED him with my eyes, the crowded Brooklyn street dissolved. Mr. V changed into an old man once again — he was bumping into a few people who stood near the front as he staggered toward the altar with his eyes awash with tears.

"Yer forgiveness is wasted on the likes o' me, God!" I heard him stammer, "I-I ain't nothin'... nothin' but a broken-down old... fool!" He reached the altar rail and collapsed to his knees, "...I got no right t' ask fer mercy Lord... but I'm beggin ya fer what I got no right to... Ain't nothin', but mercy can save me... ain't nothin' but mercy!" He was weeping like a child as he dropped his face to the altar rail and his body shook with pangs of remorse.

I saw PJ step away from the podium to kneel at the altar rail with him. Mr. V cried even harder the moment PJ placed a hand on his shoulder. He prayed silently as the old man shook and shook in uncontrollable sobs. Floodgates of remorse had been opened, releasing a torrent of sorrow and regret that had accumulated for a lifetime.

I felt a tear run down my cheek as I suddenly saw Mom urgently making her way down the aisle — her own eyes were awash with tears. She dropped to her knees beside Mr. V and put her hand beside PJ's on his shaking shoulder. In a few moments, Anna and Pete joined her, then others... so many others!

The sight was overwhelming. God was pulling out all the stops in His pursuit of this man who had resisted Him for 90 years. It was like every prayer that had been prayed for Mr. V in all those years was being answered at once on the wings of a throng of heavenly messengers. It was a massive deliverance!

Mr. V looked up at PJ through his tear-filled eyes with a pleading expression. I saw PJ lean close and speak in his ear, then saw Mr. V nod yes anxiously. Their voices were picked up by PJ's mic as he led him in the sinner's prayer, and Mr. V's broken voice could be heard as he struggled to repeat the words through his sobbing. The vast wave of intercession had spread now to the entire congregation — everyone there was joined in praying him through!

. . . In a shocking flash, I suddenly found myself at Golgotha. Once again, I saw the incredible sight of millions of desperate souls gathered around the cross as Jesus died. This time I was kneeling next to Mr. V... He was weeping bitterly under the strain of his crushing remorse. As I looked at him, a shining presence appeared to his right. To my astonishment, I recognized my Great Grandpa Moretti! Then I noticed there were others with us: Gramps Farro... and beside him was Dad's father, Lou junior. I felt a hand on my own back and glanced behind me to see my Dad. All of them acknowledged me kindly, as if to say thank you for helping to complete the work in Mr. V's life that they had each been a big part of.

We all heard Jesus cry out, announcing His finished work from the cross. Then the blinding flash of his purifying wave washed over us, making me gasp and then shout out in a spontaneous cry of joy! I saw Mr. V's filthy tattered rags being instantaneously transformed into clean, fresh robes of blinding white. He shuddered and reared back as if stunned by the sudden feeling of cleansing in his soul. The weight of 90 years of sin and guilt falling from his shoulders must have made him feel as light as a feather!

We watched in awestruck amazement as Jesus looked him in the eye and nodded to him in affirmation of his forgiveness. Mr. V reacted in the same way that we all had in the extraordinary moment when we first felt the warmth of God's acceptance. He fell forward and bowed his head to the ground in overwhelmed emotion.

I knelt in front of him as he slowly looked up ... when he saw me, his face lit with a beautiful smile, and he wrapped his arms around my neck like a rescued man. A hand on his back made him turn to see Great Grandpa Moretti smiling in welcome... "LOU!" he shouted, his face beaming. Then he noticed the others around him, and his eyes filled with tears of unbridled joy as the scene dissolved in a flash. ...

. . . Back at the tent's altar, Mr. V seemed momentarily disoriented. He looked around through his tear-filled eyes at PJ, mom, and the others, then his face filled with a thrilled expression. He climbed to his feet and hugged PJ as if he was his long-lost son, then turned toward mom, who threw her arms around him with her tears still streaming down her face.

As they finished hugging, he looked at her with an uncertain look, as if trying to decide whether to share with her what he'd just witnessed. He finally just nodded his head forward in a gesture of thanks... "I don't know how I kin ever thank ya Maria... all you've sacrificed... all you've done... I ain't worthy - not in the slightest... I owe you my whole life."

Mom looked at him with a confused expression, not understanding. "W-what have I done?" She asked.

Before he could say any more, PJ shouted into the mic — "There's a new name written down in Glory tonight!" and everyone applauded. The instruments immediately kicked in, and everyone joined in enthusiastically singing that chorus... there's a new name written![1]

Carmine reached out a hand to Mr. V, who accepted it readily with a slightly embarrassed nod of his head. Carmine smiled back and hugged him heartily. A line had begun to form with others who wanted to welcome him... all of them with huge smiles of joy on their faces.

Anna threw her arms around mom, and they embraced warmly;

the flood of emotion and gratitude that overwhelmed them both brought a new outpouring of tears to their eyes . . .

. . . I opened my eyes to look again at the darkened ceiling of my hospital room and felt a huge smile of my own sweep across my face. I let out a long, satisfied sigh and began to pray, expressing the overwhelming feeling of thanks that poured from my soul. The sense of God's spirit was strong in the room and filled my soul with an intense feeling of anticipation... something new was about to happen — I could feel it! God's next work had already begun... and it would be even more incredible than anything we'd seen so far!

The sound of Chozeq unsheathing his sword made my eyes open. I looked up at him and smiled as its light filled the room with a holy glow. He returned my gaze with an approving nod; his eyes looked the way a proud father might look when congratulating his beloved son.

"Ye have done well, Lad... thy Lord is well pleased."

"Thanks, but I know it wasn't me. Don't forget that it's God who works," I answered, half-joking as I repeated the words that he had said to me just a week ago. Chozeq smiled and nodded in a gesture of willing surrender.

He raised his sword, and I watched it ignite into a full flame.

"Now...", he said with a slight bow of his head as he smiled at me, "...I am sent to deliver thy healing. It is time for thee to be back about thy Master's work..." I happily watched his flaming sword move closer to the bandages around my chest as he lowered it... I felt no fear of its healing, salving power. This time, though, its effect was more than I expected; when it touched me, my chest was engulfed in a blinding flash of light that knocked the wind out of me — I immediately blacked out.

.   .   .

CHOZEQ SLOWLY PLACED his sword back into its sheath; "Our young friend will sleep well tonight," he said as if speaking to an unseen kinsman.

"HE WILL NEED the strength of it for the mission that our Lord has prepared for him," Ardent answered as he became visible, standing beside Chozeq.

"AYE," Chozeq replied, "but it is not the mission only that God has prepared... He has prepared *him* as well — his faith has grown strong. With his Lord's great help, he will be ready for the challenge."

ARDENT NODDED IN AGREEMENT, "he has grown to bear well the name that our Lord gave him...
    ...of a truth, he is Sterling."

⌘

THE END
OF BOOK ONE

AUTHOR'S NOTE

The opening scene begins on a radar tower beside New Jersey's Newark Airport. The inspiration for it came on a late-night drive home from working in New York City some years ago. It was a clear cold night driving along the New Jersey Turnpike. I was struck by the sight of planes lined up for approach - their landing lights visible from miles away as they stretched in a long line into the distant sky. Their distant lights seemed motionless, and the huge planes appeared to move impossibly slow as they landed, giving them the appearance of hanging in midair. As usual, the highway's twelve lanes were filled with traffic, looking like a river of light flowing along the black pavement.

The scene is meant to capture the disorientation and confusion experienced by a teenaged boy who suddenly encounters two powerful angelic warriors in a vision of the future. It is being experienced from the angels' perspective, revealing a spirit world that is shocking and more than a little terrifying to the boy.

The boy is an unlikely prophet, not unlike many examples in the Bible where God used children in remarkable ways. From Joseph's early dreams to David's courageous battle with Goliath and Jesus' selection of a young man named John, likely not more than a teenager himself, to be one of his closest Disciples. It's not much of a stretch to think that His most significant work still to come could be accomplished through some of the weakest among us. 1 Corinthians 1:27

The angel Chozeq's name is derived from the Hebrew word qzx, or kho'-zek. The noun is a masculine form, meaning strength, power, or powerful. Inspiration for much of Chozeq's advice came from the writings of Charles H. Spurgeon, especially from his Daily Devotional, Morning & Evening (public domain), initially published in 1865. An attempt was made to weave these powerful messages, which offer keen insights into God's profound nature, into the storyline to show how truly relevant they remain today.

Within & Without Time is, in essence, a story about the shocking contrast between human frailty and an infinitely powerful and sovereign God. A God who is motivated by a love that is as immense and immeasurable as His power.

Thank You for Reading!

If this book provided a blessing or encouragement,
please leave a review that will help others find it as well.

ALSO BY D. I. HENNESSEY

Books in the Within & Without Time Series:

Book 1: Within and Without Time

Book 2: The Traveler

Book 3: The Secret Door

Book 4: Evil Ascendant - Deliverance

Available on Amazon

"www.amazon.com/gp/product/B09DFDM364"

Books in the Niergel Chronicles Series:

Book 1: Niergel Chronicles - Last Hope

Book 2: Niergel Chronicles - Quest

Book 3: Niergel Chronicles - The Tenth Mantle Bearer

Book 4: Niergel Chronicles - The Dragon's Tail

For information on these and upcoming releases

Visit: www.arkharbor.press

NOTES

1. ON EARTH... AS IT IS IN HEAVEN

1. Original Word Hebrew qzx, kho'-zek, Noun Masculine: 1.strength, power, powerful

3. FUTURE SHOCK

1. Inspiration for some of Chozeq's advice was drawn from:
   Spurgeon, Charles H. Morning & Evening. 1865. pg-Mar. 16.

9. TEMPORARY

1. Psalm 103:13-16

16. MY WAYS

1. [Jonah 4:6-10]

19. BETWEEN THE BEFORE AND THE AFTER

1. [Which means, "My God, My God, Why have you forsaken me?!"].

20. ETERNITY

1. [Genesis 18]
2. [Genesis 32:24-30]
3. [Joshua 5:13]
4. [Daniel 3:19, 3:25]
5. [Spurgeon, Charles H. THE SWORD AND THE TROWEL. 1865. July]
6. [Isaiah 49:16]
7. [Spurgeon, Charles H. Morning & Evening. 1865. pg-Dec 11]

21. LEGACY

1. [Psalm 116:15]
2. [Spurgeon, Charles H. Morning & Evening. 1865. pg-July 21]

23. THE HEAVENS

1. Psalm 103

25. SAVED

1. [1 Peter 2:9]
2. Spurgeon, Charles H. Morning & Evening. 1865. pg-July 21!

26. NEW THINGS

1. [James 4:1-10]

31. GUARD DUTY

1. [Isa 5:14]

34. DEDICATION

1. [Based on 2 Chronicles 7:14-16]
2. [Matthew 18:19]

36. MARANATHA

1. [James 5:7-8]

41. STERLING

1. [Miles, C. Austin. Words & Music: A NEW NAME IN GLORY. 1910]